MARIETTA
A MAID OF VENICE

MARIETTA
A MAID OF VENICE

F. MARION CRAWFORD

WILDSIDE PRESS

MARIETTA

This edition published 2005 by Wildside Press, LLC.
www.wildsidepress.com

CHAPTER I

Very little was known about George, the Dalmatian, and the servants in the house of Angelo Beroviero, as well as the workmen of the latter's glass furnace, called him Zorzi, distrusted him, suggested that he was probably a heretic, and did not hide their suspicion that he was in love with the master's only daughter, Marietta. All these matters were against him, and people wondered why old Angelo kept the waif in his service, since he would have engaged any one out of a hundred young fellows of Murano, all belonging to the almost noble caste of the glass-workers, all good Christians, all trustworthy, and all ready to promise that the lovely Marietta should never make the slightest impression upon their respectfully petrified hearts. But Angelo had not been accustomed to consider what his neighbours might think of him or his doings, and most of his neighbours and friends abstained with singular unanimity from thrusting their opinions upon him. For this, there were three reasons: he was very rich, he was the greatest living artist in working glass, and he was of a choleric temper. He confessed the latter fault with great humility to the curate of San Piero each year in Lent, but he would never admit it to any one else. Indeed, if any of his family ever suggested that he was somewhat hasty, he flew into such an ungovernable rage in proving the contrary that it was scarcely wise to stay in the house while the fit lasted. Marietta alone was safe. As for her brothers, though the elder was nearly forty years old, it was not long since his father had given him a box on the ears which made him see simultaneously all the colours of all the glasses ever made in Murano before or since. It is true that Giovanni had timidly asked to be told one of the secrets for making fine red glass which old Angelo had learned long ago from old Paolo Godi of Pergola, the famous chemist; and these secrets were all carefully written out in the elaborate character of the late fifteenth century, and Angelo kept the manuscript in an iron box, under his own bed, and wore the key on a small silver chain at his neck.

He was a big old man, with fiery brown eyes, large features, and a very pale skin. His thick hair and short beard had once been red, and streaks of the strong colour still ran through the faded locks. His hands were large, but very skilful, and the long straight fingers were discoloured by contact with the substances he used in his experiments.

He was jealous by nature, rather than suspicious. He had been jealous of his wife while she had lived, though a more devoted woman never fell to the lot of a lucky husband. Often, for weeks together, he had locked the door upon her and taken the key with him every morning when he left the house, though his furnaces were almost exactly opposite, on the other side of the narrow canal, so that by coming to the door he could have spoken with her at her window. But instead of doing this he used to look through a little grated opening which he had caused to be made in the wall of the glass-house; and when his wife was seated at her window, at her embroidery, he could watch her unseen, for she was beautiful and he loved her. One day he saw a stranger standing by the water's edge, gazing at her, and he went out and threw the man into the canal. When she died, he said little, but he would not allow his own children to speak of her before him. After that, he became almost as jealous of his daughter, and though he did not lock her up like her mother, he used to take her with him to the glass-house when the weather was not too hot, so that she should not be out of his sight all day.

Moreover, because he needed a man to help him, and because he was afraid lest one of his own caste should fall in love with Marietta, he took Zorzi, the Dalmatian waif, into his service; and the three were often together all day in the room where Angelo had set up a little furnace for making experiments. In the year 1470 it was not lawful in Murano to teach any foreign person the art of glassmaking; for the glassblowers were a sort of nobility, and nearly a hundred years had passed since the Council had declared that patricians of Venice might marry the daughters of glass-workers without affecting their own rank or that of their children. But old Beroviero declared that he was not teaching Zorzi anything, that the young fellow was his servant and not his apprentice, and did nothing but keep up the fire in the furnace, and fetch and carry, grind materials, and sweep the floor. It was quite true that Zorzi did all these things, and he did them with a silent regularity that made him indispensable to his master, who scarcely noticed the growing skill with which the young man helped him at every turn, till he could be entrusted to perform the most delicate operations in glass-working without any especial instructions. Intent upon artistic matters, the old man was hardly aware, either, that Marietta had learned much of his art; or if he realised the fact he felt a sort of jealous satisfaction in the thought that she liked to be shut up with him for hours at a time, quite out of sight of the world and altogether out of harm's way. He fancied that she grew more like him from day to day, and he flattered himself that he understood her. She and Zorzi were the only beings in his world who never irritated him, now that he had them always under his eye and command. It was natural that he should suppose himself to be profoundly acquainted with their two natures, though he had never taken the smallest pains to test this imaginary knowledge. Possibly, in their different ways, they knew him better than he knew them.

The glass-house was guarded from outsiders as carefully as a nunnery, and somewhat resembled a convent in having no windows so situated that curious persons might see from without what went on inside. The place was entered by a low door from the narrow paved path that ran along the canal. In a little vestibule, ill-lighted by one small grated window, sat the porter, an uncouth old man who rarely answered questions, and never opened the door until he had assured himself by a deliberate inspection through the grating that the person who knocked had a right to come in. Marietta remembered him in his den when she had been a little child, and she vaguely supposed that he had always been there. He had been old then, he was not visibly older now, he would probably never die of old age, and if any mortal ill should carry him off, he would surely be replaced by some one exactly like him, who would sleep in the same box bed, sit all day in the same black chair, and eat bread, shellfish and garlic off the same worm-eaten table. There was no other entrance to the glass-house, and there could be no other porter to guard it.

Beyond the vestibule a dark corridor led to a small garden that formed the court of the building, and on one side of which were the large windows that lighted the main furnace room, while the other side contained the laboratory of the master. But the main furnace was entered from the corridor, so that the workmen never passed through the garden. There were a few shrubs in it, two or three rosebushes and a small plane-tree. Zorzi, who had been born and brought up in the country, had made a couple of flowerbeds, edged with refuse fragments of coloured and iridescent slag, and he had planted such common flowers as he could make grow in such a place, watering them from a disused rainwater cistern that was supposed to have been poisoned long ago. Here Marietta often sat in the shade, when the laboratory was too close and hot, and when the time was at hand during which even the men would not be able to work on account of the heat, and the furnace would be put out and repaired, and every one would be set to making the delicate clay pots in which the glass was to be melted. Marietta could sit silent and motionless hi her seat under the plane-tree for a long time when she was thinking, and she never told any one her thoughts.

She was not unlike her father in looks, and that was doubtless the reason why he assumed that she must be like him in character. No one would have said that she was handsome, but sometimes, when she smiled, those who saw that rare expression in her face thought she was beautiful. When it was gone, they said she was cold. Fortunately, her hair was not red, as her father's had been or she might sometimes have seemed positively ugly; it was of that deep ruddy, golden brown that one may often see in Venice still, and there was an abundance of it, though it was drawn straight back from her white forehead and braided into the smallest possible space, in the fashion of that time. There wag often a little colour in her face, though never much, and it was faint, yet very fresh, like the tint within certain delicate shells; her lips were of the same hue, but stronger and brighter, and they were very well shaped and generally closed, like her father's. But her eyes were not like his, and the lids and lashes shaded them in such a way that it was hard to guess their colour, and they had an inscrutable, reserved look that was hard to meet for many seconds. Zorzi believed that they were grey, but when he saw them in his dreams they were violet; and one day she opened them wide for an instant, at something old Beroviero said to her, and then Zorzi fancied that they were like sapphires, but before he could be sure, the lids and lashes shaded them again, and he only knew that they were there, and longed to see them, for her father had spoken of her marriage, and she had not answered a single word.

When they were alone together for a moment, while the old man was searching for more materials in the next room, she spoke to Zorzi.

"My father did not mean you to hear that," she said.

"Nevertheless, I heard," answered Zorzi, pushing a small piece of beech wood into the fire through a narrow slit on one side of the brick furnace. "It was not my fault."

"Forget that you heard it," said Marietta quietly, and as her father entered the room again she passed him and went out into the garden.

But Zorzi did not even try to forget the name of the man whom Beroviero appeared to have chosen for his daughter. He tried instead, to understand why Marietta wished him not to remember that the name was Jacopo Contarini. He glanced sideways at the girl's figure as she disappeared through the door, and he thoughtfully pushed another piece of wood into the fire. Some day, perhaps before long, she would marry this man who had been mentioned, and then Zorzi would be alone with old Beroviero in the laboratory. He set his teeth, and poked the fire with, an iron rod.

It happened now and then that Marietta did not come to the glass-house. Those days were long, and when night came Zorzi felt as if his heart were turning into a hot stone in his breast, and his sight was dull, and he ached from his work and felt scorched by the heat of the furnace. For he was not very strong of limb, though he was quick with his hands and of a very tenacious nature, able to endure pain as well as weariness when he was determined to finish what he had begun. But while Marietta was in the laboratory, nothing could tire him nor hurt him, nor make him wish that the hours were less long. He thought therefore of what must happen to him if Jacopo Contarini took Marietta away from Murano to live in a palace in Venice, and he determined at least to find out what sort of man this might be who was to receive for his own the only woman in the world for whose sake it would be perfect happiness to be burned with slow fire. He did not mean to do Contarini any harm. Perhaps Marietta already loved the man, and was glad she was to marry him. No one could have told what she felt, even from that one flashing look she had given her father. Zorzi did not try to understand her yet; he only loved her, and she was his master's daughter, and if his master found out his secret it would be a very evil day for him. So he poked the fire with his iron rod, and set his teeth, and said nothing, while old Beroviero moved about the room.

"Zorzi," said the master presently, "I meant you to hear what I said to my daughter."

"I heard, sir," answered the young man, rising respectfully, and waiting for more.

"Remember the name you heard," said Beroviero.

If the matter had been any other in the world, Zorzi would have smiled at the master's words, because they bade him do just what Marietta had forbidden. The one said "forget," the other "remember." For the first time in his life Zorzi found it easier to obey his lady's father than herself. He bent his head respectfully.

"I trust you, Zorzi," continued Beroviero, slowly mixing some materials in a little wooden trough on the table. "I trust you, because I must trust some one in order to have a safe means of communicating with Casa Contarini."

Again Zorzi bent his head, but still he said nothing.

"These five years you have worked with me in private," the old man went on, "and I know that you have not told what you have seen me do, though there are many who would pay you good money to know what I have been about."

"That is true," answered Zorzi.

"Yes. I therefore judge that you are one of those unusual beings whom God has sent into the world to be of use to their fellow-creatures instead of a hindrance. For you possess the power of holding your tongue, which I had almost believed to be extinct in the human race. I am going to send you on an errand to Venice, to Jacopo Cantarini. If I sent any one from my house, all Murano would know it tomorrow morning, but I wish no one here to guess where you have been."

"No one shall see me," answered Zorzi. "Tell me only where I am to go."

"You know Venice well by this time. You must have often passed the house of the Agnus Dei."

"By the Baker's Bridge?"

"Yes. Go there alone, tonight and ask for Messer Jacopo; and if the porter inquires your business, say that you have a message and a token from a certain Angelo. When you are admitted and are alone with Messer Jacopo, tell him from me to go and stand by the second pillar on the left in Saint Mark's, on Sunday next, an hour before noon, until he sees me; and within a week after that, he shall have the answer; and bid him be silent, if he would succeed."

"Is that all, air?"

"That is all. If he gives you any message in answer, deliver it to me tomorrow, when my daughter is not here."

"And the token?" inquired Zorzi.

"This glass seal, of which he already has an impression in wax, in case he should doubt you."

Zorzi took the little leathern bag which contained the seal. He tied a piece of string to it, and hung it round his neck, so that it was hidden in his doublet like a charm or a scapulary. Beroviero watched him and nodded in approval.

"Do not start before it is quite dark," he said. "Take the little skiff. The water will be high two hours before midnight, so you will have no trouble in getting across. When you come back, come here, and tell the porter that I have ordered you to see that my fire is properly kept up. Then go to sleep in the coolest place you can find."

After Beroviero had given him these orders, Zorzi had plenty of time for reflection, for his master said nothing more, and became absorbed in his work, weighing out portions of different ingredients and slowly mixing each with the coloured earths and chemicals that were already in the wooden trough. There was nothing to do but to tend the fire, and Zorzi pushed in the pieces of Istrian beech wood with his usual industrious regularity. It was the only part of his work which he hated, and when he was obliged to do nothing else, he usually sought consolation in dreaming of a time when he himself should be a master glassblower and artist whom it would be almost an honour for a young man to serve, even in such a humble way. He did not know how that was to happen, since there were strict laws against teaching the art to foreigners, and also against allowing any foreign person to establish a furnace at Murano; and the glass works had long been altogether banished from Venice on account of the danger of fire, at a time when two-thirds of the houses were of wood. But meanwhile Zorzi had learned the art, in spite of the law, and he hoped in time to overcome the other obstacles that opposed him.

There was strength of purpose in every line of his keen young face, strength to endure, to forego, to suffer in silence for an end ardently desired. The dark brown hair grew somewhat far back from the pale forehead, the features were youthfully sharp and clearly drawn, and deep neutral shadows gave a look of almost passionate sadness to the black eyes. There was quick perception, imagination, love of art for its own sake in the upper part of the face; its strength lay in the well-built jaw and firm lips, and a little in the graceful and assured poise of the head. Zorzi was not tall, but he was shapely, and moved without effort.

His eyes were sadder than usual just now, as he tended the fire in the silence that was broken only by the low roar of the flames within the brick furnace, and the irregular sound of the master's wooden instrument as he crushed and stirred the materials together. Zorzi had longed to see Contarini as soon as he had heard his name; and having unexpectedly obtained the certainty of seeing him that very night, he wished that the moment could be put off, he felt cold and hot, he wondered how he should behave, and whether after all he might not be tempted to do his enemy some bodily harm.

For in a few minutes the aspect of his world had changed, and Contarini's unknown figure filled the future. Until today, he had never seriously thought of Marietta's marriage, nor of what would happen to him afterwards; but now, he was to be one of the instruments for bringing the marriage about. He knew well enough what the appointment in Saint Mark's meant: Marietta was to have an opportunity of seeing Contarini before accepting him. Even that was something of a concession in those times, but Beroviero fancied that he loved his child too much to marry her against her will. This was probably a great match for the glass-worker's daughter, however, and she would not refuse it. Contarini had never seen her either; he might have heard that she was a pretty girl, but there were famous beauties in Venice, and if he wanted Marietta Beroviero it could only be for her dowry. The marriage was therefore a mere bargain between the two men, in which a name was bartered for a fortune and a fortune for a name. Zorzi saw how absurd it was to suppose that Marietta could care for a man whom she had never even seen; and worse than that, he guessed in a flash of loving intuition how wretchedly unhappy she might be with him, and he hated and despised the errand he was to perform. The future seemed to reveal itself to him with the long martyrdom of the woman he loved, and he felt an almost irresistible desire to go to her and implore her to refuse to be sold.

Nine-tenths of the marriages he had ever heard of in Murano or Venice had been made in this way, and in a moment's reflection he realised the folly of appealing even to the girl herself, who doubtless looked upon the whole proceeding as perfectly natural. She had of course expected such an event ever since she had been a child, she was prepared to accept it, and she only hoped that her husband might turn out to be young, handsome and noble, since she did not want money. A moment later, Zorzi included all marriageable young women in one sweeping condemnation: they were all hard-hearted, mercenary, vain, deceitful—anything that suggested itself to his headlong resentment. Art was the only thing worth living and dying for; the world was full of women, and they were all alike, old, young, ugly, handsome—all a pack of heartless jades; but art was one, beautiful, true, deathless and unchanging.

He looked up from the furnace door, and he felt the blood rush to his face. Marietta was standing near and watching him with her strangely veiled eyes.

"Poor Zorzi!" she exclaimed in a soft voice. "How hot you look!"

He did not remember that he had ever cared a straw whether any one noticed that he was hot or not, until that moment; but for some complicated reason connected with his own thoughts the remark stung him like an insult, and fully confirmed his recent verdict concerning women in general and their total lack of all human kindness where men were concerned. He rose to his feet suddenly and turned away without a word.

"Come out into the garden," said Marietta. "Do you need Zorzi just now?" she asked, turning to her father, who only shook his head by way of answer, for he was very busy.

"But I assure you that I am not too hot," answered Zorzi. "Why should I go out?"

"Because I want you to fasten up one of the branches of the red rose. It catches in my skirt every time I pass. You will need a hammer and a little nail."

She had not been thinking of his comfort after all, thought Zorzi as he got the hammer. She had only wanted something done for herself. He might have known it. But for the rose that caught in her skirt, he might have roasted alive at the furnace before she would have noticed that he was hot. He followed her out. She led him to the end of the walk farthest from the door of the laboratory; the sun was low and all the little garden was in deep shade. A branch of the rosebush lay across the path, and Zorzi thought it looked very much as if it had been pulled down on purpose. She pointed to it, and as he carefully lifted it from the ground she spoke quickly, in a low tone.

"What was my father saying to you a while ago?" she asked.

Zorzi held up the branch in his hand, ready to fasten it against the wall, and looked at her. He saw at a glance that she had brought him out to ask the question.

"The master was giving me certain orders," he said.

"He rarely makes such long speeches when he gives orders," observed the girl.

"His instructions were very particular."

"Will you not tell me what they were?"

Zorzi turned slowly from her and let the long branch rest on the bush while he began to drive a nail into the wall. Marietta watched him.

"Why do you not answer me?" she asked.

"Because I cannot," he said briefly.

"Because you will not, you mean."

"As you choose." Zorzi went on striking the nail.

"I am sorry," answered the young girl. "I really wish to know very much. Besides, if you will tell me, I will give you something."

Zorzi turned upon her suddenly with angry eyes.

"If money could buy your father's secrets from me, I should be a rich man by this time."

"I think I know as much of my father's secrets as you do,"

answered Marietta more coldly, "and I did not mean to offer you money."

"What then?" But as he asked the question Zorzi turned away again and began to fasten the branch.

Marietta did not answer at once, but she idly picked a rose from the bush and put it to her lips to breathe in its freshness.

"Why should you think that I meant to insult you?" she asked gently.

"I am only a servant, after all," answered Zorzi, with unnecessary bitterness. "Why should you not insult your servants, if you please? It would be quite natural."

"Would it? Even if you were really a servant?"

"It seems quite natural to you that I should betray your father's confidence. I do not see much difference between taking it for granted that a man is a traitor and offering him money to act as one."

"No," said Marietta, smelling the rose from time to time as she spoke, "there is not much difference. But I did not mean to hurt your feelings."

"You did not realise that I could have any, I fancy," retorted Zorzi, still angry.

"Perhaps I did not understand that you would consider what my father was telling you in the same light as a secret of the art," said Marietta slowly, "nor that you would look upon what I meant to offer you as a bribe. The matter concerned me, did it not?"

"Your name was not spoken. I have fastened the branch. Is there anything else for me to do?"

"Have you no curiosity to know what I would have given you?" asked Marietta.

"I should be ashamed to want anything at such a price," returned Zorzi proudly.

"You hold your honour high, even in trifles."

"It is all I have—my honour and my art."

"You care for nothing else? Nothing else in the whole world?"

"Nothing," said Zorzi.

"You must be very lonely in your thoughts," she said, and turned away.

As she went slowly along the path her hand hung by her side, and the rose she held fell from her fingers. Following her at a short distance, on his way back to the laboratory, Zorzi stooped and picked up the flower, not thinking that she would turn her head. But at that moment she had reached the door, and she looked back and saw what he had done. She stood still and held out her hand, expecting him to come up with her.

"My rose!" she exclaimed, as if surprised. "Give it back to me."

Zorzi gave it to her, and the colour came to his face a second time. She fastened it in her bodice, looking down at it as she did so.

"I am so fond of roses," she said, smiling a little. "Are you?"

"I planted all those you have here," he answered.

"Yes—I know."

She looked up as she spoke, and met his eyes, and all at once she laughed, not unkindly, nor as if at him, nor at what he had said, but quietly and happily, as women do when they have got what they want. Zorzi did not understand.

"You are gay," he said coldly.

"Do you wonder?" she asked. "If you knew what I know, you would understand."

"But I do not."

Zorzi went back to his furnace, Marietta exchanged a few words with her father and left the room again to go home.

In the garden she paused a moment by the rosebush, where she had talked with Zorzi, but there was not even the shadow of a smile in her face now. She went down the dark corridor and called the porter, who roused himself, opened the door and hailed the house opposite. A woman looked out in the evening light, nodded and disappeared. A few seconds later she came out of the house, a quiet little middle-aged creature in brown, with intelligent eyes, and she crossed the shaky wooden bridge over the canal to come and bring Marietta home. It would have been a scandalous thing if the daughter of Angelo Beroviero had been seen by the neighbours to walk a score of paces in the street without an attendant. She had thrown a hood of dark green cloth over her head, and the folds hung below her shoulders, half hiding her graceful figure. Her step was smooth and deliberate, while the little brown serving-woman trotted beside her across the wooden bridge.

The house of Angelo Beroviero hung over the paved way, above the edge of the water, the upper story being supported by six stone columns and massive wooden beams, forming a sort of portico which was at the same time a public thoroughfare; but as the house was not far from the end of the canal of San Piero which opens towards Venice, few people passed that way.

Marietta paused a moment while the woman held the door open for her. The sun had just set and the salt freshness that comes with the rising tide was already in the air.

"I wish I were in Venice this evening," she said, almost to her-self.

The serving-woman looked at her suspiciously.

CHAPTER II

The June night was dark and warm as Zorzi pushed off from the steps before his master's house and guided his skiff through the canal, scarcely moving the single oar, as the rising tide took his boat silently along. It was not until he had passed the last of the glass-houses on his right, and was already in the lagoon that separates Murano from Venice, that he began to row, gently at first, for fear of being heard by some one ashore, and then more quickly, swinging his oar in the curved crutch with that skilful, serpentine stroke which is neither rowing nor sculling, but which has all the advantages of both, for it is swift and silent, and needs scarcely to be slackened even in a channel so narrow that the boat itself can barely pass.

Now that he was away from the houses, the stars came out and he felt the pleasant land breeze in his face, meeting the rising tide. Not a boat was out upon the shallow lagoon but his own, not a sound came from the town behind him; but as the flat bow of the skiff gently slapped the water, it plashed and purled with every stroke of the oar, and a faint murmur of voices in song was borne to him on the wind from the still waking city.

He stood upright on the high stern of the shadowy craft, himself but a moving shadow in the starlight, thrown forward now, and now once more erect, in changing motion; and as he moved the same thought came back and back again in a sort of halting and painful rhythm. He was out that night on a bad errand, it said, helping to sell the life of the woman he loved, and what he was doing could never be undone. Again and again the words said themselves, the far-off voices said them, the lapping water took them up and repeated them, the breeze whispered them quickly as it passed, the oar pronounced them as it creaked softly in the crutch rowlock, the stars spelled out the sentences in the sky, the lights of Venice wrote them in the water in broken reflections. He was not alone any more, for everything in heaven and earth was crying to him to go back.

That was folly, and he knew it. The master who had trusted him would drive him out of his house, and out of Venetian land and water, too, if he chose, and he should never see Marietta again; and she would be married to Contarini just as if Zorzi had taken the message. Besides, it was the custom of the world everywhere, so far as he knew, that marriage and money should be spoken of in the same breath, and there was no reason why his master should make an exception and be different from other men.

He could put some hindrance in the way, of course, if he chose to interfere, for he could deliver the message wrong, and Contarini would go to the church in the afternoon instead of in the morning. He smiled grimly in the dark as he thought of the young nobleman waiting for an hour or two beside the pillar, to be looked at by some one who never came, then catching sight at last of some ugly old maid of forty, protected by her servant, ogling him, while she said her prayers and filling him with horror at the thought that she must be Marietta Beroviero. All that might happen, but it must inevitably be found out, the misunderstanding would be cleared away and the marriage would be arranged after all.

He had rested on his oar to think, and now he struck it deep into the black water and the skiff shot ahead. He would have a far better chance of serving Marietta in the future if he obeyed his master and delivered his message exactly; for he should see Contarini himself and judge of him, in the first place, and that alone was worth much, and afterwards there would be time enough for desperate resolutions. He hastened his stroke, and when he ran under the shadow of the overhanging houses his mood changed and he grew hopeful, as many young men do, out of sheer curiosity as to what was before him, and out of the wish to meet something or somebody that should put his own strength to the test.

It was not far now. With infinite caution he threaded the dark canals, thanking fortune for the faint starlight that showed him the turnings. Here and there a small oil lamp burned before the image of a saint; from a narrow lane on one side, the light streamed across the water, and with it came sounds of ringing glasses, and the tinkling of a lute, and laughing voices; then it was dark again as his skiff shot by, and he made haste, for he wished not to be seen.

Presently, and somewhat to his surprise, he saw a gondola before him in a narrow place, rowed slowly by a man who seemed to be in black like himself. He did not try to pass it, but kept a little astern, trying not to attract attention and hoping that it would turn aside into another canal. But it went steadily on before him, turning wherever he must turn, till it stopped where he was to stop, at the water-gate of the house of the Agnus Dei. Instantly he brought to in the shadow, with the instinctive caution of every one who is used to the water. Gondolas were few in those days and belonged only to the rich, who had just begun to use them as a means of getting about quickly, much more convenient than horses or mules; for when riding a man often had to go far out of his way to reach a bridge, and there were many canals that had no bridle path at all and where the wooden houses were built straight down into the water as the stone ones are to-day. Zorzi peered through the darkness and listened. The occupant of the gondola might be Contarini himself, coming home. Whoever it was tapped softly upon the door, which was instantly opened, but to Zorzi's surprise no light shone from the entrance. All the house above was still and dark, and he could barely make out by the starlight the piece of white marble bearing the sculptured Agnus Dei whence the house takes its name. He knew that above the high balcony there were graceful columns bearing pointed stone arches, between which are the symbols of the four Evangelists; but he could see nothing of them. Only on the balcony, he fancied he saw something less dark than the wall or the sky, and which might be a woman's dress.

Some one got out of the gondola and went in after speaking a few words in a low tone, and the door was then shut without noise. The gondola glided on, under the Baker's Bridge, but Zorzi could not see whether it went further or not; he thought he heard the sound of the oar, as if it were going away. Coming alongside the step, he knocked gently as the last comer had done, and the door opened again. He had already made his skiff fast to the step.

"Your business here?" asked a muffled voice out of the dark.

Zorzi felt that a number of persons were in the hall immediately behind the speaker.

"For the Lord Jacopo Contarini," he answered. "I have a message and a token to deliver."

"From whom?"

"I will tell that to his lordship," replied Zorzi.

"I am Contarini," replied the voice, and the speaker felt for Zorzi's face in the darkness, and brought it near his ear.

"From Angelo," whispered Zorzi, so softly that Contarini only heard the last word.

The door was now shut as noiselessly as before, but not by Contarini himself. He still kept his hold on Zorzi's arm.

"The token," he whispered impatiently.

Zorzi pulled the little leathern bag out of his doublet, slipped the string over his head and thrust the token into Contarini's hand. The latter uttered a low exclamation of surprise.

"What is this?" he asked.

"The token," answered Zorzi.

He had scarcely spoken when he felt Contarini's arms round him, holding him fast. He was wise enough to make no attempt to escape from them.

"Friends," said Contarini quickly, "the man who just came in is a spy. I am holding him. Help me!"

It seemed to Zorzi that a hundred hands seized him in the dark; by the arms, by the legs, by the body, by the head. He knew that resistance was worse than useless. There were hands at his throat, too.

"Let us do nothing hastily," said Contarini's voice, close beside him. "We must find out what he knows first. We can make him speak, I daresay."

"We are not hangmen to torture a prisoner till he confesses," observed some one in a quiet and rather indolent tone. "Strangle him quickly and throw him into the canal. It is late already."

"No," answered Contarini. "Let us at least see his face. We may know him. If you cry out," he said to Zorzi, "you will be killed instantly."

"Jacopo is right," said some one who had not spoken yet.

Almost at the same instant a door was opened and a broad bar of light shot across the hall from an inner room. Zorzi was roughly dragged towards it, and he saw that he was surrounded by about twenty masked men. His face was held to the light, and Contarini's hold on his throat relaxed.

"Not even a mask!" exclaimed Jacopo. "A fool, or a madman. Speak, man I Who are you? Who sent you here?"

"My name is Zorzi," answered the glassblower with difficulty, for he had been almost choked. "My business is with the Lord Jacopo alone. It is very private."

"I have no secrets from my friends," said Contarini. "Speak as if we were alone."

"I have promised my master to deliver the message in secret. I will not speak here."

"Strangle him and throw him out," suggested the man with the indolent voice. "His master is the devil, I have no doubt. He can take the message back with him."

Two or three laughed.

"These spies seldom hunt alone," remarked another. "While we are wasting time a dozen more may be guarding the entrance to the house."

"I am no spy," said Zorzi.

"What are you, then?"

"A glassworker of Murano."

Contarini's hands relaxed altogether, now, and he bent his ear to Zorzi's lips.

"Whisper your message," he said quickly.

Zorzi obeyed.

"Angelo Beroviero bids you wait by the second pillar on the left in Saint Mark's church, next Sunday morning, at one hour before noon, till you shall see him, and in a week from that time you shall have an answer; and be silent, if you would succeed."

"Very well," answered Contarini. "Friends," he said, standing erect, "it is a message I have expected. The name of the man who sends it is 'Angelo'—you understand. It is not this fellow's fault that he came here this evening."

"I suppose there is a woman in the case," said the indolent man. "We will respect your secret. Put the poor devil out of his misery and let us come to our business."

"Kill an innocent man!" exclaimed Contarini.

"Yes, since a word from him can send us all to die between the two red columns."

"His master is powerful and rich," said Jacopo. "If the fellow does not go back tonight, there will be trouble tomorrow, and since he was sent to my house, the inquiry will begin here."

"That is true," said more than one voice, in a tone of hesitation.

Zorzi was very pale, but he held his head high, facing the light of the tall wax candles on the table around which his captors were standing. He was hopelessly at their mercy, for they were twenty to one; the door had been shut and barred and the only window in the room was high above the floor and covered by a thick curtain. He understood perfectly that, by the accident of Angelo's name, "Angel" being the password of the company, he had been accidentally admitted to the meeting of some secret society, and from what had been said, he guessed that its object was a conspiracy against the Republic. It was clear that in self-defence they would most probably kill him, since they could not reasonably run the risk of trusting their lives in his hands. They looked at each other, as if silently debating what they should do.

"At first you suggested that we should torture him," sneered the indolent man, "and now you tremble like a girl at the idea of killing him! Listen to me, Jacopo; if you think that I will leave this house while this fellow is alive, you are most egregiously mistaken."

He had drawn his dagger while he was speaking, and before he had finished it was dangerously near Zorzi's throat. Contarini retired a step as if not daring to defend the prisoner, whose assailant, in spite of his careless and almost womanish tone, was clearly a man of action. Zorzi looked fearlessly into the eyes that peered at him through the holes in the mask.

"It is curious," observed the, other. "He does not seem to be afraid. I am sorry for you, my man, for you appear to be a fine fellow, and I like your face, but we cannot possibly let you go out of the house alive."

"If you choose to trust me," said Zorzi calmly, "I will not betray you. But of course it must seem safer for you to kill me. I quite understand."

"If anything, he is cooler than Venier," observed one of the company.

"He does not believe that we are in earnest," said Contarini.

"I am," answered Venier. "Now, my man," he said, addressing Zorzi again, "if there is anything I can do for you or your family after your death, without risking my neck, I will do it with pleasure."

"I have no family, but I thank you for your offer. In return for your courtesy, I warn you that my master's skiff is fast to the step of the house. It might be recognised. When you have killed me, you had better cast it off—it will drift away with the tide."

Venier, who had let the point of his long dagger rest against Zorzi's collar, suddenly dropped it.

"Contarini," he said, "I take back what I said. It would be an abominable shame to murder a man as brave as he is."

A murmur of approval came from all the company; but Contarini, whose vacillating nature showed itself at every turn, was now inclined to take the other side.

"He may ruin us all," he said. "One word—"

"It seems to me," interrupted a big man who had not yet spoken, and whose beard was as black as his mask, "that we could make use of just such a man as this, and of more like him if they are to be found."

"You are right," said Venier. "If he will take the oath, and bear the tests, let him be one of us. My friend," he said to Zorzi, "you see how it is. You have proved yourself a brave man, and if you are willing to join our company we shall be glad to receive you among us. Do you agree?"

"I must know what the purpose of your society is," answered Zorzi as calmly as before.

"That is well said, my friend, and I like you the better for it. Now listen to me. We are a brotherhood of gentlemen of Venice sworn together to restore the original freedom of our city. That is our main purpose. What Tiepolo and Faliero failed to do, we hope to accomplish. Are you with us in that?"

"Sirs," answered Zorzi, "I am a Dalmatian by birth, and not a Venetian. The Republic forbids me to learn the art of glass-working. I have learned it. The Republic forbids me to set up a furnace of my own. I hope to do so. I owe Venice neither allegiance nor gratitude. If your revolution is to give freedom to art as well as to men, I am with you."

"We shall have freedom for all," said Venier. "We take, moreover, an oath of fellowship which binds us to help each other in all circumstances, to the utmost of our ability and fortune, within the bounds of reason, to risk life and limb for each other's safety, and most especially to respect the wives, the daughters and the betrothed brides of all who belong to our fellowship. These are promises which every true and honest man can make to his friends, and we agree that whoso breaks any one of them, shall die by the hands of the company. And by God in heaven, it were better that you should lose your life now, before taking the oath, than that you should be false to it."

"I will take that oath, and keep it," said Zorzi.

"That is well. We have few signs and no ceremonies, but our promises are binding, and the forfeit is a painful death—so painful that even you might flinch before it. Indeed, we usually make some test of a man's courage before receiving him among us, though most of us have known each other since we were children. But you have shown us that you are fearless and honourable, and we ask nothing more of you, except to take the oath and then to keep it."

He turned to the company, still speaking in his languid way.

"If any man here knows good reason why this new companion should not be one of us, let him show it now."

Then all were silent, and uncovered their heads, but they still kept their masks on their faces. Zorzi stood out before them, and Venier was close beside him.

"Make the sign of the Cross," said Venier in a solemn tone, quite different from his ordinary voice, "and repeat the words after me."

And Zorzi repeated them steadily and precisely, holding his hand stretched out before him.

"In the name of the Holy Trinity, I promise and swear to give life and fortune in the good cause of restoring the original liberty of the people of Venice, obeying to that end the decisions of this honourable society, and to bear all sufferings rather than betray it, or any of its members. And I promise to help each one of my companions also in the ordinary affairs of life, to the best of my ability and fortune, within the bounds of reason, risking life and limb for the safety of each and all. And I promise most especially to honour and respect the wives, the daughters and the betrothed brides of all who belong to this fellowship, and to defend them from harm and insult, even as my own mother. And if I break any promise of this oath, may my flesh be torn from my limbs and my limbs from my body, one by one, to be burned with fire and the ashes thereof scattered abroad. Amen."

When Zorzi had said the last word, Venier grasped his hand, at the same time taking off the mask he wore, and he looked into the young man's face.

"I am Zuan Venier," he said, his indolent manner returning as he spoke.

"I am Jacopo Contarini," said the master of the house, offering his hand next.

Zorzi looked first at one, and then at the other; the first was a very pale young man, with bright blue eyes and delicate features that were prematurely weary and even worn; Contarini was called the handsomest Venetian of his day. Yet of the two, most men and women would have been more attracted to Venier at first sight. For Contarini's silken beard hardly concealed a weak and feminine mouth, with lips too red and too curving for a man, and his soft brown eyes had an unmanly tendency to look away while he was speaking. He was tall, broad shouldered, and well proportioned, with beautiful hands and shapely feet, yet he did not give an impression of strength, whereas Venier's languid manner, assumed as it doubtless was, could not hide the restless energy that lay in his lean frame.

One by one the other companions came up to Zorzi, took off their masks and grasped his hand, and he heard their lips pronounce names famous in Venetian history, Loredan, Mocenigo, Foscari and many others. But he saw that not one of them all was over five-and-twenty years of age, and with the keenness of the waif who had fought his own way in the world he judged that these were not men who could overturn the great Republic and build up a new government. Whatever they might prove to be in danger and revolution, however, he had saved his life by casting his lot with theirs, and he was profoundly grateful to them for having accepted him as one of themselves. But for their generosity, his weighted body would have been already lying at the bottom of the canal, and he was not just now inclined to criticise the mental gifts of those would-be conspirators who had so unexpectedly forgiven him for discovering their secret meeting.

"Sirs," he said, when he had grasped the hand of each, "I hope that in return for my life, for which I thank you, I may be of some service to the cause of liberty, and to each of you in singular, though I have but little hope of this, seeing that I am but an artist and you are all patricians. I pray you, inform me by what sign I may know you if we chance to meet outside this house, and how I may make myself known."

"We have little need of signs," answered Contarini, "for we meet often, and we know each other well. But our password is 'the Angel'—meaning the Angel that freed Saint Peter from his bonds, as we hope to free Venice from hers, and the token we give is the grip of the hand we have each given you."

Being thus instructed, Zorzi held his peace, for he felt that he was in the presence of men far above him in station, in whose conversation it would not be easy for him to join, and of whose daily lives he knew nothing, except that most of them lived in palaces and many were the sons of Councillors of the Ten, and of Senators, and Procurators and of others high in office, whereat he wondered much. But presently, as the excitement of what had happened wore off, and they sat about the table, they began to speak of the news of the day, and especially of the unjust and cruel acts of the Ten, each contributing some detail learned in his own home or among intimate friends. Zorzi sat silent in his place, listening, and he soon understood that as yet they had no definite plan for bringing on a revolution, and that they knew nothing of the populace upon whose support they reckoned, and of whom Zorzi knew much by experience. Yet, though they told each other things which seemed foolish to him, he said nothing on that first night, and all the time he watched Contarini very closely, and listened with especial attention to what he said, trying to discern his character and judge his understanding.

The splendid young Venetian was not displeased by Zorzi's attitude towards him, and presently came and sat beside him.

"I should have explained to you," he said, "that as it would be impossible for us to meet here without the knowledge of my servants, we come together on pretence of playing games of chance. My father lives in our palace near Saint Mark's, and I live here alone."

At this Foscari, the tall man with the black beard, looked at Contarini and laughed a little. Contarini glanced at him and smiled with some constraint.

"On such evenings," he continued, "I admit my guests myself, and they wear masks when they come, for though my servants are dismissed to their quarters, and would certainly not betray me for a dice-player, they might let drop the names of my friends if they saw them from an upper window."

At this juncture Zorzi heard the rattling of dice, and looking down the table he saw that two of the company were already throwing against each other. In a few minutes he found himself sitting alone near Zuan Venier, all the others having either begun to play themselves, or being engaged in wagering on the play of others.

"And you, sir?" inquired Zorzi of his neighbour.

"I am tired of games of chance," answered the pale nobleman wearily.

"But our host says it is a mere pretence, to hide the purpose of these meetings."

"It is more than that," said Venier with a contemptuous smile. "Do you play?"

"I am a poor artist, sir. I cannot."

"Ah, I had forgotten. That is very interesting. But pray do not call me 'sir' nor use any formality, unless we meet in public. At the 'Sign of the Angel' we are all brothers. Yes—yes—of course! You are a poor artist. When I expected to be obliged to cut your throat awhile ago, I really hoped that I might be able to fulfil some last wish of yours."

"I appreciated your goodness." Zorzi laughed a little nervously, now that the danger was over.

"I meant it, my friend, I do assure you. And I mean it now. One advantage of the fellowship is that one may offer to help a brother in any way without insulting him. I am not as rich as I was—I was too fond of those things once"—he pointed to the dice—"but if my purse can serve you, such as it is, I hope you will use it rather than that of another."

It was impossible to be offended, sensitive though Zorzi was.

"I thank you heartily," he answered.

"It would be a curiosity to see money do good for once," said Venier, languidly looking towards the players. "Contarini is losing again," he remarked.

"Does he generally lose much at play?" Zorzi asked, trying to seem indifferent.

Venier laughed softly.

"It is proverbial, 'to lose like Jacopo Contarini'!" he answered.

"Tell me, I beg of you, are all the meetings of the brotherhood like this one?"

"In what way?" asked Venier indifferently.

"Do you merely tell each other the news of the day, and then play at dice all night?"

"Some play cards." Venier laughed scornfully. "This is only the third of our secret sittings, I believe, but many of us meet elsewhere, during the day."

"Our host said that the society made a pretence of play in order to conspire against the State," said Zorzi. "It seems to me that this is making a pretence of conspiracy, with the chance of death on the scaffold, for the sake of dice-playing."

"To tell the truth, I think so too," answered the patrician, leaning back in his chair and looking thoughtfully at the young glassblower. "It is more interesting to break a law when you may lose your head for it than if you only risk a fine or a year's banishment. I daresay that seems complicated to you."

Zorzi laughed.

"If it is only for the sake of the danger," he said, "why not go and fight the Turks?"

"I have tried to do my share of that," replied Venier quietly. "So have some of the others."

"Contarini?" asked Zorzi.

"No. I believe he has never seen any fighting."

While the two were talking the play had proceeded steadily, and almost in silence. Contarini had lost heavily at first and had then won back his losses and twice as much more.

"That does not happen often," he said, pushing away the dice and leaning back.

Zorzi watched him. The yellow light of the wax candles fell softly upon his silky beard and too perfect features, and made splendid shadows in the scarlet silk of his coat, and flashed in the precious ruby of the ring he wore on his white hand. He seemed a true incarnation of his magnificent city, a century before the rest of all Italy in luxury, in extravagance, in the art of wasteful trifling with great things which is a rich man's way of loving art itself; and there were many others of the company who were of the same stamp as he, but whose faces had no interest for Zorzi compared with Contarini's. Beside him they were but ordinary men in the presence of a young god.

No woman could resist such a man as that, thought the poor

waif. It would be enough that Marietta's eyes should rest on him one moment, next Sunday, when he should be standing by the great pillar in the church, and her fate would be sealed then and there, irrevocably. It was not because she was only a glassmaker's daughter, brought up in Murano. What girl who was human would hesitate to accept such a husband? Contarini might choose his wife as he pleased, among the noblest and most beautiful in Italy. One or both of two reasons would explain why his choice had fallen upon Marietta. It was possible that he had seen her, and Zorzi firmly believed that no man could see her without loving her; and Angelo Beroviero might have offered such an immense dowry for the alliance as to tempt Jacopo's father. No one knew how rich old Angelo was since he had returned from Florence and Naples, and many said that he possessed the secret of making gold; but Zorzi knew better than that.

CHAPTER III

It was past midnight when Jacopo Contarini barred the door of his house and was alone. He took one of the candles from the inner room, put out all the others and was already in the hall, when he remembered that he had left his winnings on the table. Going back he opened the embroidered wallet he wore at his belt and swept the heap of heavy yellow coins into it. As the last disappeared into the bag and rang upon the others he distinctly heard a sound in the room. He started and looked about him.

It was not exactly the sound of a soft footfall, nor of breathing, but it might have been either. It was short and distinct, such a slight noise as might be made by drawing the palm of the hand quickly over a piece of stuff, or by a short breath checked almost instantly, or by a shoeless foot slipping a few inches on a thick carpet. Contarini stood still and listened, for though he had heard it distinctly he had no impression of the direction whence it had come. It was not repeated, and he began to search the room carefully.

He could find nothing. The single window, high above the floor, was carefully closed and covered by a heavy curtain which could not possibly have moved in the stillness. The tapestry was smoothly drawn and fastened upon the four walls. There was no furniture in the room but a big table and the benches and chairs. Above the tapestries the bare walls were painted, up to the carved ceiling. There was nothing to account for the noise. Contarini looked nervously over his shoulder as he left the room, and more than once again as he went up the marble staircase, candle in hand. There is probably nothing more disturbing to people of ordinary nerves than a sound heard in a lonely place and for which it is impossible to find a reason.

When he reached the broad landing he smiled at himself and looked back a last time, shading the candle with his hand, so as to throw the light down the staircase. Then he entered the apartment and locked himself in. Having passed through the large square vestibule and through a small room that led from it, he raised the latch of the next door very cautiously, shaded the candle again and looked in. A cool breeze almost put out the light.

"I am not asleep," said a sweet young voice. "I am here by the window."

He smiled happily at the words. The candlelight fell upon a

woman's face, as he went forward—such a face as men may see in dreams, but rarely in waking life.

Half sitting, half lying, she rested in Eastern fashion among the silken cushions of a low divan. The open windows of the balcony overlooked the low houses opposite, and the night breeze played with the little ringlets of her glorious hair. Her soft eyes looked up to her lover's face with infinite trustfulness, and their violet depths were like clear crystal and as tender as the twilight of a perfect day. She looked at him, her head thrown back, one ivory arm between it and the cushion, the other hand stretched out to welcome his. Her mouth was like a southern rose when there is dew on the smooth red leaves. In a maze of creamy shadows, the fine web of her garment followed the lines of her resting limbs in delicate folds, and one small white foot was quite uncovered. Her fan of ostrich feathers lay idle on the Persian carpet.

"Come, my beloved," she said. "I have waited long."

Contarini knelt down, and first he kissed the arching instep, and then her hand, that felt like a young dove just stirring under his touch, and his lips caressed the satin of her arm, and at last, with a fierce little choking cry, they found her own that waited for them, and there was no more room for words. In the silence of the June night one kiss answered another, and breath mingled with breath, and sigh with sigh.

At last the young man's head rested against her shoulder among the cushions. Then the Georgian woman opened her eyes slowly and glanced down at his face, while her hand stroked and smoothed his hair, and he could not see the strange smile on her wonderful lips. For she knew that he could not see it, and she let it come and go as it would, half in pity and half in scorn.

"I knew you would come," she said, bending her head a little nearer to his.

"When I do not, you will know that I am dead," he answered almost faintly, and he sighed.

"And then I shall go to you," she said, but as she spoke, she smiled again to herself. "I have heard that in old times, when the lords of the earth died, their most favourite slaves were killed upon the funeral pile, that their souls might wait upon their master's in the world beyond."

"Yes. It is true."

"And so I will be your slave there, as I am here, and the night that lasts for ever shall seem no longer than this summer night, that is too short for us."

"You must not call yourself a slave, Arisa," answered Jacopo.

"What am I, then? You bought me with your good gold from Aristarchi the Greek captain, in the slave market. Your steward has the receipt for the money among his accounts! And there is the Greek's written guarantee, too, I am sure, promising to take me back and return the money if I was not all he told you I was. Those are my documents of nobility, my patents of rank, preserved in your archives with your own!"

She spoke playfully, smiling to herself as she stroked his hair. But he caught her hand tenderly and brought it to his lips, holding it there.

"You are more free than I," he said. "Which of us two is the slave? You who hold me, or I who am held? This little hand will never let me go."

"I think you would come back to me," she answered. "But if I ran away, would you follow me?"

"You will not run away." He spoke quietly and confidently, still holding her hand, as if he were talking to it, while he felt the breath of her winds upon his forehead.

"No," she said, and there was a little silence.

"I have but one fear," he began, at last. "If I were ruined, what would become of you?"

"Have you lost at play again tonight?" she asked, and in her tone there was a note of anxiety.

Contarini laughed low, and felt for the wallet at his aide. He held it up to show how heavy it was with the gold, and made her take it. She only kept it a moment, but while it was in her hand her eyelids were half closed as if she were guessing at the weight, for he could not see her face.

"I won all that," he said. "Tomorrow you shall have the pearls."

"How good you are to me! But should you not keep the money? You may need it. Why do you talk of ruin?"

She knew that he would give her all he had, she almost guessed that he would commit a crime rather than lack gold to give her.

"You do not know my father!" he answered. "When he is displeased he threatens to let me starve. He will cut me off some day, and I shall have to turn soldier for a living. Would that not be ruin? You know his last scheme—he wishes me to marry the daughter of a rich glassmaker."

"I know." Arisa laughed contemptuously, "Great joy may your bride have of you! Is she really rich?"

"Yes. But you know that I will not marry her."

"Why not?" asked Arisa quite simply.

Contarini started and looked up at her face in the dim light. She was bending down to him with a very loving look.

"Why should you not marry?" she asked again. "Why do you start and look at me so strangely? Do you think I should care? Or that I am afraid of another woman for you?"

"Yes. I should have thought that you would be jealous." He still gazed at her in astonishment.

"Jealous!" she cried, and as she laughed she shook her beautiful head, and the gold of her hair glittered in the flickering candlelight. "Jealous? I? Look at me! Is she younger than I? I was eighteen years old the other day. If she is younger than I, she is a child—shall I be jealous of children? Is she taller, straighter, handsomer than I am? Show her to me, and I will laugh in her face! Can she sing to you, as I sing, in the summer nights, the songs you like and those I learned by the Kura in the shadow of Kasbek? Is her hair brighter than mine, is her hand softer, is her step lighter? Jealous? Not I! Will your rich wife be your slave? Will she wake for you, sing for you, dance for you, rise up and lie down at your bidding, work for you, live for you, die for you, as I will? Will she love you as I can love, caress you to sleep, or wake you with kisses at your dear will?"

"No—ah no! There is no woman in the world but you."

"Then I am not jealous of the rest, least of all, of your young bride. I will wager with myself against all her gold for your life, and I shall win—I have won already! Am I not trying to persuade you that you should marry?"

"I have not even seen her. Her father sent me a message tonight, bidding me go to church on Sunday and stand beside a certain pillar."

"To see and be seen," laughed Arisa. "It is not a fair exchange! She will look at the handsomest man in the world—hush! That is the truth. And you will see a little, pale, red-haired girl with silly blue eyes, staring at you, her wide mouth open and her clumsy hands hanging down. She will look like the wooden dolls they dress in the latest Venetian fashion to send to Paris every year, that the French courtiers may know what to wear! And her father will hurry her along, for fear that you should look too long at her and refuse to marry such a thing, even for Marco Polo's millions!"

Contarini laughed carelessly at the description.

"Give me some wine," he said. "We will drink her health."

Arisa rose with the grace of a young goddess, her hair tumbling over her bare shoulders in a splendid golden confusion. Contarini watched her with possessive eyes, as she went and came back, bringing him the drink. She brought him yellow wine of Chios in a glass calix of Murano, blown air-thin upon a slender stem and just touched here and there with drops of tender blue.

"A health to the bride of Jacopo Contarini!" she said, with a ringing little laugh.

Then she set the wine to her lips, so that they were wet with it, and gave him the glass; and as she stooped to give it, her hair fell forward and almost hid her from him.

"A health to the shower of gold!" he said, and he drank.

She sat down beside him, crossing her feet like an Eastern woman, and he set the empty glass carelessly upon the marble floor, as though it had been a thing of no price.

"That glass was made at her father's furnace," he said.

"A pity he could not have made his daughter of glass too," answered Arisa.

"Graceful and silent?"

"And easily destroyed! But if I say that, you will think me jealous, and I am not. She will bring you wealth. I wish her a long life, long enough to understand that she has been sold to you for your good name, like a slave, as I was sold, but that you gave gold for me because you wanted me for myself, whereas you want nothing of her but her gold."

"But for that—" Contarini seemed to be hesitating. "I never meant to marry her," he added.

"And but for that, you would not! But for that! But for the only thing which I have not to give you! I wish the world were mine, with all the rich secret things in it, the myriads of millions of diamonds in the earth, the thousand rivers of gold that lie deep in the mountain rocks, and all mankind, and all that mankind has, from end to end of it! Then you should have it all for your own, and you would not need to marry the little red-haired girl with the fish's mouth!"

Contarini laughed again.

"Have you seen her, that you can describe her so well? She may have black hair. Who knows?"

"Yes. Perhaps it is black, thin and coarse like the hair on a mule's tail; and she has black eyes, like ripe olives set in the white of a hardboiled egg; and she has a dark skin like Spanish leather which shines when she is hot and is grey when she is cold; and a black down on her upper lip; and teeth like a young horse. I hate those dark women!"

"But you have never seen her! She may be very pretty."

"Pretty, then! She shall be as you choose. She shall have a round face, round eyes, a round nose and a round mouth! Her face shall be pink and white, her eyes shall be of blue glass and her hair shall be as smooth and yellow as fresh butter. She shall have little fat white hands like a healthy baby, a double chin and a short waist. Then she will be what people call pretty."

"Yes," assented Jacopo. "That is very amusing. But just suppose, for the sake of discussion—it is impossible, of course, but suppose it—that instead of there being only one perfectly beautiful woman in the world, whose name is Arisa, there should be two, and that the name of the other chanced to be Marietta Beroviero."

Arisa raised her eyes and gazed steadily at Jacopo.

"You have seen her," she said in a tone of conviction. "She is beautiful."

"No. I give you my word that I have not seen her. I only wanted to know what you would do then."

"I do not believe that any woman is as beautiful as I am," answered the Georgian, with the quiet simplicity of a savage.

"But if there were one, and you saw her?" insisted the man, to see what she would say.

"We could not both live. One of us would kill the other."

"I believe you would," said Jacopo, watching her face.

She had forgotten his presence while she spoke; a fierce hardness had come into her eyes, and her upper lip was a little raised, in a cruel expression, just showing her teeth. He was surprised.

"I never saw you like that," he said.

"You should not make me think of killing," she answered, suddenly leaving her seat and kneeling beside him on the divan. "It is not good to think too much of killing—it makes one wish to do it."

"Then try and kill me with kisses," he said, looking into her eyes, that were growing tender again.

"You would not know you were dying," she whispered, her lips quite close to his.

As she kissed him, she loosened the collar from his white throat, and smoothed his thick hair back from his forehead upon the pillow, and she saw how pale he was, under her touch.

But by and by he fell asleep, and then she very softly drew her arm from beneath his tired head, and slipped from his side, and stood up, with a little sigh of relief. The candle had burned to the socket; she blew it out.

It was still an hour before dawn when she left the room, lifting the heavy curtain that hung before the door of her inner chamber. There, a faint light was burning before a shrine in a silver cup filled with oil. As she fastened the door noiselessly behind her, a man caught her in his arms, lifting her off her feet like a child.

Shaggy black hair grew low upon his bossy forehead, his dark eyes were fierce and bloodshot, a rough beard only half concealed the huge jaw and iron lips. He was half clad, in shirt and hose, and the muscles of his neck and arms stood out like brown ropes as he pressed the beautiful creature to his broad chest.

"I thought he would never sleep tonight," she whispered.

Her eyelids drooped, and her cheeks grew deadly white, and the strong man felt the furious beating of her heart against his own breast. He was Aristarchi, the Greek captain who had sold her for a slave, and she loved him.

In the wild days of seafighting among the Greek islands he had taken a small trading galley that had been driven out of her course. He left not a man of her crew alive to tell whether she had been Turkish or Christian, and he took all that was worth taking of her poor cargo. The only prize of any price was the captive Georgian girl who was being brought westward to be sold, like thousands of others in those days, with little concealment and no mystery, in one of the slave markets of northern Italy. Aristarchi claimed her for himself, as his share of the booty, but his men knew her value. Standing shoulder to shoulder between him and her, they drew their knives and threatened to cut her to pieces, if he would not promise to sell her as she was, when they should come to land, and share the price with them. They judged that she must be worth a thousand or fifteen hundred pieces of gold, for she was more beautiful than any woman they had ever seen, and they had already heard her singing most sweetly to herself, as if she were quite sure that she was in no danger, because she knew her own value. So Aristarchi was forced to consent, cursing them; and night and day they guarded her door against him, till they had brought her safe to Venice, and delivered her to the slave-dealers.

Then Aristarchi sold all that he had, except his ship, and it all brought far too little to buy such a slave. She would have gone with him, for she had seen that he was stronger than other men and feared neither God nor man, but she was well guarded, and he was only allowed to talk with her through a grated window, like those at convent gates.

She was not long in the dealers' house, for word was brought to all the young patricians of Venice, and many of them bid against each other for her, in the dealers' inner room, till Contarini outbid them all, saying that he could not live without her, though the price should ruin him, and because he had not enough gold he gave the dealers, besides money, a marvellous sword with a jewelled hilt, which one of his forefathers had taken at the siege of Constantinople, and which some said had belonged to the Emperor Justinian himself, nine hundred years ago.

Then Aristarchi and his men paid the dealers their commission and took the money and the sword. But before he went from the house, the Greek captain begged leave to see Arisa once more at the grating, and he told her that come what might he should steal her away. She bade him not to be in too great haste, and she promised that if he would wait, he should have with her more gold than her new master had given for her, for she would take all he had from him, little by little; and when they had enough they would leave Venice secretly, and live in a grand manner in Florence, or in Rome, or in Sicily. For she never doubted but that he would find some way of coming to her, though she were guarded more closely than in the slave-dealers' house, where the windows were grated and armed men slept before the door, and one of the dealers watched all night.

More than a year had passed since then; the strong Greek knew every corner of the house of the Agnus Dei, and every foothold under Arisa's windows, from the water to the stone sill, by which he could help himself a little as he went up hand over hand by the knotted silk rope that would have cut to the bone any hands but his. She kept it hidden in a cushioned footstool in her inner room. Many a risk he had run, and more than once in winter he had slipped down the rope with haste to let himself gently into the icy water, and he had swum far down the dark canal to a landingplace. For he was a man of iron.

So it came about that Jacopo Contarini lived in a fool's paradise, in which he was not only the chief fool himself, but was moreover in bodily danger more often than he knew. For though Aristarchi had hitherto managed to escape being seen, he would have killed Jacopo with his naked hands if the latter had ever caught him, as easily as a boy wrings a bird's neck, and with as little scruple of conscience.

The Georgian loved him for his hirsute strength, for his fearlessness, even his violence and dangerous temper. He dominated her as naturally as she controlled her master, whose vacillating nature and love of idle ease filled her with contempt. It was for the sake of gold that she acted her part daily and nightly, with a wisdom and unwavering skill that were almost superhuman; and the Greek ruffian agreed to the bargain, and had been in no haste to carry her off, as he might have done at any time. She hoarded the money she got from Jacopo, to give it by stealth to Aristarchi, who hid their growing wealth in a safe place where it was always ready; but she kept her jewels always together, in case of an unexpected flight, since she dared not sell them nor give them to the Greek, lest they should be missed.

Of late it had seemed to them both that the time for their final action was at hand, for it had been clear to Arisa that Jacopo was near the end of his resources, and that his father was resolved to force him to change his life. There were days when he was reduced to borrowing money for his actual needs, and though an occasional stroke of good fortune at play temporarily relieved him, Arisa was sure that he was constantly sinking deeper into debt. But within the week, the aspect of his affairs had changed. The marriage with Marietta had been proposed, and Arisa had made a discovery. She told Aristarchi everything, as naturally as she would have concealed everything from Contarini.

"We shall be rich," she said, twining her white arms round his swarthy neck and looking up into his murderous eyes with something like genuine adoration. "We shall get the wife's dowry for ourselves, by degrees, every farthing of it, and it shall be the dower of Aristarchi's bride instead. I shall not be portionless. You shall not be ashamed of me when you meet your old friends."

"Ashamed!" His arm pressed her to him till she longed to cry out for pain, yet she would not have had him less rough.

"You are so strong!" she gasped in a broken whisper. "Yes—a little looser—so! I can speak now. You must go to Murano tomorrow and find out all about this Angelo Beroviero and his daughter. Try to see her, and tell me whether she is pretty, but most of all learn whether she is really rich."

"That is easy enough. I will go to the furnace and offer to buy a cargo of glass for Sicily."

"But you will not take it?" asked Arisa in sudden anxiety lest he should leave her to make the voyage.

"No, no! I will make inquiries. I will ask for a sort of glass that does not exist."

"Yes," she said, reassured. "Do that. I must know if the girl is rich before I marry him to her."

"But can you make him marry her at all?" asked Aristarchi.

"I can make him do anything I please. We drank to the health of the bride tonight, in a goblet made by her father! The wine was strong, and I put a little syrup of poppies into it. He will not wake for hours. What is the matter?"

She felt the rough man shaking beside her, as if he were in an ague.

"I was laughing," he said, when he could speak. "It is a good jest. But is there no danger in all this? Is it quite impossible that he should take a liking for his wife?"

"And leave me?" Arisa's whisper was hot with indignation at the mere thought. "Then I suppose you would leave me for the first pretty girl with a fortune who wanted to marry you!"

"This Contarini is such a fool!" answered Aristarchi contemptuously, by way of explanation and apology.

Arisa was instantly pacified.

"If he should be foolish enough for that, I have means that will keep him," she answered.

"I do not see how you can force him to do anything except by his passion for you."

"I can. I was not going to tell you yet—you always make me tell you everything, like a child."

"What is it?" asked the Greek. "Have you found out anything new about him? Of course you must tell me."

"We hold his life in our hands," she said quietly, and Aristarchi knew that she was not exaggerating the truth.

She began to tell him how this was the third time that a number of masked men had come to the house an hour after dark, and had stayed till midnight or later, and how Contarini had told her that they came to play at dice where they were safe from interruption, and that on these nights the servants were sent to their quarters at sunset on pain of dismissal if Jacopo found them about the house, but that they also received generous presents of money to keep them silent.

"The man is a fool!" said Aristarchi again. "He puts himself in their power."

"He is much more completely in ours," answered Arisa. "The servants believe that his friends come to play dice. And so they do. But they come for something more serious."

Aristarchi moved his massive head suddenly to an attitude of profound attention.

"They are plotting against the Republic," whispered Arisa. "I can hear all they say."

"Are you sure?"

"I tell you I can hear every word. I can almost see them. Look here. Come with me."

She rose and he followed her to the corner of the room where the small silver lamp burned steadily before an image of Saint Mark, and above a heavy kneeling-stool.

"The foot moves," she said, and she was already on her knees on the floor, pushing the step.

It slid back with the soft sound Contarini had heard before he came upstairs. The upper part of the woodwork was built into the wall.

"They meet in the place below this," Arisa said. "When they are there, I can see a glimmer of light. I cannot get my head in. It is too narrow, but I hear as if I were with them."

"How did you find this out?" asked Aristarchi on the floor beside her, and reaching down into the dark space to explore it with his hand. "It is deep," he continued, without waiting for an answer. "There may be some passage by which one can get down."

"Only a child could pass. You see how narrow it is. But one can hear every sound. They said enough tonight to send them all to the scaffold."

"Better they than we if we ever have to make the choice," said the Greek ominously.

He had withdrawn his arm and was planted upon his hands and knees, his shaggy head hanging over the dark aperture. He was like some rough wild beast that has tracked its quarry to earth and crouches before the hole, waiting for a victim.

"How did you find this out?" he asked again, looking up.

She was standing by the corner of the stool, now, all her marvellous beauty showing in the light of the little lamp and against the wall behind her.

"I was saying my prayers here, the first night they met," she said, as if it were the most natural thing in the world. "I heard voices, as it seemed, under my feet. I tried to push away the stool, and the foot moved. That is all."

Aristarchi's jaw dropped a little as he looked up at her.

"Do you say prayers every night?" he asked in wonder.

"Of course I do. Do you never say a prayer?"

"No." He was still staring at her.

"That is very wrong," she said, in the earnest tone a mother might use to her little child. "Some harm will befall us, if you do not say your prayers."

A slow smile crossed the ruffian's face as he realised that this evil woman who was ready to commit the most atrocious deeds out of love for him, was still half a child.

CHAPTER IV

Marietta awoke before sunrise, with a smile on her lips, and as she opened her eyes, the world seemed suddenly gladder than ever before, and her heart beat in time with it. She threw back the shutters wide to let in the June morning as if it were a beautiful living thing; and it breathed upon her face and caressed her, and took her in its spirit arms, and filled her with itself.

Not a sound broke the stillness, as she looked out, and the glassy waters of the canal reflected delicate tints from the sky, palest green and faintest violet and amber with all the lovely changing colours of the dawn. By the footway a black barge was moored, piled high with round uncovered baskets of beads, white, blue, deep red and black, waiting to be taken over to Venice where they would be threaded for the East, and the colours stood out in strong contrast with the grey stones, the faint reflections in the water and the tender sky above. There were flowers on the windowsill, a young rose with opening buds, growing in a red earthen jar, and a pot of lavender just bursting into flower, with a sweet geranium beside it and some rosemary. Zorzi had planted them all for her, and her serving-woman had helped her to fasten the pots in the window, because it would have been out of the question that any man except her father should enter her room, even when she was not there. But they were Zorzi's flowers, and she bent down and smelt their fragrance. On a table behind her a single rose hung over the edge of a tall glass with a slender stem, almost the counterpart of the one in which Contarini had drunk her health at midnight. Her father had given it to her as it came from the annealing oven, still warm after long hours of cooling with many others like it. She loved it for its grace and lightness, and as for the rose, it was the one she had made Zorzi give back to her yesterday. She meant to keep it in water till it faded, and then she would press it between the first page and the binding of her parchment missal. It would keep some of its faint scent, perhaps, and if any one saw it, no one would ever guess whence it came.

It meant a great thing to her, for it had told her Zorzi's secret, which he had kept so well. He should know hers some day, but not yet, and her drooping lids could hide it if it ever came into her eyes. It was too soon to let him know that she loved him. That was one reason for hiding it, but she had another. If her father guessed that she loved the waif, it would fare ill with him. She fancied she could see the old man's fiery brown eyes and hear his angry voice. Poor Zorzi would be driven from Murano and Venice, never to set foot again within the boundaries of the Republic; for Beroviero was a man of weight and influence, of whom Venice was proud.

Youth would be very sad if it counted time and labour as it is reckoned and valued by mature age. Some day Zorzi would be no longer a mere paid helper, calling himself a servant when his humour was bitter, tending a fire on his knees and grinding coloured earths and salts in a mortar. He had the understanding of the glorious art, and the true love of it, with the magic touch; he would make a name for himself in spite of the harsh Venetian law, and some day his master would be proud to call him son. There would not be many months to wait. Months or years, what mattered, since she loved him and was at last quite sure that he loved her? Today, that was enough. She would go over to the glasshouse and sit in the garden, by the rose he had planted, and now and then she would go into the close furnace room where he worked with her father, or Zorzi would come out for something; she should be near him, she should see his face and hear his quiet voice, and she would say to herself: He loves me, he loves me—as often as she chose, knowing that it was true.

Since she knew it, she was sure that she should see it in his face, that had hidden it from her so long. There would be glances when he thought she was not watching him, his colour would come and go, as yesterday, and he would do her some little service, now and then, in which the sweet truth, against his will, should tell itself to her again and again. It would be a delicious and ever-remembered day, each minute a pearl, each hour a chaplet of jewels, from golden sunrise to golden sunset, all perfect through and through.

There were so many little things she could watch in him, now that she knew the truth, things that had long meant nothing and would mean volumes today. She would watch him, and then call him suddenly and see him try to hide the little gladness he would feel as he turned to her; and when they were alone a moment, she would ask him whether he had remembered to forget Jacopo Contarini's name; and some day, but not for a long time yet, she would drop a rose again, and she would turn as he picked it up, but she would not make him give it back to her, and in that way he should know that she loved him. She must not think of that, for it was too soon, yet she could almost see his face as it would be when he knew.

Yesterday her father had talked again of her marriage. A

whole month had passed since he had even alluded to it, but this time he had spoken of it as a certainty; and she had opened her eyes wide in surprise. She did not believe that it was to be. How could she marry a man she did not love? How could she love any man but Zorzi? They might show her twenty Venetian patricians, that she might choose among them. Meanwhile she would show her indifference. Nothing was easier than to put on an inscrutable expression which betrayed nothing, but which, as she knew, sometimes irritated her father beyond endurance.

He had always promised that she should not be married against her will, as many girls were. Then why should she marry Contarini, any more than any other man except the one she had chosen? She need only say that Contarini did not please her, and her father would certainly not try to use force. There was therefore nothing to fear, and since her first surprise was over, she felt sure of appearing quite indifferent. She would put the thought out of her mind and begin the day with the perfect certainty that the marriage was altogether impossible.

She looked out over her flowers. The door of the glass-house was open now, and the burly porter was sweeping; she could hear the cypress broom on the flagstones inside, and presently it appeared in sight while the porter was still invisible, and it whisked out a mixture of black dust and bread crumbs and bits of green salad leaves, and the old man came out and swept everything across the footway into the canal. As he turned to go back, the workmen came trooping across the bridge to the furnaces—pale men with intent faces, very different from ordinary working people. For each called himself an artist, and was one; and each knew that so far as the law was concerned the proudest noble in Venice could marry his daughter without the least derogation from patrician dignity. The workmen differed from her own father not in station, but only in the degree of their prosperity.

If Zorzi could ever have been one of them the rest would have been simple enough. But he could not, any more than a black man could turn white at will. There was no evasion of law by which a man not born a Venetian could ever be a glassblower, or could ever acquire the privileges possessed from birth by one of those shabby, pale young men who were crowding past the porter to go to their hard day's work. Yet dexterous as they were, there was not one that had his skill, there was not one that could compare with him as an artist, as a workman, as a man. No Indian caste, no ancient nobility, no mystic priesthood ever set up a barrier so impassable between itself and the outer world as that which defended the glassblowers of Murano for centuries against all who wished to be initiated. Even the boys who fed the fires all night were of the calling, and by and by would become workmen, and perhaps masters, legally almost the equals of the splendid nobles who sat in the Grand Council over there in Venice.

Zorzi's very existence was an anomaly. He had no social right to be what he was, and he knew it when he called himself a servant, for the cruel law would not allow him to be anything else so long as he helped Angelo Beroviero.

Suddenly, while Marietta watched the men, Zorzi was there among them, coming out as they went in. He must have risen early, she thought, for she did not know that he had slept in the laboratory. He looked pale and thin as he flattened himself against the doorpost to let a workman pass, and then slipped out himself. No one greeted him, even by a nod. Marietta knew that they hated him because he was in her father's confidence; and somehow, instead of pitying him, she was glad.

It seemed natural that he should not be one of them, that he should pass them with quiet indifference and that they should feel for him the instinctive dislike which most inferiors feel for those above them. Doubtless, they looked down upon him, or told themselves that they did; but in their hearts they knew that a man with such a face was born to be their teacher and their master, and the girl was proud of him. He treated them with more civility than they bestowed on him, but it was the courtesy of a superior who would not assert himself, who would scorn to thrust himself forward or in any way to claim what was his by right, if it were not freely offered. Marietta drew back a little, so that she could just see him between the flowers, without being seen.

He stood still, looking down at the canal till the last of the men had passed in. Then, before he went on, he raised his eyes slowly to Marietta's window, not guessing that her own were answering his from behind the rosemary and the geranium. His pale face was very sad and thoughtful as he looked up. She had never seen him look so tired. The porter had shut the door, which he never allowed to remain open one moment longer than was absolutely necessary, and Zorzi stood quite alone on the footway. As he looked, his face softened and grew so tender that the girl who watched him unseen stretched out her arms towards him with unconscious yearning, and her heart beat very fast, so that she felt the pulses in her throat almost choking her; yet her face was pale and her soft lips were dry and cold. For it was not all happiness that she felt; there was a sweet mysterious pain with it, which was nowhere, and yet all through her, that was weakness and yet might turn to strength, a hunger of longing for something dear and unknown and divine, without which all else was an empty shadow. Then her eyes opened to him, as he had never seen them, blue as the depth of sapphires and dewy with love mists of youth's early spring; it was impossible that he should stand there, just beyond the narrow water, and not feel that she saw him and loved him, and that her heart was crying out the true words he never hoped to hear.

But he did not know. And all at once his eyes fell, and she could almost see that he sighed as he turned wearily away and walked with bent head towards the wooden bridge. She would have given anything to look out and see him cross and come nearer, but she remembered that she was not yet dressed, and she blushed as she drew further back into the room, gathering the thin white linen up to her throat, and frightened at the mere thought that he should catch sight of her. She would not call her serving-woman yet, she would be alone a little while longer. She threw back her russet hair, and bent down to smell the rose in the tall glass. The sun was risen now and the first slanting beams shot sideways through her window from the right. The day that was to be so sweet had begun most sweetly. She had seen him already, far earlier than usual; she would see him many times before the little brown maid crossed the canal to bring her home in the evening.

The thought put an end to her meditations, and she was suddenly in haste to be dressed, to be out of the house, to be sitting in the little garden of the glass-house where Zorzi must soon pass again. She called and clapped her hands, and her serving-woman entered from the outer room in which she slept. She brought a great painted earthenware dish, on which fruit was arranged, half of a small yellow melon fresh from the cool storeroom, a little heap of dark red cherries and a handful of ripe plums. There was white wheaten bread, too, and honey from Aquileia, in a little glass jar, and there was a goblet of cold water. The maid set the big dish on the table, beside the glass that held Zorzi's rose, and began to make ready her mistress's clothes.

Marietta tasted the melon, and it was cool and aromatic, and she stood eating a slice of it, just where she could look through the flowers on the windowsill at the door of the glass-house, so that if Zorzi passed again she should see him. He did not come, and she was a little disappointed; but the melon was very good, and afterwards she ate a few cherries and spread a spoonful of honey on a piece of bread, and nibbled at it; and she drank some of the water, looking out of the window over the glass.

"Was it always so beautiful?" she asked, speaking to herself, in a sort of wonder at what she felt, as she set the glass upon the table.

Nella, the maid, turned quickly to her with a look of inquiry.

"What?" she asked. "What is beautiful? The weather? It is summer! Of course it is fine. Did you expect the north wind today, or rain from the southwest?"

Marietta laughed, sweet and low. The little maid always amused her. There was something cheerful in the queer little scolding sentences, spoken with a rising inflection on almost every word, musical and yet always seeming to protest gently against anything Marietta said.

"I know of something much more beautiful than the weather," Nella added, seeing that she got no answer except a laugh. "Do you wish to know what is more beautiful than a summer's day?"

"Oh, I know the answer to that!" cried Marietta. "You used to catch me in that way when I was a small girl."

"Well, my little lady, what is the answer? I have said nothing."

"What is more beautiful than a summer's day? Why, two summer's days, of course! I was always dreadfully disappointed when you gave me that answer, for I expected something wonderful."

Nella shook her head as she unfolded the fine linen things, and uttered a sort of little clucking sound, meant to show her disapproval of such childish jests.

"Tut, tut, tut! We are grown up now! Are we children? No, we are a young lady, beautiful and serious! Tut, tut, tut! That you should remember the nonsense I used to talk to make you stop crying for your mother, blessed soul! And I myself was so full of tears that a drop of water would have drowned me! But all passes, praise be to God!"

"I hope not," said Marietta, but so low that the woman did not hear.

"I will ask you a riddle," continued Nella presently.

"Oh no!" laughed Marietta. "I could no more guess a riddle today than I could give a dissertation on theology. Riddles are for rainy days in winter, when we sit by the fire in the evening wishing it were morning again. I know the great riddle at last—I have found it out. It is the most beautiful thing in the world."

"Then it is true," observed Nella, looking at her with satisfaction.

"What?" asked the young girl carelessly.

"That you are to be married."

"I hope so," answered Marietta. "Some day, but there is time yet—perhaps a very long time."

"As long as it will take to make a wedding gown embroidered with gold and pearls. Not a day longer than that." Nella looked very wise and watched her mistress's face.

"What do you mean?"

"The master has ordered just such a gown. That is what I mean. Do you think I would talk of such a beautiful thing, just to make you unhappy, if you were not to have one? But you will not forget poor Nella, my little lady? You will take me with you to Venice?"

"Then you think I am to marry some one from the city? What is his name?"

"The master knows. That is enough. But it must be the Doge's son, or at least the son of the Admiral of Venice. It will take two months to embroider the gown. That means that you are to be married in August, of course."

"Do you think so?" asked Marietta indifferently.

"I know it." And Nella gave a discontented little snort, for she did not like to have her conclusions questioned. "Am I halfwitted? Am I in my dotage? Am I an imbecile? The gown is ordered, and that is the truth. Do you think the master has ordered a wedding gown embroidered with gold and pearls for himself?"

Marietta tossed her hair back and shook it down her shoulders, laughing gaily at the idea.

"Ah!" cried Nella indignantly. "Now you are mocking me! You are making a laughingstock of your poor Nella! It is too bad! But you will be sorry that you laughed at me, when I am not here to bring you melons and cherries and tell you the news in the morning! You will say: 'Poor Nella! She was not such an ignorant person after all!' That is what you will say. I tell you that if your father orders a wedding gown, you are the only person in the house who can wear it, and he would not order it just to see how beautiful you would be as a bride! He is a serious man, the master, he is grave, he is wise! He does nothing without much reflection, and what he does is well done. He says, 'My daughter is to be married, therefore I will order a splendid dress for her.' That is what he says, and he orders it."

"That has an air of reason," said Marietta gravely. "I did not mean to laugh at you."

"Oh, very well! If you thought your father unreasonable, what should I say? He does not say one thing and do another, your father. And I will tell you something. They will make the gown even handsomer than he ordered it, because he is very rich, and he will grumble and scold, but in the end he will pay, for the honour of the house. Then you will wear the gown, and all Venice will see you in it on your wedding day."

"That will be a great thing for the Venetians," observed the young girl, trying not to smile.

"They will see that there are rich men in Murano, too. It will be a lesson for their intolerable vanity."

"Are the Venetians so very vain?"

"Well! Was not my husband a Venetian, blessed soul? It seems to me that I should know. Have I forgotten how he would fasten a cock's feather in his cap, almost like a gentleman, and hang his cloak over one shoulder, and pull up his hose till they almost cracked, so as to show off his leg? Ah, he had handsome legs, my poor Vito, and he never would use anything but pure beeswax to stiffen his mustaches. No, he never would use tallow. He was almost like a gentleman!"

Nella's little brown eyes were moist as she recalled her husband's small vanities; his dislike of tallow as a cosmetic seemed to affect her particularly.

"That is why I say that it will be a lesson to the pride of those Venetians to see your marriage," she resumed, after drying her eyes with the back of her hand. "And the people of Murano will be there, and all the glassblowers in their guild, since the master is the head of it. I suppose Zorzi will manage to be there, too."

Nella spoke the last words in a tone of disapproval.

"Why should Zorzi not be at my wedding?" asked Marietta carelessly.

"Why should he?" asked the serving-woman with unusual bluntness. "But I daresay the master will find something for him to do. He is clever enough at doing anything."

"Yes—he is clever," assented the young girl. "Why do you not like him? Give me some more water—you are always afraid that I shall use too much!"

"I have a conscience," grumbled Nella. "The water is brought from far, it is paid for, it costs money, we must not use too much of it. Every day the boats come with it, and the row of earthen jars in the court is filled, and your father pays—he always pays, and pays, and pays, till I wonder where the money all comes from. They say he makes gold, over there in the furnace."

"He makes glass," answered Marietta. "And if he orders gowns for me with pearls and gold, he will not grudge me a jug of water. Why do you dislike Zorzi?"

"He is as proud as a marble lion, and as obstinate as a Lombardy mule," explained Nella, with fine imagery. "If that is not enough to make one dislike a young man, you shall tell me so! But one of those days he will fall. There is trouble for the proud."

"How does his great pride show itself?" asked Marietta. "I have not noticed it."

"That would indeed be the end of everything, if he showed his pride to you!" Nella was much displeased by the mere suggestion. "But with us it is different. He never speaks to the other workmen."

"They never speak to him."

"And quite right, too, since he holds his head so high, with no reason at all! But it will not last for ever! I wonder what the master would think, for instance, if he knew that Zorzi takes the skiff in the evening, and rows himself over to Venice, all alone, and comes back long after midnight, and sleeps in the glass-house across the way because he cannot get into the house. Zorzi! Zorzi! The master cannot move without Zorzi! And where is Zorzi at night? At home and in bed, like a decent young man? No. Zorzi is away in Venice, heaven knows where, doing heaven knows what! Do you wonder that he is so pale and tired in the morning? It seems to me quite natural. Eh? What do you think, my pretty lady?"

Marietta was silent for a moment. It was only a servant's spiteful gossip, but it hurt her.

"Are you sure that he goes to Venice alone at night?" she asked, after a little pause.

"Am I sure that I live, that I belong to you, and that my name is Nella? Is not the boat moored under my window? Did I not hear the chain rattling softly last night? I got up and looked out, and I saw Zorzi, as I see you, taking the padlock off. I am not blind—praise be to heaven, I see. He turned the boat to the left, so he must have been going to Venice, and it was at least an hour after the midnight bells when I heard the chain again, and I looked out, and there he was. But he did not come into the house. And this morning I saw him coming out of the glass-house, just as the men went in. He was as pale as a boiled chicken."

Marietta had seen him, too, and the coincidence gave colour

to the rest of the woman's tale, as would have happened if the whole story had been an invention instead of being quite true. Nella was combing the girl's thick hair, an operation peculiarly conducive to a maid's chattering, for she has the certainty that her mistress cannot get away, and must therefore listen patiently.

A shadow had fallen on the brightness of Marietta's morning. She was paler, too, but she said nothing.

"Of course he was tired," continued Nella. "Did you suppose that he would come back with pink cheeks and bright eyes, like a baby from baptism, after being out half the night?"

"He is always pale," said Marietta.

"Because he goes to Venice every night," retorted Nella viciously. "That is the good reason! Oh, I am sure of it! And besides, I shall watch him, now that I know. I shall see him whenever he takes the boat."

"It is none of your business where he goes," answered Marietta. "It does not concern any one but himself."

"Oh, indeed!" sneered Nella. "Then the honour of the house does not matter! It is no concern of ours! And your father need never know that his trusty servant, his clever assistant, his faithful confidant, who shares all his secrets, is a good-for-nothing fellow who spends his nights in gambling, or drinking, or perhaps in making love to some Venetian girl as honourable and well behaved as himself!"

Marietta had grown steadily more angry while Nella was talking. She had her father's temper, though she could control it better than he.

"I will find out whether this story is true," she said coldly. "If it is not, it will be the worse for you. You shall not serve me any longer, unless you can be more careful in what you say."

Nella's jaw dropped and her hands stood still and trembled, the one holding the comb upraised, the other gathering a quantity of her mistress's hair. Marietta had never spoken to her like this in her life.

"Send me away?" faltered the woman in utter amazement. "Send me away!" she repeated, still quite dazed. "But it is impossible—" her voice began to break, as if some one were shaking her violently by the shoulders. "Oh no, no! You w-ill n-ot—no-o-o!"

The sound grew more piercing as she went on, and the words were soon lost, as she broke into a violent fit of hysterical crying.

Marietta's anger subsided as her pity for the poor creature increased. She had made a great effort to speak quietly and not to say more than she meant, and she had certainly not expected to produce such a tremendous commotion. Nella tore her hair, drew her nails down her cheeks, as if she would tear them with scratches, rocked herself forwards and backwards and from side to side, the tears poured down her brown cheeks, she screamed and blubbered and whimpered in quick alternation, and in a few moments tumbled into the corner of a big chair, a sobbing and convulsed little heap of womanhood.

Marietta tried to quiet her, and was so sorry for her that she could almost have cried too, until she remembered the detestable things which Nella had said about Zorzi, and which the woman's screams had driven out of her memory for an instant. Then she longed to beat her for saying them, and still Nella alternately moaned and howled, and twisted herself in the corner of the big chair. Marietta wondered whether her servant were going mad, and whether this might not be a judgment of heaven for telling such atrocious lies about poor Zorzi. In that case it was of course deserved, thought she, watching Nella's contortions; but it was very sudden.

She made up her mind to call the other women, and turned to go to the door. As she did so her skirt caught a comb that lay on the edge of the table and swept it off, so that it fell upon the pavement with a dry rap. Instantly Nella sat up straight and rubbed her eyes, looking about for the cause of the sound. When she saw the comb, the serving-woman's instinct returned, and with it her normal condition of mind. She picked up the comb with a quick movement, shook her head and began combing Marietta's hair again before the girl could sit down.

Peace was restored, for she did not speak again, as she helped her mistress to finish dressing; but though Marietta tried to look kindly at her once or twice, Nella quite refused to see it, and did her duty without ever raising her eyes.

It was soon finished, for the pleasure the young girl had taken in making much of the first details of the day that was to be so happy was all gone. She did not believe her woman, but there was a cloud over everything and she was in haste to get an answer to the question which it would not be easy to ask. She must know if Zorzi had been to Venice during the night, for until she knew that, all hope of peace was at an end. Nella had meant no harm, but she had played the fatal little part in which destiny loves to go masking through life's endless play.

CHAPTER V

Zorzi had slept but little after he had at last lain down upon the long bench in the laboratory, for the scene in which he had been the chief actor that night had made a profound impression upon him. There are some men who would not make good soldiers but who can face sudden and desperate danger with a calmness which few soldiers really possess, and which is generally accompanied by some marked superiority of mind; but such exceptional natures feel the reaction that follows the perilous moment far more than the average fighting man. They are those who sometimes stem the rush of panic and turn back whole armies from ruin to victorious battle; they are those who spring forward from the crowd to save life when some terrible accident has happened, as if they were risking nothing, and who generally succeed in what they attempt; but they are not men who learn to fight every day as carelessly and naturally as they eat, drink or sleep. Their chance of action may come but once or twice in a lifetime; yet when it comes it finds them far more ready and cool than the average good soldier could ever be. Like strength in some men, their courage seems to depend on quality and very little on quantity, training or experience.

Zorzi knew very well that although the young gentlemen who were playing at conspiracy in Jacopo's house did not constitute a serious danger to the Republic, they were fully aware of their own peril, and would not have hesitated to take his life if it had not occurred to them that he might be useful. His intrepid manner had saved him, but now that the night was over he felt such a weariness and lassitude as he had never known before.

The adventure had its amusing side, of course. To Zorzi, who knew the people well, it was very laughable to think that a score of dissolute young patricians should first fancy themselves able to raise a revolution against the most firmly established government in Europe, and should then squander the privacy which they had bought at a frightful risk in mere gambling and dice-playing. But there was nothing humorous about the oath he had taken. In the first place, it had been sworn in solemn earnest, and was therefore binding upon him; secondly, if he broke it, his life would not be worth a day's purchase. He was brave enough to have scorned the second consideration, but he was far too honourable to try and escape the first. He had made the promises to save his life, it was true, and under great pressure, but he would have despised himself as a coward if he had not meant to keep them.

And he had solemnly bound himself to respect "the betrothed brides" of all the brethren of the company. Marietta was not betrothed to Jacopo Contarini yet, but there was no doubt that she would be before many days; to "respect" undoubtedly meant that he must not try to win her away from her affianced husband; if he had ever dreamt that in some fair, fantastically improbable future, Marietta could be his wife, he had parted with the right to dream the like again. Therefore, when he had stood awhile looking up at her window that morning, he sighed heavily and went away.

He had never had any hope that she would love him, much less that he could ever marry her, yet he felt that he was parting with the only thing in life which he held higher than his art, and that the parting was final. For months, perhaps for years, he had never closed his eyes to sleep without calling up her face and repeating her name, he had never got up in the morning without looking forward to seeing her and hearing her voice before he should lie down again. A man more like others would have said to himself that no promise could bind him to anything more than the performance of an action, or the abstention from one, and that the right of dreaming was his own for ever. But Zorzi judged differently. He had a sensitiveness that was rather manly than masculine; he had scruples of which he was not ashamed, but which most men would laugh at; he had delicacies of conscience in his most private thoughts such as would have been more natural in a cloistered nun, living in ignorance of the world, than in a waif who had faced it at its worst, and almost from childhood. Innocent as his dream had been, he resolved to part with it, and never to dream it again. He was glad that Marietta had taken back the rose he had picked up yesterday; if she had not, he would have forced himself to throw it away, and that would have hurt him.

So he began his day in a melancholy mood, as having buried out of sight for ever something that was very dear to him. In time, his love of his art would fill the place of the other love, but on this first day he went about in silence, with hungry eyes and tightened lips, like a man who is starving and is too proud to ask a charity.

He waited for Beroviero at the door of his house, as he did every morning, to attend him to the laboratory. The old man looked at him inquiringly, and Zorzi bent his head a little to explain that he had done what had been required of him, and he followed his master across the wooden bridge. When they were alone in the laboratory, he told as much of his story as was necessary.

He had found the lord Jacopo Contarini at his house with a party of friends, he said, and he added at once that they were all men. Contarini had bidden him speak before them all, but he had whispered his message so that only Contarini should hear it. After a time he had been allowed to come away. No—Contarini had given no direct answer, he had sent no reply; he had only said aloud to his friends that the message he received was expected. That was all. The friends who were there? Zorzi answered with perfect truth that he did not remember to have seen, any of them before.

Beroviero was silent for a while, considering the story.

"He would have thought it discourteous to leave his friends," he said at last, "or to whisper an answer to a messenger in their presence. He said that he had expected the message, he will therefore come."

To this Zorzi answered nothing, for he was glad not to be questioned further about what had happened. Presently Beroviero settled to his work with his usual concentration. For many months he had been experimenting in the making of fine red glass of a certain tone, of which he had brought home a small fragment from one of his journeys. Hitherto he had failed in every attempt. He had tried one mixture after another, and had produced a score of different specimens, but not one of them had that marvellous light in it, like sunshine striking through bright blood, which he was striving to obtain. It was nearly three weeks since his small furnace had been allowed to go out, and by this time he alone knew what the glowing pots contained, for he wrote down very carefully what he did and in characters which he believed no one could understand but himself.

As usual every morning, he proceeded to make trial of the materials fused in the night. The furnace, though not large, held three crucibles, before each of which was the opening, still called by the Italian name 'bocca,' through which the materials are put into the pots to melt into glass, and by which the melted glass is taken out on the end of the blowpipe, or in a copper ladle, when it is to be tested by casting it. The furnace was arched from end to end, and about the height of a tall man; the working end was like a round oven with three glowing openings; the straight part, some twenty feet long, contained the annealing oven through which the finished pieces were made to move slowly, on iron pans, during many hours, till the glass had passed from extreme heat almost to the temperature of the air. The most delicate vessels ever produced in Murano have all been made in single furnaces, the materials being melted, converted into glass and finally annealed, by one fire. At least one old furnace is standing and still in use, which has existed for centuries, and those made nowadays are substantially like it in every important respect.

Zorzi stood holding a long-handled copper ladle, ready to take out a specimen of the glass containing the ingredients most lately added. A few steps from the furnace a thick and smooth plate of iron was placed on a heavy wooden table, and upon this the liquid glass was to be poured out to cool.

"It must be time," said Beroviero, "unless the boys forgot to turn the sand-glass at one of the watches. The hour is all but run out, and it must be the twelfth since I put in the materials."

"I turned it myself, an hour after midnight," said Zorzi, "and also the next time, when it was dawn. It runs three hours. Judging by the time of sunrise it is running right."

"Then make the trial."

Beroviero stood opposite Zorzi, his face pale with heat and excitement, his fiery eyes reflecting the fierce light from the 'bocca' as he bent down to watch the copper ladle go in. Zorzi had wrapped a cloth round his right hand, against the heat, and he thrust the great spoon through the round orifice. Though it was the hundredth time of testing, the old man watched his movements with intensest interest.

"Quickly, quickly!" he cried, quite unconscious that he was speaking.

There was no need of hurrying Zorzi. In two steps he had reached the table, and the white hot stuff spread out over the iron plate, instantly turning to a greenish yellow, then to a pale rose-colour, then to a deep and glowing red, as it felt the cool metal. The two men stood watching it closely, for it was thin and would soon cool. Zorzi was too wise to say anything. Beroviero's look of interest gradually turned into an expression of disappointment.

"Another failure," he said, with a resignation which no one would have expected in such a man.

His practised eyes had guessed the exact hue of the glass, while it still lay on the iron, half cooled and far too hot to touch. Zorzi took a short rod and pushed the round sheet till a part of it was over the edge of the table.

"It is the best we have had yet," he observed, looking at it.

"Is it?" asked Beroviero with little interest, and without giving the glass another glance. "It is not what I am trying to get.

It is the colour of wine, not of blood. Make something, Zorzi, while I write down the result of the experiment."

He took big pen and the sheet of rough paper on which he had already noted the proportions of the materials, and he began to write, sitting at the large table before the open window. Zorzi took the long iron blowpipe, cleaned it with a cloth and pushed the end through the orifice from which he had taken the specimen. He drew it back with a little lump of melted glass sticking to it.

Holding the blowpipe to his lips, he blew a little, and the lump swelled, and he swung the pipe sharply in a circle, so that the glass lengthened to the shape of a pear, and he blew again and it grew. At the 'bocca' of the furnace he heated it, for it was cooling quickly; and he had his iron pontil ready, as there was no one to help him, and he easily performed the feat of taking a little hot glass on it from the pot and attaching it to the further end of the fast-cooling pear. If Beroviero had been watching him he would have been astonished at the skill with which the young man accomplished what it requires two persons to do; but Zorzi had tricks of his own, and the pontil supported itself on a board while he cracked the pear from the blowpipe with a wet iron, as well as if a boy had held it in place for him; and then heating and reheating the piece, he fashioned it and cut it with tongs and shears, rolling the pontil on the flat arms of his stool with his left hand, and modelling the glass with his right, till at last he let it cool to its natural colour, holding it straight downward, and then swinging it slowly, so that it should fan itself in the air. It was a graceful calix now, of a deep wine red, clear and transparent as claret.

Zorzi turned to the window to show it to his master, not for the sake of the workmanship but of the colour. The old man's head was bent over his writing; Marietta was standing outside, and her eyes met Zorzi's. He did not blush as he had blushed yesterday, when he looked up from the fire and saw her; he merely inclined his head respectfully, to acknowledge her presence, and then he stood by the table waiting for the master to notice him, and not bestowing another glance on the young girl.

Beroviero turned to him at last. He was so used to Marietta's presence that he paid no attention to her.

"What is that thing?" he asked contemptuously.

"A specimen of the glass we tried," answered the young man. "I have blown it thin to show the colour."

"A man who can have such execrable taste as to make a drinking-cup of coloured glass does not deserve to know as much as you do."

"But it is very pretty," said Marietta through the window, and bending forward she rested her white hands on the table, among the little heaps of chemicals. "Anneal it, and give it to me," she added.

"Keep such a thing in my house?" asked Beroviero scornfully. "Break up that rubbish!" he added roughly, speaking to Zorzi.

Without a word Zorzi smashed the calix off the iron into an old earthen jar already half full of broken glass. Then he put the pontil in its place and went to tend the fire. Marietta left the window and entered the room.

"Am I disturbing you?" she asked gently, as she stood by her father.

"No. I have finished writing." He laid down his pen.

"Another failure?"

"Yes."

"Perhaps I do not bring you good luck with your experiments," suggested the girl, leaning down and looking over his shoulder at the crabbed writing, so that her cheek almost touched his. "Is that why you wish to send me away?"

Beroviero turned in his chair, raised his heavy brows and looked up into her face, but said nothing.

"Nella has just told me that you have ordered my wedding gown," continued Marietta.

"We are not alone," said her father in a low voice.

"Zorzi probably knows what is the gossip of the house, and what I have been the last to hear," answered the young girl. "Besides, you trust him with all your secrets."

"Yes, I trust him," assented Beroviero. "But these are private matters."

"So private, that my serving-woman knows more of them than I do."

"You encourage her to talk."

Marietta laughed, for she was determined to be good-humoured, in spite of what she said.

"If I did, that would not teach her things which I do not know myself! Is it true that you have ordered the gown to be embroidered with pearls?"

"You like pearls, do you not?" asked Beroviero with a little anxiety.

"You see!" cried Marietta triumphantly. "Nella knows all about it."

"I was going to tell you this morning," said her father in a tone of annoyance. "By my faith, one can keep nothing secret! One cannot even give you a surprise."

"Nella knows everything," returned the girl, sitting on the corner of the table and looking from her father to Zorzi. "That must be why you chose her for my serving-woman when I was a little girl. She knows all that happens in the house by day and night, so that I sometimes think she never sleeps."

Zorzi looked furtively towards the table, for he could not help hearing all that was said.

"For instance," continued Marietta, watching him, "she knows that last night some one unlocked the chain that moors the skiff, and rowed away towards Venice."

To her surprise Zorzi showed no embarrassment. He had made up the fire and now sat down at a little distance, on one of the flat arms of the glassblower's working-stool. His face was pale and quiet, and his eyes did not avoid hers.

"If I caught any one using my boat without my leave, I would make him pay dear," said Beroviero, but without anger, as if he were stating a general truth.

"Whoever it was who took the boat brought it back an hour after midnight, locked the padlock again and went away," said Marietta.

"Tell Nella that I am much indebted to her for her watchfulness. She is as good as a housedog. Tell her to come and wake me if she sees any one taking the boat again."

"She says she knows who took it last night," observed Marietta, who was puzzled by the attitude of the two men; she had now decided that it had not been Zorzi who had used the boat, but on the other hand the story did not rouse her father's anger as she had expected.

"Did she tell you the man's name?"

"Yes."

"Who was it?"

"She said it was Zorzi." Marietta laughed incredulously as she spoke, and Zorzi smiled quietly.

Beroviero was silent for a moment and looked out of the window.

"Listen to me," he said at last. "Tell your graceless gossip of a serving-woman that I will answer for Zorzi, and that the next time she hears any one taking the boat at night she had better come and call me, and open her eyes a little wider. Tell her also that I entertain proper persons to take care of my property without any help from her. Tell her furthermore that she talks too much. You should not listen to a servant's miserable chatter."

"I will tell her," replied Marietta meekly. "Did you say that the gown was to be embroidered with pearls and silver, father, or with pearls and gold?"

"I believe I said gold," answered the old man discontentedly.

"And when will it be ready? In about two months?"

"I daresay."

"So you mean to marry me in two months," concluded Marietta. "That is not a long time."

"Should you prefer two years?" inquired Beroviero with increasing annoyance. Marietta slipped from the table to her feet.

"It depends on the bridegroom," she answered. "Perhaps I may prefer to wait a lifetime!" She moved towards the door.

"Oh, you shall be satisfied with the bridegroom! I promise you that." The old man looked after her. At the door she turned her head, smiling.

"I may be hard to please," she said quietly, and she went out into the garden.

When she was gone Beroviero shut the window carefully, and though the round bull's-eye panes let in the light plentifully, they effectually prevented any one from seeing into the room. The door was already closed.

"You should have been more careful," he said to Zorzi in a tone of reproach. "You should not have let any one see you, when you took the boat."

"If the woman spent half the night looking out of her window, sir, I do not understand how I could have taken the boat without being seen by her."

"Well, well, there is no harm done, and you could not help it, I daresay. I have something else to say. You saw the lord Jacopo last night; what do you think of him? He is a fine-looking young man. Should not any girl be glad to get such a handsome husband? What do you think? And his name, too! one of the best in the Great Council. They say he has a few debts, but his father is very rich, and has promised me that he will pay everything if only his son can be brought to marry and lead a graver life. What do you think?"

"He is a very handsome young man," said Zorzi loyally. "What should I think? It is a most honourable marriage for your house."

"I hear no great harm of Jacopo," continued Beroviero more familiarly. "His father is miserly. We have spent much time in the preliminary arrangements, without the knowledge of the son, and the old man is very grasping! He would take all my fortune for the dowry if he could. But he has to do with a glassblower!"

Beroviero smiled thoughtfully. Zorzi was silent, for he was suffering.

"You may wonder why I sent that message last night," began the master again, "since matters are already so far settled with Jacopo's father. You would suppose that nothing more remained but to marry the couple in the presence of both families, should you not?"

"I know little of such affairs, sir," answered Zorzi.

"That would be the usual way," continued Beroviero. "But I will not marry Marietta against her will. I have always told her so. She shall see her future husband before she is betrothed, and persuade herself with her own eyes that she is not being deceived into marrying a hunchback."

"But supposing that after all the lord Jacopo should not be to her taste," suggested Zorzi, "would you break off the match?"

"Break off the match?" cried Beroviero indignantly. "Never! Not to her taste? The handsomest man in Venice, with a great name and a fortune to come? It would not be my fault if the girl went mad and refused! I would make her like him if she dared to hesitate a moment!"

"Even against her will?"

"She has no will in the matter," retorted Beroviero angrily.

"But you have always told her that you would not marry her against her will—"

"Do not anger me, Zorzi! Do not try your specious logic with me! Invent no absurd arguments, man! Against her will, indeed? How should she know any will but mine in the matter? I shall certainly not marry her against her will! She shall will what I please, neither more nor less."

"If that is your point of view," said Zorzi, "there is no room for argument."

"Of course not. Any reasonable person would laugh at the idea that a girl in her senses should not be glad to marry Jacopo Contarini, especially after having seen him. If she were not glad, she would not be in her senses, in other words she would not be sane, and should be treated as a lunatic, for her own good. Would you let a lunatic do as he liked, if he tried to jump out of the window? The mere thought is absurd."

"Quite," said Zorzi.

Sad as he was, he could almost have laughed at the old man's inconsequent speeches.

"I am glad that you so heartily agree with me," answered Beroviero in perfect sincerity. "I do not mean to say that I would ask your opinion about my daughter's marriage. You would not expect that. But I know that I can trust you, for we have worked together a long time, and I am used to hearing what you have to say."

"You have always been very good to me," replied Zorzi gratefully.

"You have always been faithful to me," said the old man, laying his hand gently on Zorzi's shoulder. "I know what that means in this world."

As soon as there was no question of opposing his despotic will, his kindly nature asserted itself, for he was a man subject to quick changes of humour, but in reality affectionate.

"I am going to trust you much more than hitherto," he continued. "My sons are grown men, independent of me, but willing to get from me all they can. If they were true artists, if I could trust their taste, they should have had my secrets long ago. But they are mere moneymakers, and it is better that they should enrich themselves with the tasteless rubbish they make in their furnaces, than degrade our art by cheapening what should be rare and costly. Am I right?"

"Indeed you are!" Zorzi now spoke in a tone of real conviction.

"If I thought you were really capable of making coloured drinking-cups like that abominable object you made this morning, with the idea that they could ever be used, you should not stay on Venetian soil a day," resumed the old man energetically. "You would be as bad as my sons, or worse. Even they have enough sense to know that half the beauty of a cup, when it is used, lies in the colour of the wine itself, which must be seen through it. But I forgive you, because you were only anxious to blow the glass thin, in order to show me the tint. You know better. That is why I mean to trust you in a very grave matter."

Zorzi bent his head respectfully, but said nothing.

"I am obliged to make a journey before my daughter's marriage takes place," continued Beroviero. "I shall entrust to you the manuscript secrets I possess. They are in a sealed package so that you cannot read them, but they will be in your care. If I leave them with any one else, my sons will try to get possession of them while I am away. During my last journey I carried them with me, but I am growing old, life is uncertain, especially when a man is travelling, and I would rather leave the packet with you. It will be safer."

"It shall be altogether safe," said Zorzi. "No one shall guess that I have it."

"No one must know. I would take you with me on this journey, but I wish you to go on with the experiments I have been making. We shall save time, if you try some of the mixtures while I am away. When it is too hot, let the furnace go out."

"But who will take charge of your daughter, sir?" asked Zorzi. "You cannot leave her alone in the house."

"My son Giovanni and his wife will live in my house while I am away. I have thought of everything. If you choose, you may bring your belongings here, and sleep and eat in the glass-house."

"I should prefer it."

"So should I. I do not want my sons to pry into what we are doing. You can hide the packet here, where they will not think of looking for it. When you go out, lock the door. When you are in, Giovanni will not come. You will have the place to yourself, and the boys who feed the fire at night will not disturb you. Of course my daughter will never come here while I am away. You will be quite alone."

"When do you go?" asked Zorzi.

"On Monday morning. On Sunday I shall take Marietta to Saint Mark's. When she has seen her husband the betrothal can take place at once."

Zorzi was silent, for the future looked black enough. He already saw himself shut up in the glass-house for two long months, or not much less, as effectually separated from Marietta by the narrow canal as if an ocean were between them. She would never cross over and spend an hour in the little garden then, and she would be under the care of Giovanni Beroviero, who hated him, as he well knew.

CHAPTER VI

Aristarchi rose early, though it had been broad dawn when he had entered his home. He lived not far from the house of the Agnus Dei, on the opposite side of the same canal but beyond the Baker's Bridge. His house was small and unpretentious, a little wooden building in two stories, with a small door opening to the water and another at the back, giving access to a patch of dilapidated and overgrown garden, whence a second door opened upon a dismal and unsavoury alley. One faithful man, who had followed him through many adventures, rendered him such services as he needed, prepared the food he liked and guarded the house in his absence. The fellow was far too much in awe of his terrible master to play the spy or to ask inopportune questions.

The Greek put on the rich dress of a merchant captain of his own people, the black coat, thickly embroidered with gold, the breeches of dark blue cloth, the almost transparent linen shirt, open at the throat. A large blue cap of silk and cloth was set far back on his head, showing all the bony forehead, and his coal-black beard and shaggy hair had been combed as smooth as their shaggy nature would allow. He wore a magnificent belt fully two hands wide, in which were stuck three knives of formidable length and breadth, in finely chased silver sheaths. His muscular legs were encased in leathern gaiters, ornamented with gold and silver, and on his feet he wore broad turned-up slippers from Constantinople. The dress was much the same as that which the Turks had found there a few years earlier, and which they soon amalgamated with their own. It set off the captain's vast breadth of shoulder and massive limbs, and as he stepped into his hired boat the idlers at the water-stairs gazed upon him with an admiration of which he was well aware, for besides being very splendidly dressed he looked as if he could have swept them all into the canal with a turn of his hand.

Without saying whither he was bound he directed the oarsman through the narrow channels until he reached the shallow lagoon. The boatman asked whither he should go.

"To Murano," answered the Greek. "And keep over by Saint Michael's, for the tide is low."

The boatman had already understood that his passenger knew Venice almost as well as he. The boat shot forward at a good rate under the bending oar, and in twenty minutes Aristarchi was at the entrance to the canal of San Piero and within sight of Beroviero's house.

"Easy there," said the Greek, holding up his hand. "Do you know Murano well, my man?"

"As well as Venice, sir."

"Whose house is that, which has the upper story built on columns over the footway?"

"It belongs to Messer Angelo Beroviero. His glass-house takes up all the left aide of the canal as far as the bridge."

"And beyond the bridge I can see two new houses, on the same side. Whose are they?"

"They belong to the two sons of Messer Angelo Beroviero, who have furnaces of their own, all the way to the corner of the Grand Canal."

"Is there a Grand Canal in Murano?" asked Aristarchi.

"They call it so," answered the boatman with some contempt. "The Beroviero have several houses on it, too."

"It seems to me that Beroviero owns most of Murano," observed the Greek. "He must be very rich."

"He is by far the richest. But there is Alvise Trevisan, a rich man, too, and there are two or three others. The island and all the glassworks are theirs, amongst them."

"I have business with Messer Angelo," said Aristarchi. "But if he is such a great man he will hardly be in the glass-house."

"I will ask," answered the boatman.

In a few minutes he made his boat fast to the steps before the glass-house, went ashore and knocked at the door. Aristarchi leaned back in his seat, chewing pistachio nuts, which he carried in an embroidered leathern bag at his belt. His right hand played mechanically with the short string of thick amber beads which he used for counting. The June sun blazed down upon his swarthy face.

At the grating beside the door the porter's head appeared, partially visible behind the bars.

"Is Messer Angelo Beroviero within?" inquired the boatman civilly.

"What is your business?" asked the porter in a tone of surly contempt, instead of answering the question.

"There is a rich foreign gentleman here, who desires to speak with him," answered the boatman.

"Is he the Pope?" asked the porter, with fine irony.

"No, sir," said the other, intimidated by the fellow's manner. "He is a rich—"

"Tell him to wait, then." And the surly head disappeared.

The boatman supposed that the man was gone to speak with his master, and waited patiently by the door. Aristarchi chewed his pistachio nut till there was nothing left, at which time he reached the end of his patience. He argued that it was a good sign if Angelo Beroviero kept rich strangers waiting at his gate, for it showed that he had no need of their custom. On the other hand the Greek's dignity was offended now that he had been made to wait too long, for he was hasty by nature. Once, in a fit of irritation with a Candiot who stammered out of sheer fright, the captain had ordered him to be hanged. Having finished his nut, he stood up in the boat and stepped ashore.

"Knock again," he said to the boatman, who obeyed.

There was no answer this time.

"I can hear the fellow inside," said the boatman.

The grating was too high for a man to look through it from outside. Aristarchi laid his knotty hands on the stone sill and pulled himself up till his face was against the grating. He now looked in and saw the porter sitting in his chair.

"Have you taken my message to your master?" inquired the Greek.

The porter looked up in surprise, which increased when he caught sight of the ferocious face of the speaker. But he was not to be intimidated so easily.

"Messer Angelo is not to be disturbed at his studies," he said. "If you wait till noon, perhaps he will come out to go to dinner."

"Perhaps!" repeated Aristarchi, still hanging by his hands. "Do you think I shall wait all day?"

"I do not know. That is your affair."

"Precisely. And I do not mean to wait."

"Then go away."

But the Greek had come on an exploring expedition in which he had nothing to lose. Hauling himself up a little higher, till his mouth was close to the grating, he hailed the house as he would have hailed a ship at sea, in a voice of thunder.

"Ahoy there! Is any one within? Ahoy! Ahoy!"

This was more than the porter's equanimity could bear. He looked about for a weapon with which to attack the Greek's face through the bars, heaping, upon him a torrent of abuse in the meantime.

"Son of dogs and mules!" he cried in a rising growl. "Ill befall the foul souls of thy dead and of their dead before them."

"Ahoy—oh! Ahoy!" bellowed the Greek, who now thoroughly

enjoyed the situation.

The boatman, anxious for drink money, and convinced that his huge employer would get the better of the porter, had obligingly gone down upon his hands and knees, thrusting his broad back under the captain's feet, so that Aristarchi stood upon him and was now prepared to prolong the interview without any further effort. His terrific shouts rang through the corridor to the garden.

The first person to enter the little lodge was Marietta herself, and the Greek broke off short in the middle of another tremendous yell as soon as he saw her. She turned her face up to him, quite fearlessly, and was very much inclined to laugh as she saw the sudden change in his expression.

"Madam," he said with great politeness, "I beg you to forgive my manner of announcing myself. If your porter were more obliging, I should have been admitted in the ordinary way."

"What is this atrocious disturbance?" asked Zorzi, entering before Marietta could answer. "Pray leave the fellow to me," he added, speaking to Marietta, who cast one more glance at Aristarchi and went out.

"Sir," said the captain blandly, "I admit that my behaviour may give you some right to call me 'fellow,' but I trust that my apology will make you consider me a gentleman like yourself. Your porter altogether refused to take a message to Messer Angelo Beroviero. May I ask whether you are his son, sir?"

"No, sir. You say that you wish to speak with the master. I can take a message to him, but I am not sure that he will see any one today."

Aristarchi imagined that Beroviero made himself inaccessible, in order to increase the general idea of his wealth and importance. He resolved to convey a strong impression of his own standing.

"I am the chief partner in a great house of Greek merchants settled in Palermo," he said. "My name is Charalambos Aristarchi, and I desire the honour of speaking with Messer Angelo about the purchase of several cargoes of glass for the King of Sicily."

"I will deliver your message, sir," said Zorzi. "Pray wait a minute, I will open the door."

Aristarchi's big head disappeared at last.

"Yes!" growled the porter to Zorzi. "Open the door yourself, and take the blame. The man has the face of a Turkish pirate, and his voice is like the bellowing of several bulls."

Zorzi unbarred the door, which opened inward, and Aristarchi turned a little sideways in order to enter, for his shoulders would have touched the two doorposts. The slight and gracefully built Dalmatian looked at him with some curiosity, standing aside to let him pass, before barring the door again. Aristarchi, though not much taller than himself, was the biggest man he had ever seen. He thanked Zorzi, who pushed forward the porter's only chair for him to sit on while he waited.

"I will bring you an answer immediately," said Zorzi, and disappeared down the corridor.

Aristarchi sat down, crossed one leg over the other, and took a pistachio nut from his pouch.

"Master porter," he began in a friendly tone, "can you tell me who that beautiful lady is, who came here a moment ago?"

"There is no reason why I should," snarled the porter, beginning to strip the outer leaves from a large onion which he pulled from a string of them hanging by the wall.

Aristarchi said nothing for a few moments, but watched the man with an air of interest.

"Were you ever a pirate?" he inquired presently.

"No, I never served in your crew."

The porter was not often at a loss for a surly answer. The Greek laughed outright, in genuine amusement.

"I like your company, my friend," he said. "I should like to spend the day here."

"As the devil said to Saint Anthony," concluded the porter.

Aristarchi laughed again. It was long since he had enjoyed such amusing conversation, and there was a certain novelty in not being feared. He repeated his first question, however, remembering that he had not come in search of diversion, but to gather information.

"Who was the beautiful lady?" he asked. "She is Messer Angelo's daughter, is she not?"

"A man who asks a question when he knows the answer is either a fool or a knave. Choose as you please."

"Thanks, friend," answered Aristarchi, still grinning and showing his jagged teeth. "I leave the first choice to you. Whichever you take, I will take the other. For if you call me a knave, I shall call you a fool, but if you think me a fool, I am quite satisfied that you should be the knave."

The porter snarled, vaguely feeling that the Greek had the better of him. At that moment Zorzi returned, and his coming put an end to the exchange of amenities.

"My master has no long leisure," he said, "but he begs you to come in."

They left the lodge together, and the porter watched them as they went down the dark corridor, muttering unholy things about the visitor who had disturbed him, and bestowing a few curses on Zorzi. Then he went back to peeling his onions.

As Aristarchi went through the garden, he saw Marietta sitting under the plane-tree, making a little net of coloured beads. Her face was turned from him and bent down, but when he had passed she glanced furtively after him, wondering at his size. But her eyes followed Zorzi, till the two reached the door and went in. A moment later Zorzi came out again, leaving his master and the Greek together. Marietta looked down at once, lest her eyes should betray her gladness, for she knew that Zorzi would not go back and could not leave the glass-house, so that site should necessarily be alone with him while the interview in the laboratory lasted.

He came a little way down the path, then stopped, took a short knife from his wallet and began to trim away a few withered sprigs from a rosebush. She waited a moment, but he showed no signs of coming nearer, so she spoke to him.

"Will you come here?" she asked softly, looking towards him with half closed eyes.

He slipped the knife back into his pouch and walked quickly to her side. She looked down again, threading the coloured beads that half filled a small basket in her lap.

"May I ask you a question?" Her voice had a little persuasive hesitation in it, as if she wished him to understand that the answer would be a favour of which she was anything but certain.

"Anything you will," said Zorzi.

"Provided I do not ask about my father's secret!" A little laughter trembled in the words. "You were so severe yesterday, you know. I am almost afraid ever to ask you anything again."

"I will answer as well as I can."

"Well—tell me this. Did you really take the boat and go to Venice last night?"

"Yes."

Marietta's hand moved with the needle among the beads, but she did not thread one. Nella had been right, after all.

"Why did you go, Zorzi?" The question came in a lower tone that was full of regret.

"The master sent me," answered Zorzi, looking down at her hair, and wishing that he could see her face.

His wish was almost instantly fulfilled. After the slightest pause she looked up at him with a lovely smile; yet when he saw that rare look in her face, his heart sank suddenly, instead of swelling and standing still with happiness, and when she saw how sad he was, she was grave with the instant longing to feel whatever he felt of pain or sorrow. That is one of the truest signs of love, but Zorzi had not learned much of love's sign-language yet, and did not understand.

"What is it?" she asked almost tenderly.

He turned his eyes from her and rested one hand against the trunk of the plane-tree.

"I do not understand," he said slowly.

"Why are you so sad? What is it that is always making you suffer?"

"How could I tell you?" The words were spoken almost under his breath.

"It would be very easy to tell me," she said. "Perhaps I could help you—"

"Oh no, no, no!" he cried with an accent of real pain. "You could not help me!"

"Who knows? Perhaps I am the best friend you have in the world, Zorzi."

"Indeed I believe you are! No one has ever been so good to me."

"And you have not many friends," continued Marietta. "The workmen are jealous of you, because you are always with my father. My brothers do not like you, for the same reason, and they think that you will get my father's secret from him some day, and outdo them all. No—you have not many friends."

"I have none, but you and the master. The men would kill me if they dared."

Marietta started a little, remembering how the workmen had looked at him in the morning, when he came out.

"You need not be afraid," he added, seeing her movement. "They will not touch me."

"Does my father know what your trouble is?" asked Marietta suddenly.

"No! That is—I have no trouble, I assure you. I am of a melancholy nature."

"I am glad it has nothing to do with the secrets," said the young girl, quietly ignoring the last part of his speech. "If it had, I could not help you at all. Could I?"

That morning it had seemed an easy thing to wait even two

years before giving him a sign, before dropping in his path the rose which she would not ask of him again. The minutes seemed years now. For she knew well enough what his trouble was, since yesterday; he loved her, and he thought it infinitely impossible, in his modesty, that she should ever stoop to him. After she had spoken, she looked at him with half closed eyes for a while, but he stared stonily at the trunk of the tree beside his hand. Gradually, as she gazed, her lids opened wider, and the morning sunlight sparkled in the deep blue, and her fresh lips parted. Before she was aware of it he was looking at her with a strange expression she had never seen. Then she faintly blushed and looked down at her beads once more. She felt as if she had told him that she loved him. But he had not understood. He had only seen the transfiguration of her face, and it had been for a moment as he had never seen it before. Again his heart sank suddenly, and he uttered a little sound that was more than a sigh and less than a groan.

"There are remedies for almost every kind of pain," said Marietta wisely, as she threaded several beads.

"Give me one for mine," he cried almost bitterly. "Bid that which is to cease from being, and that to be which is not earthly possible! Turn the world back, and undo truth, and make it all a dream! Then I shall find the remedy and forget that it was needed."

"There are magicians who pretend to do such things," she answered softly.

"I would there were!" he sighed.

"But those who come to them for help tell all, else the magician has no power. Would you call a physician, if you were ill, and tell him that the pain you felt was in your head, if it was really—in your heart?"

She had paused an instant before speaking the last words, and they came with a little effort.

"How could the physician cure you, if you would not tell him the truth?" she asked, as he said nothing. "How can the wizard work miracles for you, unless he knows what miracle you ask? How can your best friend help you if—if she does not know what help you need?"

Still he was silent, leaning against the tree, with bent head. The pain was growing worse, and harder to bear. She spoke so softly and kindly that it would have been easy to tell her the truth, he thought, for though she could never love him, she would understand, and would forgive him. He had not dreamed that friendship could be so kind.

"Am I right?" she asked, after a pause.

"Yes," he answered. "When I cannot bear it any longer, I will tell you, and you will help me."

"Why not now?"

The little question might have been ruinous to all his resolution, if Zorzi had not been almost like a child in his simplicity—or like a saint in his determination to be loyal. For he thought it loyalty to be silent, not only for the sake of the promise he had given in return for his life, but in respect of his master also, who put such great trust in him.

"Pray do not press me with the question," he said. "You tempt me very much, and I do not wish to speak of what I feel. Be my friend in real truth, if you can, and do not ask me to say what I shall ever after wish unsaid. That will be the best friendship."

Marietta looked across the garden thoughtfully, and suddenly a chilling doubt fell upon her heart. She could not have been mistaken yesterday, she could not be deceived in him now; and yet, if he loved her as she believed, she had said all that a maiden could to show him that she would listen willingly. She had said too much, and she felt ashamed and hurt, almost resentful. He was not a boy. If he loved her, he could find words to tell her so, and should have found them, for she had helped him to her utmost. Suddenly, she almost hated him, for what his silence made her feel, and she told herself that she was glad he had not dared to speak, for she did not love him at all. It was all a sickening mistake, it was all a miserable little dream; she wished that he would go away and leave her to herself. Not that she should shed a single tear! She was far too angry for that, but his presence, so near her, reminded her of what she had done. He must have seen, all through their talk, that she was trying to make him tell his love, and there was nothing to tell. Of course he would despise her. That was natural, but she had a right to hate him for it, and she would, with all her heart! Her thoughts all came together in a tumult of disgust and resentment. If Zorzi did not go away presently, she would go away herself. She was almost resolved to get up and leave the garden, when the door opened.

"Zorzi!" It was Beroviero's voice.

Aristarchi already stood in the doorway taking leave of Beroviero with, many oily protestations of satisfaction in having made his acquaintance. Zorzi went forward to accompany the Greek to the door.

"I shall never forget that I have had the honour of being received by the great artist himself," said Aristarchi, who held his big cap in his hand and was bowing low on the threshold.

"The pleasure has been all on my side," returned Beroviero courteously.

"On the contrary, quite on the contrary," protested his guest, backing away and then turning to go.

Zorzi walked beside him, on his left. As they reached the entrance to the corridor Aristarchi turned once more, and made an elaborate bow, sweeping the ground with his cap, for Beroviero had remained at the door till he should be out of sight. He bent his head, making a gracious gesture with his hand, and went in as the Greek disappeared. Zorzi followed the latter, showing him out.

Marietta saw the door close after her father, and she knew that Zorzi must come back through the garden in a few moments. She bent her head over her beads as she heard his step, and pretended not to see him. When he came near her he stood still a moment, but she would not look up, and between annoyance and disappointment and confusion she felt that she was blushing, which she would not have had Zorzi see for anything. She wondered why he did not go on.

"Have I offended you?" he asked, in a low voice.

Oddly enough, her embarrassment disappeared as soon as he spoke, and the blush faded away.

"No," she answered, coldly enough. "I am not angry—I am only sorry."

"But I am glad that I would not answer your question," returned Zorzi.

"I doubt whether you had any answer to give," retorted Marietta with a touch of scorn.

Zorzi's brows contracted sharply and he made a movement to go on. So her proffered friendship was worth no more than that, he thought. She was angry and scornful because her curiosity was disappointed. She could not have guessed his secret, he was sure, though that might account for her temper, for she would of course be angry if she knew that he loved her. And she was angry now because he had refused to tell her so. That was a woman's logic, he thought, quite regardless of the defect in his own. It was just like a woman! He sincerely wished that he might tell her so.

In the presence of Marietta the man who had confronted sudden death less than twenty-four hours ago, with a coolness that had seemed imposing to other men, was little better than a girl himself. He turned to go on, without saying more. But she stopped him.

"I am sorry that you do not care for my friendship," she said, in a hurt tone. She could not have said anything which he would have found it harder to answer just then.

"What makes you think that?" he asked, hoping to gain time.

"Many things. It is quite true, so it does not matter what makes me think it!"

She tried to laugh scornfully, but there was a quaver in her voice which she herself had not expected and was very far from understanding. Why should she suddenly feel that she was going to cry? It had seemed so ridiculous in poor Nella that morning. Yet there was a most unmistakable something in her throat, which frightened her. It would be dreadful if she should burst into tears over her beads before Zorzi's eyes. She tried to gulp the something: down, and suddenly, as she bent over the basket, she saw the beautiful, hateful drops falling fast upon the little dry glass things; and even then, in her shame at being seen, she wondered why the beads looked, bigger through the glistening tears—she remembered afterwards how they looked, so she must have noticed them at the time.

Zorzi knew too little of women to have any idea of what he ought to do under the circumstances. He did not know whether to turn his back or to go away, so he stood still and looked at her, which was the very worst thing he could have done. Worse still, he tried to reason with her.

"I assure you that you are mistaken," he said in a soothing tone. "I wish for your friendship with all my heart! Only, when you ask me—"

"Oh, go away! For heaven's sake go away!" cried Marietta, almost choking, and turning her face quite away, so that he could only see the back of her head.

At the same time, she tapped the ground impatiently with her foot, and to make matters worse, the little basket of beads began to slip off her knees at the same moment. She caught at it desperately, trying not to look round and half blinded by her tears, but she missed it, and but for Zorzi it would have fallen. He put it into her hands very gently, but she was not in the least grateful.

"Oh, please go away!" she repeated. "Can you not understand?"

He did not understand, but he obeyed her and turned away, very grave, very much puzzled by this new development of affairs, and sincerely wishing that some wise familiar spirit would whisper the explanation in his ear, since he could not possibly consult any living person.

She heard him go and she listened for the shutting of the laboratory door. Then she knew that she was quite alone in the garden, and she let the tears flow as they would, bending her head till it touched the trunk of the tree, and they wet the smooth bark and ran down to the dry earth.

Zorzi went in, and began to tend the fire as usual, until it should please the master to give him other orders. Old Beroviero was sitting in the big chair in which he sometimes rested himself, his elbow on one of its arms, and his hand grasping his beard below his chin.

"Zorzi," he said at last, "I have seen that man before."

Zorzi looked at him, expecting more, but for some time Beroviero said nothing. The young man selected his pieces of beech wood, laying them ready before the little opening just above the floor.

"It is very strange," said Beroviero at last. "He seems to be a rich merchant now, but I am almost quite sure that I saw him in Naples."

"Did you know him there, sir?" asked Zorzi.

"No," answered his master thoughtfully. "I saw him in a cart with his hands tied behind him, on his way to be hanged."

"He looks as if one hanging would not be enough for him," observed Zorzi.

Beroviero was silent for a moment. Then he laughed, and he laughed very rarely.

"Yes," he said. "It is not a face one could forget easily," he added.

Then he rose and went back to his table.

CHAPTER VII

The sun was high over Venice, gleaming on the blue lagoons that lightly rippled under a southerly breeze, filling the vast square of Saint Mark's with blinding light, casting deep shadows behind the church and in the narrow alleys and canals to northward, about the Merceria. The morning haze had long since blown away, and the outlines of the old church and monastery on Saint George's island, and of the buildings on the Guidecca, and on the low-lying Lido, were hard and clear against the cloudless sky, mere designs cut out in rich colours, as if with a sharp knife, and reared up against a background of violent light. In Venice only the melancholy drenching rain of a winter's day brings rest to the eye, when water meets water and sky is washed into sea and the city lies soaking and dripping between two floods. But soon the wind shifts to the northeast, out breaks the sun again, and all Venice is instantly in a glare of light and colour and startling distinctness, like the sails and rigging of a ship at sea on a clear day.

It was Sunday morning and high mass was over in Saint Mark's. The crowd had streamed out of the central door, spreading like a bright fan over the square, the men in gay costumes, red, green, blue, yellow, purple, brown, and white, their legs particoloured in halves and quarters, so that when looking at a group it was mere guesswork to match the pair that belonged to one man; women in dresses of one tone, mostly rich and dark, and often heavily embroidered, for no sumptuary laws could effectually limit outward display, and the insolent vanity of as age still almost mediaeval made it natural that the rich should attire themselves as richly as they could, and that the poor should be despised for wearing poor clothes.

Angelo Beroviero had a true Venetian's taste for splendour, but he was also deeply imbued with the Venetian love of secrecy in all matters that concerned his private life. When he bade Marietta accompany him to Venice on that Sunday morning, he was equally anxious that she should be as finely dressed as was becoming for the daughter of a wealthy citizen, and that she should be in ignorance of the object of the trip. She was not to know that Jacopo Contarini would be standing beside the second column on the left, watching her with lazily critical eyes; she was merely told that she and her father were to dine in the house of a certain Messer Luigi Foscarini, Procurator of Saint Mark, who was an old and valued friend, though a near connection of Alvise Trevisan, a rival glassmaker of Murano. All this had been carefully planned in order that during their absence Beroviero's house might be suitably prepared for the solemn family meeting which was to take place late in the afternoon, and at which her betrothal was to be announced, but of which Marietta knew nothing. Her father counted upon surprising her and perhaps dazzling her, so as to avoid all discussion and all possibility of resistance on her part. She should see Contarini in the church, and while still under the first impression of his beauty and magnificence, she should be told before her assembled family that she was solemnly bound to marry him in two months' time.

Beroviero never expected opposition in anything he wished to do, but he had always heard that young girls could find a thousand reasons for not marrying the man their parents chose for them, and he believed that he could make all argument and hesitation impossible. Marietta doubtless expected to have a week in which to make up her mind. She should have five hours, and even that was too much, thought Beroviero. He would have preferred to march her to the altar without any preliminaries and marry her to Contarini without giving her a chance of seeing him before the ceremony. After all, that was the custom of the day.

The fortunes of love were in his favour, for Marietta had spent three miserably unhappy days and nights since she had last talked with Zorzi in the garden. From that time he had avoided her moat carefully, never coming out of the laboratory when she was under the tree with her work, never raising his eyes to look at her when she came in and talked with her father. When she entered the big room, he made a solemn bow and occupied himself in the farthest corner so long as she remained. There is a stage in which even the truest and purest love of boy and maiden feeds on misunderstandings. In a burst of tears, and ashamed that she should be seen crying, Marietta had bidden him go away; in the folly of his young heart he took her at her word, and avoided her consistently. He had been hurt by the words, but by a kind of unconscious selfishness his pain helped him to do what he believed to be his duty.

And Marietta forgot that he had picked up the rose dropped by her in the path, she forgot that she had seen him stand gazing up at her window, with a look that could mean only love, she forgot how tenderly and softly he had answered her in the garden; she only remembered that she had done her utmost, and too much, to make him tell her that he loved her, and in vain. She could not forgive him that, for even after three days her cheeks burned fiercely whenever she thought of it. After that, it mattered nothing what became of her, whether she were betrothed, or whether she were married, or whether she went mad, or even whether she died—that would be the best of all.

In this mood Marietta entered the gondola and seated herself by her father on Sunday morning. She wore an embroidered gown of olive green, a little open at her dazzling throat, and a silk mantle of a darker tone hung from her shoulders, to protect her from the sun rather than from the air. Her russet hair was plaited in a thick flat braid, and brought round her head like a broad coronet of red gold, and a point lace veil, pinned upon it with stoat gold pins, hang down behind and was brought forward carelessly upon one shoulder.

Beside her, Angelo Beroviero was splendid in dark red cloth and purple silk. He was proud of his daughter, who was betrothed to the heir of a great Venetian house, he was proud of his own achievements, of his wealth, of the richly furnished gondola, of his two big young oarsmen in quartered yellow and blue hose and snowy shirts, and of his liveried man in blue and gold, who sat outside the low 'felse' on a little stool, staff in hand, ready to attend upon his master and young mistress whenever they should please to go on foot.

Marietta had got into the gondola without so much as glancing across the canal to see whether Zorzi were standing there to see them push off, as he often did when she and her father went out together. If he were there, she meant to show him that she could be more indifferent than he; if he were not, she would show herself that she did not care enough even to look for him. But when the gondola was out of sight of the house she wished she knew whether he had looked out or not.

Her father had told her that they were going to dine with the Procurator Foscarini and his wife. The pair had one daughter, of Marietta's age, and she was a cripple from birth. Marietta was fond of her, and it was a relief to get away from Murano, even for half a day. The visit explained well enough why her father had desired her to put on her best gown and most valuable lace. She really had not the slightest idea that anything more important was on foot.

Beroviero looked at her in silence as they sped along with the gently rocking motion of the gondola, which is not exactly like any other movement in the world. He had already noticed that she was paler than usual, but the extraordinary whiteness of her skin made her pallor becoming to her, and it was set off by the colour of her hair, as ivory by rough gold. He wondered whether she had guessed whither he was taking her.

"It is a long time since we were in Saint Mark's together," he said at last.

"It must be more than a year," answered Marietta. "We pass it often, but we hardly ever go in."

"It is early," observed Beroviero, speaking as indifferently as he could. "When we left home it lacked an hour and a half of noon by the dial. Shall we go into the church for a while?"

"If you like," replied Marietta mechanically.

Nothing made much difference that morning, but she knew that the high mass would be over and that the church would be quiet and cool. It was not at that time the cathedral of Venice, though it had always been the church in which the doges worshipped in state.

They landed at the low steps in the Rio del Palazzo, and the servant held out his bent elbow for Marietta to steady herself, though he knew that she would not touch it, for she was light and sure-footed as a fawn; but Beroviero leaned heavily on his man's arm. They came round the Patriarch's palace into the open square, whence the crowd had nearly all disappeared, dispersing in different directions. Just as they were within sight of the great doors of the church, Beroviero saw a very tall man in a purple silk mantle going in alone. It was Contarini, and Beroviero drew a little sigh of relief. The intended bridegroom was punctual, but Beroviero thought that he might have shown such anxiety to see his bride as should have brought him to the door a few minutes before the time.

Marietta had drawn her veil across her face, leaving only her eyes uncovered, according to custom.

"It is hot," she complained.

"It will be cool in the church," answered her father. "Throw your veil back, my dear—there is no one to see you."

"There is the sun," she said, for she had been taught that one of a Venetian lady's chief beauties is her complexion.

"Well, well—there will be no sun in the church." And the old man hurried her in, without bestowing a glance upon the bronze horses over the door, to admire which he generally stopped a few moments in passing.

They entered the great church, and the servant went before them, dipped his fingers in the basin and offered them holy water. They crossed themselves, and Marietta bent one knee, looking towards the high altar. A score of people were scattered about, kneeling and standing in the nave.

Contarini was leaning against the second pillar on the left, and had been watching the door when Marietta and her father entered. Beroviero saw him at once, but led his daughter up the opposite side of the nave, knelt down beside her a moment at the screen, then crossed and came down the aisle, and at last turned into the nave again by the second pillar, so as to come upon Contarini as it were unawares. This all seemed necessary to him in order that Marietta should receive a very strong and sudden impression, which should leave no doubt in her mind. Contarini himself was too thoroughly Venetian not to understand what Beroviero was doing, and when the two came upon him, he was drawn up to his full height, one gloved hand holding his cap and resting on his hip; the other, gloveless, and white as a woman's, was twisting his silky mustache. Beroviero had manoeuvred so cleverly that Marietta almost jostled the young patrician as she turned the pillar.

Contarini drew back with quick grace and a slight inclination of his body, and then pretended the utmost surprise on seeing his valued friend Messer Angelo Beroviero.

"My most dear sir!" he exclaimed. "This is indeed good fortune!"

"Mine, Messer Jacopo!" returned Beroviero with equally well-feigned astonishment.

Marietta had looked Contarini full in the face before she had time to draw her veil across her own. She stepped back and placed herself behind her father, protected as it were by their serving-man, who stood beside her with his staff. She understood instantly that the magnificent patrician was the man of whom her father had spoken as her future husband. Seen, as she had seen him, in the glowing church, in the most splendid surroundings that could be imagined, he was certainly a man at whom any woman would look twice, even out of curiosity, and through her veil Marietta looked again, till she saw his soft brown eyes scrutinising her appearance; then she turned quickly away, for she had looked long enough. She saw that a woman in black was kneeling by the next pillar, watching her intently with a sort of cold stare that almost made her shudder. Yet the woman was exceedingly beautiful. It was easy to see that, though the dark veil hid half her face and its folds concealed most of her figure. The mysterious, almond-shaped eyes were those of another race, the marble cheek was more perfectly modelled and turned than an Italian's, the curling golden hair was more glorious than any Venetian's. Arisa had come to see her master's bride, and he knew that she was there looking on. Why should he care? It was a bargain, and he was not going to give up Arisa and the house of the Agnus Dei because he meant to marry the rich glassblower's daughter.

Marietta imagined no connection between the woman and the man, who thus insolently came to the same place to look at her, pretending not to know one another; and when she looked back at Contarini she felt a miserable little thrill of vanity as she noticed that he was looking fixedly at her, and that his eyes did not wander to the face of that other woman, who was so much more beautiful than herself. Perhaps, after all, he would really prefer her to that matchless creature close beside her! Nothing mattered, of course, since Zorzi did not love her, but after all it was flattering to be admired by Jacopo Contarini, who could choose his wife where he pleased, through the whole world.

It all happened in a few seconds. The two men exchanged a few words, to which she paid no attention, and took leave of each other with great ceremony and much bowing on both sides. When her father turned at last, Marietta was already walking towards the door, the servant by her left side. Beroviero had scarcely joined her when she started a little, and laid her hand upon his arm.

"The Greek merchant!" she whispered.

Beroviero looked where she was looking. By the first pillar, gazing intently at Arisa's kneeling figure, stood Aristarchi, his hands folded over his broad chest, his shaggy head bent forward, his sturdy legs a little apart. He, too, had come to see the promised bride, and to be a witness of the bargain whereby he also was to be enriched.

As Marietta came out of the church, she covered her face closely and drew her silk mantle quite round her, bending her head a little. The servant walked a few paces in front.

"You have seen your future husband, my child," said Beroviero.

"I suppose that the young noble was Messer Jacopo Contarini," answered Marietta coldly.

"You are hard to please, if you are not satisfied with my choice for you," observed her father.

To this Marietta said nothing. She only bent her head a little lower, looking down as she trod delicately over the hot and dusty ground.

"And you are a most ungrateful daughter," continued

Beroviero, "if you do not appreciate my kindness and liberality of mind in allowing you to see him before you are formally betrothed."

"Perhaps he is even more pleased by your liberality of mind than I could possibly be," retorted the young girl with unbending coldness. "He has probably not seen many Venetian girls of our class face to face and unveiled. He is to be congratulated on his good fortune!"

"By my faith!" exclaimed Beroviero, "it is hard to satisfy you!"

"I have asked nothing."

"Do you mean to say that you have any objections to allege against such a marriage?"

"Have I said that I should oppose it? One may obey without enthusiasm." She laughed coldly.

"Like the unprofitable servant! I had expected something more of you, my child. I have been at infinite pains and I am making great sacrifices to procure you a suitable husband, and there are scores of noble girls in Venice who would give ten years of their lives to marry Jacopo Contarini! And you say that you obey my commands without enthusiasm! You are an ungrateful—"

"No, I am not!" interrupted Marietta firmly. "I would rather not marry at all—"

"Not marry!" repeated Beroviero, interrupting her in a tone of profound stupefaction, and standing still in the sun as he spoke. "Why—what is the matter?"

"Is it so strange that I should be contented with my girl's life?" asked Marietta. "Should I not be ungrateful indeed, if I wished to leave you and become the wife of a man I have just seen for the first time?"

"You use most extraordinary arguments, my dear," replied Beroviero, quite at a loss for a suitable retort. "Of course, I have done my best to make you happy."

He paused, for she had placed him in the awkward position of being angry because she did not wish to leave him.

"I really do not know what to say," he added, after a moment's reflection.

"Perhaps there is nothing to be said," answered Marietta, in a tone of irritating superiority, for she certainly had the best of the discussion.

They had reached the gondola by this time, and as the servant sat within hearing at the open door of the 'felse,' they could not continue talking about such a matter. Beroviero was glad of it, for he regarded the affair as settled, and considered that it should be hastened to its conclusion without any further reasoning about it. If he had sent word to young Contarini that the answer should be given him in a week, that was merely an imaginary formality invented to cover his own dignity, since he had so far derogated from it as to allow the young man to see Marietta. In reality the marriage had been determined and settled between Beroviero and Contarini's father before anything had been said to either of the young people. The meeting in the church might have been dispensed with, if the patrician had been able to answer with certainty for his wild son's conduct. Jacopo had demanded it, and his father was so anxious for the marriage that he had communicated the request to Beroviero. The latter, always for his dignity's sake, had pretended to refuse, and had then secretly arranged the matter for Jacopo, as has been seen, without old Contarini's knowledge.

Marietta leaned back under the cool, dark 'felse,' and her hands lay idly in her lap. She felt that she was helpless, because she was indifferent, and that she could even now have changed the course of her destiny if she had cared to make the effort. There was no reason for making any. She did not believe that she had really loved Zorzi after all, and if she had, it seemed today quite impossible that she should ever have married him. He was nothing but a waif, a half nameless servant, a stranger predestined to a poor and obscure life. As she inwardly repeated some of these considerations, she felt a little thrust of remorse for trying to look down on him as impossibly far below her own station, and a small voice told her that he was an artist, and that if he had chanced to be born in Venice he would have been as good as her brothers.

The future stretched out before her in a sort of dull magnificence that did not in the least appeal to her simple nature. She could not tell why she had despised Jacopo Contarini from the moment she looked into his beautiful eyes. Happily women are not expected to explain why they sometimes judge rightly at first sight, when a wise man is absurdly deceived. Marietta did not understand Jacopo, and she easily fancied that because her own character was the stronger she should rule him as easily as she managed Nella. It did not occur to her that he was already under the domination of another woman, who might prove to be quite as strong as she. What she saw was the weakness in his eyes and mouth. With such a man, she thought, there was little to fear; but there was nothing to love. If she asked, he would give, if she opposed him, he would surrender, if she lost her temper and commanded, he would obey with petulant docility. She should be obliged to take refuge in vanity in order to get any satisfaction out of her life, and she was not naturally vain. The luxuries of those days were familiar to her from her childhood. Though she had not lived in a palace, she had been brought up in a house that was not unlike one, she ate off silver plates and drank from glasses that were masterpieces of her father's art, she had coffers full of silks and satins, and fine linen embroidered with gold thread, there was always gold and silver in her little wallet-purse when she wanted anything or wished to give to the poor, she was waited on by a maid of her own like any fine lady of Venice, and there were a score of idle servants in a house where there were only two masters—there was nothing which Contarini could give her that would be more than a little useless exaggeration of what she had already. She had no particular desire to show herself unveiled to the world, as married women did, and she was not especially attracted by the idea of becoming one of them. She had been brought up alone, she had acquired tastes which other women had not, and which would no longer be satisfied in her married life, she loved the glass-house, she delighted in taking a blowpipe herself and making small objects which she decorated as she pleased, she felt a lively interest in her father's experiments, she enjoyed the atmosphere of his wisdom though it was occasionally disturbed by the foolish little storms of his hot temper. And until now, she had liked to be often with Zorzi.

That was past, of course, but the rest remained, and it was much to sacrifice for the sake of becoming a Contarini, and living on the Grand Canal with a man she should always despise.

It was clearly not the idea of marriage that surprised or repelled her, not even of a marriage with a man she did not know and had seen but once. Girls were brought up to regard marriage as the greatest thing in life, as the natural goal to which all their girlhood should tend, and at the same time they were taught from childhood that it was all to be arranged for them, and that they would in due course grow fond of the man their parents chose for them. Until Marietta had begun to love Zorzi, she had accepted all these things quite naturally, as a part of every woman's life, and it would have seemed as absurd, and perhaps as impossible, to rebel against them as to repudiate the religion in which she had been born. Such beliefs turn into prejudices, and assert themselves as soon as whatever momentarily retards them is removed. By the time the gondola drew alongside of the steps of the Foscarini palace, Marietta was convinced that there was nothing for her but to submit to her fate.

"Then I am to be married in two months?" she said, in a tone of interrogation, and regardless of the servant.

Beroviero bent his head in answer and smiled kindly; for after all, he was grateful to her for accepting his decision so quietly. But Marietta was very pale after she had spoken, for the audible words somehow made it all seem dreadfully real, and out of the shadows of the great entrance hall that opened upon the canal she could fancy Zorzi's face looking at her sadly and reproachfully. The bargain was made, and the woman he loved was sold for life. For one moment, instinctive womanhood felt the accursed humiliation, and the flushing blood rose in the girl's cool cheeks.

She would have blushed deeper had she guessed who had been witnesses of her first meeting with Contarini, and old Beroviero's temper would have broken out furiously if he could have imagined that the Greek pirate who had somehow miraculously escaped the hangman in Naples had been contemplating with satisfaction the progress of the marriage negotiations, sure that he himself should before long be enjoying the better part of Marietta's rich dowry. If the old man could have had vision of Jacopo's life, and could have suddenly known what the beautiful woman in black was to the patrician, Contarini's chance of going home alive that day would have been small indeed, for Beroviero might have strangled him where he stood, and perhaps Aristarchi would have discreetly turned his back while he was doing it. For a few minutes they had all been very near together, the deceivers and the deceived, and it was not likely that they should ever all be so near again.

Contarini had never seen the Greek, and Arisa was not aware that he was in the church. When Beroviero and Marietta were gone, Jacopo turned his back on the slave for a moment as if he meant to walk further up the church. Aristarchi watched them both, for in spite of all he did not quite trust the Georgian woman, and he had never seen her alone with Jacopo when she was unaware of his own presence. Yet he was afraid to go nearer, now, lest Arisa should accidentally see him and betray by her manner that she knew him.

Jacopo turned suddenly, when he judged that he could leave the church without overtaking Beroviero, and he walked quietly down the nave. He passed close to Arisa, and Aristarchi guessed that their eyes met for a moment. He almost fancied that

Contarini's lips moved, and he was sure that he smiled. But that was all, and Arisa remained on her knees, not even turning her head a little as her lover went by.

"Not so ugly after all," Contarini had said, under his breath, and the careless smile went with the words.

Arisa's lip curled contemptuously as she heard. She had drawn back her veil, her face was raised, as if she were sending up a prayer to heaven, and the light fell full upon the magnificent whiteness of her throat, that showed in strong relief against the black velvet and lace. She needed no other answer to what he said, but in the scorn of her curving mouth, which seemed all meant for Marietta, there was contempt for him, too, that would have cut him to the quick of his vanity.

Aristarchi walked deliberately by the pillar to the aisle, as he passed, and listened for the flapping of the heavy leathern curtain at the door. Then he stole nearer to the place where Arisa was still kneeling, and came noiselessly behind her and leaned against the column, and watched her, not caring if he surprised her now.

But she did not turn round. Listening intently, Aristarchi heard a soft quick whispering, and he saw that it was punctuated by a very slight occasional movement of her head.

He had not believed her when she had told him that she said her prayers at night, but she was undoubtedly praying now, and Aristarchi watched her with interest, as he might have looked at some rare foreign animal whose habits he did not understand. She was very intently bent on what she was saying, for he stayed there some time, scarcely breathing, before he turned away and disappeared in the shadows with noiseless steps.

CHAPTER VIII

All through the long Sunday afternoon Zorzi sat in the laboratory alone. From time to time, he tended the fire, which must not be allowed to go down lest the quality of the glass should be injured, or at least changed. Then he went back to the master's great chair, and allowed himself to think of what was happening in the house opposite.

In those days there was no formal betrothal before marriage, at which the intended bride and bridegroom joined hands or exchanged the rings which were to be again exchanged at the wedding. When a marriage had been arranged, the parents or guardians of the young couple signed the contract before a notary, a strictly commercial and legal formality, and the two families then announced the match to their respective relatives who were invited for the purpose, and were hospitably entertained. The announcement was final, and to break off a marriage after it had been announced was a deadly offence and was generally an irreparable injury to the bride.

In Beroviero's house the richest carpets were taken from the storerooms and spread upon the pavement and the stairs, tapestries of great worth and beauty were hung upon the walls, the servants were arrayed in their high-day liveries and spoke in whispers when they spoke at all, the silver dishes were piled with sweetmeats and early fruits, and the silver plates had been not only scoured, but had been polished with leather, which was not done every day. In all the rooms that were opened, silken curtains had been hung before the windows, in place of those used at other times. In a word, the house had been prepared in a few hours for a great family festivity, and when Marietta got out of the gondola, she set her foot upon a thick carpet that covered the steps and was even allowed to hang down and dip itself in the water of the canal by way of showing what little value was set upon it by the rich man.

Zorzi had known that the preparations were going forward, and he knew what they meant. He would rather see nothing of them, and when the guests were gone, old Beroviero would come over and give him some final instructions before beginning his journey; until then he could be alone in the laboratory, where only the low roar of the fire in the furnace broke the silence.

Marietta's head was aching and she felt as if the hard, hot

fingers of some evil demon were pressing her eyeballs down into their sockets. She sat in an inner chamber, to which only women were admitted. There she sat, in a sort of state, a circlet of gold set upon her loosened hair, her dress all of embroidered white silk, her shoulders covered with a wide mantle of green and gold brocade that fell in heavy folds to the floor. She wore many jewels, too, such as she would not have worn in public before her marriage. They had belonged to her mother, like the mantle, and were now brought out for the first time. It was very hot, but the windows were shut lest the sound of the good ladies' voices should be heard without; for the news that Marietta was to be married had suddenly gone abroad through Murano, and all the idlers, and the men from the furnaces, where no work was done on Sunday, as well as all the poor, were assembled on the footway and the bridge, and in the narrow alleys round the house. They all pushed and jostled each other to see Beroviero's friends and relations, as they emerged from beneath the black 'felse' of their gondolas to enter the house. In the hall the guests divided, and the men gathered in a large lower chamber, while the women went upstairs to offer their congratulations to Marietta, with many set compliments upon her beauty, her clothes and her jewels, and even with occasional flattering allusions to the vast dowry her husband was to receive with her.

She listened wearily, and her head ached more and more, so that she longed for the coolness of her own room and for Nella's soothing chatter, to which she was so much accustomed that she missed it if the little brown woman chanced to be silent.

The sun went down and wax candles were brought, instead of the tall oil lamps that were used on ordinary days. It grew hotter and hotter, the compliments of the ladies seemed more and more dull and stale, her mantle was heavy and even the gold circlet on her hair was a burden. Worse than all, she knew that every minute was carrying her further and further into the dominion of the irrevocable whence she could never return.

She had looked at the palaces she had passed in Venice that morning, some in shadow, some in sunlight, some with gay faces and some grave, but all so different from the big old house in Murano, that she did not wish to live in them at all. It would have been much easier to submit if she had been betrothed to a foreigner, a Roman, or a Florentine. She had been told that Romans were all wicked and gloomy, and that Florentines were all wicked and gay. That was what Nella had heard. But in a sense they were free, for they probably did what was good in their own eyes, as wicked people often do. Life in Venice was to be lived by rule, and everything that tasted of freedom was repressed by law. If it pleased women to wear long trains the Council forbade them; if they took refuge in long sleeves, thrown back over their shoulders, a law was passed which set a measure and a pattern for all sleeves that might ever be worn. If a few rich men indulged their fancy in the decoration of their gondolas, now that riding was out of fashion, the Council immediately determined that gondolas should be black and that they should only be gilt and adorned inside. As for freedom, if any one talked of it he was immediately tortured until he retracted all his errors, and was then promptly beheaded for fear that he should fall again into the same mistake. Nella said so, and told hideous tales of the things that had been done to innocent men in the little room behind the Council chamber in the Palace. Besides, if one talked of justice, there was Zorzi's case to prove that there was no justice at all in Venetian law. Marietta suddenly wished that she were wicked, like the Romans and the Florentines; and even when she reflected that it was a sin to wish that one were bad, she was not properly repentant, because she had a very vague notion of what wickedness really was. Righteousness seemed just now to consist in being smothered in heavy clothes, in a horribly hot room, while respectable women of all ages, fat, thin, fair, red-haired, dark, ugly and handsome, all chattered at her and overwhelmed her with nauseous flattery.

She thought of that morning in the garden, three days ago, when something she did not understand had been so near, just before disappearing for ever. Then her throat tightened and she saw indistinctly, and her lips were suddenly dry. After that, she remembered little of what happened on that evening, and by and by she was alone in her own room without a light, standing at the open window with bare feet on the cold pavement, and the night breeze stirred her hair and brought her the scent of the rosemary and lavender, while she tried to listen to the stars, as if they were speaking to her, and lost herself in her thoughts for a few moments before going to sleep.

Zorzi was still sitting in the big chair against the wall when he heard a footstep in the garden, and as he rose to look out Beroviero entered. The master was wrapped in a long cloak that covered something which he was carrying. There was no lamp in the laboratory, but the three fierce eyes of the furnace shed a low red glare in different directions. Beroviero had given orders that the night boys should not come until he sent for them.

"I thought it wiser to bring this over at night," he said, setting a small iron box on the table.

It contained the secrets of Paolo Godi, which were worth a great fortune in those times.

"Of all my possessions," said the old man, laying his hands upon the casket, "these are the most valuable. I will not hide them alone, as I might, because if any harm befell me they would be lost, and might be found by some unworthy person."

"Could you not leave them with some one else, sir?" asked Zorzi.

"No. I trust no one else. Let us hide them together tonight, for tomorrow I must leave Venice. Take up one of the large flagstones behind the annealing oven, and dig a hole underneath it in the ground. The place will be quite dry, from the heat of the oven."

Zorzi lit a lamp with a splinter of wood which he thrust into the 'bocca' of the furnace; he took a small crowbar from the corner and set to work. The laboratory contained all sorts of builder's tools, used when the furnace needed repairing. He raised one of the slabs with difficulty, turned it over, propped it with a billet of beech wood, and began to scoop out a hole in the hard earth, using a mason's trowel. Beroviero watched him, holding the box in his hands.

"The lock is not very good," he said, "but I thought the box might keep the packet from dampness."

"Is the packet properly sealed?" asked Zorzi, looking up.

"You shall see," answered the master, and he set down the box beside the lamp, on the broad stone at the mouth of the annealing oven. "It is better that you should see for yourself."

He unlocked the box and took out what seemed to be a small book, carefully tied up in a sheet of parchment. The ends of the silk cord below the knot were pinched in a broad red seal. Zorzi examined the wax.

"You sealed it with a glass seal," he observed. "It would not be hard to make another."

"Do you think it would be so easy?" asked Beroviero, who had made the seal himself many years ago.

Zorzi held the impression nearer to the lamp and scrutinised it closely.

"No one will have a chance to try," he said, with a slight gesture of indifference. "It might not be so easy."

The old man looked at him a moment, as if hesitating, and then put the packet back into the box and locked the latter with the key that hung from his neck by a small silver chain.

"I trust you," he said, and he gave the box to Zorzi, to be deposited in the hole.

Zorzi stood up, and taking a little tow from the supply used far cleaning the blowpipes, he dipped it into the oil of the lamp and proceeded to grease the box carefully before hiding it.

"It would rust," he explained.

He laid the box in the hole and covered it with earth before placing the stone over it.

"Be careful to make the stone lie quite flat," said Angelo, bending down and gathering his gown off the floor in a bunch at his knees. "If it does not lie flat, the stone will move when the boys tread on it, and they may think of taking it up."

"It is very heavy," answered the young man. "It was as much as I could do to heave it up. You need not be afraid of the boys."

"It is not a very safe place, I fear, after all," returned Beroviero doubtfully. "Be sure to leave no marks of the crowbar, and no loose earth near it."

The heavy slab slipped into its bed with a soft thud. Zorzi took the lamp and examined the edges. One of them was a little chipped by the crowbar, and he rubbed it with the greasy tow and scattered dust over it. Then he got a cypress broom and swept the earth carefully away into a heap. Beroviero himself brought the shovel and held it close to the stones while Zorzi pushed the loose earth upon it.

"Carry it out and scatter it in the garden," said the old man.

It was the first time that he had allowed his affection for Zorzi to express itself so strongly, for he was generally a very cautious person. He took the young man's hand and held it a moment, pressing it kindly.

"It was not I who made the law against strangers, and it was not meant for men like you," he added.

Zorzi knew how much this meant from such a master and he would have found words for thanks, had he been able; but when he tried, they would not come.

"You may trust me," was all he could say.

Beroviero left him, and went down the dark corridor with the firm step of a man who knows his way without light.

In the morning, when he left the house to begin his journey, Zorzi stood by the steps with the servant to steady the gondola for him. His horses were to be in waiting in Venice, whence he was to go over to the mainland. He nodded to the young man carelessly, but said nothing, and no one would have guessed how kindly he had spoken to him on the previous night. Giovanni Beroviero took ceremonious leave of his father, his cap in his hand, bending low, a lean man, twenty years older than Marietta, with an insignificant brow and clean-shaven, pointed jaw and greedy lips. Marietta stood within the shadow of the doorway, very pale. Nella was beside her, and Giovanni's wife, and further in, at a respectful distance, the serving-people, for the master's departure was an event of importance.

The gondola pushed off when Beroviero had disappeared under the 'felse' with a final wave of the hand. Zorzi stood still, looking after his master, and Marietta came forward to the doorstep and pretended to watch the gondola also. Zorzi was the first to turn, and their eyes met. He had sot expected to see her still there, and he started a little. Giovanni looked at him coldly.

"You had better go to your work," he said in a sour tone. "I suppose my father has told you what to do."

The young artist flushed, but answered quietly enough.

"I am going to my work," he said. "I need no urging."

Before he put on his cap, he bent his head to Marietta; then he passed on towards the bridge.

"That fellow is growing insolent," said Giovanni to his sister, but he was careful that Zorzi should not hear the words. "I think I shall advise our father to turn him out."

Marietta looked at her brother with something like contempt.

"Since when has our father consulted you, or taken your advice?" she asked.

"I presume he takes yours," retorted Giovanni, regretting that he could not instantly find a sharper answer, for he was not quick-witted though he was suspicious.

"He needs neither yours nor mine," said Marietta, "and he trusts whom he pleases."

"You seem inclined to defend his servants when they are insolent," answered Giovanni.

"For that matter, Zorzi is quite able to defend himself!" She turned her back on her brother and went towards the stairs, taking Nella with her.

Giovanni glanced at her with annoyance and walked along the footway in the direction of his own glass-house, glad to go back to a place where he was absolute despot. But he had been really surprised that Marietta should boldly take the Dalmatian's side against him, and his narrow brain brooded upon the unexpected circumstance. Besides the dislike he felt for the young artist, his small pride resented the thought that his sister, who was to marry a Contarini, should condescend to the defence of a servant.

Zorzi went his way calmly and spent the day in the laboratory. He was in a frame of mind in which such speeches as Giovanni's could make but little impression upon him, sensitive though he naturally was. Really great sorrows, or great joys or great emotions, make smaller ones almost impossible for the time. Men of vast ambition, whose deeds are already moving the world and making history, are sometimes as easily annoyed by trifles as a nervous woman; but he who knows that what is dearest to him is slipping from his hold, or has just been taken, is half paralysed in his sense of outward things. His own mind alone has power to give him a momentary relief.

Herein lies one of the strongest problems of human nature. We say with assurance that the mind rules the body, we feel that the spirit in some way overshadows and includes the mind. Yet if this were really true the spirit—that is, the will—should have power against bodily pain, but not against moral suffering except with some help from a higher source. But it is otherwise. If the will of ordinary human beings could hypnotise the body against material sensation, the credit due to those brave believers in all ages who have suffered cruel torments for their faith would be singularly diminished. If the mind could dominate matter by ordinary concentration of thought, a bad toothache should have no effect upon the delicate imagination of the poet, and Napoleon would not have lost the decisive battle of his life by a fit of indigestion, as has been asserted.

On the other hand, there was never yet a man of genius, or even of great talent, who was not aware that the most acute moral anguish can be momentarily forgotten, as if it did not exist for the time, by concentrating the mind upon its accustomed and favourite kind of work. Johnson wrote *Rasselas* to pay for the funeral of his yet unburied mother, and Johnson was a man of heart if ever one lived; he could not have written the book if he had had a headache. Saints and ascetics without end and of many persuasions have resorted to bodily pain as a means of deadening the imagination and exalting the will or spirit. Some great thinkers have been invalids, but in every case their food, work has been done when they were temporarily free from pain. Perhaps the truth is on the side of those mystics who say that although the mind is of a higher nature than matter, it is so closely involved with it that neither can get away from the other, and that both together tend to shut out the spirit and to forget its existence, which is a perpetual reproach to them; and any ordinary intellectual effort being produced by the joint activity of mind and the matter through which the mind acts, the condition of the spirit at the time has little or no effect upon them, nor upon what they are doing. And if one would carry the little theory further, one might find that the greatest works of genius have been produced when the effort of mind and matter has taken place under the inspiration of the spirit, so that all three were momentarily involved together. But such thoughts lead far, and it may be that they profit little. The best which a man means to do is generally better than the best he does, and it is perhaps the best he is capable of doing.

Be these things as they may, Zorzi worked hard in the laboratory, minutely carrying out the instructions he had received, but reasoning upon them with a freshness and keenness of thought of which his master was no longer capable. When he had made the trials and had added the new ingredients for future ones, he began to think out methods of his own which had suggested themselves to him of late, but which he had never been able to try. But though he had the furnace to himself, to use as long as he could endure the heat of the advancing summer, he was face to face with a difficulty that seemed insuperable.

The furnace had but three crucibles, each of which contained one of the mixtures by means of which he and Beroviero were trying to produce the famous red glass. In order to begin to make glass in his own way, it was necessary that one of the three should be emptied, but unless he disobeyed his orders this was out of the question. In his train of thought and longing to try what he felt sure must succeed, he had forgotten the obstacle. The check brought him back to himself, and he walked disconsolately up and down the long room by the side of the furnace.

Everything was against him, said the melancholy little demon that torments genius on dark days. It was not enough that he should be forced by every consideration of honour and wisdom to hide his love for his master's daughter; when he took refuge in his art and tried to throw his whole life into it, he was stopped at the outset by the most impassable barriers of impossibility. The furious desire to create, which is the strength as well as the essence of genius, surged up and dashed itself to futile spray upon the face of the solid rock.

He stood still before the hanging shelves on which he had placed the objects he had occasionally made, and which his master allowed him to keep there—light, air-thin vessels of graceful shapes: an ampulla of exquisite outline with a long curved spout that bent upwards and then outwards and over like the stalk of a lily of the valley; a large drinking-glass set on a stem so slender that one would doubt its strength to carry the weight of a full measure, yet so strong that the cup might have been filled with lead without breaking it; a broad dish that was nothing but a shadow against the light, but in the shadow was a fair design of flowers, drawn free with a diamond point; there were a dozen of such things on the shelves, not the best that Zorzi had made, for those Beroviero took to his own house and used on great occasions, while these were the results of experiments unheard of in those days, and which not long afterwards made a school.

In his present frame of mind Zorzi felt a foolish impulse to take them down and smash them one by one in the big jar into which the failures were thrown, to be melted again in the main furnace, for in a glass-house nothing is thrown away. He knew it was foolish, and he held his hands behind him as he looked at the things, wishing that he had never made them, that he had never learned the art he was forbidden by law to practise, that he had never left Dalmatia as a little boy long ago, that he had never been born.

The door opened suddenly and Giovanni entered. Zorzi turned and looked at him in silence. He was surprised, but he supposed that the master's son had a right to come if he chose, though he never showed himself in the glass-house when his father was in Murano.

"Are you alone here?" asked Giovanni, looking about him. "Do none of the workmen come here?"

"The master has left me in charge of his work," answered Zorzi. "I need no help."

Giovanni seated himself in his father's chair and looked at the table before the window.

"It is not very hard work, I fancy," he observed, crossing one leg over the other and pulling up his black hose to make it fit his lean calf better.

Zorzi suspected at once that he had come in search of information, and paused before answering.

"The work needs careful attention," he said at last.

"Most glasswork does," observed Giovanni, with a harsh little laugh. "Are you very attentive, then? Do you remember to do all that my father told you?"

"The master only left this morning. So far, I have obeyed his orders."

"I do not understand how a man who is not a glassblower can

know enough to be left alone in charge of a furnace," said Giovanni, looking at Zorzi's profile.

This time Zorzi was silent. He did not think it necessary to tell how much he knew.

"I suppose my father knows what he is about," continued Giovanni, in a tone of disapproval.

Zorzi thought so too, and no reply seemed necessary. He stood still, looking out of the window, and wishing that his visitor would go away. But Giovanni had no such intention.

"What are you making?" he asked presently.

"A certain kind of glass," Zorzi answered.

"A new colour?"

"A certain colour. That is all I can tell you."

"You can tell me what colour it is," said Giovanni. "Why are you so secret? Even if my father had ordered you to be silent with me about his work, which I do not believe, you would not be betraying anything by telling me that. What colour is he trying to make?"

"I am to say nothing about it, not even to you. I obey my orders."

Giovanni was a glassmaker himself. He rose with an air of annoyance and crossed the laboratory to the jar in which the broken glass was kept, took out a piece and held it up against the light. Zorzi had made a movement as if to hinder him, but he realised at once that he could not lay hands on his master's son. Giovanni laughed contemptuously and threw the fragment back into the jar.

"Is that all? I can do better than that myself!" he said, and he sat down again in the big chair.

His eyes fell on the shelves upon which Zorzi's specimens of work were arranged. He looked at them with interest, at once understanding their commercial value.

"My father can make good things when he is not wasting time over discoveries," he remarked, and rising again he went nearer and began to examine the little objects.

Zorzi said nothing, and after looking at them a long time Giovanni turned away and stood before the furnace. The copper ladle with which the specimens were taken from the pots lay on the brick ledge near one of the 'boccas.' Giovanni took it, looked round to see where the iron plate for testing was placed, and thrust the ladle into the aperture, holding it lightly lest the heat should hurt his hand.

"You shall not do that!" cried Zorzi, who was already beside him.

Before Giovanni knew what was happening Zorzi had struck the ladle from his hand, and it disappeared through the 'bocca' into the white-hot glass within.

CHAPTER IX

With an oath Giovanni raised his hand to strike Zorzi in the face, but the quick Dalmatian snatched up his heavy blowpipe in both hands and stood in an attitude of defence.

"If you try to strike me, I shall defend myself," he said quietly.

Giovanni's sour face turned grey with fright, and then as his impotent anger rose, the grey took an almost greenish hue that was bad to see. He smiled in a sickly fashion. Zorzi set the blowpipe upright against the furnace and watched him, for he saw that the man was afraid of him and might act treacherously.

"You need not be so violent," said Giovanni, and his voice trembled a little, as he recovered himself. "After all, my father would not have made any objection to my trying the glass. If I had, I could not have guessed how it was made."

Zorzi did not answer, for he had discovered that silence was his best weapon. Giovanni continued, in the peevish tone of a man who has been badly frightened and is ashamed of it.

"It only shows how ignorant you are of glassmaking, if you suppose that my father would care." As he still got no reply beyond a shrug of the shoulders, he changed the subject. "Did you see my father make any of those things?" he asked, pointing to the shelves.

"No," answered Zorzi.

"But he made them all here, did he not?" insisted Giovanni. "And you are always with him."

"He did not make any of them."

Giovanni opened his eyes in astonishment. In his estimation there was no man living, except his father, who could have done such work. Zorzi smiled, for he knew what the other's astonishment meant.

"I made them all," he said, unable to resist the temptation to take the credit that was justly his.

"You made those things?" repeated Giovanni incredulously.

But Zorzi was not in the least offended by his disbelief. The more sceptical Giovanni was, the greater the honour in having produced anything so rarely beautiful.

"I made those, and many others which the master keeps in his house," he said.

Giovanni would have liked to give him the lie, but he dared not just then.

"If you made them, you could make something of the kind again," he said. "I should like to see that. Take your blowpipe and try. Then I shall believe you."

"There is no white glass in the furnace," answered Zorzi. "If there were, I would show you what I can do."

Giovanni laughed sourly.

"I thought you would find some good excuse," he said.

"The master saw me do the work," answered Zorzi unconcernedly. "Ask him about it when he comes back."

"There are other furnaces in the glass-house," suggested Giovanni. "Why not bring your blowpipe with you and show the workmen as well as me what you can do?"

Zorzi hesitated. It suddenly occurred to him that this might be a decisive moment in his life, in which the future would depend on the decision he made. In all the years since he had been with Beroviero he had never worked at one of the great furnaces among the other men.

"I daresay your sense of responsibility is so great that you do not like to leave the laboratory, even for half an hour," said Giovanni scornfully. "But you have to go home at night."

"I sleep here," answered Zorzi.

"Indeed?" Giovanni was surprised. "I see that your objections are insuperable," he added with a laugh.

Zorzi was in one of those moods in which a man feels that he has nothing to lose. There might, however, be something to gain by exhibiting his skill before Giovanni and the men. His reputation as a glassmaker would be made in half an hour.

"Since you do not believe me, come," he said at last. "You shall see for yourself."

He took his blowpipe and thrust it through one of the 'boccas' to melt off the little red glass that adhered to it. Then he cooled it in water, and carefully removed the small particles that stuck to the iron here and there like spots of glazing.

"I am ready," he said, when he had finished.

Giovanni rose and led the way, without a word. Zorzi followed him, shut the door, turned the key twice and thrust it into the bosom of his doublet. Giovanni turned and watched him.

"You are really very cautious," he said. "Do you always lock the door when you go out?"

"Always," answered Zorzi, shouldering his blowpipe.

They crossed the little garden and entered the passage that led to the main furnace rooms. In the first they entered, eight or ten men and youths, masters and apprentices, were at work. The place was higher and far more spacious than the laboratory, the furnace was broader and taller and had four mouths instead of three. The sunlight streamed through a window high above the floor and fell upon the arched back of the annealing oven, the window being so placed that the sun could never shine upon the working end and dazzle the workmen.

When Giovanni and Zorzi entered, the men were working in silence. The low and steady roar of tine flames was varied by the occasional sharp click of iron or the soft sound of hot glass rolling on the marver, or by the hiss of a metal instrument plunged into water to cool it. Every man had an apprentice to help him, and two boys tended the fire. The foreman sat at a table, busy with an account, a small man, even paler than the others and dressed in shabby brown hose and a loose brown coat. The workmen wore only hose and shirts.

Without desisting from their occupations they cast surprised glances at Giovanni and his companion, whom they all hated as a favoured person. One of them was finishing a drinking-glass, rolling the pontil on the arms of the working-stool; another, a beetle-browed fellow, swung his long blowpipe with its lump of glowing glass in a full circle, high in air and almost to touch the ground; another was at a 'bocca' in the low glare; all were busy, and the air was very hot and close. The men looked grim and ill-tempered.

Giovanni explained the object of his coming in a way intended to conciliate them to himself at Zorzi's expense. Their presence gave him courage.

"This is Zorzi, the man without a name," he said, "who is come from Dalmatia to give us a lesson in glassblowing."

One of the men laughed, and the apprentices tittered. The others looked as if they did not understand. Zorzi had known well enough what humour he should find among them, but he would not let the taunt go unanswered.

"Sirs," he said, for they all claimed the nobility of the glass-blowers' caste, "I come not to teach you, but to prove to the master's son that I can make some trifle in the manner of your art."

No one spoke. The workmen in the elder Beroviero's house knew well enough that Zorzi was a better artist than they, and they had no mind to let him outdo them at their own furnace.

"Will any one of you gentlemen allow me to use his place?" asked Zorzi civilly.

Not a man answered. In the sullen silence the busy hands moved with quick skill, the furnace roared, the glowing glass grew in ever-changing shapes.

"One of you must give Zorzi his place," said Giovanni, in a tone of authority.

The little foreman turned quite round in his chair and looked on. There was no reply. The pale men went on with their work as if Giovanni were not there, and Zorzi leaned calmly on his blow-pipe. Giovanni moved a step forward and spoke directly to one of the men who had just dropped a finished glass into the bed of soft wood ashes, to be taken to the annealing oven.

"Stop working for a while," he said. "Let Zorzi have your place."

"The foreman gives orders here, not you," answered the man coolly, and he prepared to begin another piece.

Giovanni was very angry, but there were too many of the workmen, and he did not say what rose to his lips, but crossed over to the foreman. Zorzi kept his place, waiting to see what might happen.

"Will you be so good as to order one of the men to give up his place?" Giovanni asked.

The old foreman smiled at this humble acknowledgment of his authority, but he argued the point before acceding.

"The men know well enough what Zorzi can do," he answered in a low voice. "They dislike him, because he is not one of us. I advise you to take him to your own glass-house, sir, if you wish to see him work. You will only make trouble here."

"I am not afraid of any trouble, I tell you," replied Giovanni. "Please do what I ask."

"Very well. I will, but I take no responsibility before the master if there is a disturbance. The men are in a bad humour and the weather is hot."

"I will be responsible to my father," said Giovanni.

"Very well," repeated the old man. "You are a glassmaker yourself, like the rest of us. You know how we look upon for-eigners who steal their knowledge of our art."

"I wish to make sure that he has really stolen something of it."

The foreman laughed outright.

"You will be convinced soon enough!" he said. "Give your place to the foreigner, Piero," he added, speaking to the man who had refused to move at Giovanni's bidding.

Piero at once chilled the fresh lump of glass he had begun to fashion and smashed it off the tube into the refuse jar. Without a word Zorzi took his place. While he warmed the end of his blowpipe at the 'bocca' he looked to right and left to see where the working-stool and marver were placed, and to be sure that the few tools he needed were at hand, the pontil, the 'procello,'—that is, the small elastic tongs for modelling—and the shears. Piero's apprentice had retired to a distance, as he had received no special orders, and the workmen hoped that Zorzi would find himself in difficulty at the moment when he would turn in the expectation of finding the assistant at his elbow. But Zorzi was used to helping himself. He pushed his blowpipe into the melted glass and drew it out, let it cool a moment and then thrust it in again to take up more of the stuff.

The men went on with their work, seeming to pay no attention to him, and Piero turned his back and talked to the foreman in low tones. Only Giovanni watched, standing far enough back to be out of reach of the long blowpipe if Zorzi should unexpectedly swing it to its full length. Zorzi was confident and unconcerned, though he was fully aware that the men were watching every movement he made, while pretending not to see. He knew also that owing to his being partly self-taught he did certain things in ways of his own. They should see that his ways were as good as theirs, and what was more, that he needed no help, while none of them could do anything without an apprentice.

The glass grew and swelled, lengthened and contracted with his breath and under his touch, and the men, furtively watching him, were amazed to see how much he could do while the piece was still on the blowpipe. But when he could do no more they thought that he would have trouble. He did not even turn his head to see whether any one was near to help him. At the exact moment when the work was cool enough to stand he attached the pontil with its drop of liquid glass to the lower end, as he had done many a time in the laboratory, and before those who looked on could fully understand how he had done it without assistance, the long and heavy blowpipe lay on the floor and Zorzi held his piece on the lighter pontil, heating it again at the fire.

The men did not stop working, but they glanced at each other and nodded, when Zorzi could not see them. Giovanni uttered a low exclamation of surprise. The foreman alone now watched Zorzi with genuine admiration; there was no mistaking the jealous attitude of the others. It was not the mean envy of the inferior artist, either, for they were men who, in their way, loved art as Beroviero himself did, and if Zorzi had been a new companion recently promoted from the state of apprenticeship in the guild, they would have looked on in wonder and delight, even if, at the very beginning, he outdid them all. What they felt was quite different. It was the deep, fierce hatred of the mediaeval guildsman for the stranger who had stolen knowledge without apprenticeship and without citizenship, and it was made more intense because the glassblowers were the only guild that excluded every foreign-born man, without any exception. It was a shame to them to be outdone by one who had not their blood, nor their teaching, nor their high acknowledged rights.

They were peaceable men in their way, not given to quarrelling, nor vicious; yet, excepting the mild old foreman, there was not one of them who would not gladly have brought his iron blowpipe down on Zorzi's head with a two-handed swing, to strike the life out of the intruder.

Zorzi's deft hands made the large piece he was forming spin on itself and take new shape at every turn, until it had the perfect curve of those slim-necked Eastern vessels for pouring water upon the hands, which have not even now quite degenerated from their early grace of form. While it was still very hot, he took a sharp pointed knife from his belt and with a turn of his hand cut a small round hole, low down on one side. The mouth was widened and then turned in and out like the leaf of a carnation. He left the cooling piece on the pontil, lying across the arms of the stool, and took his blowpipe again.

"Has the fellow not finished his tricks yet?" asked Piero discontentedly.

It would have given him pleasure to smash the beautiful thing to atoms where it lay, almost within his reach. Zorzi began to make the spout, for it was a large ampulla that he was fashioning. He drew the glass out, widened it, narrowed it, cut it, bent it and finished off the nozzle before he touched it with wet iron and made it drop into the ashes. A moment later he had heated the thick end of it again and was welding it over the hole he had made in the body of the vessel.

"The man has three hands!" exclaimed the foreman.

"And two of them are far stealing," added Piero.

"Or all three," put in the beetle-browed man who was working next to Zorzi.

Zorzi looked at him coldly a moment, but said nothing. They did not mean that he was a thief, except in the sense that he had stolen his knowledge of their art. He went on to make the handle of the ampulla, an easy matter compared with making the spout. But the highest part of glassblowing lies in shaping graceful curves, and it is often in the smallest differences of measurement that the pieces made by Beroviero and Zorzi—preserved intact to this day—differ from similar things made by lesser artists. Yet in those little variations lies all the great secret that divides grace from awkwardness. Zorzi now had the whole vessel, with its spout and handle, on the pontil. It was finished, but he could still ornament it. His own instinct was to let it alone, leaving its perfect shape and airy lightness to be its only beauty, and he turned it thoughtfully as he looked at it, hesitating whether he should detach it from the iron, or do more.

"If you have finished your nonsense, let me come back to my work," said Piero behind him.

Zorzi did not turn to answer, for he had decided to add some delicate ornaments, merely to show Giovanni that he was a full master of the art. The dark-browed man had just collected a heavy lump of glass on the end of his blowpipe, and was blowing into it before giving it the first swing that would lengthen it out. He and Piero exchanged glances, unnoticed by Zorzi, who had become almost unconscious of their hostile presence. He began to take little drops of glass from the furnace on the end of a thin iron, and he drew them out into thick threads and heated them again and laid them on the body of the ampulla, twisting and turning each bit till he had no more, and forming a regular raised design on the surface. His neighbour seemed to get no further with what he was doing, though he busily heated and reheated his lump of glass and again and again swung his blowpipe round his head, and backward and forward. The foreman was too much interested in Zorzi to notice what the others were doing.

Zorzi was putting the last touches to his work. In a moment it would be finished and ready to go to the annealing oven, though he was even then reflecting that the workmen would certainly break it up as soon as the foreman turned his back. The man next to him swung his blowpipe again, loaded with red-hot glass.

It slipped from his hand, and the hot mass, with the full weight of the heavy iron behind it, landed on Zorzi's right foot, three paces away, with frightful force. He uttered a sharp cry of surprise and pain. The lovely vessel he had made flew from his hands and broke into a thousand tiny fragments. In excruciating agony he lifted the injured foot from the ground and stood upon the other. Not a hand was stretched out to help him, and he felt that he was growing dizzy. He made a frantic effort to hop on one leg towards the furnace, so as to lean against the brickwork. Piero laughed.

"He is a dancer!" he cried. "He is a 'ballarino'!" The others all laughed, too, and the name remained his as long as he lived—he was Zorzi Ballarin.

The old foreman came to help him, seeing that he was really injured, for no one had quite realised it at first. Savagely as they hated him, the workmen would not have tortured him, though they might have killed him outright if they had dared. Excepting Piero and the man who had hurt him, the workmen all went on with their work.

He was ghastly pale, and great drops of sweat rolled down his forehead as he reached the foreman's chair and sat down: but after the first cry he had uttered, he made no sound. The foreman could hear how his teeth ground upon each other as he mastered the frightful suffering. Giovanni came, and stood looking at the helpless foot, smashed by the weight that had fallen upon it and burned to the bone in an instant by the molten glass.

"I cannot walk," he said at last to the foreman. "Will you help me?"

His voice was steady but weak. The foreman and Giovanni helped him to stand on his left foot, and putting his arms round their necks he swung himself along as he could. The dark man had picked up his blowpipe and was at work again.

"You will pay for that when the master comes back," Piero said to him as Zorzi passed. "You will starve if you are not careful."

Zorzi turned his head and looked the dark man full in the eyes.

"It was an accident," he said faintly. "You did not mean to do it."

The man looked away shamefacedly, for he knew that even if he had not meant to injure Zorzi for life, he had meant to hurt him if he could.

As for Giovanni, he was puzzled by all that had happened so unexpectedly, for he was a dull man, though very keen for gain, and he did not understand human nature. He disliked Zorzi, but during the morning he had become convinced that the gifted young artist was a valuable piece of property, and not, as he had supposed, a clever flatterer who had wormed himself into old Beroviero's confidence. A man who could make such things was worth much money to his master. There were kings and princes, from the Pope to the Emperor, who would have given a round sum in gold for the beautiful ampulla of which only a heap of tiny fragments were now left to be swept away.

The two men brought Zorzi across the garden to the door of

the laboratory. Leaning heavily on the foreman he got the key out, and Giovanni turned it in the lock. They would have taken him to the small inner room, to lay him on his pallet bed, but he would not go.

"The bench," he managed to say, indicating it with a nod of his head.

There was an old leathern pillow in the big chair. The foreman took it and placed it under Zorzi's head.

"We must get a surgeon to dress his wound," said the foreman.

"I will send for one," answered Giovanni. "Is there anything you want now?" he asked, with an attempt to speak kindly to the valuable piece of property that lay helpless before him.

"Water," said Zorzi very faintly. "And feed the fire—it must be time."

The foreman dipped a cupful of water from an earthen jar, held up his head and helped him to drink. Giovanni pushed some wood into the furnace.

"I will send for a surgeon," he repeated, and went out.

Zorzi closed his eyes, and the foreman stood looking at him.

"Do not stay here," Zorzi said. "You can do nothing for me, and the surgeon will come presently."

Then the foreman also left him, and he was alone. It was not in his nature to give way to bodily pain, but he was glad the men were gone, for he could not have borne much more in silence. He turned his head to the wall and bit the edge of the leathern cushion. Now and then his whole body shook convulsively.

He did not hear the door open again, for the torturing pain that shot through him dulled all his other senses. He wished that he might faint away, even for a moment, but his nerves were too sound for that. He was recalled to outer things by feeling a hand laid gently on his leg, and immediately afterwards he heard a man's voice, in a quietly gruff tone that scarcely rose or fell, reciting a whole litany of the most appalling blasphemies that ever fell from human lips. For an instant, in his suffering, Zorzi fancied that he had died and was in the clutches of Satan himself.

He turned his head on the cushion and saw the ugly face of the old porter, who was bending down and examining the wounded foot while he steadily cursed everything in heaven and earth, with an earnestness that would have been grotesque had his language been less frightful. For a few moments Zorzi almost forgot that he was hurt, as he listened. Not a saint in the calendar seemed likely to escape the porter's fury, and he even went to the length of cursing the relatives, male and female, of half legendary martyrs and other good persons about whose families he could not possibly know anything.

"For heaven's sake, Pasquale!" cried Zorzi. "You will certainly be struck by lightning!"

He had always supposed that the porter hated him, as every one else did, and he could not understand. By this time he was far more helpless than he had been just after he had been hurt, and when he tried to move the injured foot to a more comfortable position it felt like a lump of scorching lead.

The porter entered upon a final malediction, which might be supposed to have gathered destructive force by collecting into itself all those that had gone before, and he directed the whole complex anathema upon the soul of the coward who had done the foul deed, and upon his mother, his sisters and his daughters if he had any, and upon the souls of all his dead relations, men, women and children, and all of his relations that should ever be born, to the end of time. He had been a sailor in his youth.

"Who did that to you?" he asked, when he had thus devoted the unknown offender to everlasting perdition.

"Give me some water, please," said Zorzi, instead of answering the question.

"Water! Oh yes!" Pasquale went to the earthen jar. "Water! Every devil in hell, old and young, will jump and laugh for joy when that man asks for water and has to drink flames!"

Zorzi drank eagerly, though the water was tepid.

"Drink, my son," said Pasquale, holding his head up very tenderly with one of his rough hands. "I will put more within reach for you to drink, while I go and get help."

"They have sent for a surgeon," answered Zorzi.

"A surgeon? No surgeon shall come here. A surgeon will divide you into lengths, fore and aft, and kill you by inches, a length each day, and for every day he takes to kill you, he will ask a piece of silver of the master! If a surgeon comes here I will throw him out into the canal. This is a burn, and it needs an old woman to dress it. Women are evil beings, a chastisement sent upon us for our sins. But an old woman can dress a burn. I go. There is the water."

Zorzi called him back when he was already at the door.

"The fire! It must not go down. Put a little wood in, Pasquale!"

The old porter grumbled. It was unnatural that a man so badly hurt should think of his duties, but in his heart he admired Zorzi all the more for it. He took some wood, and when Zorzi looked, he was trying to poke it through the 'bocca.'

"Not there!" cried Zorzi desperately. "The small opening on the side, near the floor."

Pasquale uttered several maledictions.

"How should I know?" he asked when he had found the right place. "Am I a night boy? Have I ever tended fires for two pence a night and my supper? There! I go!"

Zorzi could hear his voice still, as he went out.

"A surgeon!" he grumbled. "I should like to see the nose of that surgeon at the door!"

Zorzi cared little who came, so that he got some relief. His head was hot now, and the blood beat in his temples like little fiery hammers, that made a sort of screaming noise in his brain. He saw queer lights in circles, and the beams of the ceiling came down very near, and then suddenly went very far away, so that the room seemed a hundred feet high. The pain filled all his right side, and he even thought he could feel it in his arm.

All at once he started, and as he lay on his back his hands tried to grip the flat wood of the bench, and his eyes were wide open and fixed in a sort of frightened stare.

What if he should go mad with pain? Who would remember the fire in the master's furnace? Worse than that, what safety was there that in his delirium he should not speak of the book that was hidden under the stone, the third from the oven and the fourth from the corner?

His brain whirled but he would not go mad, nor lose consciousness, so long as he had the shadow of free will left. Rather than lie there on his back, he would get off his bench, cost what it might, and drag himself to the mouth of the furnace. There was a supply of wood there, piled up by the night boys for use during the day. He could get to it, even if he had to roll himself over and over on the floor. If he could do that, he could keep his hold upon his consciousness, the touch of the billets would remind him, the heat and the roar of the fire would keep him awake and in his right mind.

He raised himself slowly and put his uninjured foot to the floor. Then, with both hands he lifted the other leg off the bench. He was conscious of an increase of pain, which had seemed impossible. It shot through and through his whole body; and he saw flames. There was only one way to do it, he must get down upon his hands and his left knee and drag himself to the furnace in that way. It was a thing of infinite difficulty and suffering, but he did it. Inch by inch, he got nearer.

As his right hand grasped a billet of wood from the little pile, something seemed to break in his head. His strength collapsed, he fell forward from his knee to his full length in the ashes and dust, and he felt nothing more.

CHAPTER X

The porter unbarred the door and looked out. It was nearly noon and the southerly breeze was blowing. The footway was almost deserted. On the other side of the canal, in the shadow of the Beroviero house, an old man who sold melons in slices had gone to sleep under a bit of ragged awning, and the flies had their will of him and his wares. A small boy simply dressed in a shirt, and nothing else, stood at a little distance, looking at the fruit and listening attentively to the voice of the tempter that bade him help himself.

Pasquale looked at the house opposite. Everything was quiet, and the shutters were drawn together, but not quite closed. The flowers outside Marietta's window waved in the light breeze.

"Nella!" cried Pasquale, just as he was accustomed to call the maid when Marietta wanted her.

At the sound of his voice the little boy, who was about to deal effectually with his temptation by yielding to it at once, took to his heels and ran away. But no one looked out from the house. Pasquale called again, somewhat louder. The shutters of Marietta's window were slowly opened inward and Marietta herself appeared, all in white and pale, looking over the flowers.

"What is it?" she asked. "Why do you want Nella?"

The canal was narrow, so that one could talk across it almost in an ordinary tone.

"Your pardon, lady," answered Pasquale. "I did not mean to disturb you. There has been a little accident here, saving your grace."

This he added to avert possible ill fortune. Marietta instantly thought of Zorzi. She leaned forward upon the windowsill above the flowers and spoke anxiously.

"What has happened? Tell me quickly!"

"A man has had his foot badly burned—it must be dressed at once."

"Who is it?"

"Zorzi."

Pasquale saw that Marietta started a little and drew back. Then she leaned forward again.

"Wait there a minute," she said, and disappeared quickly.

The porter heard her calling Nella from an inner room, and then he heard Nella's voice indistinctly. He waited before the open door.

Nella was a born chatterer, but she had her good qualities, and in an emergency she was silent and skilful.

"Leave it to me," she said. "He will need no surgeon."

In her room she had a small store of simple remedies, sweet oil, a pot of balsam, old linen carefully rolled up in little bundles, a precious ointment made from the fat of vipers, which was a marvellous cure for rheumatism in the joints, some syrup of poppies in a stumpy phial, a box of powdered iris root, and another of saffron. She took the sweet oil, the balsam, and some linen. She also took a small pair of scissors which were among her most precious possessions. She threw her large black kerchief over her head and pinned it together under her chin.

When she came back to Marietta's room, her mistress was wrapped in a dark mantle that covered hear thin white dress entirely, and one corner of it was drawn up over her head so as to hide her hair and almost all her face. She was waiting by the door.

"I am going with you," she said, and her voice was not very steady.

"But you will be seen—" began Nella.

"By the porter."

"Your brother may see you—"

"He is welcome. Come, we are losing time." She opened the door and went out quickly.

"I shall certainly be sent away for letting you come!" protested Nella, hurrying after her.

Marietta did not even answer this, which Nella thought very unkind of her. From the main staircase Marietta turned off at the first landing, and went down a short corridor to the back stairs of the house, which led to the narrow lane beside the building. Nella snorted softly in approval, for she had feared that her mistress would boldly pass through the hall where there were always one or two idle men-servants in waiting. The front door was closed against the heat, they had met no one and they reached the door of the glass-house without being seen.

Pasquale looked at Marietta but said nothing until all three were inside. Then he took hold of Marietta's mantle at her elbow, and held her back. She turned and looked at him in amazement.

"You must not go in, lady," he said. "It is an ugly wound to see."

Marietta pushed him aside quietly, and led the way. Nella followed her as fast as she could, and Pasquale came last. He knew that the two women would need help.

Zorzi lay quite still where he had fallen, with one hand on the billet of beech wood, the other arm doubled under him, his cheek on the dusty stone. With a sharp cry Marietta ran forward and knelt beside his head, dropping her long mantle as she crossed the room. Pasquale uttered an uncompromising exclamation of surprise.

"O, most holy Mary!" cried Nella, holding up her hands with the things she carried.

Marietta believed that Zorzi was dead, for he was very white and he lay quite still. At first she opened her eyes wide in horror, but in a moment she sank down, covering her face. Pasquale knelt opposite her on one knee, and began to turn Zorzi on his back. Nella was at his feet, and she helped, with great gentleness.

"Do not be frightened, lady," said Pasquale reassuringly. "He has only fainted. I left him on the bench, but you see he must have tried to get up to feed the fire."

While he spoke he was lifting Zorzi as well as he could. Marietta dropped her hands and slowly opened her eyes, and she knew that Zorzi was alive when she saw his face, though it was ghastly and smeared with grey ashes. But in those few moments she had felt what she could never forget. It had been as if a vast sword-stroke had severed her body at the waist, and yet left her heart alive.

"Can you help a little?" asked Pasquale. "If I could get him into my arms, I could carry him alone."

Marietta sprang to her feet, all her energy and strength returning in a moment. The three carried the unconscious man easily enough to the bench and laid him down, as he had lain before, with his head on the leathern cushion. Then Nella set to work quickly and skilfully, for she hoped to dress the wound while he was still insensible. Marietta helped her, instinctively doing what was right. It was a hideous wound.

"It will heal more quickly than you think," said Nella, confidently. "The burning has cauterised it."

Marietta, delicately reared and unused to such sights, would have felt faint if the man had not been Zorzi. As it was she only felt sharp pain, each time that Nella touched the foot. Pasquale looked on, helpless but approving.

Zorzi groaned, then opened his eyes and moved one hand. Nella had almost finished.

"If only he can be kept quiet a few moments longer," she said, "it will be well done."

Zorzi writhed in pain, only half conscious yet. Marietta left

Nella to put on the last bandages, and came and looked down into his face, taking one of his hands in hers. He recognised her, and stared in wild surprise.

"You must try and not move," she said softly. "Nella has almost finished."

He forgot what he suffered, and the agonised contraction of his brows and mouth relaxed. Marietta wiped away the ashes from his forehead and cheeks, and smoothed back his thick hair. No woman's hand had touched him thus since his mother's when he had been a little child. He was too weak to question what was happening to him, but a soft light came into his eyes, and he unconsciously pressed Marietta's hand.

She blushed at the pressure, without knowing why, and first the maiden instinct was to draw away her hand, but then she pitied him and let it stay. She thought, too, that her touch helped to keep him quiet, and indeed it did.

"How did you know?" he asked at length, for in his half consciousness it had seemed natural that she should have come to him when she heard that he was hurt.

"Pasquale called Nella," she answered simply, "and I came too. Is the pain still very great?"

"It is much less. How can I thank you?"

She looked into his eyes and smiled as he had seen her smile once or twice before in his life. His memory all came back now. He knew that she ought not to have been there, since her father was away. His expression changed suddenly.

"What is the matter?" asked Marietta. "Does it hurt very much?"

"No," he said. "I was thinking—" He checked himself, and glanced at the porter.

A distant knocking was heard at the outer door, Pasquale shuffled off to see who was there.

"I will wager that it is the surgeon!" he grumbled. "Evil befall his soul! We do not want him."

"What were you going to say?" asked Marietta, bending down. "There is only Nella here now."

"Nella should not have let you come," said Zorzi. "If it is known, your father will be very angry."

"Ah, do you see?" cried Nella, rising, for she had finished. "Did I not tell you so, my pretty lady? And if your brother finds out that you have been here he will go into a fury like a wild beast! I told you so! And as for your help, indeed, I could have brought another woman, and there was Pasquale, too. I suppose he has hands. Oh, there will be a beautiful revolution in the house when this is known!"

But Marietta did not mean to acknowledge that she had done anything but what was perfectly right and natural under the circumstances; to admit that would have been to confess that she had not come merely out of pity and human kindness.

"It is absurd," she said with a little indignation. "I shall tell my brother myself that Zorzi was hurt, and that I helped you to dress his wound. And what is more, Nella, you will have to come; again, and I shall come with you as often as I please. All Murano may know it for anything I care."

"And Venice too?" asked Nella, shaking her head in disapproval. "What will they say in Casa Contarini when they hear that you have actually gone out of the house to help a wounded young man in your father's glass-house?"

"If they are human, they will say that I was quite right," answered Marietta promptly. "If they are not, why should I care what they say?"

Zorzi smiled. At that moment Pasquale passed the window, and then came in by the open door, growling. His ugly face was transfigured by rage, until it had a sort of grotesque grandeur, and he clenched his fist as he began to speak.

"Animals! Beasts! Brutes! Worse than savages! He was almost incoherent.

"Well? What has happened now?" asked. Nella. "You talk like a mad dog. Remember the young lady!"

"It would make a leaden statue speak!" answered Pasquale. "The Signer Giovanni sends a boy to say that the Surgeon was not at home, because he had gone to shave the arch-priest of San Piero!"

In spite of the great pain he still suffered, Zorzi laughed, a little.

"You said that you would throw, him into the canal if he came at all," he said.

"Yes, and so I meant to do!" cried Pasquale. "But that is no reason why the inhuman monster should be shaving the arch-priest when a man might be dying for need of him! Oh, let him come here! Oh, I advise him to come! The miserable, cowardly, bloodletting, soap-sudding, shaving little beast of a barber!"

Pasquale drew a long breath after this, and unclenched his fist, but his lips still moved, as he said things to himself which would have shocked Marietta if she could have had the least idea of what they meant.

"You cannot stay here," she said, turning to Zorzi again. "You cannot lie on this bench all day."

"I shall soon be able to stand," answered Zorzi confidently. "I am much better."

"You will not stand on that foot for many a day," said Nella, shaking her head.

"Then Pasquale must get me a pair of crutches," replied Zorzi. "I cannot lie on my back because I have hurt one foot. I must tend the furnace, I must go on with my work, I must make the tests, I must—"

He stopped short and bit his lip, turning white again as a spasm of excruciating pain shot along his right side, from his foot upwards. Marietta bent over him, full of anxiety.

"You are suffering!" she said tenderly. "You must not try to move."

"It is nothing," he answered through his closed teeth. "It will pass, I daresay."

"It will not pass today," said Nella. "But I will bring you some syrup of poppies. That will make you sleep."

Marietta seemed to feel the pain herself. She smoothed the leathern cushion under his head as well as she could, and softly touched his forehead. It was hot and dry now.

"He is feverish," she said to Nella anxiously.

"I will bring him barley water with the syrup of poppies. What do you expect? Do you think that such a wound and such a burn are cooling to the blood, and refreshing to the brain? The man is badly hurt. Of course he is feverish. He ought to be in his bed, like a decent Christian."

"Some one must help me with the work," said Zorzi faintly.

"There is no one but me," answered Marietta after a moment's pause.

"You?" cried Nella, greatly scandalised.

Even Pasquale stared at Marietta in silent astonishment.

"Yes," she said quietly. "There is no one else who knows enough about my father's work."

"That is true," said Zorzi. "But you cannot come here and work with me."

Marietta turned away and walked to the window. In her thin dress she stood there a few minutes, like a slender lily, all white and gold in the summer light.

"It is out of the question!" protested Nella. "Her brother will never allow her to come. He will lock her up in her own room for safety, till the master comes home."

"I think I shall always do just what I think right," said Marietta quietly, as if to herself.

"Lord!" cried Nella. "The young lady is going mad!"

Nella was gathering together the remains of the things she had brought. Exhausted by the pain he had suffered, and by the efforts he had made to hide it, Zorzi lay on his back, looking with half closed eyes at the graceful outline of the girl's figure, and vaguely wishing that she would never move, and that he might be allowed to die while quietly gazing at her.

"Lady," said Pasquale at last, and rather timidly, "I will take good care of him. I will get him crutches tomorrow. I will come in the daytime and keep the fire burning for him."

"It would be far better to let it go out," observed Nella, with much sense.

"But the experiments!" cried Zorzi, suddenly coming back from his dream. "I have promised the master to carry them out."

"You see what comes of your glassworking," retorted Nella, pointing to his bandaged foot.

"How did it happen?" asked Marietta suddenly. "How did you do it?"

"It was done for him," said Pasquale, "and may the Last Judgment come a hundred times over for him who did it!"

His intention was clearer than his words.

"Do you mean that it was done on purpose, out of spite?" asked Marietta, looking from Pasquale to Zorzi.

"It was an accident," said the latter. "I was in the main furnace room with your brother. The blowpipe with the hot glass slipped from a man's hand. Your brother saw it—he will tell you."

"I have been porter here for five-and-twenty years," retorted Pasquale, "and there have been several accidents in that time. But I never heard of one like that."

"It was nothing else," said Zorzi.

His voice was weak. Nella had finished collecting her belongings. Marietta saw that she could not stay any longer at present, and she went once more to Zorzi's side.

"Let Pasquale take care of you today," she said. "I will come and see how you are tomorrow morning."

"I thank you," he answered. "I thank you with all my heart. I have no words to tell you how much."

"You need none," said she quietly. "I have done nothing. It is Nella who has helped you."

"Nella knows that I am very grateful."

"Of course, of course!" answered the woman kindly. "You

have made him talk too much," she added, speaking to Marietta. "Let us go away. I must prepare the barley water. It takes a long time."

"Is he to have nothing but barley water?" asked Pasquale.

"I will send him what he is to have," answered Nella, with an air of superiority.

Marietta looked back at Zorzi from the door, and his eyes were following her. She bent her head gravely and went out, followed by the others, and he was alone again. But it was very different now. The spasms of pain came back now and then, but there was rest between them, for there was a potent anodyne in the balsam with which Nella had soaked the first dressing. Of all possible hurts, the pain from burning is the most acute and lasting, and the wise little woman, who sometimes seemed so foolish, had done all that science could have done for Zorzi, even at a much later day. He could think connectedly now, he had been able to talk; had it been possible for him to stand, he might even have gone on for a time with the preparations for the next experiment. Yet he felt an instinctive certainty that he was to be lame for life.

He was not thinking of the experiments just then; he could think of nothing but Marietta. Four or five days had passed since he had talked with her in the garden, and she was now formally promised to Jacopo Contarini. He wondered why she had come with Nella, and he remembered her earnest offer of friendship. She meant to show him that she was still in earnest, he supposed. It had been perfect happiness to feel her cool young hand on his forehead, to press it in his own. No one could take that from him, as long as he lived. He remembered it through the horrible pain it had soothed, and it was better than the touch of an angel, for it was the touch of a loving woman. But he did not know that, and be fancied that if she had ever guessed that he loved her, she would not have come to him now. She would feel that the mere thought in his heart was an offence. And besides, she was to marry Contarini, and she was not of the kind that would promise to marry one man and yet encourage love in another. It was well, thought Zorzi, that she had never suspected the truth.

When Marietta reached her room again she listened patiently to Nella's scolding and warning, for she did not hear a word the good woman said to her. Nella brushed the dust from the silk mantle and from Marietta's white skirt very industriously, lest it should betray the secret to Giovanni or any other member of the household. For they had escaped being seen, even when they came back.

Nella scolded on in a little singsong voice, with many rising inflections. In her whole life, she said, she had never connived at anything more utterly shameless than this! She was humble, indeed, and of no account in the world, but if she had run out in the middle of the day to visit a young man when she was betrothed to her poor Vito, blessed soul, and the Lord remember him, her poor Vito would have gone to her father, might the Lord refresh his soul, and would have said, "What ways are these? Do you think I will marry a girl who runs about in this fashion?" That was what Vito would have said. And he would have said, "Give me back the gold things I gave your daughter, and let me go and find a wife who does not run about the city." And it would have been well said. Did Marietta suppose that an educated person like the lord Jacopo Contarini would be less particular about his bride's manners than that good soul Vito? Not that Vito had been ignorant. Nella should have liked any one to dare to say that she had married an ignorant man! And so forth. And so on.

Marietta heard the voice without listening to the words, and the gentle, half complaining, half reproving tone was rather soothing than otherwise. She sat by the half closed window with her bead work, while Nella talked, and brushed, and moved about the room, making imaginary small tasks in order to talk the more. But Marietta threaded the red and blue beads and fastened them in patterns upon the piece of stuff she was ornamenting, and when Nella looked at her every now and then, she seemed quite calm and indifferent. There had always been something inscrutable about her.

She was wondering why she had submitted to be betrothed to Contarini, when she loved Zorzi; and the answer did not come. She could not understand why it was that although she loved Zorzi with all her heart she had been convinced that she hated him, during four long, miserable days. Then, too, it was very strange that she should feel happy, that she should know that she was really happy, her heart brimming over with sunshine and joy, while Zorzi, whom she loved, was lying on that uncomfortable bench in dreadful pain. It was true that when she thought of his wound, the pain ran through her own limbs and made her move in her seat. But the next moment she was perfectly happy again, and yet was displeased with herself for it, as if it were not quite right.

Nella stood still at last, close to her, and spoke to her so directly that she could not help hearing.

"My little lady," said the woman, "do not forget that the

women are coming early tomorrow morning to show you the stuffs which your father has chosen for your wedding gown."

"Yes. I remember."

Marietta laid down her work in the little basket of beads and looked away towards the window. Between the shutters she could just see one of the scarlet flowers of the sweet geranium, waving in the sunlight. It was true. The women were coming in the morning to begin the work. They would measure her, and cut out patterns in buckram and fit them on her, making her stand a long time. They would spread out silks and satins on the bed and on the table, they would hold them up and make long draperies with them, and make the light flash in the deep folds, and they would tell her how beautiful she would be as a bride, and that her skin was whiter than lilies and milk and snow, and her hair finer than silk and richer than ropes of spun red gold. While they were saying those things she would look very grave and indifferent, and nothing they could show her would make her open her eyes wide; but her heart would laugh long and sweetly, for she should be infinitely happy, though no one would know it. She would give no opinion about the gown, no matter how they pressed her with questions.

After that the pieces that were to be embroidered would be very carefully weighed, the silk and the satin, and the weights of the pieces would be written down. Also, each of the hired women who were to make the embroidery would receive a certain amount of silver and gold thread, of which the weight would be written down under that of the stuff, and the two figures added together would mean just what the finished piece of embroidery ought to weigh. For if this were not done, the women would of course steal the gold and silver thread, a little every day, and take it away in their mouths, because the housekeeper would always search them every evening, in spite of the weighing. But they were well paid for the work and did not object to being suspected, for it was part of their business.

In time, Marietta would go to see the work they were doing, in the great cool loft where they would sit all day, where the linen presses stood side by side, and the great chests which held the hangings and curtains and carpets that were used on great occasions. The housekeeper had her little room up there, and could watch the sewing-women at their work and scold them if they were idle, noting how much should be taken from their pay. The women would sing long songs, answering each other for an hour at a time, but no one would hear them below, because the house was so big.

By and by the work would be almost finished, and then it would be quite done, and the wedding day would be very near. There Marietta's vision of the future suddenly came to a climax, as she tried to imagine what would happen when she should boldly declare that neither her father, nor the Council of Ten, nor the Doge himself, nor even His Holiness Pope Paul, who was a Venetian too, could ever make her marry Jacopo Contarini. There would be such a convulsion of the family as had never taken place since she was born. In her imagination she fancied all Murano taking sides for her or against her; even Venice itself would be amazed at the temerity of a girl who dared to refuse the husband her father had chosen for her. It would be an outrage on all authority, a scandal never to be forgotten, an unheard-of rebellion against the natural law by which unmarried children were held in bondage as slaves to their parents. But Marietta was not frightened by the tremendous consequences her fancy deduced from her refusal to marry. She was happy. Some day, the man she loved would know that she had faced the world for him, rather than be bound to any one else, and he would love her all the more dearly for having risked so much. She had never been so happy before. Only, now and then, when she thought of Zorzi's hurt, she felt a sharp thrill of pain run through her.

All day the tide of joy was high in her heart. Towards evening, she sent Nella over to the glass-house to see how Zorzi was doing, and as soon as the woman was gone she stood at the open window, behind her flowers, to watch her go in, Pasquale would look out, the door would be open for a moment, she would be a little nearer.

Even in that small anticipation she was not disappointed. It was a new joy to be able to look from her window into the dark entry that led to the place where Zorzi was. Tomorrow, or the next day, he would perhaps come to the door, helped by Pasquale, but tomorrow morning she would go and see him, come what might. She was not afraid of her brother Giovanni, and it might be long before her father came back. Till then, at all events, she would do what she thought right, no matter how Nella might be scandalised.

Nella came back, and said that Zorzi was better, that he had slept all the afternoon and now had very little pain, and he was not in any anxiety about the furnace, for Pasquale had kept the fire burning properly all day. Zorzi had begged Nella to deliver a message of thanks.

"Try and remember just what he told you," said Marietta.

"There was nothing especial," answered Nella with exasperating indifference. "He said that I was to thank you very much. Something like that—nothing else."

"I am sure that those were not his words. Why did you forget them?"

"If it had been an account of money spent, I should remember it exactly," answered Nella. "A pennyworth of thread, beeswax a farthing, so much for needles; I should forget nothing. But when a man says 'I thank you,' what is there to remember? But you are never satisfied! Nella may work her hands to the bone for you, Nella may run errands for you till she is lame, you are never pleased with what Nella does! It is always the same."

She tossed her brown head to show that she was offended. But Marietta laughed softly and patted the little woman's cheek affectionately.

"You are a dear little old angel," she said.

Nella was pacified.

CHAPTER XI

The porter kept his word, and took good care of Zorzi. When the night boys had come, he carried him into the inner room and put him to bed like a child. Zorzi asked him to tell the boys to wake him at the watches, as they had done on the previous night, and Pasquale humoured him, but when he went away he wisely forgot to give the message, and the lads, who knew that he had been hurt, supposed that he was not to be disturbed. It was broad daylight when he awoke and saw Pasquale standing beside him.

"Are the boys gone already?" he asked, almost as he opened his eyes.

"No, they are all asleep in a corner," answered the porter.

"Asleep!" cried Zorzi, in sudden anxiety. "Wake them, Pasquale, and see whether the sand-glass has been turned and is running, and whether the fire is burning. The young good-for-nothings!"

"I will wake them," answered Pasquale. "I supposed that they were allowed to sleep after daylight."

A moment later Zorzi heard him apostrophising the three lads with his usual vigour of language. Judging from the sounds that accompanied the words he was encouraging their movements by other means also. Presently one of the three set up a howl.

"Oh, you sons of snails and codfish, I will teach you!" growled Pasquale; and he proceeded to teach them, till they were all three howling at once.

Zorzi knew that they deserved a beating, but he was naturally tender-hearted.

"Pasquale!" he called out. "Let them alone! Let them make up the fire!"

Pasquale came back, and the yells subsided.

"I have knocked their empty heads together," he observed. "They will not sleep for a week. Yes, the sand-glass has run out, but the fire is not very low. I will bring you water, and when you are dressed I will carry you out into the laboratory."

The boys did not dare to go away till they had made up the fire. Then they took themselves off, and as Pasquale let them out he treated them to a final expression of his opinion. The tallest of the three was bleeding from his nose, which had been brought into violent conjunction with the skull' of one of his companions.

When the door was shut, and they had gone a few steps along the footway, he stopped the others.

"We are glassblowers' sons," he said, "and we have been beaten by that swine of a porter. Let us be revenged on him. Even Zorzi would not have dared to touch us, because he is a foreigner."

"We can do nothing," answered the smallest boy disconsolately. "If I tell my father that we went to sleep, he will say that the porter served us right, and I shall get another beating."

"You are cowards," said the first speaker. "But I am wounded," he continued proudly, pointing to his nose. "I will go to the master and ask redress. I will sit down before the door and wait for him."

"Do what you please," returned the others. "We will go home."

"You have no spirit of honour in you," said the tall boy contemptuously.

He turned his back on them in disdain, crossed the bridge and sat down under the covered way in front of Beroviero's house. He smeared the blood over his face till he really looked as if he might be badly hurt, and he kept up a low, tremulous moaning. His nose really hurt him, and as he was extremely sorry for himself some real tears came into his eyes now and then. He waited a long time. The front door was opened and two men came out with brooms and began to sweep. When they saw him they were for making him go away, but he cried out that he was waiting for the Signor Giovanni, to show him how a free glassblower's son had been treated by a dog of a foreigner and a swine of a porter over there in the glass-house. Then the servants let him stay, for they feared the porter and hated Zorzi for being a Dalmatian.

At last Giovanni came out, and the boy at once uttered a particularly effective moan. Giovanni stopped and looked at him, and he gulped and sobbed vigorously.

"Get up and go away at once!" said Giovanni, much disgusted by the sight of the blood.

"I will not go till you hear me, sir," answered the boy dramatically. "I am a free glassblower's son and I have been beaten like this by the porter of the glass-house! This is the way we are treated, though we work to learn the art as our fathers worked before us."

"You probably went to sleep, you little wretch," observed Giovanni. "Get out of my way, and go home!"

"Justice, sir! Justice!" moaned the boy, dropping himself on his knees.

"Nonsense! Go away!" Giovanni pushed him aside, and began

to walk on.

The boy sprang up and followed him, and running beside him as Giovanni tried to get away, touched the skirt of his coat respectfully, and then kissed the back of his own hand.

"If you will listen to me, sir," he said in a low voice, "I will tell you something you wish to know."

Giovanni stopped short and looked at him with curiosity.

"I will tell you of something the master did on the Sunday night before he went on his journey," continued the lad. "I am one of the night boys in the laboratory, and I saw with my eyes while the others were asleep, for we had been told to wait till we were called."

Giovanni looked about, to see whether any one was within hearing. They were still in the covered footway above which the first story of the house was built, but were near the end, and the shutters of the lower windows were closed.

"Tell me what you saw," said Giovanni, "but do not speak loud."

At this moment the other two boys came running up with noisy lamentations. With the wisdom of their kind they had patiently watched to see whether their companion would get a hearing of the master, and judging that he had been successful at last, they came to enjoy the fruit of his efforts.

"We also have been beaten!" they wailed, but they bore no outward and visible signs of ill-treatment on them.

The elder boy turned upon them with righteous fury, and to their unspeakable surprise began to drive them away with kicks and blows. They could not stand against him, and after a brief resistance, they turned and ran at full speed. The victor came back to Giovanni's side.

"They are cowardly fellows," he said, with disdain. "They are ignorant boys. What do you expect? But they will not come back."

"Go on with your story," said Giovanni impatiently, "but speak low."

"It was on Sunday night, sir. The master came to talk with Zorzi in the laboratory. I was in the garden, at the entrance of the other passage. When the door opened there was not much light, and the master was wrapped in his cloak, and he turned a little, and went in sideways, so I knew that he had something under his arm, for the door is narrow."

"He was probably bringing over some valuable materials," said Giovanni.

"I believe he was bringing the great book," said the boy confidently, but almost in a whisper.

"What great book?"

The lad looked at Giovanni with an expression of cunning on his face, as much as to say that he was not to be deceived by such a transparent pretence of ignorance.

"He was afraid to leave it in his house," he said, "lest you should find it and learn how to make the gold as he does. So he took it over to the laboratory at night."

Giovanni began to understand, though it was the first time he had heard that the boys, like the common people, suspected Angelo Beroviero of being an alchemist. It was clear that the boy meant the book that contained the priceless secrets for glass-making which Giovanni and his brother had so long coveted. His interest increased.

"After all," he said, "you saw nothing distinctly. My father went in and shut the door, I suppose."

"Yes," answered the boy. "But after a long time the door opened again."

He stopped, resolved to be questioned, in order that his information should seem more valuable. The instinct of small boys is often as diabolically keen as that of a grown woman.

"Go on!" said Giovanni, more and more interested. "The door opened again, you say? Then my father came out—"

"No, sir. Zorzi came out into the light that fell from the door. The master was inside."

"Well, what did Zorzi do? Be quick!"

"He brought out a shovel full of earth, sir, and he carefully scattered it about over the flowerbed, and then he went back, and presently he came out with the shovel again, and more earth; and so three times. They had buried the great book somewhere in the laboratory."

"But the laboratory is paved," objected Giovanni, to gain time, for he was thinking.

"There is earth under the stones, sir. I remember seeing it last year when the masons put down several new slabs. The great book is somewhere under the floor of the laboratory. I must have stepped over it in feeding the fire last night, and that is why the devils that guard it inspired the porter to beat me this morning. It was the devils that sent us to sleep, for fear that we should find it."

"I daresay," said Giovanni with much gravity, for he thought it better that the boy should be kept in awe of an object that possessed such immense value. "You should be careful in future, or ill may befall you."

"Is it true, sir, that I have told you something you wished to know?"

"I am glad to know that the great book is safe," answered Giovanni ambiguously.

"Zorzi knows where it is," suggested, the boy in a tone meant to convey the suspicion that Zorzi might use his knowledge.

"Yes—yes," repeated Giovanni thoughtfully, "and he is ill. He ought to be brought over to the house until he is better."

"Then the furnace could be allowed to get out, sir, could it not?"

"Yes. The weather is growing warm, as it is. Yes—the furnace may be put out now." Giovanni hardly knew that he was speaking aloud. "Zorzi will get well much sooner if he is in a good room in the house. I will see to it."

The boy stood still beside him, waiting patiently for some reward.

"Are we to come as usual tonight, sir, or will there be no fire?" he asked.

"Go and ask at the usual time. I have not decided yet. There—you are a good boy. If you hold your tongue there will be more."

Giovanni offered the lad a piece of money, but he would not take it.

"We are glassblowers' sons, sir, we are not poor people," he said with theatrical pride, for he would have taken the coin without remark if he had not felt that he possessed a secret of great value, which might place Giovanni in his power before long.

Giovanni was surprised.

"What do you want, then?" he asked.

"I am old enough to be an apprentice, sir."

"Very well," answered Giovanni. "You shall be an apprentice. But hold your tongue about what you saw. You told me every-thing, did you?"

"Yes, sir. And I thank you for your kindness, sir. If I can help you, sir—" he stopped.

"Help me!" exclaimed Giovanni. "I do not work at the fur-naces! Wash your face and come by and by to my glass-house, and you shall have an apprentice's place."

"I shall serve you well, sir. You shall see that I am grateful," answered the boy.

He touched Giovanni's sleeve and kissed his own hand, and ran back to the steps before the front door. There he knelt down, leaning over the water, and washed his face in the canal, well pleased with the price he had got for his bruising.

Giovanni did not look at him, but turned to go on, past the corner of the house, in deep thought. From the narrow line into which the back door opened, Marietta and Nella emerged at the same moment. Nella had made sure that Giovanni had gone out, but she could not foresee that he would stop a long time to talk with the boy in the covered footway. She ran against him, as he passed the corner, for she was walking on Marietta's left side. The young girl's face was covered, but she knew that Giovanni must recognise her instantly, by her cloak, and because Nella was with her.

"Where are you going?" he asked sharply.

"To church, sir, to church," answered Nella in great perturbation. "The young lady is going to confession."

"Ah, very good, very good!" exclaimed Giovanni, who was very attentive to religious forms. "By all means go to confession, my sister. You cannot be too conscientious in the performance of your duties."

But Marietta laughed a little under her veil.

"I had not the least intention of going to confession this morning," she said. "Nella said so because you frightened her."

"What? What is this?" Giovanni looked from one to the other. "Then where are you going?"

"To the glass-house," answered Marietta with perfect coolness.

"You are not going to the laboratory? Zorzi is living there alone. You cannot go there."

"I am not afraid of Zorzi. In the first place, I wish to know how he is. Secondly, this is the hour for making the tests, and as he cannot stand he cannot try the glass alone."

Giovanni was amazed at her assurance, and immediately assumed a grave and authoritative manner befitting the eldest brother who represented the head of the house.

"I cannot allow you to go," he said. "It is most unbecoming. Our father would be shocked. Go back at once, and never think of going to the laboratory while Zorzi is there. Do you hear?"

"Yes. Come, Nella," she added, taking her serving-woman by the arm.

Before Giovanni realised what she was going to do, she was walking quickly across the wooden bridge towards the glass-house, holding Nella's sleeve, to keep her from lagging, and Nella trotted beside her mistress like a frightened lamb, led by a string. Giovanni did not attempt to follow at first, for he was utterly nonplussed by his sister's behaviour. He rarely knew what to do when any one openly defied him. He stood still, staring after the two, and saw Marietta tap upon the door of the glass-house. It opened almost immediately and they disappeared within.

As soon as they were out of sight, his anger broke out, and he made a few quick steps on the bridge. Then he stopped, for he was afraid to make a scandal. That at least was what he said to himself, but the fact was that he was afraid to face his sister, who was infinitely braver and cooler than he. Besides, he reflected that he could not now prevent her from going to the laboratory, since she was already there, and that it would be very undignified to make a scene before Zorzi, who was only a servant after all. This last consideration consoled him greatly. In the eyes of the law, and therefore in Giovanni's, Zorzi was a hired servant. Now, socially speaking, a servant was not a man; and since Zorzi was not a man, and Marietta was therefore gone with one servant to a place, belonging to her father, where there was another servant, to go thither and forcibly bring her back would either be absurd, or else it would mean that Zorzi had acquired a new social rank, which was absurd also. There is no such consolation to a born coward as a logical reason for not doing what he is afraid to do.

But Giovanni promised himself that he would make his sister pay dearly for having defied him, and as he had also made up his mind to have Zorzi removed to the house, on pretence of curing his hurt, but in reality in order to search for the precious manuscripts, it would be impossible for Marietta to commit the same piece of folly a second time. But she should pay for the affront she had put upon him.

He accordingly came back to the footway and walked along toward his own glass-house; and the boy, who had finished washing his face, smoothed his hair with his wet fingers and followed him, having seen and understood all that had happened.

Marietta sent Pasquale on, to tell Zorzi that she was coming, and when she reached the laboratory he was sitting in the master's big chair, with his foot on a stool before him. His face was pale and drawn from the suffering of the past twenty-four hours, and from time to time he was still in great pain. As Marietta entered, he looked up with a grateful smile.

"You seem glad to see us after all," she said. "Yet you protested that I should not come today!"

"I cannot help it," he answered.

"Ah, but if you had been with us just now!" Nella began, still frightened.

But Marietta would not let her go on.

"Hold your tongue, Nella," she said, with a little laugh. "You should know better than to trouble a sick man's fancy with such stories."

Nella understood that Zorzi was not to know, and she began examining the foot, to make sure that the bandages had not been displaced during the night.

"Tomorrow I will change them," she said. "It is not like a scald. The glass has burned you like red-hot iron, and the wound will heal quickly."

"If you will tell me which crucible to try," said Marietta, "I will make the tests for you. Then we can move the table to your side and you can prepare the new ingredients according to the writing."

Pasquale had left them, seeing that he was not wanted.

"I fear it is of little use," answered Zorzi, despondently. "Of course, the master is very wise, but it seems to me that he has added so much, from time to time, to the original mixture, and so much has been taken away, as to make it all very uncertain."

"I daresay," assented Marietta. "For some time I have thought so. But we must carry out his wishes to the letter, else he will always believe that the experiments might have succeeded if he had stayed here."

"Of course," said Zorzi. "We should make tests of all three crucibles today, if it is only to make more room for the things that are to be put in."

"Where is the copper ladle?" asked Marietta. "I do not see it in its place."

"I have none—I had forgotten. Your brother came here yesterday morning, and wanted to try the glass himself in spite of me. I knocked the ladle out of his hand and it fell through into the crucible."

"That was like you," said Marietta. "I am glad you did it."

"Heaven knows what has happened to the thing," Zorzi answered. "It has been there since yesterday morning. For all I know, it may have melted by this time. It may affect the glass, too."

"Where can I get another?" asked Marietta, anxious to begin.

Zorzi made an instinctive motion to rise. It hurt him badly and he bit his lip.

"I forgot," he said. "Pasquale can get another ladle from the main glass-house."

"Go and call Pasquale, Nella," said Marietta at once. "Ask him to get a copper ladle."

Nella went out into the garden, leaving the two together. Marietta was standing between the chair and the furnace, two or three steps from Zorzi. It was very hot in the big room, for the window was still shut.

"Tell me how you really feel," Marietta said, almost at once.

Every woman who loves a man and is anxious about him is sure that if she can be alone with him for a moment, he will tell her the truth about his condition. The experience of thousands of years has not taught women that if there is one person in the world from whom a man will try to conceal his ills and aches, it is the woman he loves, because he would rather suffer everything than give her pain.

"I feel perfectly well," said Zorzi.

"Indeed you are not!" answered Marietta, energetically. "If you were perfectly well you would be on your feet, doing your work yourself. Why will you not tell me?"

"I mean, I have no pain," said Zorzi.

"You had great pain just now, when you tried to move," retorted Marietta. "You know it. Why do you try to deceive me? Do you think I cannot see it in your face?"

"It is nothing. It comes now and then, and goes away again almost at once."

Marietta had come close to him while she was speaking. One hand hung by her side within his reach. He longed to take it, with such a longing as he had never felt for anything in his life; he resisted with all the strength he had left. But he remembered that he had held her hand in his yesterday, and the memory was a force in itself, outside of him, drawing him in spite of himself, lifting his arm when he commanded it to lie still. His eyes could not take themselves from the beautiful white fingers, so delicately curved as they hung down, so softly shaded to pale rose colour at their tapering tips. She stood quite still, looking down at his bent head.

"You would not refuse my friendship, now," she said, in a low voice, so low that when she had spoken she doubted whether he could have understood.

He took her hand then, for he had no resistance left, and she let him take it, and did not blush. He held it in both his own and silently drew it to him, till he was pressing it to his heart as he had never hoped to do.

"You are too good to me," he said, scarcely knowing that he pronounced the words.

Nella passed the window, coming back from her errand.

Instantly Marietta drew her hand away, and when the serving-woman entered she was speaking to Zorzi in the most natural tone in the world.

"Is the testing plate quite clean?" she asked, and she was already beside it.

Zorzi looked at her with amazement. She had almost been seen with her hand in his, a catastrophe which he supposed would have entailed the most serious consequences; yet there she was, perfectly unconcerned and not even faintly blushing, and she had at once pretended that they had been talking about the glass.

"Yes—I believe it is clean," he answered, almost hesitating. "I cleaned it yesterday morning."

Nella had brought the copper ladle. There were always several in the glassworks for making tests. Marietta took it and went to the furnace, while Nella watched her, in great fear lest she should burn herself. But the young girl was in no danger, for she had spent half her life in the laboratory and the garden, watching her father. She wrapped the wet cloth round her hand and held the ladle by the end.

"We will begin with the one on the right," she said, thrusting the instrument through the aperture.

Bringing it out with some glass in it, she supported it with both hands as she went quickly to the iron table, and she instantly poured out the stuff and began to watch it.

"It is just what you had the other day," she said, as the glass rapidly cooled.

Zorzi was seated high enough to look over the table.

"Another failure," he said. "It is always the same. We have scarcely had any variation in the tint in the last week."

"That is not your fault," answered Marietta. "We will try the next."

As if she had been at the work all her life, she chilled the ladle and chipped off the small adhering bits of glass from it, and slipped the last test from the table, carrying it to the refuse jar with tongs. Once more she wrapped the damp cloth round her hand and went to the furnace. The middle crucible was to be tried next. Nella, looking on with nervous anxiety, was in a profuse perspiration.

"I believe that is the one into which the ladle fell," said Zorzi. "Yes, I am quite sure of it."

Marietta took the specimen and poured it out, set down the ladle on the brick work, and watched the cooling glass, expecting to see what she had often seen before. But her face changed, in a look of wonder and delight.

"Zorzi!" she exclaimed. "Look! Look! See what a colour!"

"I cannot see well," he answered, straining his neck. "Wait a minute!" he cried, as Marietta took the tongs. "I see now! We have got it! I believe we have got it! Oh, if I could only walk!"

"Patience—you shall see it. It is almost cool. It is quite stiff now."

She took the little flat cake up with the tongs, very carefully, and held it before his eyes. The light fell through it from the window, and her head was close to his, as they both looked at it together.

"I never dreamed of such a colour," said Zorzi, his face flushing with excitement.

"There never was such a colour before," answered Marietta. "It is like the juice of a ripe pomegranate that has just been cut, only there is more light in it."

"It is like a great ruby—the rubies that the jewellers call 'pigeon's blood.'"

"My father always said it should be blood-red," said Marietta. "But I thought he meant something different, something more scarlet."

"I thought so, too. What they call pigeon's blood is not the colour of blood at all. It is more like pomegranates, as you said at first. But this is a marvellous thing. The master will be pleased."

Nella came and looked too, convinced that the glass had in some way turned out more beautiful by the magic of her mistress's touch.

"It is a miracle!" cried the woman of the people. "Some saint must have made this."

The glass glowed like a gem and seemed to give out light of its own. As Zorzi and Marietta looked, its rich glow spread over their faces. It was that rare glass which, from old cathedral windows, casts such a deep stain upon the pavement that one would believe the marble itself must be dyed with unchanging color.

"We have found it together," said Marietta.

Zorzi looked from the glass to her face, close by his, and their eyes met for a moment in the strange glow and it was as if they knew each other in another world.

"Do not let the red light fall on your faces," said Nella, crossing herself. "It is too much like blood—good health to you," she added quickly for fear of evil.

Marietta lowered her hand and turned the piece of glass sideways, to see how it would look.

"What shall we do with it?" she asked. "It must not be left any longer in the crucible."

"No. It ought to be taken out at once. Such a colour must be kept for church windows. If I were able to stand, I would make most of it into cylinders and cut them while hot. There are men who can do it, in the glass-house. But the master does not want them here."

"We had better let the fires go out," said Marietta. "It will cool in the crucible as it is."

"I would give anything to have that crucible empty, or an empty one in the place," answered Zorzi. "This is a great discovery, but it is not exactly what the master expected. I have an idea of my own, which I should like to try."

"Then we must empty the crucible. There is no other way. The glass will keep its colour, whatever shape we give it. Is there much of it?"

"There may be twenty or thirty pounds' weight," answered Zorzi. "No one can tell."

Nell listened in mute surprise. She had never seen Marietta with old Beroviero, and she was amazed to hear her young mistress talking about the processes of glassmaking, about crucibles and cylinders and ingredients as familiarly as of domestic things. She suddenly began to imagine that old Beroviero, who was probably a magician and an alchemist, had taught his daughter the same dangerous knowledge, and she felt a sort of awe before the two young people who knew such a vast deal which she herself could never know.

She asked herself what was to become of this wonderful girl, half woman and half enchantress, who brought the colour of the saints' blood out of the white flames, and understood as much as men did of the art which was almost all made up of secrets. What would happen when she was the wife of Jacopo Contarini, shut up in a splendid Venetian palace where there were no glass furnaces to amuse her? At first she would grow pale, thought Nella, but by and by would weave spells in her chamber which would bring all Venice to her will, and turn it all to gold and precious stones and red glass, and the people to fairies subject to her will, her husband, the Council of Ten, even the Doge himself.

Nella roused herself, and passed her hand over her eyes, as if she were waking from a dream. And indeed she had been dreaming, for she had looked too long into the wonderful depths of the new colour, and it had dazed her wits.

CHAPTER XII

On that day Marietta felt once more the full belief that Zorzi loved her; but the certainty did not fill her with happiness as on that first afternoon when she had seen him stoop to pick up the rose she had dropped. The time that had seemed so very distant had come indeed; instead of years, a week had scarcely passed, and it was not by letting a flower fall in his path that she had told him her love, as she had meant to do. She had done much more. She had let him take her hand and press it to his heart, and she would have left it there if Nella had not passed the window; she had wished him to take it, she had let it hang by her side in the hope that he would be bold enough to do so, and she had thrilled with delight at his touch; she had drawn back her hand when the woman came, and she had put on a look of innocent indifference that would have deceived one of the Council's own spies. Could any language have been more plain?

It was very strange, she thought, that she should all at once have gone so far, that she should have felt such undreamt joy at the moment and then, when it was hers, a part of her life which nothing could ever undo nor take from her, it was stranger still that the remembrance of this wonderful joy should make her suddenly sad and thoughtful, that she should lie awake at night, wishing that it had never been, and tormenting herself with the idea that she had done an almost irretrievable wrong. At the very moment when the coming day was breaking upon her heart's twilight, a wall of darkness arose between her and the future.

Much that is very good and true in the world is built upon the fanciful fears of evil that warn girls' hearts of harm. There are dangers that cannot be exaggerated, because the value of what they threaten cannot be reckoned too great, so long as human goodness rests on the dangerous quicksands of human nature.

Marietta had not realised what it meant to be betrothed to Jacopo Contarini, until she had let her hand linger in Zorzi's. But after that, one hour had not passed before she felt that she was living between two alternatives that seemed almost equally terrible, and of which she must choose the one or the other within two months. She must either marry Contarini and never see Zorzi again, or she must refuse to be married and face the tremendous consequences of her unheard-of wilfulness, her father's anger, the just resentment of all the Contarini family, the humiliation which her brothers would heap upon her, because, in the code of those days, she would have brought shame on them and theirs. In those times such results were very real and inevitable when a girl's formal promise of marriage was broken, though she herself might never have been consulted.

It was no wonder that Marietta was sleepless at night, and spent long hours of the day sitting listless by her window without so much as threading a score of beads from the little basket that stood beside her. Nella came and went often, looked at her, and shook her head with a wise smile.

"It is the thought of marriage," said the woman of the people to herself. "She pines and grows pale now, because she is thinking that she must leave her father's house so soon, and she is afraid to go among strangers. But she will be happy by and by, like the swallows in spring."

Nella remembered how frightened she herself had been when she was betrothed to her departed Vito, and she was thereby much comforted as to Marietta's condition. But she said nothing, after Marietta had coldly repelled her first attempt to talk of the marriage, though she forgave her mistress's frigid order to be silent, telling herself that no right-minded young girl could possibly be natural and sweet tempered under the circumstances. She was more than compensated for what might have seemed harshness, by something that looked very much like a concession. Marietta had not gone back to the laboratory since the discovery of the new glass, and a week had passed since then.

Nella went every other day and did all that was necessary for Zorzi's recovery. Each time she came he asked her about Marietta, in a rather formal tone, as was becoming when he spoke of his master's daughter, but hoping that Nella might have some message to deliver, and he was more and more disappointed as he realised that Marietta did not mean to send him any. She had gone away on that morning with a sort of intimation that she would come back every day, but Nella did not so much as hint that she ever meant to come back at all.

Zorzi went about on crutches, swinging his helpless foot as he walked, for it still hurt him when he put it to the ground. He was pale and thin, both from pain and from living shut up almost all day in the close atmosphere of the laboratory. For a change, he began to come out into the little garden, sometimes walking up and down on his crutches for a few minutes, and then sitting down to rest on the bench under the plane-tree, where Marietta had so often sat. Pasquale came and talked with him sometimes, but

Zorzi never went to the porter's lodge.

He felt that if he got as far as that he should inevitably open the door and look up at Marietta's window, and he would not do it, for he was hurt by her apparent indifference, after having allowed him to hold her hand in his. She had not even asked through Nella what had become of the beautiful glass. What he pretended to say to himself was that it would be very wrong to go and stand outside the glass-house, where the porter would certainly see him, and where he might be seen by any one else, staring at the window of his master's daughter's room on the other side of the canal. But what he really felt was that Marietta had treated him capriciously and that if he had a particle of self-respect he must show her that he did not care. For if Marietta was very like other carefully brought up girls of her age, Zorzi was nothing more than a boy where love was concerned, and like many boys who have struggled for existence in a more or less corrupt world, he had heard much more of the faithlessness and caprices of women in general than of the sensitiveness and delicate timidity of innocent young girls.

Marietta was his perfect ideal, the most exquisite, the most beautiful and the most lovable creature ever endowed with form and sent into the world by the powers of good. He believed all this in his heart, with the certainty of absolute knowledge. But he was quite incapable of discerning the motives of her conduct towards him, and when he tried to understand them, it was not his heart that felt, but his reason that argued, having very little knowledge and no experience at all to help it; and since his erring reason demonstrated something that offended his self-esteem, his heart was hurt and nursed a foolish, small resentment against what he truly loved better than life itself. At one time or another most very young men in love have found themselves in that condition, and have tormented themselves to the verge of fever and distraction over imaginary hurts and wrongs. Was there ever a true lyric poet who did not at least once in his early days believe himself the victim of a heartless woman? And though long afterwards fate may have brought him face to face with the tragedy of unhappy love, fierce with passion and terrible with violent death, can he ever quite forget the fancied sufferings of first youth, the stab of a thoughtless girl's first unkind word, the sickening chill he felt under her first cold look? And what would first love be, if young men and maidens came to it with all the reason and cool self-judgment that long living brings?

Zorzi sought consolation in his art, and as soon as he could stand and move about with his crutches he threw his whole pent-up energy into his work. The accidental discovery of the red glass had unexpectedly given him an empty crucible with which to make an experiment of his own, and while the materials were fusing he attempted to obtain the new colour in the other two, by dropping pieces of copper into each regardless of the master's instructions. To his inexpressible disappointment he completely failed in this, and the glass he produced was of the commonest tint.

Then he grew reckless; he removed the two crucibles that had contained what had been made according to Beroviero's theories until he had added the copper, and he began afresh according to his own belief.

On that very morning Giovanni Beroviero made a second visit to the laboratory. He came, he said, to make sure that Zorzi was recovering from his hurt, and Zorzi knew from Nella that Giovanni had made inquiries about him. He put on an air of sympathy when he saw the crutches.

"You will soon throw them aside," he said, "but I am sorry that you should have to use them at all."

When he entered, Zorzi was introducing a new mixture, carefully powdered, into one of the glass-pots with a small iron shovel. It was clear that he must put it all in at once, and he excused himself for going on with his work. Giovanni looked at the large quantity of the mixed ingredients with an experienced eye, and at once made up his mind that the crucible must have been quite empty. Zorzi was therefore beginning to make some kind of glass on his own account. It followed almost logically, according to Giovanni's view of men, fairly founded on a knowledge of himself, that Zorzi was experimenting with the secrets of Paolo Godi, which he and old Beroviero had buried together somewhere in that very room. Now, ever since the boy had told his story, Giovanni had been revolving plans for getting the manuscript into his possession during a few days, in order to copy it. A new scheme now suggested itself, and it looked so attractive that he at once attempted to carry it out.

"It seems a pity," he said, "that a great artist like yourself should spend time on fruitless experiments. You might be making very beautiful things, which would sell for a high price."

Without desisting from his occupation Zorzi glanced at his visitor, whose manner towards him had so entirely changed within a little more than a week. With a waif's quick instinct he guessed that Giovanni wanted something of him, but the generous instinct of the brave man towards the coward made him accept what seemed to be meant for an advance after a quarrel. It had never occurred to Zorzi to blame Giovanni for the accident in the glass-house, and it would have been very unjust to do so.

"I can blow glass tolerably, sir," Zorzi answered. "But none of you great furnace owners would dare to employ me, in the face of the law. Besides, I am your father's man. I owe everything I know to his kindness."

"I do not see what that has to do with it," returned Giovanni; "it does not diminish your merit, nor affect the truth of what I was saying. You might be doing better things. Any one can weigh out sand and kelp-ashes, and shovel them into a crucible!"

"Do you mean that the master might employ me for other work?" asked Zorzi, smiling at the disdainful description of what he was doing.

"My father—or some one else," answered Giovanni. "And besides your astonishing skill, I fancy that you possess much valuable knowledge of glassmaking. You cannot have worked for my father so many years without learning some of the things he has taken great pains to hide from his own sons."

He spoke the last words in a somewhat bitter tone, quite willing to let Zorzi know that he felt himself injured.

"If I have learned anything of that sort by looking on and helping, when I have been trusted, it is not mine to use elsewhere," said Zorzi, rather proudly.

"That is a fine moral sentiment, my dear young friend, and does you credit," replied Giovanni sententiously. "It is impossible not to respect a man who carries a fortune in his head and refuses to profit by it out of a delicate sense of honour."

"I should have very little respect for a man who betrayed his master's secrets," said Zorzi.

"You know them then?" inquired the other with unusual blandness.

"I did not say so." Zorzi looked at him coldly.

"Oh no! Even to admit it might not be discreet. But apart from Paolo Godi's secrets, which my father has left sealed in my care—"

At this astounding falsehood Zorzi started and looked at Giovanni in unfeigned surprise.

"—but which nothing would induce me to examine," continued Giovanni with perfect coolness, "there must be many others of my father's own, which you have learned by watching him. I respect you for your discretion. Why did you start and look at me when I said that the manuscript was in my keeping?'"

The question was well put, suddenly and without warning, and Zorzi was momentarily embarrassed to find an answer. Giovanni judged that his surprise proved the truth of the boy's story, and his embarrassment now added certainty to the proof. But Zorzi rarely lost his self-possession when he had a secret to keep.

"If I seemed astonished," he said, "it may have been because you had just given me the impression that the master did not trust you, and I know how careful he is of the manuscript."

"You know more than that, my friend," said Giovanni in a playful tone.

Zorzi had now filled the crucible and was replacing the clay rings which narrow the aperture of the 'bocca.' He plastered more wet clay upon them, and it pleased Giovanni to see how well he knew every detail of the art, from the simplest to the most difficult operations.

"Would anything you can think of induce you to leave my father?" Giovanni asked, as he had received no answer to his last remark. "Of course, I do not mean to speak of mere money, though few people quite despise it."

"That may be understood in more than one way," answered Zorzi cautiously. "In the first place, do you mean that if I left the master, it would be to go to another master, or to set up as a master myself?"

"Let us say that you might go to another glass-house for a fixed time, with the promise of then having a furnace of your own. How does that strike you?"

"No one can give such a promise and keep it," said Zorzi, scraping the wet clay from his hands with a blunt knife.

"But suppose that some one could," insisted Giovanni.

"What is the use of supposing the impossible?" Zorzi shrugged his shoulders and went on scraping.

"Nothing is impossible in the Republic, except what the Ten are resolved to hinder. And that is really impossible."

"The Ten will not make new laws nor repeal old ones for the benefit of an unknown Dalmatian."

"Perhaps not," answered Giovanni. "But on the other hand there is no very great penalty if you set up a furnace of your own. If you are discovered, your furnace will be put out, and you may have to pay a fine. It is no great matter. It is a civil offence, not a criminal one."

"What is it that you wish of me?" asked Zorzi with sudden directness. "You are a busy man. You have not come here to pass a morning in idle conversation with your father's assistant. You want something of me, sir. Speak out plainly. If I can do what you wish, I will do it. If I cannot, I will tell you so, frankly."

Giovanni was a little disconcerted by this speech. Excepting where money was concerned directly, his intelligence was of the sort that easily wastes its energy in futile cunning. He had not meant to reach the point for a long time, if he had expected to reach it at all at a first attempt.

"I like your straightforwardness," he said evasively. "But I do not think your conversation idle. On the contrary, I find it highly instructive."

"Indeed?" Zorzi laughed. "You do me much honour, sir! What have you learned from me this morning?"

"What I wished to know," answered Giovanni with a change of tone, and looking at him keenly.

Zorzi returned the glance, and the two men faced each other in silence for a moment. Zorzi knew what Giovanni meant, as soon as the other had spoken. The quick movement of surprise, which was the only indiscretion of which Zorzi had been guilty, would have betrayed to any one that he knew where the manuscript was, even if it were not in his immediate keeping. His instinct was to take the offensive and accuse his visitor of having laid a trap for him, but his caution prevailed.

"Whatever you may think that you have learned from me," he said, "remember that I have told you nothing."

"Is it here, in this room?" asked Giovanni, not heeding his last speech, and hoping to surprise him again.

But he was prepared now, and his face did not change as he replied.

"I cannot answer any questions," he said.

"You and my father hid it together," returned Giovanni. "When you had buried it under the stones in this room, you carried the earth out with a shovel and scattered it about on a flowerbed. You took out three shovelfuls of earth in that way. You see, I know everything. What is the use of trying to hide your secret from me?"

Zorzi was now convinced that Giovanni himself had been lurking in the garden.

"Sir," he said, with ill-concealed contempt for a man capable of such spy's work, "if you have more to say of the same nature, pray say it to your father, when he comes back."

"You misunderstand me," returned Giovanni with sudden mildness. "I had no intention of offending you. I only meant to warn you that you were watched on that night. The person who informed me has no doubt told many others also. It would have been very ill for you, if my father had returned to find that his secret was public property, and if you had been unable to explain that you had not betrayed him. I have given you a weapon of defence. You may call upon me to repeat what I have said, when you speak with him."

"I am obliged to you, sir," said Zorzi coldly. "I shall not need to disturb you."

"You are not wise," returned Giovanni gravely. "If I were curious—fortunately for you I am not!—I would send for a mason and have some of the stones of the pavement turned over before me. A mason would soon find the one you moved by trying them all with his hammer."

"Yes," said Zorzi. "If this were a room in your own glass-house, you could do that. But it is not."

"I am in charge of all that belongs to my father, during his absence," answered Giovanni.

"Yes," said Zorzi again. "Including Paolo Godi's manuscript, as you told me," he added.

"You understand very well why I said that," Giovanni answered, with visible annoyance.

"I only know that you said it," was the retort. "And as I cannot suppose that you did not know what you were saying, still less that you intentionally told an untruth, I really cannot see why you should suggest bringing a mason here to search for what must be in your own keeping."

Zorzi spoke with a quiet smile, for he felt that he had the best of it. Be was surprised when Giovanni broke into a peal of rather affected laughter.

"You are hard to catch!" he cried, and laughed again. "You did not really suppose that I was in earnest? Why, every one knows that you have the manuscript here."

"Then I suppose you spoke ironically," suggested Zorzi.

"Of course, of course! A mere jest! If I had known that you would take it so literally—" he stopped short.

"Pray excuse me, sir. It is the first time I have ever heard you say anything playful."

"Indeed! The fact is, my dear Zorzi, I never knew you well enough to jest with you, till today. Paolo Godi's secrets in my keeping? I wish they were! Oh, not that anything would induce me to break the seals. I told you that. But I wish they were in my possession. I tell you, I would pay down half my fortune to have them, for they would bring me back four times as much within the year. Half my fortune! And I am not poor, Zorzi."

"Half your fortune?" repeated Zorzi. "That is a large sum, I imagine. Pray, sir, how much might half your fortune be, in round numbers? Ten thousand silver lires?"

"Silver!" sneered Giovanni contemptuously.

"Gold, then?" suggested Zorzi, drawing him on.

"Gold? Well—possibly," admitted Giovanni with caution. "But of course I was exaggerating. Ten thousand gold pounds would be too much, of course. Say, five thousand."

"I thought you were richer than that," said Zorzi coolly.

"Do you mean that five thousand would not be enough to pay for the manuscript?" asked Giovanni.

"The profits of glassmaking are very large when one possesses a valuable secret," said Zorzi. "Five thousand—" He paused, as though in doubt, or as if making a mental calculation. Giovanni fell into the trap.

"I would give six," he said, lowering his voice to a still more confidential tone, and watching his companion eagerly.

"For six thousand gold lires," said Zorzi, smiling, "I am quite sure that you could hire a ruffian to break in and cut the throat of the man who has charge of the manuscript."

Giovanni's face fell, but he quickly assumed an expression of righteous indignation.

"How can you dare to suggest that I would employ such means to rob my father?" he cried.

"If it were your intention to rob your father, sir, I cannot see that it would matter greatly what means you employed. But I was only jesting, as you were when you said that you had the manuscript. I did not expect that you would take literally what I said."

"I see, I see," answered Giovanni, accepting the means of escape Zorzi offered him. "You were paying me back in my own coin! Well, well! It served me right, after all. You have a ready wit."

"I thought that if my conversation were not as instructive as you had hoped, I could at least try to make it amusing—light, gay, witty! I trust you will not take it ill."

"Not I!" Giovanni tried to laugh. "But what a wonderful thing is this human imagination of ours! Now, as I talked of the secrets, I forgot that they were my father's, they seemed almost within my grasp, I was ready to count out the gold, to count out six thousand gold lires. Think of that!"

"They are worth it," said Zorzi quietly.

"You should know best," answered the other. "There is no such glass as my father's for lightness and strength. If he had a dozen workmen like you, my brother and I should be ruined in trying to compete with him. I watched you very closely the other day, and I watched the others, too. By the bye, my friend, was that really an accident, or does the man owe you some grudge? I never saw such a thing happen before!"

"It was an accident, of course," replied Zorzi without hesitation.

"If you knew that the man had injured you intentionally, you should have justice at once," said Giovanni. "As it is, I have no doubt that my father will turn him out without mercy."

"I hope not." Zorzi would say nothing more.

Giovanni rose to go away. He stood still a moment in thought, and then smiled suddenly as if recollecting himself.

"The imagination is an extraordinary thing!" he said, going back to the past conversation. "At this very moment I was thinking again that I was actually paying out the money—six thousand lires in gold! I must be mad!"

"No," said Zorzi. "I think not."

Giovanni turned away, shaking his head and still smiling. To tell the truth, though he knew Zorzi's character, he had not believed that any one could refuse such a bribe, and he was trying to account for the Dalmatian's integrity by reckoning up the expectations the young man must have, to set against such a large sum of ready money. He could only find one solution to the problem: Zorzi was already in full possession of the secrets, and would therefore not sell them at any price, because he hoped before long to set up for himself and make his own fortune by them. If this were true, and he could not see how it could be otherwise, he and his brother would be cheated of their heritage when their father died.

It was clear that something must be done to hinder Zorzi from carrying out his scheme. After all, Zorzi's own jesting proposal, that a ruffian should be employed to cut his throat, was not to be rejected. It was a simple plan, direct and conclusive. It might not be possible to find the manuscript after all, but the only man who knew its contents would be removed, and Beroviero's sons would inherit what should come to them by right. Against this project there was the danger that the murderer might some day betray the truth, under torture, or might come back again and again, and demand more money; but the killing of a man who was not even a Venetian, who was an interloper, who could be proved to have abused his master's confidence, when he should be no longer alive to defend himself, did not strike Giovanni as a very serious matter, and as for any one ever forcing him to pay money which he did not wish to pay, he knew that to be a feat beyond the ability of an ordinary person.

One other course suggested itself at once. He could forestall Zorzi by writing to his father and telling him what he sincerely believed to be the truth. He knew the old man well, and was sure that if once persuaded that Zorzi had betrayed him by using the manuscript, he would be merciless. The difficulty would lie in making Beroviero believe anything against his favourite. Yet in Giovanni's estimation the proofs were overwhelming. Besides, he had another weapon with which to rouse his father's anger against the Dalmatian. Since Marietta had defied him and had gone to see Zorzi in the laboratory, he had not found what he considered a convenient opportunity of speaking to her on the subject; that is to say, he had lacked the moral courage to do so at all. But it would need no courage to complain of her conduct to their father, and though Beroviero's anger might fall chiefly upon Marietta, a portion of it would take effect against Zorzi. It would be one more force acting in the direction of his ruin.

Giovanni went away to his own glass-house, meditating all manner of evil to his enemy, and as he reckoned up the chances of success, he began to wonder how he could have been so weak as to offer Zorzi an enormous bribe, instead of proceeding at once to his destruction.

Unconscious of his growing danger, Zorzi fed the fire of the furnace, and then sat down at the table before the window, laid his crutches beside him, and began to write out the details of his own experiments, as the master had done for years. He wrote the rather elaborate characters of the fifteenth century in a small but clear hand, very unlike old Beroviero's. The window was open, and the light breeze blew in, fanning his heated forehead; for the weather was growing hotter and hotter, and the order had been given to let the main furnaces cool after the following Saturday, as the workmen could not bear the heat many days longer. After that, they would set to work in a shed at the back of the glass-house to knead the clay for making new crucibles, and the night boys would enjoy their annual holiday, which consisted in helping the workmen by treading the stiff clay in water for several hours every day.

A man's shadow darkened the window while Zorzi was writing, and he looked up. Pasquale was standing outside.

"There is a pestering fellow at the door," he said, "who will not be satisfied till he has spoken with you. He says he has a message for you from some one in Venice, which he must deliver himself."

"For me?" Zorzi rose in surprise.

CHAPTER XIII

Zorzi swung himself along the dark corridor on his crutches after Pasquale, who opened the outer door with his usual deliberation. A little man stood outside in grey hose and a servant's dark coat, gathered in at the waist by a leathern belt. He was clean shaven and his hair was cropped close to his head, which was bare, for he held his black hat in his hand. Zorzi did not like his face. He waited for Zorzi to speak first.

"Have you a message for me?" asked the Dalmatian. "I am Zorzi."

"That is the name, sir," answered the man respectfully. "My master begs the honour and pleasure of your company this evening, as usual."

"Where?" asked Zorzi.

"My master said that you would know the place, sir, having been there before."

"What is your master's name?"

"The Angel," answered the man promptly, keeping his eyes on Zorzi's face.

The latter nodded, and the servant at once made an awkward obeisance preparatory to going away.

"Tell your master," said Zorzi, "that I have hurt my foot and am walking on crutches, so that I cannot come this evening, but that I thank him for his invitation, and send greeting to him and to the other guests."

The man repeated some of the words in a tone hardly audible, evidently committing the message to memory.

"Signor Zorzi—hurt his foot—crutches—thanks—greeting," he mumbled. "Yes, sir," he added in his ordinary voice, "I will say all that. Your servant, sir."

With another awkward bow, he turned away to the right and walked very quickly along the footway. He had left his boat at the entrance to the canal, not knowing exactly where the glass-house was. Zorzi looked after him a moment, then turned himself on his sound foot and set his crutches before him to go in. Pasquale was there, and must have heard what had passed. He shut the door and followed Zorzi back a little way.

"It is no concern of mine," he said roughly. "You may amuse yourself as you please, for you are young, and your host may be the Archangel Michael himself, or the holy Saint Mark, and the house to which you are bidden may be a paradise full of other angels! But I would as soon sit down before the grating and look at the hooded brother, while the executioner slipped the noose over my head to strangle me, as to go to any place on a bidding delivered by a fellow with such a jailbird's head. It is as round as a bullet and as yellow as cheese. He has eyes like a turtle's and teeth like those of a young shark."

"I am quite of your opinion," said Zorzi, halting at the entrance to the garden.

"Then why did you not kick him into the canal?" inquired the porter, with admirable logic.

"Do I look as if I could kick anything?" asked Zorzi, laughing and glancing at his lame foot.

"And where should I have been?" inquired Pasquale indignantly. "Asleep, perhaps? If you had said 'kick,' I would have kicked. Perhaps I am a statue!"

Zorzi pointed out that it was not usual to answer invitations in that way, even when declining them.

"And who knows what sort of invitation it was?" retorted the old porter discontentedly. "Since when have you friends in Venice who bid you come to their houses at night, like a thief? Honest men, who are friends, say 'Come and eat with me at noon, for today we have this, or this'—say, a roast sucking pig, or tripe with garlic. And perhaps you go; and when you have eaten and drunk and it is the cool of the afternoon, you come home. That is what Christians do. Who are they that meet at night? They are thieves, or conspirators, or dice-players, or all three."

Pasquale happened to have been right in two guesses out of three, and Zorzi thought it better to say nothing. There was no fear that the surly old man would tell any one of the message; he had proved himself too good a friend to Zorzi to do anything which could possibly bring him into trouble, and Zorzi was willing to let him think what he pleased, rather than run the smallest risk of betraying the society of which he had been obliged to become a member. But he was curious to know why Contarini kept such a singularly unprepossessing servant, and why, if he chose to keep him, he made use of him to deliver invitations. The fellow had the look of a born criminal; he was just such a man as Zorzi had thought of when he had jestingly proposed to Giovanni to hire a murderer. Indeed, the more Zorzi thought of his face, the more he was inclined to doubt that the man came from Contarini at all.

But in this he was mistaken. The message was genuine, and moreover, so far as Contarini and the society were concerned, the man was perfectly trustworthy. Possibly there were reasons why Contarini chose to employ him, and also why the servant was so consistently faithful to his master. After all, Zorzi reflected, he was certainly ignorant of the fact that the noble young idlers who met at the house of the Agnus Dei were playing at conspiracy and revolution.

But that night, when Contarini's friends were assembled and had counted their members, some one asked what had become of the Murano glassblower, and whether he was not going to attend their meetings in future; and Contarini answered that Zorzi had hurt his foot and was on crutches, and sent a greeting to the guests. Most of them were glad that he was not there, for he was not of their own order, and his presence caused a certain restraint in their talk. Besides, he was poor, and did not play at dice.

"He works with Angelo Beroviero, does he not?" asked Zuan Venier in a tone of weary indifference.

"Yes," answered Contarini with a laugh. "He is in the service of my future father-in-law."

"To whom may heaven accord a speedy, painless and Christian death!" laughed Foscari in his black beard.

"Not till I am one of his heirs, if you please," returned Contarini. "As soon after the wedding day as you like, for besides her rich dowry, the lady is to have a share of his inheritance."

"Is she very ugly?" asked Loredan. "Poor Jacopo! You have the sympathy of the brethren."

"How does he know?" sneered Mocenigo. "He has never seen her. Besides, why should he care, since she is rich?"

"You are mistaken, for I have seen her," said Contarini, looking down the table. "She is not at all ill-looking, I assure you. The old man was so much afraid that I would not agree to the match that he took her to church so that I might look at her."

"And you did?" asked Mocenigo. "I should never have had the courage. She might have been hideous, and in that case I should have preferred not to find it out till I was married."

"I looked at her with some interest," said Contarini, smiling in a self-satisfied way. "I am bound to say, with all modesty, that she also looked at me," he added, passing his white hand over his thick hair.

"Of course," put in Foscari gravely. "Any woman would, I should think."

"I suppose so," answered Contarini complacently. "It is not my fault if they do."

"Nor your misfortune," added Fosoari, with as much gravity

as before.

Zuan Venier had not joined in the banter, which seemed to him to be of the most atrocious taste. He had liked Zorzi and had just made up his mind to go to Murano the next day and find him out.

On that evening there was not so much as a mention of what was supposed to bring them together. Before they had talked a quarter of an hour, some one began to throw dice on the table, playing with his right hand against his left, and in a few moments the real play had begun.

High up in Arisa's room the Georgian woman and Aristarchi heard all that was said, crouching together upon the floor beside the opening the slave had discovered. When the voices were no longer heard except at rare intervals, in short exclamations of satisfaction or disappointment, and only the regular rattling and falling of the dice broke the silence, the pair drew back from the praying-stool.

"They will say nothing more tonight," whispered Arisa. "They will play for hours."

"They had not said a word that could put their necks in danger," answered Aristarchi discontentedly. "Who is this fellow from the glass-house, of whom they were speaking?"

Arisa led him away to a small divan between the open windows. She sat down against the cushions at the back, but he stretched his bulk upon the floor, resting his head against her knee. She softly rubbed his rough hair with the palm of her hand, as she might have caressed a cat, or a tame wild animal. It gave her a pleasant sensation that had a thrill of danger in it, for she always expected that he would turn and set his teeth into her fingers.

She told him the story of the last meeting, and how Zorzi had been made one of the society in order that they might not feel obliged to kill him for their own safety.

"What fools they are!" exclaimed Aristarchi with a low laugh, and turning his head under her hand.

"You would have killed him, of course," said Arisa, "if you had been in their place. I suppose you have killed many people," she added thoughtfully.

"No," he answered, for though he loved her savagely, he did not trust her. "I never killed any one except in fair fight."

Arisa laughed low, for she remembered.

"When I first saw you," she said, "your hands were covered with blood. I think the reason why I liked you was that you seemed so much more terrible than all the others who looked in at my cabin door."

"I am as mild as milk and almonds," said Aristarchi. "I am as timid as a rabbit."

His deep voice was like the purring of a huge cat. Arisa looked down at his head. Then her hands suddenly clasped his throat and she tried to make her fingers meet round it as if she would have strangled him, but it was too big for them. He drew in his chin a little, the iron muscles stiffened themselves, the cords stood out, and though she pressed with all her might she could not hurt him, even a little; but she loved to try.

"I am sure I could strangle Contarini," she said quietly. "He has a throat like a woman's."

"What a murderous creature you are!" purred the Greek, against hex knee. "You are always talking of killing."

"I should like to see you fighting for your life," she answered, "or for me."

"It is the same thing," he said.

"I should like to see it. It would be a splendid sight."

"What if I got the worst of it?" asked Aristarchi, his vast mouth grinning at the idea.

"You?" Arisa laughed contemptuously. "The man is not born who could kill you. I am sure of it."

"One very nearly succeeded, once upon a time," said Aristarchi.

"One man? I do not believe it!"

"He chanced to be an executioner," answered the Greek calmly, "and I had my hands tied behind me."

"Tell me about it."

Arisa bent down eagerly, for she loved to hear of his adventures, though he had his own way of narrating them which always made him out innocent of any evil intention.

"There is nothing to tell. It was in Naples. A woman betrayed me and they bound me in my sleep. In the morning I was condemned to death, thrown into a cart and dragged off to be hanged. I thought it was all over, for the cords were new, so that I could not break them. I tried hard enough! But even if I had broken loose, I could never have fought my way through the crowd alone. The noose was around my neck."

He stopped, as if he had told everything.

"Go on!" said Arisa. "How did you escape? What an adventure!"

"One of my men saved me. He had a little learning, and could pass for a monk when he could get a cowl. He went out before it was daylight that morning, and exchanged clothes with a burly friar whom he met in a quiet place."

"But how did the friar agree to that?" asked Arisa in surprise.

"He had nothing to say. He was dead," answered Aristarchi.

"Do you mean to say that he chanced to find a dead friar lying in the road?" asked the Georgian.

"How should I know? I daresay the monk was alive when he met my man, and happened to die a few minutes afterwards—by mere chance. It was very fortunate, was it not?"

"Yes!" Arisa laughed softly. "But what did he do? Why did he take the trouble to dress the monk in his clothes?"

"In order to receive his dying confession, of course. I thought you would understand! And his dying confession was that he, Michael Pandos, a Greek robber, had killed the man for whose murder I was being hanged that morning. My man came just in time, for as the friar's head was half shaved, as monks' heads are, he had to shave the rest, as they do for coolness in the south, and he had only his knife with which to do it. But no one found that out, for he had been a barber, as he had been a monk and most other things. He looked very well in a cowl, and spoke Neapolitan. I did not know him when he came to the foot of the gallows, howling out that I was innocent."

"Were you?" asked Arisa.

"Of course I was," answered Aristarchi with conviction.

"Who was the man that had been killed?"

"I forget his name," said the Greek. "He was a Neapolitan gentleman of great family, I believe. I forget the name. He had red hair."

Arisa laughed and stroked Aristarchi's big head. She thought she had made him betray himself.

"You had seen him then?" she said, with a question. "I suppose you happened to see him just before he died, as your man saw the monk."

"Oh no!" answered Aristarchi, who was not to be so easily caught. "It was part of the dying confession. It was necessary to identify the murdered person. How should Michael Parados, the Greek robber, know the name of the gentleman he had killed? He gave a minute description of him. He said he had red hair."

"You are not a Greek for nothing," laughed Arisa.

"Did you ever hear of Odysseus?" asked Aristarchi.

"No. What should I know of your Greek gods? If you were a good Christian, you would not speak of them."

"Odysseus was not a god," answered Aristarchi, with a grin. "He was a good Christian. I have often thought that he must have been very like me. He was a great traveller and a tolerable sailor."

"A pirate?" inquired Arisa.

"Oh no! He was a man of the most noble and upright character, incapable of deception! In fact he was very like me, and had nearly as many adventures. If you understood Greek, I would repeat some verses I know about him."

"Should you love me more, if I understood Greek?" asked Arisa softly. "If I thought so, I would learn it."

Aristarchi laughed roughly, so that she was almost afraid lest he should be heard far down in the house.

"Learn Greek? You? To make me like you better? You would be just as beautiful if you were altogether dumb! A man does not love a woman for what she can say to him, in any language."

He turned up his face, and his rough hands drew her splendid head down to him, till he could kiss her. Then there was silence for a few minutes.

He shook his great shoulders at last.

"Everything else is a waste of time," he said, as if speaking to himself.

Her head lay on the cushions now, and she watched him with half closed eyes in the soft light, and now and then the thin embroideries that covered her neck and bosom rose and fell with a long, satisfied sigh. He rose to his feet and slowly paced the marble floor, up and down before her, as he would have paced the little poop-deck of his vessel.

"I am glad you told me about that glassblower," he said suddenly. "I have met him and talked with him, and I may meet him again. He is old Beroviero's chief assistant. I fancy he is in love with the daughter."

"In love with the girl whom Contarini is to marry?" asked Arisa, suddenly opening her eyes.

"Yes. I told you what I said to the old man in his private room—it was more like a brick-kiln than a rich man's counting-house! While I was inside, the young man was talking to the girl under a tree. I saw them through a low window as I sat discussing business with Beroviero."

"You could not hear what they said, I suppose."

"No. But I could see what they looked." Aristarchi laughed at his own conceit. "The girl was doing some kind of work. The young man stood beside her, resting one hand against the tree. I could not see his face all the time, but I saw hers. She is in love with him. They were talking earnestly and she said something that had a strong effect upon him, for I saw that he stood a long time looking at the trunk of the tree, and saying nothing. What can you make of that, except that they are in love with each other?"

"That is strange," said Arisa, "for it was he that brought the message to Contarini, bidding him go and see her in Saint Mark's. That was how he chanced upon them, downstairs, at their last meeting."

"How do you know it was that message, and not some other?"

"Contarini told me."

"But if the boy loves her, as I am sure he does, why should he have delivered the message?" asked; the cunning Greek. "It would have been very easy for him to have named another hour, and Contarini would never have seen her. Besides, he had a fine chance then to send the future husband to Paradise! He needed only to name a quiet street, instead of the Church, and to appoint the hour at dusk. One, two and three in the back, the body to the canal, and the marriage would have been broken off."

"Perhaps he does not wish it broken off," suggested Arisa, taking an equally amiable but somewhat different point of view. "He cannot marry the girl, of course—but if she is once married and out of her father's house, it will be different."

"That is an idea," assented Aristarchi. "Look at us two. It is very much the same position, and Contarini will be indifferent about her, which he is not, where you are concerned. Between the glassblower and me, and his wife and you, he will not be a man to be envied. That is another reason for helping the marriage as much as we can."

"What if the glassblower makes her give him money?" asked the Georgian woman. "If she loves him she will give him everything she has, and he will take all he can get, of course."

"Of course, if she had anything to give," said Aristarchi. "But she will only have what you allow Contarini to give her. The young man knows well enough that her dowry will all be paid to her husband on the day of the marriage. It does not matter, for if he is in love he will not care much about the money."

"I hope he will be careful. Any one else may see him with her, as you did, and may warn old Contarini that his intended daughter-in-law is in love with a boy belonging to the glass-house. The marriage would be broken off at once if that happened."

"That is true."

So they talked together, judging Zorzi and Marietta according to their views of human nature, which they deduced chiefly from their experience of themselves. From time to time Arisa went and listened at the hole in the floor, and when she heard the guests beginning to take their leave she hid Aristarchi in the embrasure of a disused window that was concealed by a tapestry, and she went into the larger room and lay down among the cushions by the balcony. When Contarini came, a few minutes later, she seemed to have fallen asleep like a child, weary of waiting for him.

So far both she and Aristarchi looked upon Zorzi, who did not know of their existence, with a friendly eye, but their knowledge of his love for Marietta was in reality one more danger in his path. If at any future moment he seemed about to endanger the success of their plans, the strong Greek would soon find an opportunity of sending him to another world, as he had sent many another innocent enemy before. They themselves were safe enough for the present, and it was not likely that they would commit any indiscretion that might endanger their future flight. They had long ago determined what to do if Contarini should accidentally find Aristarchi in the house. Long before his body was found, they would both be on the high seas; few persons knew of Arisa's existence, no one connected the Greek merchant captain in any way with Contarini, and no one guessed the sailing qualities of the unobtrusive vessel that lay in the Giudecca waiting for a cargo, but ballasted to do her best, and well stocked with provisions and water. The crew knew nothing, when other sailors asked when they were to sail; the men could only say that their captain was the owner of the vessel and was very hard to please in the matter of a cargo.

In one way or another the two were sure of gaining their end, as soon as they should have amassed a sufficient fortune to live in luxury somewhere in the far south.

A change in the situation was brought about by the appearance of Zuan Venier at the glass-house on the following morning. Indolent, tired of his existence, sick of what amused and interested his companions, but generous, true and kind-hearted, he had been sorry to hear that Zorzi had suffered by an accident, and he felt impelled to go and see whether the young fellow needed help. Venier did not remember that he had ever resisted an impulse in his life, though he took the greatest pains to hide the fact that he ever felt any. He perhaps did not realise that although he had done many foolish things, and some that a confessor would not have approved, he had never wished to do anything that was mean, or unkind, or that might give him an unfair advantage over others.

He fancied Zorzi alone, uncared for, perhaps obliged to work in spite of his lameness, and it occurred to him that he might help him in some way, though it was by no means clear what direction his help should take. He did not know that Beroviero was absent, and he intended to call for the old glassmaker. It would be easy to say that he was an old friend of Jacopo Contarini and wished to make the acquaintance of Marietta's father before the wedding. He would probably have an opportunity of speaking to Zorzi without showing that he already knew him, and he trusted to Zorzi's discretion to conceal the fact, for he was a good judge of men.

It turned out to be much easier to carry out his plan than he had expected.

"My name is Zuan Venier," he said, in answer to Pasquale's gruff inquiry.

Pasquale eyed him a moment through the bars, and immediately understood that he was not a person to be kicked into the canal or received with other similar amenities. The great name alone would have awed the old porter to something like civility, but he had seen the visitor's face, and being quite as good a judge of humanity as Venier himself, he opened the door at once.

Venier explained that he wished to pay his respects to Messer Angelo Beroviero, being an old friend of Messer Jacopo Contarini. Learning that the master was absent on a journey, he asked whether there were any one within to whom he could deliver a message. He had heard, he said, that the master had a trusted assistant, a certain Zorzi. Pasquale answered that Zorzi was in the laboratory, and led the way.

Zorzi was greatly surprised, but as Venier had anticipated, he said nothing before Pasquale which could show that he had met his visitor before. Venier made a courteous inclination of the head, and the porter disappeared immediately.

"I heard that you had been hurt," said Venier, when they were alone. "I came to see whether I could do anything for you. Can I?"

Zorzi was touched by the kind words, spoken so quietly and sincerely, for it was only lately that any one except Marietta had shown him a little consideration. He had not forgotten how his master had taken leave of him, and the unexpected friendliness of old Pasquale after his accident had made a difference in his life; but of all men he had ever met, Venier was the one whom he had instinctively desired for a friend.

"Have you come over from Venice on purpose to see me?" he

asked, in something like wonder.

"Yes," answered Venier with a smile. "Why are you surprised?"

"Because it is so good of you."

"You have solemnly sworn to do as much for me, and for all the companions of our society," returned Venier, still smiling. "We are to help each other under all circumstances, as far as we can, you know. You are standing, and it must tire you, with those crutches. Shall we sit down? Tell me quite frankly, is there anything I can do for you?"

"Nothing you could ever do could make me more grateful than I am to you for coming," answered Zorzi sincerely.

Venier took the crutches from his hands and helped him to sit on the bench.

"You are very kind," Zorzi said.

Venier sat down beside him and asked him all manner of questions about his accident, and how it had happened. Zorzi had no reason for concealing the truth from him.

"They all hate me here," he said. "It happened like an accident, but the man made it happen. I do not think that he intended to maim me for life, but he meant to hurt me badly, and he did. There was not a man or a boy in the furnace room who did not understand, for no workman ever yet let his blowpipe slip from his hand in swinging a piece. But I do not wish to make matters worse, and I have said that I believed it was an accident."

"I should like to come across the man who did it," said Venier, his eyes growing hard and steely.

"When I tried to hop to the furnace on one leg to save myself from falling, one of the men cried out that I was a dancer, and laughed. I hear that the name has stuck to me among the workmen. I am called the 'Ballarin.'"

The ignoble meanness of Zorzi's tormentors roused Venier's generous blood.

"You will yet be their master," he said. "You will some day have a furnace of your own, and they will fawn to you. Your nickname will be better than their names in a few years!"

"I hope so," answered Zorzi.

"I know it," said the other, with an energy that would have surprised those who only knew the listless young nobleman whom nothing could amuse or interest.

He did not stay very long, and when he went away he said nothing about coming again. Zorzi went with him to the door. He had asked the Dalmatian to tell old Beroviero of his visit. Pasquale, who had never done such a thing in his life, actually went out upon the footway to the steps and steadied the gondola by the gunwale while Venier got in.

Giovanni Beroviero saw Venier come out, for it was near noon, and he had just come back from his own glass-house and was standing in the shadow of his father's doorway, slowly fanning himself with his large cap before he went upstairs, for it had been very hot in the sun. He did not know Zuan Venier by sight, but there was no mistaking the Venetian's high station, and he was surprised to see that the nobleman was evidently on good terns with Zorzi.

CHAPTER XIV

Zorzi had not left the glass-house since he had been hurt, but he foresaw that he might be obliged to leave the laboratory for an hour or more, now that he was better. He could walk, with one crutch and a stick, resting a little on the injured foot, and he felt sure that in a few days he should be able to walk with the stick alone. He had the certainty that he was lame for life, and now and then, when it was dusk and he sat under the plane-tree, meditating upon the uncertain future, he felt a keen pang at the thought that he might never again walk without limping; for he had been light and agile, and very swift of foot as a boy.

He fancied that Marietta would pity him, but not as she had pitied him at first. There would be a little feeling of repulsion for the cripple, mixed with her compassion for the man. It was true that, as matters were going now, he might not see her often again, and he was quite sure that he had no right to think of loving her. Zuan Venier's visit had recalled very clearly the obligations by which he had solemnly bound himself, and which he honestly meant to fulfil; and apart from them, when he tried to reason about his love, he could make it seem absurd enough that he should dream of winning Marietta for his wife.

But love itself does not argue. At first it is seen far off, like a beautiful bird of rare plumage, among flowers, on a morning in spring; it comes nearer, it is timid, it advances, it recedes, it poises on swiftly beating wings, it soars out of sight, but suddenly it is nearer than before; it changes shapes, and grows vast and terrible, till its flight is like the rushing of the whirlwind; then all is calm again, and in the stillness a sweet voice sings the chant of peace or the melancholy dirge of an endless regret; it is no longer the dove, nor the eagle, nor the storm that leaves ruin in its track—it is everything, it is life, it is the world itself, for ever and time without end, for good or evil, for such happiness as may pass all understanding, if God will, and if not, for undying sorrow.

Zorzi had forgotten his small resentment against Marietta, for not having given him a sign nor sent one word of greeting. He knew only that he loved her with all his heart and would give every hope he had for the pressure of her hand in his and the sound of her answering voice; and he dreaded lest she should pity him, as one pities a hurt creature that one would rather not touch.

It would not be in the hope of seeing her that he might leave the laboratory before long. He felt quite sure that Giovanni would make some further attempt to get possession of the little book that meant fortune to him who should possess it; and Giovanni evidently knew where it was. It would he easy for him to send Zorzi on an errand of importance, as soon as he should be so far recovered as to walk a little. The great glass-houses had dealings with the banks in Venice and with merchants of all countries, and Beroviero had more than once sent Zorzi to Venice on business of moment. Giovanni would come in some morning and declare that he could trust no one but Zorzi to collect certain sums of money in the city, and he would take care that the matter should keep him absent several hours. That would be ample time in which to try the flagstones with a hammer and to turn over the right one. Zorzi had convinced himself that it gave a hollow sound when he tapped it and that Giovanni could find it easily enough.

It was therefore folly to leave the box in its present place any longer, and he cast about in his mind for some safer spot in which to hide it. In the meantime, fearing lest Giovanni might think of sending him out at any moment, he waited till Pasquale had brought him water in the morning, and then raised the stone, as he had done before, took the box out of the earth and hid it in the cool end of the annealing oven, while he replaced the slab. The effort it cost him to move the latter told him plainly enough that his injury had weakened him almost as an illness might have done, but he succeeded in getting the stone into its bed at last. He tapped it with the end of his crutch as he knelt on the floor, and the sound it gave was even more hollow than before. He smiled as he thought how easily Giovanni would find the place, and how grievously disappointed he would be when he realised that it was empty.

It occurred at once to Zorzi that Giovanni's first impression would naturally be that Zorzi had taken the book himself in order to use it during the master's absence; and this thought perplexed him for a time, until he reflected that Giovanni could not accuse him of the deed without accusing himself of having searched for the box, a proceeding which his father would never forgive. Zorzi did not intend to tell the master of his conversation with Giovanni, nor of his suspicions. He would only say that the hiding-place had not seemed safe enough, because the stone gave a hollow sound which even the boys would notice if anything fell upon it.

But for Nella, it would be safest to give the box into Marietta's keeping, since no one could possibly suspect that it could have found its way to her room. At the mere thought, his heart beat fast. It would be a reason for seeing her alone, if he could, and for talking with her. He planned how he would send her a message by Nella, begging that he might speak to her on some urgent business of her father's, and she would come as she had come before; they would talk in the garden, under the plane-tree, where Pasquale and Nella could see them, and he would explain what he wanted. Then he would give her the box. He thought of it with calm delight, as he saw it all in a beautiful vision.

But there was Nella, and there was Pasquale, the former indiscreet, the latter silent but keen-sighted, and quick-witted in spite of his slow and surly ways. Every one knew that the book existed somewhere, and the porter and the serving-woman would guess the truth at once. At present no one but himself knew positively where the thing was. If he carried out his plan, three other persons would possess the knowledge. It was not to be thought of.

He looked about the laboratory. There were the beams and crossbeams, and the box would probably just fit into one of the shadowy interstices between two of the latter. But they were twenty feet from the ground, he had no ladder, and if there had been one at hand he could not have mounted it yet. His eye fell on the big earthen jar, more than half a man's height and as big round as a hogshead, half full of broken glass from the experiments. No one would think of it as a place for hiding anything, and it would not be emptied till it was quite full, several months hence. Besides, no one would dare to empty it without Beroviero's orders, as it contained nothing but fine red glass, which was valuable and only needed melting to be used at once.

It was not an easy matter to take out half the contents, and he was in constant danger of interruption. At night it would have been impossible owing to the presence of the boys. If Pasquale appeared and saw a heap of broken glass on the floor, he would surely suspect something. Zorzi calculated that it would take two hours to remove the fragments with the care necessary to avoid cutting his hands badly, and to put them back again, for the shape of the jar would not admit of his employing even one of the small iron shovels used for filling the crucibles.

With considerable difficulty he moved a large chest, that contained sifted white sand, out of the dark corner in which it stood and placed it diagonally so as to leave a triangular space behind it. To guard against the sound of the broken glass being heard from without, he shut the window, in spite of the heat, and having arranged in the corner one of the sacks used for bringing the cakes of kelp-ashes from Egypt, he began to fill it with the broken glass he brought from the jar in a bucket. When he judged that he had taken out more than half the contents, he took the iron box from the annealing oven. It was hard to carry it under the arm by which he walked with a stick, the other hand being necessary to move the crutch, and as he reached the jar he felt that it was slipping. He bent forward and it fell with a crash, bedding itself in the smashed glass. Zorzi drew a long breath of satisfaction, for the hardest part of the work was done.

He tried to heave up the sack from the corner, but it was far too heavy, and he was obliged to bring back more than half of what it held by bucketfuls, before he was able to bring the rest, dragging it after him across the floor. It was finished at last, he had shaken out the sack carefully over the jar's mouth, and he had moved the sand-chest back to its original position. No one would have imagined that the broken glass had been removed and put back again. The box was safely hidden now.

He was utterly exhausted when he dropped into the big chair, after washing the dust and blood from his hands—for it had been impossible to do what he had done without getting a few scratches, though none of them could have been called a cut. He sat quite still and closed his eyes. The box was safe now. It was not to be imagined that any one should ever suspect where it was, and on that point he was well satisfied. His only possible cause of anxiety now might be that if anything should happen to him, the master would be in ignorance of what he had done. But he saw no reason to expect anything so serious and his mind was at rest about a matter which had much disturbed him ever since Giovanni's visit.

The plan which he had attributed to the latter was not, however, the one which suggested itself to the younger Beroviero's mind. It would have been easy to carry out, and was very simple, and for that very reason Giovanni did not think of it. Besides, in his estimation it would be better to act in such a way as to get rid of Zorzi for ever, if that were possible.

On the Saturday night after Zorzi had hidden the box in the jar, the workmen cleared away the litter in the main furnace rooms and the order was given to let the fires go out. Zorzi sent word to the night boys who tended the fire in the laboratory that they were to come as usual. They appeared punctually, and to his surprise made no objection to working, though he had expected that they would complain of the heat and allege that their fathers would not let them go on any longer. On Sunday, according to the old rule of the house, no work was done, and Zorzi kept up the fire himself, spending most of the long day in the garden. On Sunday night the boys came again and went to work without a word, and in the morning they left the usual supply of chopped billets piled up and ready for use. Zorzi had rested himself thoroughly and went back to his experiments on that Monday with fresh energy.

The very first test he took of the glass that had been fusing since Saturday night was successful beyond his highest expectations. He had grown reckless after having spoiled the original mixtures by adding the copper in the hope of getting more of the wonderful red, and carried away by the love of the art and by the certainty of ultimate success which every man of genius feels almost from boyhood, he had deliberately attempted to produce the white glass for which Beroviero was famous. He followed a theory of his own in doing so, for although he was tolerably sure of the nature of the ingredients, as was every workman in the house, neither he nor they knew anything of the proportions in which Beroviero mixed the substances, and every glassmaker knows by experience that those proportions constitute by far the most important element of success.

Zorzi had not poured out the specimen on the table as he had done when the glass was coloured; on the contrary he had taken some on the blowpipe and had begun to work with it at once, for the three great requisites were transparency, ductility, and lightness. In a few minutes he had convinced himself that his glass possessed all these qualities in an even higher degree than the master's own, and that was immeasurably superior to anything which the latter's own sons or any other glassmaker could produce. Zorzi had taken very little at first, and he made of it a thin phial of graceful shape, turned the mouth outward, and dropped the little vessel into the bed of ashes. He would have set it in the annealing oven, but he wished to try the weight of it, and he let it cool. Taking it up when he could touch it safely, it felt in his hand like a thing of air. On the shelf was another nearly like it in size, which he had made long ago with Beroviero's glass. There were scales on the table; he laid one phial in each, and the old one was by far the heavier. He had to put a number of pennyweights into the scale with his own before the two were balanced.

His heart almost stood still, and he could not believe his good fortune. He took the sheet of rough paper on which he had written down the precise contents of the three crucibles, and he carefully went over the proportions of the ingredients in the one from which he had just taken his specimen. He made a strong effort of memory, trying to recall whether he had been careless and in-exact in weighing any of the materials, but he knew that he had been most precise. He had also noted the hour at which he had put the mixture into the crucible on Saturday, and he now glanced at the sand-glass and made another note. But he did not lay the paper upon the table, where it had been lying for two days, kept in place by a little glass weight. It had become his most precious pos-session; what was written on it meant a fortune as soon as he could get a furnace to himself; it was his own, and not the mas-ter's; it was wealth, it might even be fame. Beroviero might call him to account for misusing the furnace, but that was no capital offence after all, and it was more than paid for by the single cru-cible of magnificent red glass. Zorzi was attempting to reproduce that too, for he had the master's notes of what the pot had con-tained, and it was almost ready to be tried; he even had the piece of copper carefully weighed to be equal in bulk with the ladle that had been melted. If he succeeded there also, that was a new secret for Beroviero, but the other was for himself.

All that morning he revelled in the delight of working with the new glass. A marvellous dish with upturned edge and orna-mented foot was the next thing he made, and he placed it at once in the annealing oven. Then he made a tall drinking glass such as he had never made before, and then, in contrast, a tiny ampulla, so small that he could almost hide it in his hand, with its spout, yet decorated with all the perfection of a larger piece. He worked on, careless of the time, his genius all alive, the rest a distant dream.

He was putting the finishing touches to a beaker of a new shape when the door opened, and Giovanni entered the labora-tory. Zorzi was seated on the working stool, the pontil in one hand, the 'porcello' in the other. He glanced at Giovanni absently and went on, for it was the last touch and the glass was cooling quickly.

"Still working, in this heat?" asked Giovanni, fanning himself with his cap as was his custom.

There was a moment's silence. Then a sharp clicking sound and the beaker fell finished into the soft ashes.

"Yes, I am still at work, as you see," answered Zorzi, not real-ising that Giovanni would particularly notice what he was doing.

He rose with some difficulty and got his crutch under one arm. With a forked stick he took the beaker from the ashes and placed it in the annealing oven. Giovanni watched him, and when the broad iron door was open, he saw the other pieces already standing inside on the iron tray.

"Admirable!" cried Giovanni. "You are a great artist, my dear Zorzi! There is no one like you!"

"I do what I can," answered Zorzi, closing the door quickly, lest the hot end of the oven should cool at all.

"I should say that you do what no one else can," returned Giovanni. "But how lame you are! I had expected to find you walking as well as ever by this time."

"I shall never walk again without limping."

"Oh, take courage!" said Giovanni, who seemed determined to be both cheerful and flattering. "You will soon be as light on your feet as ever. But it was a shocking accident."

He sat down in the big chair and Zorzi took the small one by the table, wishing that he would go away.

"It is a pity that you had no white glass in the furnace on that particular day," Giovanni continued. "You said you had none, if I remember. How is it that you have it now? Have you changed one of the crucibles?"

"Yes. One of the experiments succeeded so well that it seemed better to take out all the glass."

"May I see a piece of it?" inquired Giovanni, as if he were asking a great favour.

It was one thing to let him test the glass himself, it was quite another to show him a piece of it. He would see it sooner or later, and he could guess nothing of its composition.

"The specimen is there, on the table," Zorzi answered.

Giovanni rose at once and took the piece from the paper on which it lay, and held it up against the light. He was amazed at the richness of the colour, and gave vent to all sorts of exclamations.

"Did you make this?" he asked at last.

"It is the result of the master's experiments."

"It is marvellous! He has made another fortune."

Giovanni replaced the specimen where it had lain, and as he did so, his eye fell on the phial Zorzi had made that morning. Zorzi had not put it into the annealing oven because it had been allowed to get quite cold, so that the annealing would have been imperfect. Giovanni took it up, and uttered a low exclamation of surprise at its lightness. He held it up and looked through it, and then he took it by the neck and tapped it sharply with his fingernail.

"Take care," said Zorzi; "it is not annealed. It may fly."

"Oh!" exclaimed Giovanni. "Have you just made it?"

"Yes."

"It is the finest glass I ever saw. It is much better than what they had in the main furnaces the day you were hurt. Did you not find it so yourself, in working with it?"

Zorzi began to feel anxious as to the result of so much questioning. Whatever happened he must hide from Giovanni the fact that he had discovered a new glass of his own.

"Yes," he answered, with affected indifference. "I thought it was unusually good. I daresay there may be some slight difference in the proportions."

"Do you mean to say that my father does not follow any exact rule?"

"Oh yes. But he is always making experiments."

"He mixes all the materials for the main furnaces himself, does he not?" inquired Giovanni.

"Yes. He does it alone, in the room that is kept locked. When he has finished, the men come and carry out the barrows. The materials are stirred and mixed together outside."

"Yes. I do it in the same way myself. Have you ever helped my father in that work?"

"No, certainly not. If I had helped him once, I should know the secret." Zorzi smiled.

"But if you do not know the secret," said Giovanni unexpectedly, "how did you make this glass?"

He held up the phial.

"Why do you suppose that I made it?" Zorzi felt himself growing pale. "The master has supplies of everything here in the laboratory and in the little room where I sleep."

"Is there white glass here too?"

"Of course!" answered Zorzi readily. "There is half a jar of it in my room. We keep it there so that the night boys may not steal it a little at a time."

"I see," answered Giovanni. "That is very sensible."

He was firmly convinced that if he asked Zorzi any more direct question, the answer would be a falsehood, and he applauded himself for stopping at the point he had reached in his inquiries. For he was an experienced glassmaker and was perfectly sure that the phial was not made from Beroviero's ordinary glass. It followed that Zorzi had used the precious book, and Giovanni inferred that the rest was a lucky accident.

"Will you sell me one of those beautiful things you have in the oven?" Giovanni asked, in an insinuating tone.

Zorzi hesitated. The master had often paid him a fair price for objects he had made, and which were used in Beroviero's house, as has been told. Zorzi did not wish to irritate Giovanni by refusing, and after all, there was no great difference between being paid by old Beroviero or by his son. The fact that he worked in glass, which had been an open secret among the workmen for a long time, was now no secret at all. The question was rather as to his right, being Beroviero's trusted assistant, to sell anything out of the house.

"Will you?" asked Giovanni, after waiting a few moments for an answer.

"I would rather wait until the master comes back," said Zorzi doubtfully. "I am not quite sure about it."

"I will take all the responsibility," Giovanni answered cheerfully. "Am I not free to come to my father's glass-house and buy a beaker or a dish for myself, if I please? Of course I am. But there is no real difference between buying from you, on one side of the garden, or from the furnace on the other. Is there?"

"The difference is that in the one case you buy from the master and pay him, but now you are offering to pay me, who am already well paid by him for any work I may do."

"You are very scrupulous," said Giovanni in a disappointed tone. "Tell me, does my father never give you anything for the things you make, and which you say are in the house?"

"Oh yes," answered Zorzi promptly. "He always pays me for them."

"But that shows that he does not consider them as part of the work you are regularly paid to do, does it not?"

"I suppose so," Zorzi said, turning over the question in his mind.

Giovanni took a small piece of gold from the purse he carried at his belt, and he laid it on the flat arm of the chair beside him, and put down one of his crooked forefingers upon it.

"I cannot see what objection you can have, in that case. You know very well that young painters who work for masters help them, but are always allowed to sell anything they can paint in their leisure time."

"Yes. That is true. I will take the money, sir, and you may choose any of the pieces you like. When the master comes, I will tell him, and if I have no right to the price he shall keep it himself."

"Do you really suppose that my father would be mean enough to take the money?" asked Giovanni, who would certainly have taken it himself under the circumstances.

"No. He is very generous. Nevertheless, I shall certainly tell him the whole story."

"That is your affair. I have nothing to say about it. Here is the money, for which I will take the beaker I saw you finishing when I came in. Is it enough? Is it a fair price?"

"It is a very good price," Zorzi answered. "But there may be a piece among those in the oven which you will like better. Will you not come tomorrow, when they are all annealed, and make your choice?"

"No. I have fallen in love with the piece I saw you making."

"Very well. You shall have it, and many thanks."

"Here is the money, and thanks to you," said Giovanni, holding out the little piece of gold.

"You shall pay me when you take the beaker," objected Zorzi. "It may fly, or turn out badly."

"No, no!" answered Giovanni, rising, and putting the money into Zorzi's hand. "If anything happens to it, I will take another. I am afraid that you may change your mind, you see, and I am very anxious to have such a beautiful thing."

He laughed cheerfully, nodded to Zorzi and went out at once, almost before the latter had time to rise from his seat and get his crutch under his arm.

When he was alone, Zorzi looked at the coin and laid it on the table. He was much puzzled by Giovanni's conduct, but at the same time his artist's vanity was flattered by what had happened. Giovanni's admiration of the glass was genuine; there could be no doubt of that, and he was a good judge. As for the work, Zorzi knew quite well that there was not a glassblower in Murano who could approach him either in taste or skill. Old Beroviero had told him so within the last few months, and he felt that it was true.

He would have been neither a natural man nor a born artist if he had refused to sell the beaker, out of an exaggerated scruple. But the transaction had shown him that his only chance of success for the future lay in frankly telling old Beroviero what he had done in his absence, while reserving his secret for himself. The master was proud of him as his pupil, and sincerely attached to him as a man, and would certainly not try to force him into explaining how the glass was made. Besides, the glass itself was there, easily distinguished from any other, and Zorzi could neither hide it nor throw it away.

Giovanni went out upon the footway, and as he passed, Pasquale thought he had never seen him so cheerful. The sour look had gone out of his face, and he was actually smiling to himself. With such a man it would hardly have been possible to attribute his pleased expression to the satisfaction he felt in having bought Zorzi's beaker. He had never before, in his whole life, parted with a piece of gold without a little pang of regret; but he had felt the most keen and genuine pleasure just now, when Zorzi had at last accepted the coin.

Pasquale watched him cross the wooden bridge and go into his father's house opposite. Then the old porter shut the door and went back to the laboratory, walking slowly with his ugly head bent a little, as if in deep thought. Zorzi had already resumed his occupation and had a lump of hot glass swinging on his blowpipe, his crutch being under his right arm.

"Half a rainbow to windward," observed the old sailor. "There will be a squall before long."

"What do you mean?" asked Zorzi.

"If you had seen the Signor Giovanni smile, as he went out, you would know what I mean," answered Pasquale. "In our seas, when we see the stump of a rainbow low down in the clouds, we say it is the eye of the wind, looking out for us, and I can tell you that the wind is never long in coming!"

"Did you say anything to make him smile?" asked Zorzi, going on with his work.

"I am not a mountebank," growled the porter. "I am not a strolling player at the door of his booth at a fair, cracking jokes with those who pass! But perhaps it was you who said something amusing to him, just before he left? Who knows? I always took you for a grave young man. It seems that I was mistaken. You make jokes. You cause a serious person like the Signor Giovanni to die of laughing."

CHAPTER XV

Giovanni sat in his father's own room at home, with shut doors, and he was writing. He had received as good an education as any young nobleman or rich merchant's son in Venice, but writing was always irksome to him, and he generally employed a scribe rather than take the pen himself. Today he preferred to dispense with help, instead of trusting the discretion of a secretary; and this is what he was setting down.

"I, Giovanni Beroviero, the son of Angelo, of Murano, the glassmaker, being in my father's absence and in his stead the Master of our honourable Guild of Glassmakers, do entreat your Magnificence to interfere and act for the preservation of our ancient rights and privileges and for the maintenance of the just laws of Venice, and for the honour of the Republic, and for the public good of Murano. There is a certain Zorzi, called the Ballarin, who was a servant of the aforesaid Angelo Beroviero, a Dalmatian and a foreigner and a fellow of no worth, who formerly swept the floor of the said Angelo's furnace room, which the said Angelo keeps for his private use. This fellow therefore, this foreigner, the said Angelo being absent on a long journey, was left by him to watch the fire in the said room, there being certain new glass in the crucibles of the said furnace, which the said Zorzi, called the Ballarin, was to keep hot a certain number of days. And now in the torrid heat of summer, the canicular days being at hand, the furnaces in the glass-house of the said Angelo have been extinguished. But this Zorzi, called the Ballarin, although he has removed from the furnace of the said Angelo the glass which was to be kept hot, does insolently and defiantly refuse to put out the fire in the said furnace, and forces the boys to make the fire all night, to the great injury of their health, because the canicular days are approaching. But the said Zorzi, called the Ballarin, like a raging devil come upon earth from his master Satan, heeds no heat. And he has no respect of laws, nor of persons, nor of the honourable Guild, nor of the Republic, working day and night at the glassblower's art, just as if he were not a Dalmatian, and a foreigner, and a low fellow of no worth. Moreover, he has made glass himself, which it is forbidden for any foreigner to make throughout the dominions of the Republic. Moreover, it is a good white glass, which he could not have made if he had not wickedly, secretly and feloniously stolen a book which is the property of the aforesaid Angelo, and which contains many things concerning the making of glass. Moreover, this Zorzi, called the Ballarin, is a liar, a thief and an assassin, for of the good white glass which he has melted by means of the said Angelo's secrets, he makes vessels, such as phials, ampullas and dishes, which it is not lawful for any foreigner to make. Moreover, in the vile wickedness of his shameless heart, the said Zorzi, called the Ballarin, has the presumption and effrontery to sell the said vessels, openly admitting that he has made them. And they are well made, with diabolical skill, and the sale of the said vessels is a great injury to the glassblowers of Murano, and to the honourable Guild, besides being an affront to the Republic. I, the aforesaid Giovanni, was indeed unable to believe that such monstrous wickedness could exist. I therefore went into the furnace room myself, and there I found the said Zorzi, called the Ballarin, working alone and making a certain piece in the form of a beaker. And though he knows me, that I am the son of his master, he is so lost to all shame, that he continued to work before me, as if he were a glassblower, and though I fanned myself in order not to die of heat, he worked before the fire, and felt nothing, raging like a devil. I therefore offered to buy the beaker he was making and I put down a piece of money, and the said Zorzi, called the Ballarin, a liar, a thief and an assassin, took the said piece of money, and set the said beaker within the annealing oven of the said furnace, wherein I saw many other pieces of fine workmanship, and he said that I should have the said beaker when it was annealed. Wherefore I, being for the time the Master of the honourable Guild in the stead of the said Angelo, entreat your Magnificence on behalf of the said Guild to interfere and act for the preservation of our ancient rights and privileges, and for the honour of the Republic. Moreover, I entreat your Magnificence to send a force by night, in order that there may be no scandal, to take the said Zorzi, called the Ballarin, and to bind him, and carry him to Venice, that he may be tried for his monstrous crimes, and be questioned, even with torture, as to others which he has certainly committed, and be exiled from all the dominions of the Republic for ever on pain of being hanged, that in this way our laws may be maintained and our privileges preserved. Moreover, I will give any further information of the same kind which your Magnificence may desire. At Murano, in the house of Angelo Beroviero, my father, this third day of July, in the year of the Salvation of the World fourteen hundred and seventy, Giovanni Beroviero, the glass-maker."

Giovanni had taken a long time in the composition of this remarkable document. He sat in his linen shirt and black hose, but he had paused often to fan himself with a sheet of paper, and to wipe the perspiration from his forehead, for although he was a lean man he suffered much from the heat, owing to a weakness of his heart.

He folded the two sheets of his letter and tied them with a silk string, of which he squeezed the knot into pasty red wax, which he worked with his fingers, and upon this he pressed the iron seal of the guild, using both his hands and standing up in order to add his weight to the pressure. The missive was destined for the Podestà of Murano, which is to say, for the Governor, who was a patrician of Venice and a most high and mighty personage. Giovanni did not mean to trust to any messenger. That very afternoon, when he had slept after dinner, and the sun was low, he would have himself rowed to the Governor's house, and he would deliver the letter himself, or if possible he would see the dignitary and explain even more fully that Zorzi, called the Ballarin, was a liar, a thief and an assassin. He felt a good deal of pride in what he had written so carefully, and he was sure that his case was strong. In another day or two, Zorzi would be gone for ever from Murano, Giovanni would have the precious manuscript in his possession, and when old Beroviero returned Giovanni would use the book as a weapon against his father, who would be furiously angry to find his favourite assistant gone. It was all very well planned, he thought, and was sure to succeed. He would even take possession of the beautiful red glass, and of the still more wonderful white glass which Zorzi had made for himself. By the help of the book, he should soon be able to produce the same in his own furnaces. The vision of a golden future opened before him. He would outdo all the other glassmakers in every market, from Paris to Palermo, from distant England to Egyptian Alexandria, wheresoever the vast trade of Venice carried those huge bales of delicate glass, carefully packed in the dried seaweed of the lagoons. Gold would follow gold, and his wealth would increase, till it became greater than that of any patrician in Venice. Who could tell but that, in time, the great exception might be made for him, and he might be admitted to sit in the Grand Council, he and his heirs for ever, just as if he had been born a real patrician and not merely a member of the half noble caste of glassblowers? Such things were surely possible.

In the cooler hours of the afternoon he got into his father's gondola, for he was far too economical to keep one of his own, and he had himself rowed to the house of the Governor, on the Grand Canal of Murano. But at the door he was told that the official was in Venice and would not return till the following day. The liveried porter was not sure where he might be found, but he often went to the palace of the Contarini, who were his near relations. The Signor Giovanni, to whom the porter was monstrously civil, might give himself the fatigue of being taken there in his gondola. In any case it would be easy to find the Governor. He would perhaps be on the Grand Canal in Venice at the hour when all the patricians were taking the air. It was very probable indeed.

The porter bowed low as the gondola pushed off, and Giovanni leaned back in the comfortable seat, to repeat again and again in his mind what he meant to say if he succeeded in speaking with the Governor. He had his letter of complaint safe in his wallet, and he could remember every word he had written. In order to go to Venice, the nearest way was to return from the Grand Canal of Murano by the canal of San Piero, and to pass the glass-house. The door was shut as usual, and Giovanni smiled as he thought of how the city archers would go in, perhaps that very night, to take Zorzi away. He would not be with them, but when they were gone, he would go and find the book under one of the stones. When he had got it, his father might come home, for all Giovanni cared.

Before long the gondola was winding its way through the narrow canals, now shooting swiftly along a short straight stretch, between a monastery and a palace, now brought to by a turn of the hand at a corner, as the man at the oar shouted out a direction meant for whoever might be coming, by the right or left, as one should say "starboard helm" or "port helm," and both doing the same, two vessels pass clear of one another; and to this day the gondoliers of Venice use the old words, and tell long-winded stories of their derivation and first meaning, which seem quite unnecessary. But in Beroviero's time, the gondola had only lately come into fashion, and every one adopted it quickly because it was much cheaper than keeping horses, and it was far more pleasant to be taken quickly by water, by shorter ways, than to ride in the narrow streets, in the mud in winter and in the dust in summer, jostling those who walked, and sometimes quarrelling with those who rode, because the way was too narrow for one horse to pass another, when both had riders on their backs. Moreover, it was law that after nine o'clock in the morning no man who had reached the fig-tree that grew in the open space before San Salvatore, should ride to Saint Mark's by the Merceria, so that people had to walk the rest of the way, leaving their horses to grooms. The gondola was therefore a great convenience, besides being a notable economy, and old Francesco Sansovino says that in his day, which was within a lifetime of Angelo Beroviero's, there were nine or ten thousand gondolas in Venice. But at first they had not the high peaked stem of iron, and stem and stern were made almost alike, as in the Venetian boats and skiffs of our own time.

Giovanni got out at the steps of the Contarini palace, which, of the many that even then belonged to different branches of that great house, was distinguished above all others by its marvellous outer winding staircase, which still stands in all its beauty and slender grace. But near the great palace there were little wooden houses of two stories, some new and straight and gaily painted, but some old and crooked, hanging over the canals so that they seemed ready to topple down, with crazy outer balconies half closed in by lattices behind which the women sat for coolness, and sometimes even slept in the hot months. For the great city of stone and brick was not half built yet, and the space before Saint Mark's was much larger than it is now, for the Procuratie did not yet exist, nor the clock, but the great belltower stood almost in the middle of an open square, and there were little wooden booths at its base, in which all sorts of cheap trinkets were sold. There were also such booths and small shops at the base of the two columns. Also, the bridge of Rialto was a broad bridge of boats, on which shops were built on each side of the way, and the middle of the bridge could be drawn out, for the great Bucentoro to pass through, when the Doge went out in state to wed the sea.

Giovanni Beroviero was well known to Contarini's household, for all knew of the approaching marriage, and the servants were not surprised when he inquired for the Governor of Murano, saying that his business was urgent. But the Governor was not there, nor the master of the house. They were gone to the Grand Canal. Would the Signor Giovanni like to speak with Messer Jacopo, who chanced to be in the palace and alone? It was still early, and Giovanni thought that the opportunity was a good one for ingratiating himself with his future brother-in-law. He would go in, if he should not disturb Messer Jacopo. He was announced and ushered respectfully into the great hall, and thence up the broad staircase to the hall of reception above. And below, his gondoliers gossiped with the servants, talking about the coming marriage, and many indiscreet things were said, which it was better that their masters should not hear; as for instance that Jacopo was really living in the house of the Agnus Dei, where he kept a beautiful Georgian slave in unheard-of luxury, and that this was a great grief to his father, who was therefore very desirous of hastening the marriage with Marietta. The porter winked one eye solemnly at the head gondolier, as who should imply that the establishment at the Agnus Dei would not be given up for twenty marriages; but the gondolier said boldly that if Jacopo did not change his life after he had married Marietta, something would happen to him. Upon this the porter inquired superciliously what, in the name of a great many beings, celestial and infernal, could possibly happen to any Contarini who chose to do as he pleased. The gondolier answered that there were laws, the porter retorted that the laws were made for glassblowers but not for patricians, and the two might have come to blows if they had not just then heard their masters' voices from the landing of the great staircase; and of coarse it was far more important to overhear all they could of the conversation than to quarrel about a point of law.

Giovanni was too full of his plan for Zorzi's destruction to resist the temptation of laying the whole case before Contarini, who was so soon to be a member of the family, and as Jacopo, who was himself going out, accompanied his guest downstairs, Giovanni continued to talk of the matter earnestly, and Contarini answered him by occasional monosyllables and short sentences, much interested by the whole affair, but wishing that Giovanni would go away, now that he had told all. He was in constant fear lest Zorzi should say something which might betray the meetings at the house of the Agnus Dei, and had often regretted that he had not been put quietly out of the way, instead of being admitted to the society. Now after hearing what Giovanni had to say, he had not the slightest doubt but that Zorzi had really broken the laws, and it seemed an admirable solution of the whole affair that the Dalmatian should be exiled from the Republic for life. That being settled, he wished to get rid of his visitor, as Arisa was waiting for him.

"I assure you," Giovanni said, "that this miserable Zorzi is a liar, a thief and an assassin."

"Yes," assented Contarini carelessly, "I have no doubt of it."

"The best thing is to arrest him at once, this very night, if possible, and have him brought before the Council."

"Yes."

Contarini had agreed with Giovanni on this point already, and made a movement to descend, but Giovanni loved to stand still in order to talk, and he would not move. Contarini waited for him.

"It is important that some member of the Council should be informed of the truth beforehand," he continued. "Will you speak to your father about it, Messer Jacopo?"

"Yes," answered Contarini, and he spoke the word intentionally with great emphasis, in the hope that Giovanni would be finally satisfied and go away.

"You will be conferring a benefit on the city of Murano," said Giovanni in a tone of gratitude, and this time he began to come down the steps.

The gondolier had heard every word that had been said, as well as the servants in the lower hall; but to them the conversation had no especial meaning, as they knew nothing of Zorzi. To the gondolier, on the other hand, who was devoted to his master and detested his master's son, it meant much, though his stolid, face did not betray the slightest intelligence.

Giovanni took leave of Contarini with much ceremony, a little too much, Jacopo thought.

"To the Grand Canal," said Giovanni as the gondolier helped him to get in, and he backed under the 'felse.' "Try and find the Governor of Murano, and if you see him, take me alongside his gondola."

The sun was now low, and as the light craft shot out at last upon the Grand Canal, the breeze came up from the land, cool and refreshing. Scores of gondolas were moving up and down, some with the black 'felse,' some without, and in the latter there were beautiful women, whose sun-dyed hair shone resplendent under the thin embroidered veils that loosely covered it. They wore silk and satin of rich hues, and jewels, and some were clad in well-fitting bodices that were nets of thin gold cord drawn close over velvet, with lawn sleeves gathered to the forearm and the upper arm by netting of seed pearls. Beside some of them sat their husbands or their fathers, in robes and mantles of satin and silk, or in wide coats of rich stuff, open at the neck; bearded men, straight-featured, and often very pale, wearing great puffed caps set far back on their smooth hair, their white hands playing with their gloves, their dark eyes searching out from afar the faces of famous beauties, or, if they were grey-haired men, fixed thoughtfully before them.

Overall the evening light descended like a mist of gold, reflected from the sculptured walls of palaces, where marble columns and light traceries of stone were dyed red and orange and almost purple by the setting sun, and nestling among the carved beams and far-projecting balconies of wooden houses that over-hung the canal, gilding the water itself where the broad-bladed oars struck deep and churned it, and swept aft, and steered with a poising, feathering backstroke, or where tiny waves were dashed up by a gondola's bright iron stem. Slowly the water turned to wine below, the clear outlines of the palaces stood out less sharply against the paling sky, the golden cloudlets, floating behind the great tower of Saint Mark's presently faded to wreaths of delicate mist. The bells rung out from church and monastery, far and near, till the air was filled with a deep music, telling all Venice that the day was done.

Then the many voices that had echoed in greeting and in laughter, from boat to boat, were hushed a moment, and almost every man took off his hat or cap, the robed Councillor and the gondolier behind him; and also a good number of the great ladies made the sign of the cross and were silent a while. It was the hour when Venice puts forth her stealing charm, when the terrible dis-tinctness of her splendour grows gentle and almost human, and the little mystery of each young life rises from the heart to hold converse with the sweet, mysterious all. Through the long day the palaces look down consciously at themselves, mirrored in the calm water where they stand, and each seems to say "I am finer than you," or "My master is still richer than yours," or "You are going to ruin faster than I am," or "I was built by a Lombardo," or "I by Sansovino," and the violent light is ever there to bear wit-ness of the truth of what each says. Within, without, in hall and church and gallery, there is perpetual brightness and perpetual silence. But at the evening hour, now, as in old times, a spirit takes Venice and folds it in loving arms, whispering words that are not even guessed by day.

The Ave Maria had not ceased ringing when Giovanni's gon-dolier came up with the Governor of Murano. He was alone, and at his invitation Giovanni left his own craft and sat down beside the patrician, whose gondola was uncovered for coolness. Gio-vanni talked earnestly in low tones, holding his sealed letter in his hand, while his own oarsman watched him closely in the advancing dusk, but was too wise to try to overhear what was said. He knew well enough now what Giovanni wanted of the Gov-ernor, and what he obtained.

"Not tonight," the Governor said audibly, as Giovanni re-turned to his own gondola. "Tomorrow."

Giovanni turned before getting under the 'felse,' bowed low as he stood up and said a few words of thanks, which the Governor could hardly have heard as his boat shot ahead, though he made one more gracious gesture with his hand. The shadows descended quickly now, and everywhere the little lights came out, from latticed balconies and palace windows left open to let in the cool air, and from the silently gliding gondolas that each carried a small lamp; and here and there between tall houses the young summer moon fell across the black water, rippling under the freshening breeze, and it was like a shower of silver falling into a widow's lap.

But Giovanni saw none of these things, and if he had looked out of the small windows of the 'felse,' he would not have cared to see them, for beauty did not appeal to him in nature any more than in art, except that in the latter it was a cause of value in things. Besides, as he suffered from the heat all day, he was afraid of being chilled at evening; so he sat inside the 'felse,' gloating over the success of his trip. The Governor, who knew nothing of Zorzi but was well aware of Giovanni's importance in Murano, had readily consented to arrest the poor Dalmatian who was represented as such a dangerous person, besides being a liar and other things, and Giovanni had particularly requested that the force sent should be sufficient to overpower the "raging devil" at once and without scandal. He judged that ten men would suffice for this, he said. The fact was that he feared some resistance on the part of Pasquale, whom he knew to be a friend to Zorzi. He had carefully abstained from alluding to Zorzi's lameness, lest the mere mention of it should excite some compassion in his hearer. He had in fact done everything to assure the success of his scheme, except the one thing which was the most necessary of all. He had allowed himself to speak of it in the hearing of the gondolier who hated him, and who lost no time in making use of the information.

It was nearly suppertime when he deposited Giovanni at the steps of the house and took the gondola round to the narrow canal in which the boats lay, and which was under Nella's window. The shutters were wide open, and there was a light within. He called the serving-woman by name, and she looked out, and asked what he wanted. Then, as now, gondoliers worked indoors like the servants when not busy with the boats, and slept in the house. The man was on friendly terms with Nella, who liked him because he thought her mistress the most perfect creature in the world.

"I have ripped the arm of my doublet," he said. "Can you mend it for me this evening?"

"Bring it up to me now," answered Nella. "There is time before supper. You can wait outside my room while I do it. My mistress is already gone downstairs."

"You are an angel," observed the gondolier from below. "The only thing you need is a husband."

"You have guessed wrong," answered Nella with a little laugh. "That is the only thing I do not need."

She disappeared, and the gondolier went round by the back of the house to the side door, in order to go upstairs. In a quarter of an hour, while she stood in her doorway, and he in the passage without, he had told her all he knew of Giovanni's evil intentions against Zorzi, including the few words which the Governor had spoken audibly. The torn sleeve was an invention.

Giovanni was visibly elated at supper, a circumstance which pleased his wife but inspired Marietta with some distrust. She had never felt any sympathy for the brother who was so much older than herself, and who took a view of things which seemed to her sordid, and she did not like to see him sitting in her father's place, often talking of the house as if it were already his, and dictating to her upon matters of conduct as well as upon questions of taste. Everything he said jarred on her, but as yet she had no idea that he had any plans against Zorzi, and being of a reserved character she often took no trouble to answer what he said, except to bend her head a little to acknowledge that he had said it. When she was alone with her father, she loved to sit with him after supper in the big room, working by the clear light of the olive oil lamp, while he sat in his great chair and talked to her of his work. He had told her far more than he realised of his secret processes as well as of his experiments, and she had remembered it, for she alone of his children had inherited his true love and understanding of the noble art of glassmaking.

But now that he was away, Giovanni generally spent the evening in instructing his wife how to save money, and she listened meekly enough to what he told her, for she was a modest little woman, of colourless character, brought up to have no great opinion of herself, though her father was a rich merchant; and she looked upon her husband as belonging to a superior class. Marietta found the conversation intolerable and she generally left the couple together a quarter of an hour after supper was over and went to her own room, where she worked a little and listened to Nella's prattle, and sometimes answered her. She was living in a state of half-suspended thought, and was glad to let the time pass as it would, provided it passed at all.

This evening, as usual, she bade her brother and his wife good night, and went upstairs. Nella had learned to expect her and was waiting for her. To her surprise, Nella shut the window as soon as she entered.

"Leave it open," she said. "It is hot this evening. Why did you shut it? You never do."

"A window is an ear," answered Nella mysteriously. "The nights are still and voices carry far."

"What great secret are you going to talk of?" inquired Marietta, with a careless smile, as she drew the long pins from her hair and let the heavy braids fall behind her.

"Bad news, bad news!" Nella repeated. "The young master is doing things which he ought not to do, because they are very unjust and spiteful. I am only a poor serving-woman, but I would bite off my fingers, like this"—and she bit them sharply and shook them—"before I would let them do such things!"

"What do you mean, Nella?" asked Marietta. "You must not speak of my brother in that way."

"Your brother! Eh, your brother!" cried Nella in a low and angry voice, quite unlike her own. "Do you know what your brother has done? He has been to Messer Jacopo Contarini, your betrothed husband, and he has told him that Zorzi is a liar, a thief and an assassin, and that he will have him arrested tonight, if he can, and Messer Jacopo promised that his father, who is of the Council, shall have Zorzi condemned! And your brother has seen the Governor of Murano in Venice, and has given him a great letter, and the Governor said that it should not be tonight, but tomorrow. That is the sort of man your brother is."

Marietta was standing. She had turned slowly pale while Nella was speaking, and grasped the back of a chair with both hands. She thought she was going to faint.

CHAPTER XVI

Marrietta's heart stood still, as she bent over the back of the chair holding it with both her hands, but feeling that she was falling. She had expected anything but this, when Nella had begun to speak. The blow was sudden and heavy, and she herself had never known how much she could be hurt, until that moment.

Nella looked at her in astonishment. The serving-woman had changed her mind about Zorzi of late, and had grown fond of him in taking care of him. But her anger against Giovanni was roused rather because what he was about to do was an affront to his father, her master, than out of mere sympathy for the intended victim. She was far from understanding what could have so deeply moved Marietta.

"You see," she said triumphantly, "what sort of a brother you have!"

The sound of her voice recalled the young girl just when she felt that she was losing consciousness. Her first instinct was to go to Zorzi and warn him. He must escape at once. The Governor had said that it should be tomorrow, but he might change his mind and send his men tonight. There was no time to be lost, she must go instantly. As she stood upright she could see the porter's light shining through the small grated window, for Pasquale was still awake, but in a few minutes the light would go out. She had often been at her own window at that hour, and had watched it, wondering whether Zorzi would work far into the night, and whether he was thinking of her.

It would be easy to slip out by the side door and run across. No one would know, except Nella and Pasquale, but she would have preferred that only the latter should be in the secret. She was still dressed, though her hair was undone, and the hood of a thin silk mantle would hide that. Her mind reasoned by instantaneous flashes now, and she had full control of herself again. She would tell Nella that she was going downstairs again for a little while, and she would also tell her to make an infusion of lime flowers and to bring it in half an hour and wait for her. Down the main staircase to the landing, down the narrow stairs in the dark, out into the street—it would not take long, and she would tap very softly at the door of the glass-house.

When she said that she would go down again, Nella suspected nothing. On the contrary she thought her mistress was wise.

"You will lead on the Signor Giovanni to talk of Zorzi," she said. "You will learn something."

"And make me a drink of lime flowers," continued Marietta. "The housekeeper has plenty."

"I know, I know," answered Nella. "Shall you come up again soon?"

"Be here in half an hour with the drink, and wait for me. You had better go for the lime flowers before the housekeeper is asleep. I will twist my hair up again before I go down."

Nella nodded and disappeared, for the housekeeper generally went to bed very early. As soon as she was out of the room Marietta took her silk cloak and wrapped herself in it, drawing the end over her head, so as to hide her hair and shade her face. She was pale still, but her lips were tightly closed and her eyelids a little drawn together, as she left the room. She met no one on the stairs. In the dark, when she reached the door, she could feel the oak bar that was set across it at night, and she slipped it back into its hole in the wall, without making much noise. She lifted the latch and went out.

The night was still and clear, and the young moon was setting. If any one had been looking out she must have been seen as she crossed the wooden bridge, and she glanced nervously back at the open windows. There were lights in the big room, and she heard Giovanni's monotonous voice, as he talked to his wife. But there was shadow under the glass-house, and a moment later she was tapping softly at the door. Pasquale looked down from the grating, and was about to say something uncomplimentary when he recognised her, for he could see very well when there was little light, like most sailors. He opened the door at once, and stood aside to let Marietta enter.

"Shut the door quickly," she whispered, "and do not open it for anybody, till I come out."

Pasquale obeyed in silence. He knew as well as she did that Giovanni was sitting in the big room, with open windows, within easy hearing of ordinary sounds. A feeble light came through the open door of the porter's lodge.

"Is Zorzi awake?" Marietta asked in a low tone, when both had gone a few steps down the corridor.

"Yes. He will sleep little tonight, for the boys have not come, and he must tend the fire himself."

Marietta guessed that her brother had given the order, so that Zorzi might be left quite alone.

"Pasquale," she said, "I can trust you, I am sure. You are a good friend to Zorzi."

The porter growled something incoherent, but she understood what he meant.

"Yes," she continued, "I trust you, and you must trust me. It is absolutely necessary that I should speak with Zorzi alone tonight. No one knows that I have left the house, and no one must know that I have been here."

The old sailor had seen much in his day, but he was profoundly astonished at Marietta's audacity.

"You are the mistress," he said in a grave and quiet voice that Marietta had never heard before. "But I am an old man, and I cannot help telling you that it is not seemly for a young girl to be alone at night with a young man, in the place where he lives. You will forgive me for saying so, because I have served your father a long time."

"You are quite right," answered Marietta. "But in matters of life and death there is nothing seemly or unseemly. I have not time to explain all this. Zorzi is in great danger. For my father's sake I must warn him, and I cannot stay out long. Not even Nella must know that I am here. Be ready to let me out."

She almost ran down the corridor to the garden. The moon was already too low to shine upon the walk, but the beams silvered the higher leaves of the plane-tree, and all was clear and distinct. Even in her haste, she glanced at the place where she had so often sat, before her life had began to change.

There was a strong light in the laboratory and the window was open. She looked in and saw Zorzi sitting in the great chair, his head leaning back and his eyes closed. He was so pale and worn that, she felt a sharp pain as her eyes fell on his face. His crutch was beside him, and he seemed to be asleep. It was a pity to wake him, she thought, yet she could not lose time; she had lost too much already in talking with Pasquale.

"Zorzi!" She called him softly.

He started in his sleep, opened his eyes wide, and tried to spring up without his crutch, for he fancied himself in a dream. She had thrown back the drapery that covered her head and the bright light fell upon her face. It hurt her again to see how he staggered and put out his hand for his accustomed support.

"I am coming in," she said quietly. "Do not move, unless the door is locked."

She met him before he was half across the room. Instinctively she put out her hand to help him back to his chair. Then she understood that he did not need it, for he was much better now. She saw that he looked to the window, expecting to see Nella, and she smiled.

"I am alone," she said. "You see how I trust you. Only Pasquale knows that I am here. You must sit down, and I will sit beside you, for I have much to say."

He looked at her in silent wonder for a moment, happy beyond words to be with her, but very anxious as to the reasons which could have brought her to him at such an hour and quite alone. Her manner was so quiet and decided that it did not even occur to him to protest against her coming, and he sat down as she bade him, but on the bench, and she seated herself in the chair, turning in it so that she could see his face. They were near enough to speak in low tones.

"My brother Giovanni hates you," she began. "He means to ruin you, if he can, before my father comes home."

"I am not afraid of him," said Zorzi, speaking for the first time since she had entered. "Let him do his worst."

"You do not know what his worst is," answered Marietta, "and he has got Messer Jacopo Contarini to help him. You are surprised? Yes. My betrothed husband has promised to speak with his father against you, at once. You know that he is of the Council."

Zorzi's face expressed the utmost astonishment.

"Are you quite sure that it is Jacopo Contarini?" he asked, as if unable to believe what she said.

"Is it likely that I should be mistaken? My brother was with him this afternoon at the palace, our gondolier heard them talking on the stairs as they came down. He told Nella, and she has just told me. Giovanni heaped all sorts of abuse on you, and Messer Jacopo agreed with all he said. Then they spoke of arresting you and bringing you to justice, and they talked of the Council. After that Giovanni met the Governor of Murano and got into his gondola, and they talked in a low tone. My brother gave him a sealed document, and the Governor said that it should not be tonight, but tomorrow. That is all I know, but it is enough."

Zorzi half closed his eyes for a moment, in deep thought; and in a flash he understood that Contarini wished him out of the way, and was taking the first means that offered to get rid of him. To keep faith with such a man would be as foolish as to expect any faithfulness from him. Zorzi opened his eyes again, and looked at the face of the woman he loved. His oath to the society had stood between him and her, and he knew that it was no longer binding on him, since Jacopo Contarini was helping to send him to destruction. Yet now that it was gone, he saw also that it had been the least of the obstacles that made up the barrier.

"Of what do they accuse me?" he asked, after a moment's silence. "What can they prove against me?"

"I cannot tell. It matters very little. Do you understand? Tomorrow, if not tonight, the Governor's men will come here to arrest you, and if you have not escaped, you will be imprisoned and taken before the Council. They may accuse you of being involved in a conspiracy—they may torture you."

She shivered at the thought, and looked into his dark eyes with fear and pity. His lip curled a little disdainfully.

"Do you think that I shall run away?" he asked.

"You will not stay here, and let them arrest you!" cried Marietta anxiously.

"Your father left me here to take care of what belongs to him, and there is much that is valuable. I thank you very much for warning me, but I know what your brother means to do, and I shall not go away of my own accord. If he can have me taken off by force, he will come here alone and search the place. If he searches long enough, he may find what he wants."

"Is Paolo Godi's manuscript in this room?" asked Marietta quietly.

Zorzi stared at her in surprise.

"How did you know that your father left it with me?" he asked.

"He would not have entrusted it to any one else. That is natural. My brother wants it. Is that the reason why you will not escape? Or is there any other?"

"That is the principal reason," answered Zorzi. "Another is that there is valuable glass here, which your brother would take."

"Which he would steal," said Marietta bitterly. "But Pasquale can bury it in the garden after you are gone. The principal thing is the book. Give it to me. I will take care of it till my father comes back. Until then you must hide somewhere, for it is madness to stay here. Give me the book, and let me take it away at once."

"I cannot give it to you," Zorzi said, with a puzzled expression which Marietta did not understand.

"You do not trust me," she answered sadly.

He did not reply at once, for the words made no impression on him when he heard them. He trusted her altogether, but there was a material difficulty in the way. He remembered how long it had taken to hide the iron box under broken glass, and he knew how long it would take to get it out again. Marietta could not stay in the laboratory, late into the night, and yet if she did not take the box with her now, she might not be able to take it at all, since neither she nor Nella could have carried it to the house by day, without being seen.

Marietta rested her elbow on the arm of the big chair, and her hand supported her chin, in an attitude of thought, as she looked steadily at Zorzi's face, and her own was grave and sad.

"You never trusted me," she said presently. "Yet I have been a good friend to you, have I not?"

"A friend? Oh, much more than that!" Zorzi turned his eyes from her. "I trust you with all my heart."

She shook her head incredulously.

"If you trusted me, you would do what I ask," she said. "I have risked something to help you—perhaps to save your life—who knows? Do you know what would happen if my brother found me here alone with you? I should end my life in a convent. But if you will not save yourself, I might as well not have come."

"I would give you the book if I could," answered Zorzi. "But I cannot. It is hidden in such a way that it would take a long time to get it out. That is the simple truth. Your father and I had buried it here under the stones, but somehow your brother suspected that, and I have changed the hiding place. It took a whole morning to do it."

Still Marietta did not quite believe that he could not give it to her if he chose. It seemed as if there must always be a shadow between them, when they were together, always the beginning of a misunderstanding.

"Where is it?" she asked, after a moment's hesitation. "If you are in earnest you will tell me."

"It is better that you should know, in case anything happens to me," answered Zorzi. "It is buried in that big jar, in some three feet of broken glass. I had to take the glass out bit by bit, and put it all back again."

As Marietta looked at the jar, a little colour rose in her face again.

"Thank you," she said. "I know you trust me, now."

"I always have," he answered softly, "and I always shall, even when you are married to Jacopo Contarini."

"That is still far off. Let us not talk of it. You must get ready to leave this place before morning. You must take the skiff and get away to the mainland, if you can, for till my father comes you will not be safe in Venice."

"I shall not go away," said Zorzi firmly. "They may not try to arrest me after all."

"But they will, I know they will!" All her anxiety for him came back in a moment. "You must go at once! Zorzi, to please me—for my sake—leave tonight!"

"For your sake? There is nothing I would not do for your sake, except be a coward."

"But it is not cowardly!" pleaded Marietta. "There is nothing else to be done, and if my father could know what you risk by staying, he would tell you to go, as I do. Please, please, please—"

"I cannot," he answered stubbornly.

"Oh, Zorzi, if you have the least friendship for me, do what I ask! Do you not see that I am half mad with anxiety? I entreat you, I beg you, I implore you—"

Their eyes met, and hers were wide with fear for him, and earnestness, and they were not quite dry.

"Do you care so much?" asked Zorzi, hardly knowing what he said. "Does it matter so much to you what becomes of me?"

He moved nearer on the bench. Leaning towards her, where he sat, he could rest his elbow on the broad arm of the low chair, and so look into her face. She covered her eyes, and shook a little, and her mantle slipped from her shoulders and trembled as it settled down into the chair. He leaned farther, till he was close to her, and he tried to uncover her eyes, very gently, but she resisted. His heart beat slowly and hard, like strokes of a hammer, and his hands were shaking, when he drew her nearer. Presently he himself sat upon the arm of the chair, holding her close to him, and she let him press her head to his breast, for she could not think any more; and all at once her hands slipped down and she was resting in the hollow of his arm, looking up to his face.

It seemed a long time, as long as whole years, since she had meant to drop another rose in his path, or even since she had suffered him to press her hand for a moment. The whole tale was told now, in one touch, in one look, with little resistance and less fear.

"I love you," he said slowly and earnestly, and the words were strange to his own ears.

For he had never said them before, nor had she ever heard them, and when they are spoken in that way they are the most wonderful words in the world, both to speak and to hear.

The look he had so rarely seen was there now, and there was no care to hide what was in her eyes, for she had told him all, without a word, as women can.

"I have loved you very long," he said again, and with one hand he pressed back her hair and smoothed it.

"I know it," she answered, gazing at him with lips just parted. "But I have loved you longer still."

"How could I guess it?" he asked. "It seems so wonderful, so very strange!"

"I could not say it first." She smiled. "And yet I tried to tell you without words."

"Did you?"

She nodded as her head lay in his arm, and closed her smiling lips tightly, and nodded again.

"You would not understand," she said. "You always made it hard for me."

"Oh, if I had only known!"

She lay quietly on his arm for a few seconds, and neither spoke. Only the low roar of the furnace was heard in the hot stillness. Marietta looked up steadily into his face, with unwinking eyes.

"How you look at me!" he said, with a happy smile.

"I have often wanted to look at you like this," she answered gravely. "But until you had told me, how could I?"

He bent down rather timidly, but drawn to her by a power he could not resist. His first kiss touched her forehead lightly, with a sort of boyish reverence, while a thrill ran through every nerve and fibre of his body. But she turned in his arms and threw her own suddenly round his neck, and in an instant their lips met.

Zorzi was in a dream, where Marietta alone was real. All thought and recollection of danger vanished, the very room was not the laboratory where he had so long lived and worked, and thought and suffered. The walls were gold, the stone pavement was a silken carpet, the shadowy smoke-stained beams were the carved ceiling of a palace, he was himself the king and master of the whole world, and he held all his kingdom in his arms.

"You understand now," Marietta said at last, holding his face before her with her hands.

"No," he answered lovingly. "I do not understand, I will not even try. If I do, I shall open my eyes, and it will suddenly be daylight, and I shall put out my hands and find nothing! I shall be alone, in my room, just awake and aching with a horrible longing for the impossible. You do not know what it is to dream of you, and wake in the grey dawn! You cannot guess what the emptiness is, the loneliness!"

"I know it well," said Marietta. "I have been perfectly happy, talking to you under the plane-tree, your hand in mine, and mine in yours, our eyes in each other's eyes, our hearts one heart! And then, all at once, there was Nella, standing at the foot of my bed with a big dish in her hands, laughing at me because I had been sleeping so soundly! Oh, sometimes I could kill her for waking me!"

She drew his face to hers, with a little laugh that broke off short. For a kiss is a grave matter.

"How much time we have wasted in all these months!" she said presently. "Why would you never understand?"

"How could I guess that you could ever love me?" Zorzi asked.

"I guessed that you loved me," objected Marietta. "At least," she added, correcting herself, "I was quite sure of it for a little while. Then I did not believe it all. If I had believed it quite, they should never have betrothed me to Jacopo Contarini!"

The name recalled all realities to Zorzi, though she spoke it very carelessly, almost with scorn. Zorzi sighed and looked up at last, and stared at the wall opposite.

"What is it?" asked Marietta quickly. "Why do you sigh?"

"There is reason enough. Are you not betrothed to him, as you say?"

Marietta straightened herself suddenly, and made him look at her. A quick light was in her eyes, as she spoke.

"Do you know what you are saying? Do you think that if I meant to marry Messer Jacopo, I should be here now, that I should let you hold me in your arms, that I would kiss you? Do you really believe that?"

"I could not believe it," Zorzi answered. "And yet—"

"And yet you almost do!" she cried. "What more do you need, to know that I love you, with all my heart and soul and will, and that I mean to be your wife, come what may?"

"How is it possible?" asked Zorzi almost disconsolately. "How could you ever marry me? What am I, after all, compared with you? I am not even a Venetian! I am a stranger, a waif, a man with neither name nor fortune! And I am half a cripple, lame for life! How can you marry me? At the first word of such a thing your father will join his son against me, I shall be thrown into prison on some false charge and shall never come out again, unless it be to be hanged for some crime I never committed."

"There is a very simple way of preventing all those dreadful things," answered Marietta.

"I wish I could find it."

"Take me with you," she said calmly.

Zorzi looked at her in dumb surprise, for she could not have said anything which he had expected less.

"Listen to me," she continued. "You cannot stay here—or rather, you shall not, for I will not let you. No, you need not smile and shake your head, for I will find some means of making you go."

"You will find that hard, dear love, for that is the only thing I will not do for you."

"Is it? We shall see. You are very brave, and you are very, very obstinate, but you are not very sensible, for you are only a man, after all. In the first place, do you imagine that even if Giovanni were to spend a whole week in this room, he would think of looking for the box amongst the broken glass?"

"No, I do not think he would," answered Zorzi. "That was sensible of me, at all events." She laughed.

"Oh, you are clever enough! I never said that you were not that. I only said that you had no sense. As for instance, since you are sure that my brother cannot find the box, why do you wish to stay here?"

"I promised your father that I would. I will keep my promise, at all costs."

"In which of two ways shall you be of more use to my father? If you hide in a safe place till he comes home, and if you then come back to him and help him as before? Or if you allow yourself to be thrown into prison, and tried, and perhaps hanged or banished, for something you never did? And if any harm comes to you, what do you think would become of me? Do you see? I told you that you had no common sense. Now you will believe me. But if all this is not enough to make you go, I have another plan, which you cannot possibly oppose."

"What is that?" asked Zorzi.

"I will go alone. I will cross the bridge, and take the skiff, and row myself over to Venice and from Venice I will get to the mainland."

"You could not row the skiff," objected Zorzi, amused at the idea. "You would fall off, or upset her."

"Then I should drown," returned Marietta philosophically. "And you would be sorry, whether you thought it was your fault or not. Is that true?"

"Yes."

"Very well. If you will not promise me faithfully to escape to the mainland tonight, I swear to you by all that you and I believe in, and most of all by our love for each other, that I will do what I said, and run away from my father's house, tonight. But you will not let me go alone, will you?"

"No!"

"There! You see! Of course you would not let me go alone, me, a poor weak girl, who have never taken a step alone in my life, until tonight! And they say that the world is so wicked! What would become of me if you let me go away alone?"

"If I thought you meant to do that!"

He laughed again, and drew her to him, and would have kissed her; but she held him back and looked at him earnestly.

"I mean it," she said. "That is what I will do. I swear that I will. Yes—now you may."

And she kissed him of her own accord, but quickly withdrew herself from his arms again.

"You have your choice," she said, "and you must choose quickly, for I have been here too long—it must be nearly half an hour since I left my room, and Nella is waiting for me, thinking that I am with my brother and his wife. Promise me to do what I ask, and I will go back, and when my father comes home I will tell him the whole troth. That is the wisest thing, after all. Or, I will go with you, if you will take me as I am."

"No," he answered, with an effort. "I will not take you with me."

It cost him a hard struggle to refuse. There she was, resting against his arm, in the blush and wealth of unspent love, asking to go with him, who loved her better than his life. But in a quick vision he saw her with him, she who was delicately nurtured and used from childhood to all that care and money could give, he saw her with him, sharing his misery, his hunger and his wandering, suffering silently for love's sake, but suffering much, and he could not bear the fancied sight.

"I should be in your way," she said. "Besides, they would send all over Italy to find me."

"It is not that," he answered. "You might starve."

She looked up anxiously to his face.

"And you?" she asked. "Have you no money?"

"No. How should I have money? I believe I have one piece of gold and a little silver. It will be enough to keep me from starvation till I can get work somewhere. I can live on bread and water, as I have many a time."

"If I had only thought!" exclaimed Marietta. "I have so much! My father left me a little purse of gold that I shall never need."

"I would not take your father's money," answered Zorzi. "But have no fear. If I go at all, I shall do well enough. Besides, there is a man in Venice—" He stopped short, not wishing to speak of Zuan Venier.

"You must not make any condition," she answered, not heeding the unfinished sentence. "You must go at once."

She rose as she spoke.

"Every minute I stay here makes it more dangerous for me to go back," she said. "I know that you will keep your promise. We must say good-bye."

He had risen, too, and stood facing her, his crutch under his arm. In all her anxiety for his safety she had half forgotten that his wound was barely healed, and that he still walked with great difficulty. And now, at the thought of leaving him she forgot everything else. They had been so cruelly short, those few minutes of perfect happiness between the long misunderstanding that had kept them apart and the parting again that was to separate them, perhaps for months. As they looked at each other, they both grew pale, and in an instant Zorzi's young face looked haggard and his eyes seemed to grow hollow, while Marietta's filled with tears.

"Good-bye!" she cried in a broken voice. "God keep you, my dear love!"

Then her face was buried in the hollow of his shoulder and her tears flowed fast and burning hot.

CHAPTER XVII

It was over at last, and Zorzi stood alone by the table, for Marietta would not let him go with her to the door. She could not trust herself before Pasquale, even in the gloom. He stood by the table, leaning on it heavily with one hand, and trying to realise all that had come into his lonely life within the half hour, and all that might happen to him before morning. The glorious and triumphant certainty which first love brings to every man when it is first returned, still swelled his heart and filled the air he breathed, so that while breathing deep, he could not breathe enough. In such a mood all dangers dwindled, all obstacles sank out of sight as shadows sink at dawn. And yet the parting had hurt him, as if his body had been wrenched in the middle by some resistless force.

Women feel parting differently. Shall we men ever understand them? To a man, first love is a victory, to a girl it is a sweet wonder, and a joy, and a tender longing, all in one. And when partings come, as come they must in life until death brings the last, it is always the man who leaves, and the woman who is left, even though in plain fact it be the man that stays behind; and we men feel a little contemptuous pity for one who seems to cry out after the woman he loves, asking why she has left him, and beseeching her to come back to him, but our compassion for the woman in like case is always sincere. In such small things there are the great mysteries of that prime difference, which neither man nor woman can ever fully understand, but which, if not understood a little, is the cause of much miserable misunderstanding in life.

Zorzi had to face the future at once, for it was upon him, and the old life was over, perhaps never to come again. He stood still, where he was, for any useless movement was an effort, and he tried to collect his thoughts and determine just what he should do, and how it was to be done. His eye fell on the piece of gold Giovanni had paid for the beaker. In the morning, if he drew the iron tray further down the annealing oven, the glass would be ready to be taken out, and Giovanni could take it if he pleased, for he knew whose it was. But starvation itself could not have induced Zorzi to take the money now. He turned from it with contempt. All he needed was enough to buy bread for a week, and mere bread cost little. That little he had, and it must suffice.

Besides that he would make a bundle small enough to be easily carried. His chief difficulty would be in rowing the skiff. To use the single oar at all it was almost indispensable to stand, and to stand chiefly on the right foot, since the single rowlock, as in every Venetian boat, was on the starboard side and could not be shifted to port. He fancied that in some way he could manage to sit on the thwart, and use the oar as a paddle. In any case he must get away, since flight was the wisest course, and since he had promised Marietta that he would go. His reflections had occupied scarce half a minute.

He began to walk towards the small room where he slept, and where he kept his few possessions. He had taken two steps from the table, when he stopped short, turned round and listened.

He heard the sound of light footsteps, running along the path and coming nearer. In another moment Marietta was at the window, her face deadly white, her eyes wide with fear.

"They are there!" she cried wildly. "They have come tonight! Hide yourself quickly! Pasquale will keep them out as long as he can."

She had found Pasquale stoutly refusing to open the door. Outside stood a lieutenant of the archers with half a dozen men, demanding admittance in the name of the Governor. Pasquale answered that they might get in by force if they could, but that he had no orders to open the door to them. The lieutenant was in doubt whether his warrant authorised him to break in or not.

Zorzi knew that Marietta was in even more danger than he. The situation was desperate and the time short. She was still at the window, looking in.

"You know your way to the main furnace rooms," Zorzi said quickly, but with great coolness. "Run in there, and stand still in the dark till everything is quiet. Then slip out and get home as quickly as possible."

"But you? What will become of you?" asked Marietta in an agony of anxiety.

"If they do not take me at once, they will search all the buildings and will find you," answered Zorzi. "I will go and meet them, while you are hiding."

He opened the door beside the window and put his crutch forward upon the path. At the same moment the sound of a tremendous blow echoed down the dark corridor. The moon was low but had not set and there was still light in the garden.

"Quickly!" Zorzi exclaimed. "They are breaking down the door."

But Marietta clung to him almost savagely, when he tried to push her in the direction of the main furnace rooms on the other side of the garden.

"I will not leave you," she cried. "They shall take me with you, wherever you are going!"

She grasped his hand with both her hands, and then, as he moved, she slipped her arm round him. At the street door the pounding blows succeeded each other in quick succession, but apparently without effect.

Zorzi saw that he must make her understand her extreme danger. He took hold of her wrist with a quiet strength that recalled her to herself, and there was a tone of command in his voice when he spoke.

"Go at once," he said. "It will be worse for both of us if you are found here. They will hang me for stealing the master's daughter as well as his secrets. Go, dear love, go! Good-bye!"

He kissed her once, and then gently pushed her from him. She understood that she must obey, and that if he spoke of his own danger it was for the sake of her good name. With a gesture of despair she turned and left him, crossed the patch of light without looking back, and disappeared into the shadows beyond. She was safe now, for he would go and meet the archers, opening the door to give himself up. Using his crutch he swung himself along into the dark corridor without another moment's hesitation.

But matters did not turn out as he expected. When the force came down the footway from the dilution of San Piero, Giovanni was still talking to his wife about household economies and censuring what he called the reckless extravagance of his father's housekeeping. As he talked, he heard the even tread of a number of marching men. He sprang to his feet and went to the window, for he guessed who was coming, though he could not imagine why the Governor had not waited till the next day, as had been agreed. He could not know that on leaving him Jacopo Contarini had seen his father and had told him of Zorzi's misdeeds; and that the Governor had supped with old Contarini, who was an uncompromising champion of the law, besides being one of the Ten and therefore the Governor's superior in office; and that Contarini had advised that Zorzi should be taken on that same night, as he might be warned of his danger and find means to escape. Moreover, Contarini offered a trusty and swift oarsman to take the order to Murano, and the Governor wrote it on the supper table, between two draughts of Greek wine, which he drank from a goblet made by Angelo Beroviero himself in the days when he still worked at the art.

In half an hour the warrant was in the hands of the officer, who immediately called out half-a-dozen of his men and marched them down to the glass-house.

Giovanni saw them stop and knock at the door, and he heard Pasquale's gruff inquiry.

"In the Governor's name, open at once!" said the officer.

"Any one can say that," answered the porter. "In the devil's name go home and go to bed! Is this carnival time, to go masquerading by the light of the moon and waking up honest people?"

"Silence!" roared the lieutenant. "Open the door, or it will be the worse for you."

"It will be the worse for you, if the Signor Giovanni hears this disturbance," answered Pasquale, who could see Giovanni at the window opposite in the moonlight. "Either get orders from him, or go home and leave me in holy peace, you band of braying jackasses, you mob of blobber-lipped Barbary apes, you pack of doltish, droiling, doddered joltheads! Be off!"

This eloquence, combined with Pasquale's assured manner, caused the lieutenant to hesitate before breaking down the door, an operation for which he had not been prepared, and for which he had brought no engines of battery.

"Can you get in?" he inquired of his men, without deigning to answer the porter's invectives. "If not, let one of you go for a sledge hammer. Try it with the butts of your halberds against the lock, one, two, three and all at once."

"Oh, break down the door!" cried Pasquale derisively. "It is of oak and iron, and it cost good money, and you shall pay for it, you lubberly ours."

But the men pounded away with a good will.

"Open the door!" cried Giovanni from the opposite window, at the top of his lungs.

The sight of the destruction of property for which he might have to account to his father was very painful to him. But he could not make himself heard in the terrific din, or else Pasquale suspected the truth and pretended that he could not hear. The porter had seen Marietta a moment in the gloom, and he knew that she had gone back to warn Zorzi. He hoped to give them both time to hide themselves, and he now retired from the grating and began to strengthen the door, first by putting two more heavy oak bars in their places across it near the top and bottom, and further by bringing the scanty furniture from his lodge and piling it up against the panels.

Meanwhile the pounding continued at a great rate, and Giovanni thought it better to go down and interfere in person, since he could not make himself heard. The servants were all roused by this time, and many heads were looking out of upper windows, not only from Beroviero's house, but from the houses higher up, beyond the wooden bridge. Two men who were walking up the footway from the opposite direction stopped at a little distance and looked on, their hoods drawn over their eyes.

Giovanni came out hurriedly and crossed the bridge. He laid his hand on the lieutenant's shoulder anxiously and spoke close to his ear, for the pounding was deafening. The six men had strapped their halberds firmly together in a solid bundle with their belts, and standing three on each side they swung the whole mass of wood and iron like a battering ram, in regular time.

"Stop them, sir! Stop them, pray!" cried Giovanni. "I will have the door opened for you."

Suddenly there was silence as the officer caught one of his men by the arm and bade them all wait.

"Who are you, sir?" he inquired.

"I am Giovanni Beroviero," answered Giovanni, sure that his name would inspire respect.

The officer took off his cap politely and then replaced it. The two men who were looking on nudged each other.

"I have a warrant to arrest a certain Zorzi," began the lieutenant.

"I know! It is quite right, and he is within," answered Giovanni. "Pasquale!" he called, standing on tiptoe under the grating. "Pasquale! Open the door at once for these gentlemen."

"Gentlemen!" echoed one of the men softly, with a low laugh and digging his elbow into his companion's side.

No one else spoke for a moment. Then Pasquale looked through the grating.

"What did you say?" he asked.

"I said open the door at once!" answered Giovanni. "Can you not recognise the officers of the law when you see them?"

"No," grunted Pasquale, "I have never seen much of them. Did you say I was to open the door?"

"Yes!" cried Giovanni angrily, for he wished to show his zeal before the officer. "Blockhead!" he added with emphasis, as Pasquale disappeared again and was presumably out of hearing.

They all heard him dragging the furniture away again, the box-bed and the table and the old chair.

Zorzi came up as Pasquale was clearing the stuff away.

"They want you," said the old sailor, seeing him and hearing him at the same time. "What have you been doing now? Where is the young lady?"

"In the main furnace room," whispered Zorzi. "Do not let them go there whatever they do."

Pasquale gave vent to his feelings in a low voice, as he dragged the last things back and began to unbar the door. Zorzi leaned against the wall, for his lameness prevented him from helping. At last the door was opened, and he saw the figures of the men outside against the light. He went forward as quickly as he could, pushing past Pasquale to get out. He stood on the threshold, leaning on his crutch.

"I am Zorzi," he said quietly.

"Zorzi the Dalmatian, called the Ballarin?" asked the lieutenant.

"Yes, yes!" cried Giovanni, anxious to hasten matters, "They call him the dancer because he is lame. This is that foreign liar, that thief, that assassin! Take him quickly!"

The archers, who in the changes of time had become halberdiers, had dropped the bundle of spears they had made for a battering-ram. Two of them took Zorzi by the arms roughly, and prepared to drag him along with them. He made no resistance, but objected quietly.

"I can walk better, if you do not hold me," he said. "I cannot run away, as you see."

"Let him walk between you," ordered the officer. "Good night, sir," he said to Giovanni.

Two of the men lifted the bundle of halberds and began to carry it between them, trying to undo the straps as they walked, for they could not stay behind. Giovanni saluted the officer and stood aside for the party to pass. The two men who had looked on had separated, and one had already gone forward and disappeared beyond the bridge. The other lingered, apparently still interested in the proceedings. Pasquale, dumb with rage at last, stood in the doorway.

"Let me pass," said Giovanni, as soon as the archers had gone on a few steps, surrounding Zorzi.

With a growl, Pasquale came out and stood on the pavement a moment, and Giovanni went in. Instantly, the man who had lingered made a step towards the porter, whispered something in his ear, and then made off as fast as he could in the direction taken by the archers. Pasquale looked after him in surprise, only half understanding the meaning of what he had said. Then he went in, but left the door ajar. The people who had been looking out of the windows of Beroviero's house had disappeared, when they had seen that Giovanni was on the footway. All was silent now; only, far off, the tramp of the archers could still be heard.

They could not go very fast, with Zorzi in their midst, but the two men who were busy unfastening the bundle of halberds lagged in the rear, talking in a low voice. They did not notice quick footsteps behind them, but they heard a low whistle, answered instantly by another, just as the main party was nearing the corner by the church of San Piero. That was the last the two loiterers remembered, for at the next instant they lay in a heap upon the halberds, which had fallen upon the pavement with a tremendous clatter. A couple of well-delivered blows with a stout stick had thoroughly stunned them almost at the same instant. It would be some time before they recovered their senses.

While the man who had whispered to Pasquale was doing effectual work in the rear, his companion was boldly attacking the main party in front. As the lieutenant stopped short and turned his head when the halberds dropped, a blow under the jaw from a fist like a sledge hammer almost lifted him off his feet and sent him reeling till he fell senseless, half a dozen paces away. Before the two archers who were guarding Zorzi could defend themselves, unarmed as they were, another blow had felled one of them. The second, springing forward, was caught up like a child by his terrible assailant and whirled through the air, to fall with a noisy splash into the shallow waters of the canal. The other companion attacked the remaining two from behind with his club and knocked one of them down. The last sprang to one side and ran on a few steps as fast as he could. But swifter feet followed him, and in an instant iron fingers were clutching his throat and squeezing his breath out. He struggled a moment, and then sank down. His captor deliberately knocked him on the head with his fist, and he rolled over like a stone.

Utterly bewildered, Zorzi stood still, where he had stopped. Never in his life had he dreamed that two men could dispose of seven, in something like half a minute, with nothing but a stick for a weapon between them. But he had seen it with his eyes, and he was not surprised when he felt himself lifted from his feet, with his crutch beside him, and carried along the footway at a sharp run, in the direction of the glass-house. His reason told him that he had been rescued and was being quickly conveyed to a place of safety, but he could not help distrusting the means that accomplished the end, for he had unconsciously watched the two men in what could hardly be called a fight, though he could not see their faces, and a more murderous pair of ruffians he had never seen. Men not well used to such deeds could not have done them at all, thought Zorzi, as he was borne along, his breath almost shaken out of him by the strong man's movements.

All was quiet, as they passed the glass-house, and no one was looking out, for Giovanni's wife feared him far too much to seem to be spying upon his doings, and the servants were discreet. Only Nella, hiding behind the flowers in Marietta's window, and supposing that Marietta was with her sister-in-law, was watching the door of the glass-house to see when Giovanni would come out. She now heard the steps of the two men, running down the footway. The rescue had taken place too far away for her to hear anything but a splash in the canal. She saw that one of the men was carrying what seemed to be the body of a man. She instinctively crossed herself, as they ran on towards the end of the canal, and when she could see them no longer in the shadow, she drew back into the room, momentarily forgetting Giovanni, and already running over in her head the wonderful conversation she was going to have with her mistress as soon as the young girl came back to her room.

Pasquale, meanwhile, withdrew his feet from the old leathern slippers he wore, and noiselessly stole down the corridor and along the garden path, to find out what Giovanni was doing. When he came to the laboratory, he saw that the window was now shut, as well as the door, and that Giovanni had set the lamp on the floor behind the further end of the annealing oven. Its bright light shot upwards to the dark ceiling, leaving the front of the laboratory almost in the dark. Pasquale listened and he heard the sharp tapping of a hammer on stone. He understood at once that Giovanni had shut himself in to search for something, and would therefore be busy some time.

Without noise he crossed the garden to the entrance of the main furnace room and went into the passage.

"Come out quickly!" he whispered, as his seaman's eyes made out Marietta's figure in a gloom that would have been total darkness to a landsman; and he took hold of the girl's arm to lead her away.

"Your brother is in the laboratory, and will not come out," he whispered. "By this time Zorzi may be safe."

"Safe!" She spoke the word aloud, in her relief.

"Hush, for heaven's sake. The door is open. You can get home now without being seen. Make no noise."

She followed him quickly. They had to cross the patch of dim light in the garden, and she glanced at the closed window of the laboratory. It had all happened as Zorzi had foreseen, and Giovanni was already searching for the manuscript. The only thing she could not understand was that Zorzi should have escaped the archers. Even as she crossed the garden, the two man were passing the door, bearing Zorzi he knew not where, but away from the nearest danger. A moment later she was on the footway, hurrying towards the bridge. Pasquale stood watching her, to be sure that she was safe, and he glanced up at the windows, too, fearing lest some one might still be looking out.

But chance had saved Marietta this time. She carefully barred the side door after she had gone in, and groped her way up the dark stairs. On the landing there was light from below, and she paused for breath, her bosom heaving as she leaned a moment on the balustrade. She passed one hand over her brows, as if to bring herself back to present consciousness, and then went quickly on.

"Safe," she repeated under her breath as she went, "safe, safe, safe!"

It was to give herself courage, for she could hardly believe it, though she knew that Pasquale would not deceive her and must have some strong good reason for what he said. There had not been time to question him.

All he knew himself was that a man whose face he could not see had whispered to him that Zorzi was in no danger. But he had recognised the other man who had gone up the footway first, in spite of his short cloak and hood, and he felt well assured that Charalambos Aristarchi could throw the officer and his six men into the canal without anybody's help, if he chose, though why the Greek ruffian was suddenly inspired to interfere on Zorzi's behalf was a mystery past his comprehension.

Marietta entered her room, and Nella, who had been revelling in the coming conversation, was suddenly very busy, stirring the drink of lime flowers which Marietta had ordered. She was so sure that her mistress had been all the time in the house, and so anxious not to have it thought that she could possibly have been idle, even for a moment, that she looked intently into the cup and stirred the contents in a most conscientious manner. Marietta turned from her almost immediately and began to undo the braids of hair, that Nella might comb it out and plait it again for the night. Nella immediately began to talk, and to tell all that she had seen from the window, with many other things which she had not seen.

"But of course you were looking out, too," she said presently. "They were all at the windows for some time."

"No," Marietta answered. "I was not looking out."

"Well, it was tonight, and not tomorrow, you see. Do you think the Governor is stupid? If he had waited till tomorrow, we should have told Zorzi. Poor Zorzi! I saw them taking him away, loaded with chains."

"In chains!" cried Marietta, starting painfully.

"I could not see the chains," continued Nella apologetically, "but I am sure they were there. It was too dark to see. Poor Zorzi! Poor Zorzi! By this time he is in the prison under the Governor's house, and he wishes that he had never been born. A little straw, a little water! That is all he has."

Marietta moved in her chair, as if something hurt her, but she knew that it would be unwise to stop the woman's talk. Besides, Nella was evidently sorry for Zorzi, though she thought his arrest very interesting. She went on for a long time, combing more and more slowly, after the manner of talkative maids, when they fear that their work may be finished before their story. But for Pasquale's reassuring words, Marietta felt that she must have gone mad. Zorzi was safe, somewhere, and he was not in the Governor's prison, on the straw. She told herself so again and again as Nella went on.

"There is one thing I did not tell you," said the latter, with a sudden increase of vigour at the thought.

"I think you have told me enough, Nella," said Marietta wearily. "I am very tired."

"You cannot go to bed till I have plaited your hair," answered Nella mercilessly, but at the same time laying down the comb. "Just before you came in, I was looking out of the window. It was just an accident, for I was very busy with your things, of course. Well, as I was saying, in passing I happened to glance out of the window, and I saw—guess what I saw, my pretty lady!"

Marietta trembled, thinking that Nella had seen her, and perhaps recognised her, and was about to bring her garrulous tale to a dramatic climax by telling her so.

"Perhaps you saw a woman," she suggested desperately.

"A woman indeed!" cried Nella. "That must be a nice woman who would be seen in the street at such a time of night, and the Governor's archers there, too! Woman? I would not look at such a woman, I tell you! No. What I saw was this, since you cannot guess. There came two big men, running fast, and they were carrying a dead body between them! Eh! They were at no good, I tell you. One could see that."

Marietta could bear no more, now. She bent her head and bit her finger to keep herself from crying out.

"If you will not be still, how in the world am I to plait your hair?" asked Nella querulously.

"Do it quickly, please," Marietta succeeded in saying. "I am so very tired tonight."

Her head bent still further forward.

"Indeed," said Nella, much annoyed that her tale should not have been received with more interest, "you seem to be half asleep already."

But Nella was much too truly attached to her mistress not to feel some anxiety when she saw her white face and noticed how uncertainly she walked. Nella had her in bed at last, however, and gave her more of the soothing drink, smoothed the cool pillow under her head, looked round the room to see that all was in order before going away, then took the lamp and at last went out.

"Good night, my pretty lady," said Nella cheerfully from the door, "good rest and pleasant dreams!"

She was gone at last, and she would not come back before morning.

Marietta sat up in bed in the dark and pressed her hands to her temples in utter despair.

"I shall go mad! I shall go mad!" she whispered to herself.

She remembered that she had left her light silk mantle in the laboratory, on the great chair.

CHAPTER XVIII

Aristarchi's interference to rescue Zorzi had not been disinterested, and so far as justice was concerned he was quite ready to believe that the Dalmatian had done all the things of which he was accused. The fact was not of the slightest importance in the situation. It was much more to the point that in the complicated and dangerous plan which the Greek captain and Arisa were carrying out, Zorzi could be of use to them, without his own knowledge. As has been told, the two had decided that he was in love with Marietta, and she with him. The rest followed naturally.

After meeting his father and telling him Giovanni's story, Jacopo Contarini had gone to the house of the Agnus Dei for an hour, and during that time he had told Arisa everything, according to his wont. No sooner was he gone than Arisa made the accustomed signal and Aristarchi appeared at her window, for it was then already night. He judged rightly that there was no time to be lost, and having stopped at his house to take his trusted man, the two rowed themselves over to Murano, and were watching the glass-house from, a distance, fully half an hour before the archers appeared.

The officer and his men came to their senses, one by one, bruised and terrified. The man who had been thrown into the shallow canal got upon his feet, standing up to his waist in the water, sputtering and coughing from the ducking. Before he tried to gain the shore, he crossed himself three times and repeated all the prayers he could remember, in a great hurry, for he was of opinion that Satan must still be in the neighbourhood. It was not possible that any earthly being should have picked him up like a puppy and flung him fully ten feet from the spot where he had been standing. He struggled to the bank, his feet sinking at each step in the slimy bottom; and after that he was forced to wade some thirty yards to the stairs in front of San Piero before he could get out of the water, a miserable object, drenched from head to foot and coated with black mud from his knees down. Yet he was in a better case than his companions.

They came to themselves slowly, the officer last of all, for Aristarchi's blow under the jaw had nearly killed him, whereas the other five men had only received stunning blows on different parts of their thick skulls. In half an hour they were all on their feet, though some of them were very unsteady, and in a forlorn train they made the best of their way back to the Governor's palace. Their discomfiture had been so sudden and complete that none of them had any idea as to the number of their assailants; but most of them agreed that as they came within sight of the church, Zorzi had slackened his pace, and that an unholy fire had issued from his eyes, his mouth and his nostrils, while he made strange signs in the air with his crutch, and suddenly grew to a gigantic stature. The devils who were his companions had immediately appeared in great numbers, and though the archers had fought against their supernatural adversaries with the courage of heroes, they had been struck down senseless where they stood; and when they had recovered their sight and their other understanding, Zorzi had long since vanished to the kingdom of darkness which was his natural abode.

Those things the officer told the Governor on the next day, and the men solemnly swore to them, and they were all written down by the official scribe. But the Governor raised one eyebrow a little, and the corners of his mouth twitched strangely, though he made no remark upon what had been said. He remembered, however, that Giovanni had advised him to send a very strong force to arrest the lame young man, from which he argued that Zorzi had powerful friends, and that Giovanni knew it. He then visited the scene of the fight, and saw that there were drops of blood on dry stones, which was not astonishing and which gave no clue whatever to the identity of the rescuers. He pointed out quietly to his guide, the man who had only received a ducking, that there were no signs of fire on the pavement nor on the walls of the houses, which was a strong argument against any theory of diabolical intervention; and this the man was reluctantly obliged to admit. The strangest thing, however, was that the people who lived near by seemed to have heard no noise, though one old man, who slept badly, believed that he had heard the clatter of wood and iron falling together, and then a splashing in the canal; and indeed those were almost the only sounds that had disturbed the night. The whole affair was shrouded in mystery, and the Governor, who knew that his men were to be trusted as far as their limited intelligence could go, resolved to refer the matter to the Council of Ten without delay. He therefore bade the archers hold their tongues and refuse to talk of their misadventure.

On that night Giovanni had suffered the greatest disappointment he remembered in his whole life. He had found without much trouble the stone that rang hollow, but it had cost him great pains to lift it, and the sweat ran down from his forehead and dropped upon the slab as he slowly got it up. His heart beat so that he fancied he could hear it, both from the effort he made, and from his intense excitement, now that the thing he had most desired in the world was within his grasp. At last the big stone was raised upright, and the light of the lamp that stood on the floor fell slanting across the dark hole. Giovanni brought the lamp to the edge and looked in. He could not see the box, but a quantity of loose earth lay there, under which it was doubtless buried. He knelt down and began to scoop the earth out, using his two hands together. Then he thrust one hand in, and felt about for the box. There was nothing there. He cleared out the cavity thoroughly, and tried to loosen the soil at the bottom, tearing his nails in his excitement. It must be there, he was sure.

But it was not. When he realised that he had been tricked, he collapsed, kneeling as he was, and sat upon his heels, and his crooked hands all dark with the dusty earth clutched at the stones beside him. He remained thus a long time, staring at the empty hole. Then caution, which was even stronger in his nature than greed, brought him to himself. His thin face was grey and haggard as he carefully swept the earth back to its place, removing all traces of what he had done. Then he knew how foolish he had been to let Zorzi know what he had partly heard and partly guessed.

Of course, as soon as Zorzi understood that Giovanni had found out where the book was, he had taken it out and put it away in a safer place, to which Giovanni had no clue at all. Zorzi was diabolically clever, and would not have been so foolish as to hide the treasure again in the same room or in the same way. It was probably in the garden now, but it would take a strong man a day or two to dig up all the earth there to the depth at which the book must have been buried. Zorzi must have done the work at night, after the furnaces were out, and when there were no night boys to watch him. But then, the boys had been feeding the fires in the laboratory until the previous night, and it followed that he must have bailed the box this very evening.

Giovanni got the slab back into its place without injuring it, and he rubbed the edges with dust, and swept the place with a broom, as Zorzi had done twice already. Then he took the lamp and set it on the table before the window. The light fell on the gold piece that lay there. He took it, examined it carefully, and slipped it into his wallet with a sort of mechanical chuckle. He glanced at the furnace next, and recollected that the precious pieces Zorzi had made were in the annealing oven. But that did not matter, for the fires would now go out and the whole furnace would slowly cool, so that the annealing would be very perfect. No one but he could enter the laboratory, now that Zorzi was gone, and he could take the pieces to his own house at his leisure. They were substantial proofs of Zorzi's wickedness in breaking the laws of Venice, however, and it would perhaps be wiser to leave them where they were, until the Governor should take cognizance of their existence.

His first disappointment turned to redoubled hatred of the man who had caused it, and whom it was safer to hate now than formerly, since he was in the clutches of the law; moreover, the defeat of Giovanni's hopes was by no means final, after the first shock was over. He could make an excuse for having the garden dug over, on pretence of improving it during his father's absence; the more easily, as he had learned that the garden had always been under Zorzi's care, and must now be cultivated by some one else. Giovanni did not believe it possible that the precious box had been taken away altogether. It was therefore near, and he could find it, and there would be plenty of time before his father's return. Nevertheless, he looked about the laboratory and went into the small room where Zorzi had slept. There was water there, and Spanish soap, and he washed his hands carefully, and brushed the dust from his coat and from the knees of his fine black hose. He knew that his patient wife would be waiting for him when he went back to the house.

He searched Zorzi's room carefully, but could find nothing. An earthen jar containing broken white glass stood in one corner. The narrow truckle-bed, with its single thin mattress and flattened pillow, all neat and trim, could not have hidden anything. On a line stretched across from wall to wall a few clothes were hanging—a pair of disconsolate brown hose, the waistband on the one side of the line hanging down to meet the feet on the other, two clean shirts, and a Sunday doublet. On the wall a cap with a black eagle's feather hung by a nail. Here and there on the white plaster, Zorzi had roughly sketched with a bit of charcoal some pieces of glass which he had thought of making. That was all. The floor was paved with bricks, and a short examination showed that none of them had been moved.

Giovanni turned back into the laboratory, stood a moment looking disconsolately at the big stone which it had cost him so much fruitless labour to move, and then passed round by the other side of the furnace, along the wall against which the bench and the easy chair were placed. His eye fell on Marietta's silk mantle, which lay as when it had slipped down from her shoulders, the skirts of it trailing on the floor. His brows contracted suddenly. He came nearer, felt the stuff, and was sure that he recognised it. Then he looked at it, as it lay. It had the unmistakable appearance of having been left, as it had been, by the person who had last sat in the chair.

Two explanations of the presence of the mantle in the laboratory suggested themselves to him at once, but the idea that Marietta could herself have been seated in the chair not long ago was so absurd that he at once adopted the other. Zorzi had stolen the mantle, and used it for himself in the evening, confident that no one would see him. Tonight he had been surprised and had left it in the chair, another and perhaps a crowning proof of his atrocious crimes. Was he not a thief, as well as a liar and an assassin? Giovanni knew well enough that the law would distinguish between stealing the art of glass-making, which was merely a civil offence, though a grave one, and stealing a mantle of silk which he estimated to be worth at least two or three pieces of gold. That was theft, and it was criminal, and it was one of many crimes which Zorzi had undoubtedly committed. The hangman would twist the rest out of him with the rack and the iron boot, thought Giovanni gleefully. The Governor should see the mantle with his own eyes.

Before he went away, he was careful to fasten the window securely inside, and he locked the door after him, taking the key. He carried the brass lamp with him, for the corridor was very dark and the night was quite still.

Pasquale was seated on the edge of his box-bed in his little lodge when Giovanni came to the door. He was more like a big and very ugly watchdog crouching in his kennel than anything else.

"Let no one try to go into the laboratory," said Giovanni, setting down the lamp. "I have locked it myself."

Pasquale snarled something incomprehensible, by way of reply, and rose to let Giovanni out. He noticed that the latter had brought nothing but the lamp with him. When the door was open Pasquale looked across at the house, and saw that although there was still light in some of the other windows, Marietta's window was now dark. She was safe in bed, for Giovanni's search had occupied more than an hour.

Marietta might have breathed somewhat more freely if she had known that her brother did not even suspect her of having been to the laboratory, but the knowledge would have been more than balanced by a still greater anxiety if she had been told that Zorzi could be accused of a common theft.

She sat up in the dark and pressed her throbbing temples with her hands. She thought, if she thought at all, of getting up again and going back to the glass-house. Pasquale would let her in, of course, and she could get the mantle back. But there was Nella, in the next room, and Nella seemed to be always awake, and would hear her stirring and come in to know if she wanted anything. Besides, she was in the dark. The night light burned always in Nella's room, a tiny wick supported by a bit of split cork in an earthen cup of oil, most carefully tended, for if it went out, it could only be lighted by going down to the hall where a large lamp burned all night.

Marietta laid her head upon the pillow and tried to sleep, repeating over and over again to herself that Zorzi was safe. But for a long time the thought of the mantle haunted her. Giovanni had found it, of course, and had brought it back with him. In the morning he would send for her and demand an explanation, and she would have none to give. She would have to admit that she had been in the laboratory—it mattered little when—and that she had forgotten her mantle there. It would be useless to deny it.

Then all at once she looked the future in the face, and she saw a little light. She would refuse to answer Giovanni's questions, and when her father came back she would tell him everything. She would tell him bravely that nothing could make her marry Contarini, that she loved Zorzi and would marry him, or no one. The mantle would probably be forgotten in the angry discussion that would follow. She hoped so, for even her father would never forgive her for having gone alone at night to find Zorzi. If he ever found it out, he would make her spend the rest of her life in a convent, and it would break his heart that she should have thus cast all shame to the winds and brought disgrace on his old age. It never occurred to her that he could look upon it in any other way.

She dreaded to think of the weeks that might pass before he returned. He had spoken of making a long journey and she knew that he had gone southward to Rimini to please the great Sigismondo Malatesta, who had heard of Beroviero's stained glass windows and mosaics in Florence and Naples, and would not be outdone in the possession of beautiful things. But no one knew more than that. She was only sure that he would come back some time before her intended marriage, and there would still be time to break it off. The thought gave her some comfort, and toward morning she fell into an uneasy sleep. Of all who had played a part in that eventful night she slept the least, for she had the most at stake; her fair name, Zorzi's safety, her whole future life were in the balance, and she was sure that Giovanni would send for her in the morning.

She awoke weary and unrefreshed when the sun was already high. She scarcely had energy to clap her hands for Nella, and after the window was open she still lay listlessly on her pillow. The little woman looked at her rather anxiously but said nothing at first, setting the big dish with fruit and water on the table as usual, and busying herself with her mistress's clothes. She opened the great carved wardrobe, and she hung up some things and took out others, in a methodical way.

"Where is your silk mantle?" she asked suddenly, as she missed the garment from its accustomed place.

"I do not know," answered Marietta quite naturally, for she had expected the question.

Her reply was literally true, since she had every reason for believing that Giovanni had brought it back with him in the night, but could have no idea as to where he had put it. Nella began to search anxiously, turning over everything in the wardrobe and the few things that hung over the chairs.

"You could not have put it into the chest, could you?" she asked, pausing at the foot of the bed and looking at Marietta.

"No. I am sure I did not," answered the girl. "I never do."

"Then it has been stolen," said Nella, and her face darkened wrathfully.

"How is such a thing possible?" asked Marietta carelessly. "It must be somewhere."

This appeared to be certain, but Nella denied it with energy, her eyes fixed on Marietta almost as angrily as if she suspected her of having stolen her own mantle from herself.

"I tell you it is not," she replied. "I have looked everywhere. It has been stolen."

"Have you looked in your own room?" inquired Marietta indifferently, and turning her head on her pillow, as if she were tired of meeting Nella's eyes, as indeed she was.

"My own room indeed!" cried the maid indignantly. "As if I did not know what is in my own room! As if your new silk mantle could hide itself amongst my four rags!"

Why Nella and her kind, to this day, use the number four in contempt, rather than three or five, is a mystery of what one might call the psychical side of the Italian language. Marietta did not answer.

"It has been stolen," Nella repeated, with gloomy emphasis. "I trust no one in this house, since your brother and his wife have been here, with their servants."

"My sister-in-law was obliged to bring one of her women," objected Marietta.

"She need not have brought that sour-faced shrew, who walks about the house all day repeating the rosary and poking her long nose into what does not belong to her. But I am not afraid of the Signor Giovanni. I will tell the housekeeper that your mantle has been stolen, and all the women's belongings shall be searched before dinner, and we shall find the mantle in that evil person's box."

"You must do nothing of the sort," answered Marietta in a tone of authority.

She sat up in bed at last, and threw the thick braid of hair behind her, as every woman does when her hair is down, if she means to assert herself.

"Ah," cried Nella mockingly, "I see that you are content to lose your best things without looking for them! Then let us throw everything out of the window at once! We shall make a fine figure!"

"I will speak to my brother about it myself," said Marietta.

Indeed she thought it extremely likely that Giovanni would oblige her to speak of it within an hour.

"You will only make trouble among the servants," she added.

"Oh, as you please!" snorted Nella discontentedly. "I only tell you that I know who took it. That is all. Please to remember that I said so, when it is too late. And as for trouble, there is not one of us in the house who would not like to be searched for the sake of sending your sister-in-law's maid to prison, where she belongs!"

"Nella," said Marietta, "I do not care a straw about the mantle. I want you to do something very important. I am sure that Zorzi has been arrested unjustly, and I do not believe that the Governor will keep him in prison. Can you not get your friend the gondolier to go to the Governor's palace before midday, and ask whether Zorzi is to be let out?"

"Of course I can. By and by I will call him. He is busy cleaning the gondola now."

Marietta had spoken quite quietly, though she had expected that her voice would shake, and she had been almost sure that she was going to blush. But nothing so dreadful happened, though she had prepared for it by turning her back on Nella. She sat on the edge of the bed, slowly feeling her way into her little yellow leathern slippers. It was a relief to know that even now she could speak of Zorzi without giving any outward sign of emotion, and she felt a little encouraged, as she began the dreaded day.

She took a long time in dressing, for she expected at every moment that her sister-in-law's maid would knock at the door with a message from Giovanni, bidding her come to him before he went out. But no one came, though it was already past the hour at which he usually left the house. All at once she heard his unmistakable voice through the open window, and on looking out through the flowers she saw him standing at the open door of the glass-house, talking with the porter, or rather, giving instructions about the garden which Pasquale received in surly silence.

Marietta listened in surprise. It seemed impossible that Giovanni should not take her to task at once if he had found the mantle. He was not the kind of man to put off accusing any one when he had proof of guilt and was sure that the law was on his side, and Marietta felt sure that the evidence against her was overwhelming, for she had yet to learn what amazing things can be done with impunity by people who have the reputation of perfect innocence.

Giovanni was telling Pasquale, in a tone which every one might hear, that he had sent for a gardener, who would soon come with a lad to help him, that the two must be admitted at once, and that he himself would be within to receive them; but that no one else was to be allowed to go in, as he should be extremely busy all the morning. Having said these things three or four times over, in order to impress them on Pasquale's mind, he went in. The porter looked up at Marietta's window a moment, and then followed him and shut the door. It was clear that Giovanni had no intention of speaking to his sister before the midday meal. She breathed more freely, since she was to have a respite of several hours.

When she was dressed, Nella called the gondolier from her own window, and met him in the passage when he came up. He at once promised to make inquiries about Zorzi and went off to the palace to find his friend and crony, the Governor's head boatman. The latter, it is needless to say, knew every detail of the supernatural rescue from the archers, who could talk of nothing else in spite of the Governor's prohibition. They sat in a row on the stone bench within the main entrance, a rueful crew, their heads bound up with a pleasing variety of bandages. In an hour the gondolier returned, laden with the wonderful story which Nella was the first, but not the last, to hear from him. Her brown eyes seemed to be starting from her head when she came back to tell it to her mistress.

Marietta listened with a beating heart, though Nella began

at once by saying that Zorzi had mysteriously disappeared, and was certainly not in prison. When all was told, she drew a long breath, and wished that she could be alone to think over what she had heard; but Nella's imagination was roused, and she was prepared to discuss the affair all the morning. The details of it had become more and more numerous and circumstantial, as the men with the bandaged heads recalled what they had seen and heard. The devils that had delivered Zorzi all had blue noses, brass teeth and fiery tails. A peculiarity of theirs was that they had six fingers with six iron claws on each hand, and that all their hoofs were red-hot. As to their numbers, they might be roughly estimated at a thousand or so, and their roaring was like the howling of the south wind and the breaking of the sea on the Lido in a winter storm. It was horrible to hear, and would alone have put all the armies of the Republic to ignominious flight. Nella thought these things very interesting. She wished that she might talk with one of the men who had seen a real devil.

"I do not believe a word of all that nonsense," said Marietta. "The most important thing is that Zorzi got away from them and is not in prison."

"If he escaped by selling his soul to the fiends," said Nella, shaking her head, "it is a very evil thing."

Her mistress's disbelief in the blue noses and fiery tails was disconcerting, and had a chilling effect on Nella's talkative mood. The gondolier had crossed the bridge, to tell his story to Pasquale, whose view of the case seemed to differ from Nella's. He listened with approving interest, but without comment, until the gondolier had finished.

"I could tell you many such stories," he said. "Things of this kind often happen at sea."

"Really!" exclaimed the gondolier, who was only a boatman and regarded real sailors with a sort of professional reverence.

"Yes," answered Pasquale. "Especially on Sundays. You must know that when the priests are all saying mass, and the people are all praying, the devils cannot bear it, and are driven out to sea for the day. Very strange things happen then, I assure you. Some day I will tell you how the boatswain of a ship I once sailed in rove the end of the devil's tail through a link of the chain, made a Flemish knot at the end to stop it, and let go the anchor. So the devil went to the bottom by the run. We unshackled the chain and wore the ship to the wind, and after that we had fair weather to the end of the voyage. It happened on a Sunday."

"Marvellous!" cried the gondolier. "I should like to hear the whole story! But if you will allow me, I will go in and tell the Signor Giovanni what has happened, for he does not know yet."

Pasquale grinned as he stood in the doorway.

"He has given strict orders that no one is to be admitted this morning, as he is very busy."

"But this is a very important matter," argued the gondolier, who wished to have the pleasure of telling the tale.

"I cannot help it," answered Pasquale. "Those are his orders, and I must obey them. You know what his temper is, when he is not pleased."

Just then a skiff came up the canal at a great rate, so that the quick strokes of the oar attracted the men's attention. They saw that the boat was one of those that could be hired everywhere in Venice. The oarsman backed water with a strong stroke and brought to at the steps before the glass-house.

"Are you not Messer Angelo Beroviero's gondolier?" he inquired civilly.

"Yes," answered the man addressed, "I am the head gondolier, at your service."

"Thank you," replied the boatman. "I am to tell you that Messer Angelo has just arrived in Venice by sea, from Rimini, on board the *Santa Lucia*, a Neapolitan galliot now at anchor in the Giudecca. He desires you to bring his gondola at once to fetch him, and I am to bring over his baggage in my skiff."

The gondolier uttered an exclamation of surprise, and then turned to Pasquale.

"I go," he said. "Will you tell the Signor Giovanni that his father is coming home?"

Pasquale grinned again. He was rarely in such a pleasant humour.

"Certainly not," he answered. "The Signor Giovanni is very busy, and has given strict orders that he is not to be disturbed on any account."

"That is your affair," said the gondolier, hurrying away.

CHAPTER XIX

A little more than an hour later, the gondola came back and stopped alongside the steps of the house. The gondolier had made such haste to obey the summons that he had not thought of going into the house to give the servants warning, and as most of the shutters were already drawn together against the heat, no one had been looking out when he went away. He had asked Pasquale to tell the young master, and that was all that could be expected of him. There was therefore great surprise in the household when Angelo Beroviero went up the steps of his house, and his own astonishment that no one should be there to receive him was almost as great. The gondolier explained, and told him what Pasquale had said.

It was enough to rouse the old man's suspicions at once. He had left Zorzi in charge of the laboratory, enjoining upon him not to encourage Giovanni to go there; but now Giovanni was shut up there, presumably with Zorzi, and had given orders that he was not to be disturbed. The gondolier had not dared to say anything about the Dalmatian's arrest, and Beroviero was quite ignorant of all that had happened. He was not a man who hesitated when his suspicions or his temper were at work, and now he turned, without even entering his home, and crossed the bridge to the glass-house. Pasquale was looking through the grating and saw him coming, and was ready to receive him at the open door. For the third time on that morning, he grinned from ear to ear. Beroviero was pleased by the silent welcome of his old and trusted servant.

"You seem glad to see me again," he said, laying his hand kindly on the old porter's arm as he passed in.

"Others will be glad, too," was the answer.

As he went down the corridor Beroviero heard the sound of spades striking into the earth and shovelling it away. The gardener and his lad had been at work nearly two hours, and had turned up most of the earth in the little flowerbeds to a depth of two or three feet during that time, while Giovanni sat motionless under the plane-tree, watching every movement of their spades. He rose nervously when he heard footsteps in the corridor, for he did not wish any one to find him seated there, apparently watching a most commonplace operation with profound interest. He had made a step towards the door of the laboratory, when he saw his father emerge from the dark passage. He was a coward, and he trembled from head to foot, his teeth chattered in his head, and the cold sweat moistened his forehead in an instant. The old man stood still four or five paces from him and looked from him to the men who had been digging. On seeing the master they stopped working and pulled off their knitted caps. As a further sign of respect they wiped their dripping faces with their shirt sleeves.

"What are you doing here?" asked Beroviero in a tone of displeasure. "The garden was very well as it was."

"I—I thought," stammered Giovanni, "that it would—that it might be better to dig it—"

"It would not be better," answered the old man. "You may go," he added, speaking to the men, who were glad enough to be dismissed.

Beroviero passed his son without further words and tried the door of the laboratory, but found it locked.

"What is this?" he asked angrily. "Where is Zorzi? I told him not to leave you here alone."

"You had great confidence in him," answered Giovanni, recovering himself a little. "He is in prison."

He took the key from his wallet and thrust it into the lock as he spoke.

"In prison!" cried Beroviero in a loud voice. "What do you mean?"

Giovanni held the door open for him.

"I will tell you all about Zorzi, if you will come in," he said.

Beroviero entered, stood still a moment and looked about. Everything was as Zorzi had left it, but the glassmaker's ear missed the low roar of the furnace. Instinctively he made a step towards the latter, extending his hand to see whether it was already cold, but at that moment he caught sight of the silk mantle in the chair. He glanced quickly at his son.

"Has Marietta been here with you this morning?" he asked sharply.

"Oh no!" answered Giovanni contemptuously. "Zorzi stole that thing and had not time to hide it when they arrested him last night. I left it just where it was, that the Governor might see it."

Beroviero's face changed slowly. His fiery brown eyes began to show a dangerous light and he stroked his long beard quickly, twisting it a little each time.

"If you say that Zorzi stole Marietta's silk mantle," he said slowly, "you are either a fool or a liar."

"You are my father," answered Giovanni in some perturbation. "I cannot answer you."

Beroviero was silent for a long time. He took the mantle from the chair, examined it and assured himself that it was Marietta's own and no other. Then he carefully folded it up and laid it on the bench. His brows were contracted as if he were in great pain, and his face was pale, but his eyes were still angry.

Giovanni knew the signs of his father's wrath and dared not speak to him yet..

"Is this the evidence on which you have had my man arrested?" asked Beroviero, sitting down in the big chair and fixing his gaze on his son.

"By no means," answered Giovanni, with all the coolness he could command. "If it pleases you to hear my story from the beginning I will tell you all. If you do not hear all, you cannot possibly understand."

"I am listening," said old Beroviero, leaning back and laying his hands on the broad wooden arms of the chair.

"I shall tell you everything, exactly as it happened," said Giovanni, "and I swear that it is all true."

Beroviero reflected that in his experience this was usually the way in which liars introduced their accounts of events. For truth is like a work of genius: it carries conviction with it at once, and therefore needs no recommendation, nor other artificial support.

"After you left," Giovanni continued, "I came here one morning, out of pure friendliness to Zorzi, and as we talked I chanced to look at those things on the shelf. When I admired them, he admitted rather reluctantly that he had made them, and other things which you have in your house."

Beroviero gravely nodded his assent to the statement.

"I asked him to make me something," Giovanni went on to say, "but he told me that he had no white glass in the furnace, and that what was there was the result of your experiments."

Again Beroviero bent his head.

"So I asked him to bring his blowpipe to the main furnace room, where they were still working at that time, and we went there together. He at once made a very beautiful piece, and was just finishing it when a bad accident happened to him. Another man let his blowpipe fly from his hand and it fell upon Zorzi's foot with a large lump of hot glass."

Beroviero looked keenly at Giovanni.

"You know as well as I that it could not have been an accident," he said. "It was done out of spite."

"That may be," replied Giovanni, "for the men do not like him, as you know. But Zorzi accepted it as being an accident, and said so. He was badly hurt, and is still lame. Nella dressed the wound, and then Marietta came with her."

"Are you sure Marietta came here?" asked Beroviero, growing paler.

"Quite sure. They were on their way here together early in the morning when I stopped them, and asked Marietta where she was going, and she boldly said she was going to see Zorzi. I could not prevent her, and I saw them both go in."

"Do you mean to say that although Zorzi was so badly hurt you did not have him brought to the house?"

"Of course I proposed that at once," Giovanni answered. "But he said that he would not leave the furnace."

"That was like him," said old Beroviero.

"He knew what he was doing. It was on that same day that a night boy told me how he had seen you and Zorzi burying something in the laboratory the night before you left."

Beroviero started and leaned forward. Giovanni smiled thoughtfully, for he saw how his father was moved, and he knew that the strongest part of his story was yet untold.

"It would have been better to leave Paolo Godi's manuscript with me," he said, in a tone of sympathy. "I grew anxious for its safety as soon as I knew that Zorzi had charge of it. Yesterday morning I came in again. Zorzi was sitting on the working-stool, finishing a beautiful beaker of white glass."

"White glass?" repeated Beroviero in evident surprise. "White glass? Here?"

"Yes," answered Giovanni, enjoying his triumph. "I pointed out that when I had last come, there had been no white glass in the furnace. He answered that as one of the experiments had produced a beautiful red colour which he thought must be valuable, he had removed the crucible. He also showed me a specimen of it."

"Is it here?" asked Beroviero anxiously. "Where is it?"

Giovanni took the specimen from the table, for Zorzi had left it lying there, and he handed it to his father. The latter took it, held it up to the light, and uttered an exclamation of astonishment and anger.

"There is only one way of making that," he said, without hesitation.

"Yes," Giovanni answered coolly. "I supposed it was made according to one of your secrets."

A quick look was the only reply to this speech. Giovanni continued.

"I asked him to sell me the piece of glass he had been making when he came in, and at first he pretended that he was not sure whether you would allow it, but at last he took a piece of gold for it, and I was to have it as soon as it was annealed. When you see it, you will understand why I was so anxious to get it."

"Where is it?" asked the old man. "Show it to me."

Giovanni went to the other end of the annealing oven, and came back a moment later carrying the iron tray on which stood the pieces Zorzi had made on the previous morning. Beroviero looked at them critically, tried their weight, and noticed their transparency.

"That is not my glass," he said in a tone of decision.

"No," said Giovanni, "I saw that it was not your ordinary glass. It seems much better. Now Zorzi must have made it in a new crucible, and if he did, he made it with some secret of yours, for it is impossible that he should have discovered it himself. I said to myself that if he had made it, and the red glass there, he must have opened the book which you had buried together in this room, and that there was only one way of hindering him from learning everything in it, and ruining you and us by setting up a furnace of his own."

Beroviero was looking hard at Giovanni, but he was now thoroughly alarmed for the safety of his treasured manuscript, and listened with attention and without any hostility. The proofs seemed at first sight very strong, and after all Zorzi was only a Dalmatian and a foreigner, who might have yielded to temptation.

"What did you do?" asked Beroviero.

Giovanni told him the truth, how he had written a letter to the Governor, and had seen him in person, as well as Jacopo Contarini.

"Of course," Giovanni concluded, "you know best. If you find the book as you and he hid it together, he must have learned your secrets in some other way."

"We can easily see," answered old Beroviero, rising quickly. "Come here. Get the crowbar from the corner, and help me to lift the stone."

Giovanni took pains to look for the crowbar exactly where it was not, for he thought that this would divert any lingering suspicion from himself, but Beroviero was only annoyed.

"There, there!" he cried, pointing. "It is in that corner. Quickly!"

"It would be like the clever scoundrel to have copied what he wanted and then to have put the book back into the hiding place," said Giovanni, pausing.

"Do not waste words, my son!" cried Beroviero in the greatest anxiety. "Here! This is the stone. Get the crowbar in at this side. So. Now we will both heave. There! Wedge the stone up with that bit of wood. That will do. Now let us both get our hands under it, and lift it up."

It was done, while he was speaking. A moment later Giovanni had scooped out the loose earth, and Beroviero was staring down into the empty hole, just as Giovanni had done on the previous night. Giovanni was almost consoled for his own disappointment when he saw his father's face.

"It is certainly gone," he said. "You did not bury it deeper, did you? The soil is hard below."

"No, no! It is gone!" answered the old man in a dull voice. "Zorzi has got it."

"You see," said Giovanni mercilessly, "when I saw the red and white glass which he had made himself I was so sure of the truth that I acted quickly. I saw him arrested, and I do not think he could have had anything like a book with him, for he was in his doublet and hose. And as he is safe in prison now, he can be made to tell where he has put the thing. How big was it?"

"It was in an iron box. It was heavy." Beroviero spoke in low tones, overcome by his loss, and by the apparent certainty that Zorzi had betrayed him.

"You see why I should naturally suspect him of having stolen the mantle," observed Giovanni. "A man who would betray your confidence in such a way would do anything."

"Yes, yes," answered the old master vaguely. "Yes—I must go and see him in prison. I was kind to him, and perhaps he may confess everything to me."

"We might ask Marietta when she first missed her mantle," suggested Giovanni. "She must have noticed that it was gone."

"She will not remember," answered Beroviero. "Let us go to the Governor's house at once. There is just time before midday. We can speak to Marietta at dinner."

"But you must be tired, after your journey," objected Giovanni, with unusual concern for his father's comfort.

"No. I slept well on the ship. I have done nothing to tire me. The gondola may be still there. Tell Pasquale to call it over, and we will go directly. Go on! I will follow you."

Giovanni went forward, and Beroviero stayed a moment to

look again at the beautiful objects of white glass, examining them carefully, one by one. The workmanship was marvellous, and he could not help admiring it, but it was the glass itself that disturbed him. It was like his own, but it was better, and the knowledge of its composition and treatment was a fortune. Then, too, the secret of dropping a piece of copper into a certain mixture in order to produce a particularly beautiful red colour was in the book, and the colour could not be mistaken and was not the one which Beroviero had been trying to produce. He shook his head sadly as he went out and locked the door behind him, convinced against his will that he had been betrayed by the man whom he had most trusted in the world.

Pasquale watched the two, father and son, as they got into the gondola. Old Beroviero had not even looked at him as he came out, and it was not the porter's business to volunteer information, nor the gondolier's either. But when the latter was ordered to row to the Governor's house as fast as possible, he turned his head and looked at Pasquale, who slowly nodded his ugly head before going in again.

On reaching their destination they were received at once, and the Governor told them what had happened, in as few words as possible. Nothing could exceed old Beroviero's consternation, and his son's disappointment. Zorzi had been rescued at the corner of San Piero's church by men who had knocked senseless the officer and the six archers. No one knew who these men were, nor their numbers, but they were clearly friends of Zorzi's who had known that he was to be arrested.

"Accomplices," suggested Giovanni. "He has stolen a valuable book of my father's, containing secrets for making the finest glass. By this time he is on his way to Milan, or Florence."

"I daresay," said the Governor. "These foreigners are capable of anything."

"I had trusted him so confidently," said Beroviero, too much overcome to be angry.

"Exactly," answered the Governor. "You trusted him too much."

"I always thought so," put in Giovanni wisely.

"There is nothing to be said," resumed Beroviero. "I do not wish to believe it of him, but I cannot deny the evidence of my own senses."

"I have already sent a report to the Council of Ten," said the Governor. "The most careful search will be made in Venice for Zorzi and his companions, and if they are found, they will suffer for what they have done."

"I hope so!" replied Giovanni heartily.

"I remember that you recommended me to send a strong force," observed the Governor. "Perhaps you knew that a rescue was intended. Or you were aware that the fellow had daring accomplices."

"I only suspected it," Giovanni answered. "I knew nothing. He was always alone."

"He has hardly been out of my sight for five years," said old Beroviero sadly.

He and his son took their leave, the Governor promising to keep them informed as to the progress of the search. At present nothing more could be done, for Zorzi has disappeared altogether, and old Beroviero was much inclined to share his son's opinion that the fugitive was already on his way to Milan, or Florence, where the possession of the secrets would insure him a large fortune, very greatly to the injury of Beroviero and all the glassworkers of Murano. The two men returned to the house in silence, for the elder was too much absorbed by his own thoughts to speak, and Giovanni was too wise to interrupt reflections which undoubtedly tended to Zorzi's destruction.

Marietta was awaiting her father's return with much anxiety, for every one knew that the master had gone first to the laboratory and then to the Governor's palace, with Giovanni, so that the two must have been talking together a long time. Marietta waited with her sister-in-law in the lower hall, slowly walking up and down.

When her father came up the low steps at last, she went forward to meet him, and a glance told her that he was in the most extreme anxiety. She took his hand and kissed it, in the customary manner, and he bent a little and touched her forehead with his lips. Then, to her surprise, he put one hand under her chin, and laid the other on the top of her head, and with gentle force made her look at him. Giovanni's wife was there, and most of the servants were standing near the foot of the staircase to welcome their master.

Beroviero said nothing as he gazed into his daughter's eyes. They met his own fearlessly enough, and she opened them wide, as she rarely did, as if to show that she had nothing to conceal; but while he looked at her the blood rose blushing in her cheeks, telling that there was something to hide after all, and as she would not turn her eyes from his, they sparkled a little with vexation. Beroviero did not speak, but he let her go and went on towards the stairs, bending his head graciously to the other persons who were assembled to greet him.

He was a man of strong character and of much natural dignity, far too proud to break down under a great loss or a bitter disappointment, and at dinner he sat at the head of the table and spoke affably of the journey he had made, explaining his unexpectedly early return by the fact that the Lord of Rimini had at once approved his designs and accepted his terms. Occasionally Giovanni asked a respectful question, but neither his wife nor Marietta said much during the meal. Zorzi was not mentioned.

"You are welcome at my house, my son," Beroviero said, when they had finished, "but I suppose that you will go back to your own this evening."

This was of course a command, and Marietta thought it a good omen. She had felt sure, when her father made her look at him, that Giovanni had spoken to him of the mantle, but in what way she could not tell. Perhaps, though it seemed incredible, he would not make such a serious case of it as she had expected.

He said nothing, when he withdrew to rest during the hot hours of the afternoon, and she went to her own room as every one did at that time. Little as she had slept that night, she felt that it would be intolerable to lie down; so she took her little basket of beads and tried to work. Nella was dozing in the next room. From time to time the young girl leaned back in her chair with half closed eyes, and a look of pain came over her face; then with an effort she took her needle once more, and picked out the beads, threading them one by one in a regular succession of colours.

She was sure that if Zorzi were near he would have already found some means of informing her that he was really in safety. He must have friends of whom she knew nothing, and who had rescued him at great risk. He would surely trust one of them to take a message, or to make a signal which she could understand. She sat near the window, and the shutters were half closed so as to leave a space through which she could look out. From time to time she glanced at the white line of the footway opposite, over which the shadow of the glass-house was beginning to creep as the sun moved westward. But no one appeared. When it was cool Pasquale would probably come out and look three times up and down the canal as he always did. Giovanni would not go to the laboratory again. Perhaps her father would go, when, he was rested. Then, if she chose, she could take Nella and join him, and since there was to be an explanation with him, she would rather have it in the laboratory, where they would be quite alone.

She had fully made up her mind to tell him at the very first interview that she would not marry Jacopo Contarini under any circumstances, but she had not decided whether she would add that she loved Zorzi. She hated anything like cowardice, and it would be cowardly to put off telling the truth any longer; but what concerned Zorzi was her secret, and she had a right to choose the most favourable moment for making a revelation on which her whole life, and Zorzi's also, must immediately depend. She felt weak and tired, for she had eaten little and hardly slept at all, but her determination was strong and she would act upon it.

Occasionally she rose and moved wearily about the room, looked out between the shutters and then sat down again. She was in one of those moments of life in which all existence seems drawn out to an endless quivering thread, a single throbbing nerve stretched to its utmost point of strain.

The silence was broken by a man's footstep in the passage, coming towards her door. A moment later she heard her father's voice, asking if he might come in. Almost at the same time she opened and Beroviero stood on the threshold. Nella had heard him speaking, too, and she started up, wide awake in an instant, and came in, to see if she were needed.

"Will you go with me to the laboratory, my dear?" asked the old man quietly.

She answered gravely that she would. There was no gladness in her tone, but no reluctance. She was facing the most difficult situation she had ever known, and perhaps the most dangerous.

"Very well," said her father. "Let Nella give you your silk mantle and we will go at once."

Before Marietta could have answered, even if she had known what to say, Nella had begun her tale of woe. The mantle was stolen, the sour-faced shrew of a maid who belonged to the Signor Giovanni's wife had stolen it, the house ought to be searched at once, and so much more to the same effect that Nella was obliged to pause for breath.

"When did you miss it?" asked Beroviero, looking hard at the serving-woman.

"This morning, sir. It was here last night, I am quite sure."

The truthful little brown eyes did not waver.

"And it cannot have been any one else," continued Nella. "This is a very evil person, sir, and she sometimes comes here with a message, or making believe that she is helping me. As if I needed help, indeed!"

"Do not accuse people of stealing when you have no evidence

against them," answered Beroviero somewhat sternly. "Give your mistress something else to throw over her."

"Give me the green silk cloak," said Marietta, who was anxious not to be questioned about the mantle.

"It has a spot in one corner," Nella answered discontentedly, as she went to the wardrobe.

The spot turned out to be no bigger than the head of a pin. A moment later Marietta and her father were going downstairs. At the door of the glass-house Pasquale eyed them with approbation, and Marietta smiled and said a word to him as she passed. It seemed strange that she should have trusted the ugly old man with a secret which she dared not tell her own father.

Beroviero did not speak as she followed him down the path and stood waiting while he unlocked the door. Then they both entered, and he laid his cap upon the table.

"There is your mantle, my dear," he said quietly, and he pointed to it, neatly folded and lying on the bench.

Marietta started, for she was taken unawares. While in her own room, her father had spoken so naturally as to make it seem quite possible that Giovanni had said nothing about it to him, yet he had known exactly where it was. He was facing her now, as he spoke.

"It was found here last night, after Zorzi had been arrested," said Beroviero. "Do you understand?"

"Yes," Marietta answered, gathering all her courage. "We will talk about it by and by. First, I have something to say to you which is much more important than anything concerning the mantle. Will you sit down, father, and hear me as patiently as you can?"

"I am learning patience today," said Beroviero, sitting down in his chair. "I am learning also the meaning of such words as ingratitude, betrayal and treachery, which were never before spoken in my house."

He sighed and leaned back, looking at the wall. Marietta dropped her cloak beside the mantle on the bench and began to walk up and down before him, trying to begin her speech. But she could not find any words.

"Speak, child," said her father. "What has happened? It seems to me that I could bear almost anything now."

She stood still a moment before him, still hesitating. She now saw that he had suffered more than she had suspected, doubtless owing to Zorzi's arrest and disappearance, and she knew that what she meant to tell him would hurt him much more.

"Father," she began at last, with a great effort, "I know that what I am going to say will displease you very, very much. I am sorry—I wish it were not—"

Suddenly her set speech broke down. She fell on her knees and took his hands, looking up beseechingly to his face.

"Forgive me!" she cried. "Oh, for God's sake forgive me! I cannot marry Jacopo Contarini!"

Beroviero had not expected that. He sat upright in the chair, in his amazement, and instinctively tried to draw his hands out of hers, but she held them fast, gazing earnestly up to him. His look was not angry, nor cold, nor did he even seem hurt. He was simply astonished beyond all measure by the enormous audacity of what she said. As yet he did not connect it with anything else.

"I think you must be mad!"

That was all he could find to say.

CHAPTER XX

Marietta shook her head. She still knelt at her father's feet, holding his hands.

"I am not mad," she said. "I am in earnest. I cannot marry him. It is impossible."

"You must marry him," answered Beroviero. "You are betrothed to him, and it would be an insult to his family to break off the marriage now. Besides, you have no reason to give, not the shadow of a reason."

Marietta dropped his hands and rose to her feet lightly. She had expected a terrific outburst of anger, which would gradually subside, after which she hoped to find words with which to influence him. But like many hot-tempered men, he was sometimes unexpectedly calm at critical moments, as if he were really able to control his nature when he chose. She now almost wished that he would break out in a rage, as women sometimes hope we may, for they know it is far easier to deal with an angry man than with a determined one.

"I will not marry him," she said at last, with strong emphasis, and almost defiantly.

"My child," Beroviero answered gravely, "you do not know what you are saying."

"I do!" cried Marietta with some indignation. "I have thought of it a long time. I was very wrong not to make up my mind from the beginning, and I ask your forgiveness. In my heart I always knew that I could not do it in the end, and I should have said so at once. It was a great mistake."

"There is no question of your consent," replied Beroviero with conviction. "If girls were consulted as to the men they were to marry, the world would soon come to an end. This is only a passing madness, of which you should be heartily ashamed. Say no more about it. On the appointed day, the wedding will take place."

"It will not," said Marietta firmly; "and you will do better to let it be known at once. It is of no use to take heaven to witness, and to make a solemn oath. I merely say that I will not marry Jacopo Contarini. You may carry me to the church, you may drag me before the altar, but I will resist. I will scream out that I will not, and the priest himself will protect me. That will be a much greater scandal than if you go to the Contarini family and tell them that your daughter is mad—if you really think I am."

"You are undoubtedly beside yourself at the present moment," Beroviero answered. "But it will pass, I hope."

"Not while I am alive, and I shall certainly resist to the end. It would be much wiser of you to send me to a convent at once, than to count on forcing me to go through the marriage ceremony."

Beroviero stared at her, and stroked his beard. He began to believe that she might possibly be in earnest. Since she talked so quietly of going to a convent, a fate which most girls considered the most terrible that could be imagined. He bent his brows in thought, but watched her steadily.

"You have not yet given me a single reason for all this wild talk," he said after a pause. "It is absurd to think that without some good cause you are suddenly filled with repulsion for marriage, or for Jacopo Contarini. I have heard of young women who were betrothed, but who felt a religious vocation, and refused to marry for that reason. It never seemed a very satisfactory one to me, for if there is any condition in which a woman needs religion, it is the marriage state."

He paused in his speech, pleased with his own idea, in spite of all his troubles. Marietta had moved a few steps away from him and stood beside the table, looking down at the things on it, without seeing them.

"But you do not even make religion a pretext," pursued her father. "Have you no reason to give? I do not expect a good one, for none can have any weight. But I should like to hear the best you have."

"It is a very convincing one to me," Marietta replied, still looking down at the table. "But I think I had better not tell it to you today," she added. "It would make you angry."

"No," said Beroviero. "One cannot be angry with people who are really out of their senses."

"I am not so mad as you think," answered the girl. "I have told you of my decision, because it was cowardly of me not to tell you what I felt before you went away. But it might be a mistake to tell you more today. You have had enough to harass you already, since you came back."

"You are suddenly very considerate."

"No, I have not been considerate. I could not be, without acting a lie to you, by letting you believe that I meant to marry Messer Jacopo, and I will not do that any longer, since I know that it is a lie. But I cannot see the use of saying anything more."

"You had better tell me the whole truth, rather than let me

think something that may be much worse," answered Beroviero, changing his attitude.

"There is nothing in the truth of which I am ashamed," said Marietta, holding up her head proudly. "I have done nothing which I did not believe to be right, however strange it may seem to you."

Once more their eyes met and they gazed steadily at each other; and again the blush spread over her cheeks. Beroviero put out his hand and touched the folded mantle.

"Marietta," he said, "Zorzi has stolen my precious book of secrets, and has disappeared with it. They tell me that he also stole this mantle, for it was found here just after he was arrested last night. Is it true, or has he stolen my daughter instead?"

Marietta's face had darkened when he began to accuse the absent man. At the question that followed she started a little, and drew herself up.

"Zorzi is neither a thief nor a traitor," she answered. "If you mean to ask me whether I love him—is that what you mean?" She paused, with flashing eyes.

"Yes," answered her father, and his voice shook.

"Then yes! I love him with all my heart, and I have loved him long. That is why I will not marry Jacopo Contarini. You know my secret now."

Beroviero groaned aloud, and his head sank as he grasped the arms of the chair. His daughter loved the man who had cheated him, betrayed him and robbed him. It was almost too much to bear. He had nothing to say, for no words could tell what he felt then, and he silently bowed his head.

"As for the accusations you bring against him," Marietta said after a moment, "they are false, from first to last, and I can prove to you that every one of them is an abominable lie."

"You cannot make that untrue which I have seen with my eyes."

"I can, though Zorzi has the right to prove his innocence himself. I may say too much, for I am not as generous as he is. Do you know that when they tried to kill him in the furnace room, and lamed him for life, he told every one, even me, that it was an accident? He is so brave and noble that when he comes here again, he will not tell you that it was your own son who tried to rob you, who did everything in his power to get Zorzi away from this room, in order to search for your manuscript, and who at last, as everything else failed, persuaded the Governor to arrest him. He will not tell you that, and he does not know that before they had taken him twenty paces from the door, Giovanni was already here, locked in and trying the stones with a hammer to find out which one covered the precious book. Did Giovanni tell you that this morning? No. Zorzi would not tell you all the truth, and I know some of it even better than he. But Zorzi was always generous and brave."

Beroviero had lifted his head now and was looking hard at her.

"And your mantle? How came it here?" he asked.

There was nothing to be done now, but to speak the truth.

"It is here," said Marietta, growing paler, "because I came here, unknown to any one except Pasquale who let me in, because I came alone last night to warn the man I love that Giovanni had planned his destruction, and to save him if I could. In my haste I left the mantle in that chair of yours, in which I had been sitting. It slipped from my shoulders as I sat, and there Giovanni must have found it. If you had seen it there you would know that what I say is true."

"I did see it," said Beroviero. "Giovanni left it where it was, and I folded it myself this morning. Zorzi did not steal the mantle. I take back that accusation."

"Nor has he stolen your secrets. Take that back, too, if you are just. You always were, till now."

"I have searched the place where he and I put the book, and it is not there."

"Giovanni searched it twelve hours earlier, and it was already gone. Zorzi saved it from your son, and then, in his rage, I suppose that Giovanni accused him of stealing it. He may even have believed it, for I can be just, too. But it is not true. The book is safe."

"Zorzi took it with him," said Beroviero.

"You are mistaken. Before he was arrested, he said that I ought to know where it was, in case anything happened to him, in order to tell you."

Beroviero rose slowly, staring at her, and speaking with an effort.

"You know where it is? He told you? He has not taken it away?"

Marietta smiled, in perfect certainty of victory.

"I know where it is," she said.

"Where is it?" he asked in extreme anxiety, for he could hardly believe what he heard.

"I will not tell you yet," was the unexpected answer Marietta gave him. "And you cannot possibly find it unless I do."

The veins stood out on the old man's temples in an instant, and the old angry fire came back to his eyes.

"Do you dare to tell me that you will not show me the place where the book is, on the very instant?" he cried.

"Oh yes," answered Marietta. "I dare that, and much more. I am not a coward like my brother, you know. I will not tell you the secret till you promise me something."

"You are trying to sell me what is my own!" he answered angrily. "You are in league with Zorzi against me, to break off your marriage. But I will not do it—you shall tell me where the book is—if you refuse, you shall repent it as long as you live—I will—"

He stopped short in his speech as he met her disdainful look.

"You never threatened me before," she said. "Why do you think that you can frighten me?"

"Give me what is mine," said the old man angrily. "That is all I demand. I am not threatening."

"Set me free from Messer Jacopo, and you shall have it," answered Marietta.

"No. You shall marry him."

"I will not. But I will keep your book until you change your mind, or else—but no I If I gave it to Zorzi, he is so honourable that he would bring it back to you without so much as looking into it. I will keep it for myself. Or I will burn it!"

She felt that if she had been a man, she could not have taken such an unfair advantage of him; but she was a defenceless girl, fighting for the liberty of her whole life. That might excuse much, she thought. By this time Beroviero was very angry; he stalked up and down beside the furnace, trailing his thin silk gown behind him, stroking his beard with a quick, impatient movement, and easting fierce glances at Marietta from time to time.

He was not used to being at the mercy of circumstances, still less to having his mind made up for him by his son and his daughter. Giovanni had made him believe that Zorzi had turned traitor and thief, after five years of faithful service, and the conviction had cut him to the quick; and now Marietta had demonstrated Zorzi's innocence almost beyond doubt, but had made matters worse in other ways, and was taking the high hand with him. He did not realise that from the moment when she had boldly confessed what she had done and had declared her love for Zorzi, his confidence in her had returned by quick degrees, and that the atrocious crime of having come secretly at night to the laboratory had become in his eyes, and perhaps against his will, a mere pardonable piece of rashness; since if Zorzi was innocent, anything which could save him from unjust imprisonment might well be forgiven. He had borne what seemed to him very great misfortunes with fortitude and dignity; but his greatest treasures were safe, his daughter and Paolo Godi's manuscript, and he became furiously angry with Marietta, because she had him in her power.

If a man is seated, a woman who intends to get the better of him generally stands; but if he loses his temper and begins to walk about, she immediately seats herself and assumes an exasperating calmness of manner. Accordingly Marietta sat down on a small chair near the table and watched her father in silence, persuaded that he would be obliged to yield in the end.

"No one has ever dared to browbeat me in this way, in my whole life!" cried the old man fiercely, and his voice shook with rage.

"Will you listen to me?" asked Marietta with sudden meekness.

"Listen to you?" he repeated instantly. "Have I not been listening to you for hours?"

"I do not know how long it may have been," answered the girl, "but I have much more to say. You are so angry that you will not hear me."

"Angry? I? Are you telling me that I am so beside myself with rage, that I cannot understand reason?"

"I did not say that."

"You meant it, then! What did you say? You have forgotten what you said already! Just like a girl! And you pretend to argue with me, with your own father! It is beyond belief! Silence, I say! Do not answer me!"

Marietta sat quite still, and began to look at her nails, which were very pink and well shaped. After a short silence Beroviero stopped before her.

"Well!" he cried. "Why do you not speak?" His eyes blazed and he tapped the pavement with his foot. She raised her eyebrows, smiled a little wearily and sighed.

"I misunderstood you," she said, with exasperating patience. "I thought you told me to be silent."

"You always misunderstand me," he answered angrily and walking off again. "You always did, and you always will! I believe you do it on purpose. But I will make you understand! You shall know what I mean!"

"I should be so glad," said Marietta. "Pray tell me what you mean."

This was too much. He turned sharply in his walk.

"I mean you to marry Contarini," he cried out, with a stamp of the foot.

"And you mean never to see Paolo Godi's manuscript again," suggested Marietta quietly.

"Perdition take the accursed thing!" roared the old man. "If I only knew where you have put it—"

"It is where you can never, never find it," Marietta answered. "So it is of no use to be angry with me, is it? The more angry you are, the less likely it is that I shall tell you. But I will tell you something else, father—something you never understood before. My marriage was to have been a bargain, a great name for a fortune, half your fortune for a great name and an alliance with the Contarini. Perhaps one was worth the other. I know very little of such things. But it chances that I can have a word to say about the bargain, too. Would any one say that I was doing very wrong if I gave that book to my brother, for instance? Giovanni would not give it back to you, as Zorzi would, I am quite sure."

"What abominable scheme is this?" Beroviero fairly trembled in his fury.

"I offer you a simple bargain," Marietta answered, unmoved. "I will give you your manuscript for my freedom. Will you take it, father? Or will you insist upon trying to marry me by force, and let me give the book to Giovanni? Yes, that is what I will do. Then I will marry Zorzi, and go away."

"Silence, child! You! Marry a stranger, a Dalmatian—a servant!"

"But I love him. You may call him a servant, if you choose. It would make no difference to me if it were true. He would not be less brave, less loyal or less worthy if he were forced to clean your shoes in order to live, instead of sharing your art with you. Did he ever lie to you?"

"No!" cried the old man. "I would have broken his bones!"

"Did he ever betray a secret, since you know that the book is safe?"

"No."

"Have you trusted him far more than your own sons, for many years?"

"Yes—of course—"

"Then call him your servant if you like, and call your sons what you please," concluded Marietta, "but do not tell me that such a man is not good enough to be the husband of a glass-blower's daughter, who does not want a great name, nor a palace, nor a husband who sits in the Grand Council. Do not say that, father, for it would not be true—and you never told a lie in your life."

"I tell you that marriage has nothing to do with all this!" He began walking again, to keep his temper hot, for he was dimly conscious that he was getting the worst of the encounter, and that her arguments were good.

"And I tell you that a marriage that has nothing to do with love, and with honour, and with trust, is no marriage at all!" answered the girl. "Say what you please of customs, and traditions, and of station, and all that! God never meant that an innocent girl should be bought and sold like a slave, or a horse, for a name, nor for money, nor for any imaginary advantage to herself or to her father! I know what our privilege is, that the patricians may marry us and not lose their rank. I would rather keep my own, and marry a glass-worker, even if I were to be sold! Do you know what your money would buy for me in Venice? The privilege of being despised and slighted by patricians and great ladies. You know as well as I that it would all end there, in spite of all you may give. They want your money, you want their name, because you are rich and you have always been taught to think that the chief use of money is to rise in the world."

"Will you teach me what I am to think?" asked old Beroviero, amazed by her sudden flow of words.

"Yes," she answered, before he could say more. "I will teach you what you should think, what you should have always thought—a man as brave and upright and honest in everything as you are! You should think, you should know, that your daughter has a right to live, a right to be free, and a right to love, like every living creature God ever made!"

"This is the most abominable rebellion!" retorted Beroviero. "I cannot imagine where you learned—"

"Rebellion?" she cried, interrupting him in ringing tones. "Yes, it is rank rebellion, sedition and revolt against slavery, for life and love and freedom! You wonder where I have learned to turn and face this oppression of the world, instead of yielding to it, one more unhappy woman among the thousands that are bought and sold into wifehood every year! I have learned nothing, my heart needed no teaching for that! It is enough that I love an honest man truly—I know that it is wrong to promise my faith to another, and that it is a worse wrong in you to try to get that promise from me by force. A vow that could be nothing but a solemn lie! Would the ring on my finger be a charm to make me forget? Would the priest's words and blessing be a spell to root out of my heart what is the best part of my life? Better go to a nunnery, and weep for the truth, than to hope for peace in such a lie as that—better a thousand, thousand times!"

She had risen now, and was almost eloquent, facing her father with flashing eyes.

"Oh, you have always been kind to me, good to me, dear to me," she went on quickly. "It is only in this that you will not understand. Would it not hurt you a little to feel that you had sent me to a sort of living death from which I could never come back to life? That I was imprisoned for ever among people who looked down upon me and only tolerated me for my fortune's sake? Yet that would be the very least part of it all! I could bear all that, if it were for any good. But to become the creature, the possession, the plaything of a man I do not lobe, when I love another with all my heart—oh, no, no, no! You cannot ask me that!"

His anger had slowly subsided, and he was listening now, not because she had him in her power, but because what she said was true. For he was a just and honourable man.

"I wish that you might have loved any man but Zorzi," he said, almost as if speaking to himself.

"And why another?" she asked, following up her advantage instantly. "You would have had me marry a Trevisan, perhaps, or the son of any of the other great glassmakers? Is there one of them who can compare with Zorzi as an artist, let alone as a man? Look at those things he has made, there, on the table! Is there a man living who could make one of them? Not you, yourself; you know it better than I do!"

"No," answered Beroviero. "That is true. Nor is there any one who could make the glass he used for them without the secrets that are in the book—and more too, for it is better than my own."

Marietta looked at him in surprise. This was something she had not known.

"Is it not your glass?" she asked.

"It is better. He must have added something to the composition set down in the book."

"You believe that although the book itself is safe, he has made use of it."

"Yes. I cannot see how it could be otherwise."

"Was the book sealed?"

"Yes, and looked in an iron box. Here is the key. I always

wear it."

He drew out the small iron key, and showed it to her.

"If you find the box locked, and the seals untouched, will you believe that Zorzi has not opened the manuscript?" asked Marietta.

"Yes," answered Beroviero after a moment's thought. "I showed him the seal, and I remember that he said a man might make one like it. But I should know by the wax. I am sure I could tell whether it had been tampered with. Yes, I should believe he had not opened the book, if I found it as I left it."

"Then you will be convinced that Zorzi is altogether innocent of all the charges Giovanni made against him. Is that true?"

"Yes. If he has learnt the art in spite of the law, that is my fault, not his. He was unwise in selling the beaker to Giovanni. But what is that, after all?"

"Promise me then," said Marietta, laying her hand upon her father's arm, "promise me that if Zorzi comes back, he shall be safe, and that you will trust him as you always have."

"Though he dares to be in love with you?"

"Though I dare to love him—or apart from that. Say that if it were not for that, you would treat him just as before you went away."

"Yes, I would," answered Beroviero thoughtfully.

"The book is there," said Marietta.

She pointed to the big earthen jar that contained the broken glass, and her father's eyes followed her land.

"It is for Zorzi's sake that I tell you," she continued. "The book is buried deep down amongst the broken bits. It will take a long time to get it out. Shall I call Pasquale to help us?"

"No," answered her father.

He went to the other end of the room and brought back the crowbar. Then he placed himself in a good position for striking, and raised the iron high in air with both his hands.

"Stand back!" he cried as Marietta came nearer.

The first blow knocked a large piece of earthenware from the side of the strong jar, and a quantity of broken red glass poured out, as red as blood from a wound, and fell with little crashes upon the stone floor. Beroviero raised the crowbar again and again and brought it down with all his might. At the fourth stroke the whole jar went to pieces, leaving nothing but a red heap of smashed glass, round about which lay the big fragments of the jar. In the middle of the heap, the corner of the iron box appeared, sticking up like a black stone.

"At last!" exclaimed the old man, flushed with satisfaction. "Giovanni had not thought of this."

He cleared away the shivers and gently pushed the box out of its bed with the crowbar. He soon got it out on the floor, and with some precaution, lest any stray splinter should cut his fingers, he set it upon the table. Then he took the key from his neck and opened it.

Marietta's belief in Zorzi had never wavered, from the first, but Beroviero was more than half sure that the book had been opened. He took it up with care, turned it over and over in his hands, scrutinised the seal, the strings, the knots, and saw that they were all his own.

"It is impossible that this should have been undone and tied up again," he said confidently.

"Any one could see that at once," Marietta answered. "Do you believe that Zorzi is innocent?"

"I cannot help believing. But I do not understand. There is the red glass, made by dropping the piece of copper into it. That is in the book, I am sure."

"It was an accident," said Marietta. "The copper ladle fell into the glass. Zorzi told me about it."

"Are you sure? That is possible. The very same thing happened to Paolo Godi, and that was how he discovered the colour. But there is the white glass, which is so like mine, though it is better. That may have been an accident too. Or the boy may have tried an experiment upon mine by adding something to it."

"It is at least sure that the book has not been touched, and that is the main thing. You admit that he is quite innocent, do you not? Quite, quite innocent?"

"Yes, I do. It would be very unjust not to admit it."

Marietta drew a long breath of relief, for she had scarcely hoped to accomplish so much in so short a time. The rest would follow, she felt sure.

"I would give a great deal to see Zorzi at once," said her father, at last, as he replaced the manuscript in the box and shut the lid.

"Not half as much as I would!" Marietta almost laughed, as she spoke. "Father," she added gently, and resting one hand upon his shoulder, "I have given you back your book, I have given you back the innocent man you trusted, instead of the villain invented by my brother. What will you give me?"

She smiled and rubbed her cheek against his shoulder. He shook his head a little, and would not answer.

"Would it be so hard to say that you ask another year's time before the marriage? And then, you know, you could ask it again, and they would soon be tired of waiting and would break it off themselves."

"Do not suggest such woman's tricks to me," answered her father; but he could not help smiling.

"Oh, you may find a better way," Marietta said. "But that would be so easy, would it not? Your daughter is so young—her health is somewhat delicate—"

She was interrupted by a knock at the door, and Pasquale entered.

"The Signor Giovanni is without, sir," said the porter. "He desires to take leave of you, as he is returning to his own house today."

"Let him come in," said Beroviero, his face darkening all at once.

CHAPTER XXI

Giovanni entered the laboratory confidently, not even knowing that Marietta was with her father, and not suspecting that he could have anything to fear from her.

"I have come to take my leave of you, sir," he began, going towards his father at once.

He did not see the broken jar, which was at some distance from the door.

"Before you go," said Beroviero coldly, "pray look at this."

Giovanni saw the box on the table, but did not understand, as he had never seen it before. His father again took the key from his neck and opened the casket.

"This is Paolo Godi's manuscript," he said, without changing his tone. "You see, here is the book. The seal is unbroken. It is exactly as I left it when Zorzi and I buried it together. You suspected him of having opened it, and I confess that you made me suspect him, too. For the sake of justice, convince yourself."

Giovanni's face was drawn with lines of vexation and anxiety.

"It was hidden in the jar of broken glass," Beroviero explained. "You did not think of looking there."

"No—nor you, sir."

"I mean that you did not look there when you searched for it alone, immediately after Zorzi was arrested."

Giovanni was pale now, but he raised both hands and turned up his eyes as if calling upon heaven to witness his innocence.

"I swear to you," he began, "on the body of the blessed Saint Donatus—"

Beroviero interrupted him.

"I did not ask you to swear by anything," he said. "I know the truth. The less you say of what has happened, the better it will be for you in the end."

"I suppose my sister has been poisoning your mind against me as usual. Can she explain how her mantle came here?"

"It does not concern you to know how it came here," answered Beroviero. "By your wholly unjustifiable haste, to say nothing worse, you have caused an innocent man to be arrested, and his rescue and disappearance have made matters much worse. I do not care to ask what your object has been. Keep it to yourself, pray, and do not remind me of this affair when we meet, for after all, you are my son. You came to take your leave, I think. Go home, then, by all means."

Without a word, Giovanni went out, biting his thin lip and reflecting mournfully upon the change in his position since he had talked with his father in the morning. While they had been speaking Marietta had gone to a little distance, affecting to unfold the mantle and fold it again according to feminine rules. As she heard the door shut again she glanced at her father's face, and saw that he was looking at her.

"I told you that I was learning patience today," he said. "I longed to lay my hands on him."

"You frightened him much more by what you said," answered Marietta.

"Perhaps. Never mind! He is gone. The question is how to find Zorzi. That is the first thing, and then we must undo the mischief Giovanni has done."

"I think Pasquale must have some clue by which we may find Zorzi," suggested Marietta.

Pasquale was called at once. He stood with his legs bowed, holding his old cap in both hands, his small bloodshot eyes fixed on his master's face with a look of inquiry. He was more than ever like a savage old watchdog.

"Yes, sir," he said in answer to Beroviero's question, "I can tell you something. Two men were looking on last night when the Signor Giovanni made me open the door to the Governor's soldiers. They wore hoods over their eyes, but I am certain that one of them was that Greek captain who came here one morning before you went away. When Zorzi came out, the Greek walked off, up the footway and past the bridge. The other waited till they were all gone and till Signor Giovanni had come in. He whispered quickly in my ear, 'Zorzi is safe.' Then he went after the others. I could see that he had a short staff hidden under his cloak, and that he was a man with bones like an ox. But he was not so big a man as the captain. Then I knew that two such men, who were seamen accustomed to using their hands, quick on their feet and seeing well in the dark, as we all do, could pitch the officer over the tower of San Piero, if they chose, with all his sleazy crew of lubberly, dressed-up boobies, armed with overgrown boat-hooks. This I thought, and so it happened. That is what I know."

"But why should Captain Aristarchi care whether Zorzi were arrested or not?" asked Beroviero.

"This the saints may know in paradise," answered Pasquale, "but not I."

"Has the captain been here again?" asked Beroviero, completely puzzled.

"No, sir. But I should have told you that one morning there came a patrician of Venice, Messer Zuan Venier, who wished to see you, being a friend of Messer Jacopo Contarini, and when he heard that you were away he desired to see Zorzi, and stayed some time."

"I know him by name," said Beroviero, nodding. "But there can be no connection between him and this Greek."

Pasquale snarled and showed his teeth at the mere idea, for his instinct told him that Aristarchi was a pirate, or had been one, and he was by no means sure that the Greek had carried off Zorzi for any good purpose.

"Pasquale," said Beroviero, "it is long since you have had a holiday. Take the skiff tomorrow morning, and go over to Venice. You are a seaman and you can easily find out from the sailors about the Giudecca who this Aristarchi really is, and where he lives. Then try to see him and tell him that Zorzi is innocent of all the charges against him, and that if he will come back I will protect him. Can you do that?"

Pasquale gave signs of great satisfaction, by growling and grinning at the same time, and his lids drew themselves into a hundred wrinkles till his eyes seemed no bigger than two red Murano beads.

Then Beroviero and Marietta went back to the house, and the young girl carried the folded mantle under her cloak. Before going to her own room she opened it out, as if it had been worn, and dropped it behind a bench-box in the large room, as if it had fallen from her shoulders while she had been sitting there; and in due time it was found by one of the men-servants, who brought it back to Nella.

"You are so careless, my pretty lady!" cried the serving-woman, holding up her hands.

"Yes," answered Marietta, "I know it."

"So careless!" repeated Nella. "Nothing has any value for you! Some day you will forget your face in the mirror and go away without it, and then they will say it is Nella's fault!"

Marietta laughed lightly, for she was happy. It was clear that everything was to end well, though it might be long before her father would consent to let her marry Zorzi. She felt quite sure that he was safe, though he might lie far away by this time.

Beroviero returned at once to the Governor's house, and did his best to undo the mischief. But to his unspeakable disappointment he found that the Governor's report had already gone to the Council of Ten, so that the matter had passed altogether oat of his hands. The Council would certainly find Zorzi, if he were in Venice, and within two or three days, at the utmost, if not within a few hours; for the Signors of the Night were very vigilant and their men knew every hiding-place in Venice. Zorzi, said the Governor, would certainly be taken into custody unless he had escaped to the mainland. Beroviero could have wrung his hands for sheer despair, and when he told Marietta the result of his second visit to the Governor, her heart sank, for Zorzi's danger was greater than ever before, and it was not likely that a man who had been so mysteriously rescued, to the manifest injury and disgrace of those who were taking him to prison, could escape torture. He would certainly be suspected of connivance with secret enemies of the Republic.

Beroviero bethought him of the friends he had in Venice, to whom he might apply for help in his difficulty. In the first place there was Messer Luigi Foscarini, a Procurator of Saint Mark; but he had not been long in office, and he would probably not wish to be concerned in any matter which tended to oppose authority. And there was old Contarini, who was himself one of the Ten; Beroviero knew his character well and judged that he would not be lenient towards any one who had been forcibly rescued, no matter how innocent he might be. Moreover the law against foreigners who attempted to work in glass was in force, and very stringent. Contarini, like many over-wise men who have no control whatever over their own children, was always for excessive severity in all processes of the law. Beroviero thought of some others, but against each one he found some real objection.

Sitting in his chair after supper, he talked earnestly of the matter with Marietta, who sat opposite him with her work, by the large brass lamp. For the present he had almost forgotten the question of her marriage, for all his former affection for Zorzi had returned, with the conviction of his innocence, and the case was very urgent. That very night Zorzi might be found, and on the next morning he might be brought before the Ten to be examined. Marietta thought with terror of the awful tales Nella had told her about the little torture chamber behind the hall of the Council.

"Who is that Messer Zuan Venier, who came to see Zorzi?" asked Marietta suddenly.

"A young man who fought very bravely in the East, I believe," answered Beroviero. "His father was the Admiral of the Republic for some time."

"He has talked with Zorzi," said Marietta. "Pasquale said so. He must have liked him, of course; and none of the other patricians you have mentioned have ever seen him. Messer Zuan is not in office, and has nothing to lose. Perhaps he will be willing to use his influence with his father. If only the Ten could know the whole truth before Zorzi is brought before them, it would be very different."

Beroviero saw that there was some wisdom in applying to a younger man, like Zuan Venier, who had nothing at stake, and since Venier had come to visit him, there could be nothing strange in his returning the courtesy as soon as he conveniently could.

On the following morning therefore the master betook himself to Venice in his gondola. Pasquale was already gone in the skiff, on the errand entrusted to him. He had judged it best not to put on his Sunday clothes, nor his clean shirt, nor to waste time in improving his appearance at the barber's, for he had been shaved on Saturday night as usual and the week was not yet half over. Hidden in the bow of the little boat there lay his provision for the day, half a loaf of bread, a thick slice of cheese and two onions, with an earthen bottle of water. With these supplies the old sailor knew that he could roam the canals of Venice for twenty-four hours if he chose, and he also had some money in case it should seem wise to ply an acquaintance with a little strong wine in order to promote conversation.

The morning was sultry and a light haze hung over the islands at sunrise, which is by no means usual. Pasquale sniffed the air as he rowed himself through the narrow canals. There was a mingled smell of stagnant salt water, cabbage stalks, watermelons and wood smoke long unfamiliar to him, and reminding him pleasantly of his childhood. Wherever a bit of stone pier ran along by an open space, scores of olive-skinned boys were bathing, and as he passed they yelled at him and splashed him. Many a time he had done the same, long ago, and had sometimes got a sharp knock from the blade of an oar for his pains.

The high walls made brown shadows, that struck across the greenish water, shivering away to long streaks of broken light and shade, and trying to dance and rock themselves together for a moment before a passing boat disturbed them again. In the shade boats were moored, laden with fresh vegetables, and with jars of milk brought in from the islands and the mainland before dawn. From open windows, here and there, red-haired women with dark eyes looked down idly, and breathed the morning air for a few minutes before beginning their household work. The bells of Saint

John and Saint Paul were ringing to low mass, and a few old women with black shawls over their heads, and wooden clogs on their feet, made a faint clattering as they straggled to the door.

It was long since Pasquale had been in Venice. He could not remember exactly how many years had passed, but the city had changed little, and still after many centuries there is but little and slow change. The ways and turnings were as familiar to him as ever, and would have been unforgotten if he had never taken the trouble to cross the lagoon again, to his dying day. The soft sounds, the violent colours, the splendid gloom of deep-arched halls that went straight from the great open door at the water's edge to the shadowy heart of the palace within; the boatmen polishing the metal work of their gondolas with brick dust and olive oil; the servants, still in rough working clothes, sweeping the steps, and trimming off the charred hemp-wicks of torches that had been used in the night; the single woman's voice far overhead that broke the silence of some narrow way, singing its song for sheer gladness of an idle heart; it was all as it used to be, and Pasquale had a dim consciousness that he loved it better than his dreary little den in Murano, and better than his Sunday walk as far as San Donato, when all the handsome women and pretty girls of the smaller people were laughing away the cool hours and showing off their little fineries. It was but a vague suggestion of a sentiment with him, and no more. He knew that he should starve if he came back to Venice, and what was the pleasant smell of the cabbage stalks and watermelons that it should compare with the security of daily bread and lodging, with some money to spare, and two suits of clothes every year, which his master gave him in return for keeping a single door shut?

He pushed out upon the Grand Canal, where as yet there were few boats and no gondolas at all, and soon he turned the corner of the Salute and rowed out slowly upon the Giudecca, where the merchant vessels lay at anchor, large and small, galliots and feluccas and many a broad 'trabacolo' from the Istrian coast, with huge spreading bows, and hawse ports painted scarlet like great red eyes. The old sailor's heart was gladdened by the sight of them, and as he rested on his single oar, he gently cursed the land, and all landlocked places, and rivers and fresh water, and all lakes and inland canals, and wished himself once more on the high seas with a stout vessel, a lazy captain, a dozen hard-fisted shipmates and a quarter of a century less to his account of years.

He had been dreaming a little, and now he bent to the oar

again and sent the skiff quietly along by the pier, looking out for any idle seamen who might be led into conversation. Before long he spied a couple, sitting on the edge of the stones near some steps and fishing with long canes. He passed them, of course, without looking at them, lest they should suspect that he had come their way purposely, and he made the skiff fast by the stair, after which he sat down on a thwart and stared vacantly at things in general, being careful not to bestow a glance on the two men. Presently one of them caught a small fish, and Pasquale judged that the moment for scraping an acquaintance had begun. He turned his head and watched how the man unhooked the fish and dropped it flapping into a basket made of half dried rushes.

"There are no whales in the canal," he observed. "There are not even tunny fish. But what there is, it seems that you know how to catch."

"I do what I can, according to my little skill," answered the man. "It passes the time, and then it is always something to eat with the bread."

"Yes," Pasquale answered. "A roasted fish on bread with a little oil is very savoury. As for passing the time, I suppose that you are looking for a ship."

"Of course," the man replied. "If we had a ship we should not be here fishing! It is a bad time of the year, you must know, for most of the Venetian vessels are at sea, and we do not care to ship with any Neapolitan captain who chances to have starved some of his crew to death!"

"I have heard of a rich Greek merchant captain who has been in Venice some time," observed Pasquale carelessly. "He will be looking out for a crew before long."

"Is Captain Aristarchi going to sea at last?" asked the man who had not spoken yet. "Or do you mean some other captain?"

"That is the name, I believe," said Pasquale. "It was an outlandish name like that. Do you ever see him about the docks? I saw him once, a piece of man, I tell you, with bones like a bull and a face like a bear."

"He is not often seen," answered the man who had spoken last. "That is his ship; over there, between the 'trabacolo' and the dismasted hulk."

"I see her," returned Pasquale at once. "A thorough Greek she is, too, by her looks, but well kept enough if she is only, waiting for a cargo, with two or three hands on board."

The men laughed a little at Pasquale's ignorance concerning the vessel.

"She has a full crew," said one. "She is always ready for sea at any moment, with provisions and water. No one can understand what the captain means, nor why he is here, nor why he is willing to pay twenty men for doing nothing."

"Does the captain live on board of her?" inquired Pasquale indifferently.

"Not he! He is amusing himself in Venice. He has hired a house by the month, not far from the Baker's Bridge, and there he has been living for a long time."

"He must be very rich," observed Pasquale, who had found out what he wished to know, but was too wise to let the conversation drop too abruptly. "From what you say, however, he needs no more hands on his vessel," he added.

"It is not for us," answered the man. "We will ship with a captain we know, and with shipmates from our own country, who are Christians and understand the compass."

This he said because all seagoing vessels did not carry a compass in those days.

"And until we can pick up a ship we like," added the other man, "we will live on bread and water, and if we can catch a fish now and then in the canal, so much the better."

Pasquale cast off the bit of line that moored his skiff, shipped his single oar, and with a parting word to the men, he pushed off.

"You are quite right!" he said. "Eh! A roast fish is a savoury thing."

They nodded to him and again became intent on their pastime. Pasquale rowed faster than before, and he passed close under the stern of the Greek vessel. The mate was leaning over the taffrail under the poop awning. He was dressed in baggy garments of spotless white, his big blue cap was stuck far back on his head, and his strong brown arms were bare to the elbow. He looked as broad as he was long.

"Is the captain on board, sir?" asked Pasquale, at a venture, but looking at the mate with interest.

He expected that he would answer the question in the negative, by sticking out his jaw and throwing his head a little backward. To his surprise the mate returned his gaze a moment, and then stood upright.

"Keep under the counter," he said in fairly good Italian. "I will go and see if the captain is in his cabin."

Pasquale waited, and in a few moments the mate returned, dropped a Jacob's ladder over the taffrail and made it fast on board. Pasquale hitched the painter of the skiff to the end that hung down, and went up easily enough in spite of his age and stiffened joints. He climbed over the rail and stood beside the mate. The instant his feet touched the white deck he wished he had put on his Sunday hose and his clean shirt. He touched his cap, as he assuredly would not have done ashore, to any one but his master.

"You seem to have been a sailor," said the Greek mate, in an approving tone.

"Yes, sir," answered Pasquale. "Is Zorzi still safe?"

"The captain will tell you about Zorzi," was the mate's answer, as he led the way.

Aristarchi was seated with one leg under him on a inroad transom over which was spread a priceless Persian silk carpet, such as the richest patrician in Venice would have hung on the wall like a tapestry of great value. He looked at Pasquale, and the latter heard the door shut behind him. At the same instant a well-known voice greeted him by name, as Zorzi himself appeared from the inner cabin.

"I did not expect to find you so soon," said the porter with a growl of satisfaction.

"I wish you had found him sooner," laughed Aristarchi carelessly. "And since you are here, I hope you will carry him off with you and never let me see his face again, till all this disturbance is over! I would rather have carried off the Doge himself, with his precious velvet nightcap on his head, than have taken this fellow the other night. All Venice is after him. I was just going to drown him, to get rid of him."

There was a sort of savage good-nature in the Greek's tone which was reassuring, in spite of his ferocious looks and words.

"You would have been hanged if you had," observed Pasquale in answer to the last words.

Zorzi was evidently none the worse for what had happened to him since his arrest and unexpected liberation. He was not of the sort that suffer by the imagination when there is real danger, for he had plenty of good sense. Pasquale told him that the master had returned.

"We knew it yesterday," Zorzi answered. "The captain seems to know everything."

"Listen to me, friend porter," Aristarchi said. "If you will take this young fellow with you I shall be obliged to you. I took him from the Governor's men out of mere kindness of heart, because I liked him the first time I saw him, but the Ten are determined to get him into their hands, and I have no fancy to go with him and answer for the half-dozen crowns my mate and I broke in that frolic at Murano."

Pasquale's small eyes twinkled at the thought of the discomfited archers.

"We have changed our lodgings three times since yesterday afternoon," continued Aristarchi, "and I am tired of carrying this lame bottle-blower up and down rope ladders, when the Signors of the Night are at the door. So drop him over the rail into your boat and let me lead a peaceful life."

"Like an honest merchant captain as you are," added Pasquale with a grin. "We have been anxious for you," he added, looking at Zorzi. "The master is in Venice this morning, to see his friends on your behalf, I think."

"If we go back openly," said Zorzi, "we may both be taken at any moment."

"If they catch me," answered Pasquale, "they will heave me overboard. I am not worth salting. But they need not catch either of us. Once in the laboratory at Murano, they will never find you. That is the one place where they will not look for you."

The mate put his head down through the small hatch overhead.

"I do not like the look of a boat that has just put off from Saint George's," he said.

Aristarchi sprang to his feet.

"Pick him up and drop him into the porter's skiff," he said. "I am sick of dancing with the fellow in my arms."

With incredible ease Aristarchi took Zorzi round the waist, mounted the cabin table and passed him up through the hatch to the mate, who had already brought him to the Jacob's ladder at the stern before Pasquale could get there by the ordinary way.

"Quick, man!" said the mate, as the old sailor climbed over the rail.

At the same time he slipped the bight of short rope round Zorzi's body under his arms and got a turn round the rail with both parts, so as to lower him easily. Zorzi helped himself as well as he could, and in a few moments he was lying in the bottom of the skiff, covered with a piece of sacking which the mate threw down, the rope ladder was hauled up and disappeared, and when Pasquale glanced back as he rowed slowly away, the mate was leaning over the taffrail in an attitude of easy unconcern.

The old porter had smuggled more than one bale of rich goods ashore in his young days, for a captain who had a dislike of the customs, and he knew that his chance of safety lay not in speed, but in showing a cool indifference. He might have dropped down the Giudecca at a good rate, for the tide was fair, but he preferred a direction that would take him right across the course of the boat which the mate had seen coming, as if he were on his way to the Lido.

The officer of the Ten, with four men in plain brown coats and leathern belts, sat in the stern of the eight-oared launch that swept swiftly past the skiff towards the vessels at anchor. Pasquale rested on his oar a moment and turned to look, with an air of interest that would have disarmed any suspicions the officer might have entertained. But he had none, and did not bestow a second glance on the little craft with its shabby oarsman. Then Pasquale began to row again, with a long even stroke that had no air of haste about it, but which kept the skiff at a good speed. When he saw that he was out of hearing of other boats, and heading for the Lido, he began to tell what he intended to do next, in a low monotonous tone, glancing down now and then at Zorzi's face that cautiously peered at him out from the folds of the sack-cloth.

"I will tell you when to cover yourself," he said, speaking at the horizon. "We shall have to spend the day under one of the islands. I have some bread and cheese and water, and there are onions. When it is night I will just slip into our canal at Murano, and you can sleep in the laboratory, as if you had never left it."

"If they find me there, they cannot say that I am hiding," said Zorzi with a low laugh.

"Lie low," said Pasquale softly. "There is a boat coming."

For ten minutes neither spoke, and Zorzi lay quite still, covering his face. When the danger was past Pasquale began to talk again, and told him all he himself knew of what had happened, which was not much, but which included the assurance that the master was for him, and had turned against Giovanni.

"As for me," said Zorzi, by and by, when they were moored to a stake, far out in the lagoon, "I was whirled from place to place by those two men, till I did not know where I was. When they first carried me off, they made me lie in the bottom of their boat as I am lying now, and they took me to a house somewhere near the Baker's Bridge. Do you know the house of the Agnus Dei?"

Pasquale grunted.

"It was not far from that," Zorzi continued. "Aristarchi lives there. The mate went back to the ship, I suppose, and Aristarchi's servant gave us supper. Then we slept quietly till morning and I stayed there all day, but Aristarchi thought it would not be safe to keep me in his house the next night—that was last night. He said he feared that a certain lady had guessed where I was. He is a mysterious individual, this Greek! So I was taken somewhere else in the bottom of a boat, after dark. I do not know where it was, but I think it must have been the garret of some tavern where they play dice. After midnight I heard a great commotion below me, and presently Aristarchi appeared at the window with a rope. He always seems to have a coil of rope within reach! He tied me to him—it was like being tied to a wild horse—and he got us safely down from the window to the boat again, and the mate was in it, and they took me to the ship faster than I was ever rowed in my life. You know the rest."

All through the long July day they lay in the fierce sun, shading themselves with the sacking as best they could. But when it was dark at last, Pasquale cast off and headed the skiff for Murano.

CHAPTER XXII

Jacopo Contarini's luck at dice had changed of late, and his friends no longer spoke of losing like him, but of winning as he did, on almost every throw.

"Nevertheless," said the big Foscari to Zuan Venier, "his love affairs seem to prosper! The Georgian is as beautiful as ever, and he is going to marry a rich wife."

It was the afternoon of the day on which Zorzi had left Aristarchi's ship, and the two patricians were lounging in the shady Merceria, where the overhanging balconies of the wooden houses almost met above, and the merchants sat below in the windows of their deep shops, on the little platforms which were at once counters and windowsills. The street smelt of Eastern silks and Spanish leather, and of the Egyptian pastils which the merchants of perfumery continually burnt in order to attract custom.

"I am not qualmish," answered Venier languidly, "yet it sickens me to think of the life Jacopo means to lead. I am sorry for the glassmaker's daughter."

Foscari laughed carelessly. The idea that a woman should be looked upon as anything more than a slave or an object of prey had never occurred to him. But Venier did not smile.

"Since we speak of glassmakers," he said, "Jacopo is doing his best to get that unlucky Dalmatian imprisoned and banished. Old Beroviero came to see me this morning and told me a long story about it, which I cannot possibly remember; but it seems to me—you understand!"

He spoke in low tones, for the Merceria was crowded. Foscari, who was one of those who took most seriously the ceremonial of the secret society, while not caring a straw for its political side, looked very grave.

"It is of no use to say that the poor fellow is only a glass-blower," Venier continued. "There are men besides patricians in the world, and good men, too. I mean to tell Contarini what I think of it tonight."

"I will, too," said Foscari at once.

"And I intend to use all the influence my family has, to obtain a fair hearing for the Dalmatian. I hope you will help me. Amongst us we can reach every one of the Council of Ten, except old Contarini, who has the soul of a schoolmaster and the intelligence of a crab. If I did not like the fellow, I suppose I should let him be hanged several times rather than take so much trouble. Sins of omission are my strongest point. I have always surprised my confessor at Easter by the extraordinary number of things I have left undone."

"I daresay," laughed Foscari, "but I remember that you were not too lazy to save me from drowning when I fell into the Grand Canal in carnival."

"I forgot that the water was so cold," said Venier. "If I had guessed how chilly it was, I should certainly not have pulled you out. There is old Hossein at his window. Let us go in and drink sherbet."

"We shall find Mocenigo and Loredan there," answered Foscari. "They shall promise to help the glassblower, too."

They nodded to the Persian merchant, who saluted them by extending his hand towards the ground as if to take up dust, and then bringing it to his forehead. He was very fat, and his pear-shaped face might have been carved out of white cheese. The two young men went in by a small door at the side of the window-counter and disappeared into the interior. At the back of the shop there was a private room with a latticed window that looked out upon a narrow canal. It was one of many places where the young Venetians met in the afternoon to play at dice undisturbed, on pretence of examining Hossein's splendid carpets and Oriental silks. Moreover Hossein's wife, always invisible but ever near, had a marvellous gift for making fruit sherbets, cooled with the snow that was brought down daily from the mountains on the mainland in dripping bales covered with straw matting.

Loredan and Mocenigo were already there, as Foscari had anticipated, eating pistachio nuts and sipping sherbet through rice straws out of tall glasses from Murano. It was a very safe place, for Hossein's knowledge of the Italian language was of a purely commercial character, embracing every numeral and fraction, common or uncommon, and the names of all the hundreds of foreign coins that passed current in Venice, together with half a dozen necessary phrases; and his invisible but occasionally audible wife understood no Italian at all. Also, Hossein was always willing to lend any young patrician money with which to pay his losses, at the modest rate of seven ducats to be paid every week for the use of each hundred; which one of the youths, who had a turn for arithmetic, had discovered to be only about 364 per cent yearly, whereas Casadio, the Hebrew, had a method of his own by which he managed to get about 580. It was therefore a real economy to frequent Hossein's shop.

In spite of his pretended forgetfulness, Venier remembered every word that Beroviero had told him, and indolently as he talked, his whole nature was roused to defend Zorzi. In his heart he despised Contarini, and hoped that his marriage might never take place, for he was sincerely sorry for Marietta; but it was Jacopo's behaviour towards Zorzi that called forth his wrath, it was the man's disdainful assumption that because Zorzi was not a patrician, the oath to defend every companion of the society was not binding where he was concerned; it was the insolent certainty that the others should all be glad to be rid of the poor Dalmatian, who after all had not troubled them over-much with his company. On that very evening they were to meet at the house of the Agnus Dei, and Venier was determined to speak his mind. When he chose to exert himself, his influence over his companions was very great, if not supreme.

He soon brought Mocenigo and Loredan to share his opinion and to promise the support of all their many relations in Zorzi's favour, and the four began to play, for lack of anything better to do. Before long others of the society came in, and as each arrived Venier, who only played in order not to seem as unsociable as he generally felt, set down the dice box to gain over a new ally. An hour had passed when Contarini himself appeared, even more magnificent than usual, his beautiful waving beard most carefully trimmed and combed as if to show it to its greatest advantage against the purple silk of a surcoat cut in a new fashion and which he was wearing for the first time. His white hands were splendid with jewelled rings, and he wore at his belt a large wallet-purse embroidered in Constantinople before the coming of the Turks and adorned with three enamelled images of saints. Hossein himself ushered him in, as if he were the guest of honour, as the Persian merchant indeed considered him, for none of the others had ever paid him half so many seven weekly ducats for money borrowed in all their lives, as Jacopo had often paid in a single year.

There are men whom no one respects very highly, who are not sincerely trusted, whose honour is not spotless and whose ways are far from straight, but who nevertheless hold a certain ascendancy over others, by mere show and assurance. When Contarini entered a place where many were gathered together, there was almost always a little hush in the talk, followed by a murmur that was pleasant in his ear. No one paused to look at Zuan Venier when he came into a room, though there was not one of his friends who would not have gone to him in danger or difficulty, without so much as thinking of Contarini as a possible helper in trouble. But it was almost impossible not to feel a sort of artistic surprise at Jacopo's extraordinary beauty of face and figure, if not at the splendid garments in which he delighted to array himself.

It was with a slight condescension that he greeted the group of players, some of whom at once made a place for him at the table. They had been ready enough to stand by Venier against him in Zorzi's defence, but unless Venier led the way, there was not one of them who would think of opposing him, or taking him to task for what was very like a betrayal. Venier returned his greeting with some coldness, which Contarini hardly noticed, as his reception by the others had been sufficiently flattering. Then they began to play.

Jacopo won from the first. Foscari bent his heavy eyebrows and tugged at his beard angrily, as he lost one throw after another; the cold sweat stood on Mocenigo's forehead in beads, as he risked more and more, and Loredan's hand trembled when it was his turn to take up the dice box against Contarini; for they played a game in which each threw against all the rest in succession.

"You cannot say that the dice are loaded," laughed Contarini at last, "for they are your own!"

"The delicacy of the thought is only exceeded by the good taste that expresses it," observed Venier.

"You are sarcastic, my friend," answered Jacopo, shaking the dice. "It is your turn with me."

Jacopo threw first. Venier followed him and lost.

"That is my last throw," he said, as he pushed the remains of his small heap of gold across to Contarini. "I have no more money today, nor shall I have tomorrow."

"Hossein has plenty," suggested Foscari, who hoped that Contarini's luck would desert him before long.

"At this rate you will need all he has," returned Venier with a careless laugh.

Before long more than one of the players was obliged to call in the ever-complacent Persian merchant, and the heap of gold grew in front of Jacopo, till he could hardly keep it together.

"It is true that you have been losing for years," said Mocenigo, trying to laugh, "but we did not think you would win back all your losses in a day."

"You shall have your revenge tonight," answered Contarini, rising. "I am expected at a friend's house at this hour."

His large wallet was so full of gold that he could hardly draw the strong silken strings together and tie them.

"A friend's house!" laughed Loredan, who had lost somewhat less than the others. "It would give us much delight to know the colour of the lady's hair!"

To this Contarini answered only by a smile, which was not devoid of satisfaction.

"Take care!" said Foscari, gloomily contemplating the bare table before him, over which so much of his good gold had slipped away. "Take care! Luck at play, mischance in love, says the proverb."

"Oh! In that case I congratulate you, my dear friend!" returned Contarini gaily.

The others laughed at the retort, and the party broke up, though all did not go at once. Venier went out alone, while two or three walked with Contarini to his gondola. The rest stayed behind in the shop and made old Hossein unroll his choicest carpets and show them his most precious embroideries, though he protested that it was already much too dark to appreciate such choice things. But they did not wish to be seen coming away in a body, for such playing was very strictly forbidden, and the spies of the Ten were everywhere.

Contarini dismissed his gondola at the house of the Agnus Dei, and was admitted by the trusted servant who had once taken a message to Zorzi. He found Arisa waiting for him in her favourite place by the open window, and the glow of the setting sun made little fires in her golden hair. She could tell by his face that he had been fortunate at play, and her smile was very soft and winning. As he sank down beside her in the luxurious silence of satisfaction, her fingers were stealthily trying the weight of his laden wallet. She could not lift it with one hand. She smiled again, as she thought how easily Aristarchi would carry the money in his teeth, well tied and knotted in a kerchief, when he slipped down the silk rope from her window, though it would be much wiser to exchange it for pearls and diamonds which Contarini might see and admire, and which she could easily take with her in her final flight.

He trusted her, too, in his careless way, and that night, when he was ready to go down and admit his companions, he would empty most of the gold into a little coffer in which he often left the key, taking but just enough to play with, and almost sure of winning more.

She was very gentle on that evening, when the sun had gone

down, and they sat in the deepening dusk, and she spoke sadly of not seeing him for several hours. It would be so lonely, she said, and since he could play in the daytime, why should he give up half of one precious night to those tiresome dice? He laughed indolently, pleased that she should not even suspect the real object of the meetings.

By and by, when it was an hour after dark, and they had eaten of delicate things which a silent old woman brought them on small silver platters, Contarini went down to let in his guests, and Arisa was alone, as usual on such evenings. For a long time she lay quite still among the cushions, in the dark, for Jacopo had taken the light with him. She loved to be in darkness, as she always told him, and for very good reasons, and she had so accustomed herself to it as to see almost as well as Aristarchi himself, for whom she was waiting.

At last she heard the expected signal of his coming, the soft and repeated splashing of an oar in the water just below the window. In a moment she was in the inner room, to receive him in her straining arms, longing to be half crushed to death in his. But tonight, even as he held her in the first embrace of meeting, she felt that something had happened, and that there was a change in him. She drew him to the little light that burned in her chamber before the image, and looked into his face, terrified at the thought of what she might see there. He smiled at her and raised his shaggy eyebrows as if to ask if she really distrusted him.

"Yes," he said, nodding his big head slowly, "something has happened. You are quick at guessing. We are going tonight. There is moonlight and the tide will serve in two or three hours. Get ready what you need and put together the jewels and the money."

"Tonight!" cried Arisa, very much surprised. "Tonight? Do you really mean it?"

"Yes. I am in earnest. Michael has emptied my house of all my belongings today and has taken the keys back to the owner. We have plenty of time, for I suppose those overgrown boys are playing at dice downstairs, and I think I shall take leave of Contarini in person."

"You are capable of anything!" laughed Arisa. "I should like to see you tear him into little strips, so that every shred should keep alive to be tortured!"

"How amiable! What gentle thoughts you have! Indeed, you women are sweet creatures!"

With her small white hand she jestingly pretended to box his huge ears.

"You would be well paid if I refused to go with you," she said with a low laugh. "But I should like to know why you have decided so suddenly. What is the matter? What is to become of all our plans, and of Contarini's marriage? Tell me quickly!"

"I have had a visit from an officer of the Ten today," he said. "The Ten send me greeting, as it were, and their service, and kindly invite me to leave Venice within twenty-four hours. As the Ten are the only persons in Venice for whom I have the smallest respect, I shall show it by accepting their invitation."

"But why? What have you done?"

"Of course it is not a serious matter to give a sound beating to an officer of justice and six of his men," answered Aristarchi, "but it is not the custom here, and they suspect me of having done it. To tell the truth, I think I am hardly treated. I have sent Zorzi back to Murano, and if the Ten have the sense to look for him where he has been living for five years, they will find him at once, at work in that stifling furnace-room. But I fancy that is too simple for them."

He told her how Pasquale had come in the morning, and how the officer who had been in pursuit of him had searched the ship for Zorzi in vain. The order to leave Venice had come an hour later. The anchors were now up, and the vessel was riding to a kedge by a light hawser, well out in the channel. As soon as Arisa could be brought on board Aristarchi meant to make sail, for the strong offshore breeze would blow all night.

"We may as well leave nothing behind," said Aristarchi coolly. "Michael will wait for us below, in one of the ship's boats. There is room for all Contarini's possessions, if we could only get at them."

"Would it not be better to be content with what we have already, and to go at once?" asked Arisa rather timidly.

"No," replied Aristarchi. "I am going to say good-bye to your old friend in my own way."

"Do you mean to kill him?" asked Arisa in a whisper, though it was quite safe for them to talk in natural tones. "I could go behind him and throw something over his head."

Aristarchi grinned, and pressed her beautiful head to his breast, caressing her with his rough hands.

"You are as bloodthirsty as a little tigress," he said. "No. I do not even mean to hurt him."

"Oh, I hoped you would," answered the Georgian woman. "I have hated him so long. Will you not kill him, just to please me? We could wind him in a sheet with a weight, you know, and drop him into the canal, and no one would ever know. I have often thought of it."

"Have you, my gentle little sweetheart?" Aristarchi chuckled with delight as he stroked her hair. "I am sorry," he continued. "The fact is, I am not a Georgian like you. I have been brought up among people of civilisation, and I have scruples about killing any one. Besides, sweet dove, if we were to kill the son of one of the Council of Ten, the Council would pursue us wherever we went, for Venice is very powerful. But the Ten will not lift a hand to revenge a good-for-nothing young gamester whose slave has run away with her first love! Every one will laugh at Contarini if he tries to get redress. It is better to laugh than to be laughed at, it is better to be laughed at than to cry, it is better to cry one's eyes blind than to be hanged."

Having delivered himself of these opinions Aristarchi began to look about him for whatever might be worth the trouble of carrying off, and Arisa collected all her jewels from the caskets in which they were kept, and little bags of gold coins which she had hidden in different places. She also lit a candle and brought Aristarchi to the small coffer in which Contarini kept ready gold for play, and which was now more than half full.

"The dowry of the glassmaker's daughter!" observed the Greek as he carried it off.

There were small objects of gold and silver on the tables in the large room, there was a dagger with a jewelled hilt, an illuminated mass book in a chased silver case.

"You will need it on Sundays at sea," said Aristarchi.

"I cannot read," said the Georgian slave regretfully. "But it will be a consolation to have the missal."

Aristarchi smiled and tossed the book upon the heap of things.

"It would be amusing to pay a visit to those young fools downstairs, and to take all their money and leave them locked up for the night," he said, as if a thought had struck him.

"There are too many of them," answered Arisa, laying her hand anxiously upon his arm. "And they are all armed. Please do nothing so foolish."

"If they are all like Contarini, I do not mind twenty of them or so," laughed Aristarchi. "They must have more than a thousand gold ducats amongst them. That would be worth taking."

"They are not all like Contarini," said Arisa. "There is Zuan Venier, for instance."

"Zuan Venier? Is he one of them? I have heard of him. I

should like to see whether he could be frightened, for they say it is impossible."

Aristarchi scratched his head, pushing his shaggy hair forward over his forehead, as he tried to think of an effectual scheme for producing the desired result.

"The Ten might pursue us for that, as well as for a murder," said Arisa.

Meanwhile the friends assembled in the room downstairs had been occupied for a long time in hearing what Zuan Venier had to say to Jacopo Contarini, concerning the latter's treatment of Zorzi. For Venier had kept his word, and as soon as all were present he had boldly spoken his mind, in a tone which his friends were not accustomed to hear. At first Contarini had answered with offended surprise, asking what concern it could be of Venier's whether a miserable glassblower were exiled or not, and he appealed to the others, asking whether it would not be far better for them all that such an outsider as Zorzi should be banished from Venice. But Venier retorted that the Dalmatian had taken the same oath as the rest of the company, that he was an honest man, besides being a great artist as his master asseverated, and that he had the same right to the protection of each and all of them as Contarini himself. To the latter's astonishment this speech was received with unanimous approbation, and every man present, except Contarini, promised his help and that of his family, so far as he might obtain it.

"I have advised Beroviero," Venier then continued, "if he can find the young artist, to make him go before the Council of Ten of his own free will, taking some of his works with him. And now that this question is settled, I propose to you all that our society cease to have any political or revolutionary aim whatever, for I am of opinion that we are risking our necks for a game at dice and for nothing else, which is childish. The only liberty we are vindicating, so far as I can see, is that of gaming as much as we please, and if we do that, and nothing more, we shall certainly not go between the red columns for it. A fine or a few months of banishment to the mainland would be the worst that could happen. As things are now, we are not only in danger of losing our heads at any moment, which is an affair of merely relative importance, but we may be tempted to make light of a solemn promise, which seems to me a very grave matter."

Thereupon Venier looked round the table, and almost all the men were of his opinion. Contarini flushed angrily, but he knew himself to be in the wrong and though he was no coward, he had not the sort of temper that faces opposition for its own sake. He therefore began to rattle the dice in the box as a hint to all that the discussion was at an end.

But his good fortune seemed gone, and instead of winning at almost every throw, as he had won in the afternoon, he soon found that he had almost exhausted the heap of gold he had laid on the table, and which he had thought more than enough. He staked the remainder with Foscari, who won it at a cast, and laughed.

"You offered us our revenge," said the big man. "We mean to take it!"

But though Contarini was not a good fighter, he was a good gamester, and never allowed himself to be disturbed by ill-luck. He joined in the laugh and rose from the table.

"You must forgive me," he said, "if I leave you for a moment. I must fill my purse before I play again."

"Do not stay too long!" laughed Loredan. "If you do, we shall come and get you, and then we shall know the colour of the lady's hair."

Contarini laughed as he went to the door, opened it and stealthily set the key in the lock on the outside.

"I shall lock you in while I am gone!" he cried. "You are far too inquisitive!"

Laughing gaily he turned the key on the whole company, and he heard their answering laughter as he went away, for they accepted the jest, and continued playing.

He entered the large room upstairs, just as Aristarchi had finished tying up the heavy bundle in the inner chamber. Arisa heard the well-known footstep, and placed one hand over Aristarchi's mouth, lest he should speak, while the other pointed to the curtained door. The Greek held his breath.

"Arisa! Arisa!" Contarini called out. "Bring me a light, sweetest!"

Without hesitation Arisa took the lighted candle, and making a gesture of warning to Aristarchi went quickly to the other room. The Greek crept towards the door, the big veins standing out like knots on his rugged temples, his great hands opened wide, with the tips of the fingers a little turned in. He was like a wrestler ready to get his hold with a spring.

"I want some more money," Contarini was saying, in explanation. "They said they would follow me if I stayed too long, so I have locked them in! I think I shall keep them waiting a while. What do you say, love?"

He laughed again, aloud, and on the other side of the curtain

Aristarchi grinned from ear to ear and noiselessly loosened the black sash he wore round his waist. For once in his life, as Zorzi would have said, he had not a coil of rope at hand when he needed it, but the sash was strong and would serve the purpose. He pushed the curtain aside, a very little, in order to see before springing.

Contarini stood half turned away from the door, clasping Arisa to his breast and kissing her hair. The next moment he was sprawling on the floor, face downwards, and Arisa was pressing one of the soft cushions from the divan upon his head to smother his cries, while Aristarchi bound his hands firmly together behind him with one end of the long sash, and in spite of his desperate struggle got a turn with the rest round both his feet, drew them back as far as he could and hitched the end twice. Jacopo was now perfectly helpless, but he was not yet dumb. Aristarchi had brought his tools with him, in the bosom of his doublet.

Kneeling on Contarini's shoulders he took out a small iron instrument, shaped exactly like a pear, but which by a screw, placed where the stem would be, could be made to open out in four parts that spread like the petals of a flower. Arisa looked on with savage interest, for she believed that it was some horrible instrument of torture; and indeed it was the iron gag, the 'pear of anguish,' which the torturers used in those days, to silence those whom they called their patients.

Holding the instrument closed, Aristarchi pushed his hand under the cushion. He knew that Contarini's mouth would be open, as he must be half suffocated and gasping for breath. In an instant the iron pear had slipped between his teeth and had opened its relentless leaves, obedient to the screw.

"Take the pillow away," said Aristarchi quietly. "We can say good-bye to your old acquaintance now, but he will have to content himself with nodding his head in a friendly way."

He turned the helpless man upon his side, for owing to the position of his heels and hands Contarini could not lie on his back. Then Aristarchi set the candle on the floor near his face and looked at him and indulged himself in a low laugh. Contarini's face was deep red with rage and suffocation, and his beautiful brown eyes were starting from their sockets with a terror which increased when he saw far the first time the man with whom he had to deal, or rather who was about to deal with him, and most probably without mercy. Then he caught sight of Arisa, smiling at him, but not as she had been wont to smile. Aristarchi spoke at last, in an easy, reassuring tone.

"My friend," he said, "I am not going to hurt you any more. You may think it strange, but I really shall not kill you. Arisa and I have loved each other for a long time, and since she has lived here, I have come to her almost every night. I know your house almost as well as you do, and you have kindly told me that your friends are all looked in. We shall therefore not have the trouble of leaving by the window, since we can go out by the front door, where my boat will be waiting for us. You will never see us again."

Contarini's eyes rolled wildly, and still Arisa smiled.

"You have made him suffer," she said. "He loved me."

"Before we go," continued the Greek, folding his arms and looking down upon his miserable enemy, "I think it fair to warn you that under the praying-stool in Arisa's room there is an air shaft through which we have heard all your conversation, during these secret meetings of yours. If you try to pursue us, I shall send information to the Ten, which will cut off most of your heads. As they are so empty it might seem to be scarcely worth while to take them, but the Ten know best. I can rely on your discretion. If I were not sure of it I would accede to this dear lady's urgent request and cut you up into small pieces."

Contarini writhed and sputtered, but could make no sound.

"I promised not to hurt you any more, my friend, and I am a man of my word. But I have long admired your hair and beard. You see I was in Saint Mark's when you went there to meet the glassmaker's daughter, and I have seen you at other times. I should be sorry never to see such a beautiful beard again, so I mean to take it with me, and if you will keep quiet, I shall really not hurt you."

Thereupon he produced from his doublet a bright pair of shears, and knelt down by the wretched man's head. Contarini twisted himself as be might and tried instinctively to draw his head away.

"I have heard that pirates sometimes accidentally cut off a prisoner's ear," said Aristarchi. "If you will not move, I am quite sure that I shall not be so awkward as to do that."

Contarini now lay motionless, and Aristarchi went to work. With the utmost neatness he cropped off the silky hair, so close to Jacopo's skull that it almost looked as if it had been shaved with a razor. In the same way he clipped the splendid beard away, and even the brown eyebrows, till there was not a hair left on Contarini's head or face. Then he contemplated his work, and laughed at the weak jaw and the womanish mouth.

"You look like an ugly woman in man's clothes," he said, by

way of consoling his victim.

He rose now, for he feared lest Contarini's friends might break open the door downstairs. He shouldered the heavy bundle with ease, set his blue cap on the back of his head and bade Arisa go with him. She had her mantle ready, but she could not resist casting delighted glances at her late owner's face. Before going, she knelt down one moment by his side, and inclined her face to his, with a very loving gaze. Lower and lower she bent, as if she would give him a parting kiss, till Aristarchi uttered an exclamation. Then she laughed cruelly, and with the back of her hand struck the lips that had so often touched her own.

A few moments later Aristarchi had placed her in his boat, the heavy bundle of spoils lay at her feet, and the craft shot swiftly from the door of the house of the Agnus Dei. For Michael Pandos, the mate, had been waiting under the window, and a stroke of the oars brought him to the steps.

In the closed room where the friends were playing dice, there began to be some astonishment at the time needed by Jacopo to replenish his purse. When more than half an hour had passed one pair stopped playing, and then another, until they were all listening for some sound in the silent house. The perfect stillness had something alarming in it, and none of them fully trusted Contarini.

"I think," said Venier with all his habitual indolence, "that it is time to ascertain the colour of the lady's hair. Can you break the lock?"

He spoke to Foscari, who nodded and went to the door with two or three others. In a few seconds it flew open before their combined attack, and they almost lost their balance as they staggered out into the dark hall. The rest brought lights and they all began to go up the stairs together. The first to enter the room was Foscari. Venier, always indifferent, was among the last.

Foscari started at the extraordinary sight of a man in magnificent clothes, lying on one shoulder, with his heels tied up to his hands and his shorn head and face moving slowly from side to side in the bright light of the wax candle that stood on the floor. The other men crowded into the room, but at first no one recognised the master of the house. Then all at once Foscari saw the rings on his fingers.

"It is Contarini," he cried, "and somebody has shaved his head!"

He burst into a fit of uncontrollable laughter, in which the others joined, till the house rang again, and the banished servants came running down to see what was the matter.

Only Zuan Venier, a compassionate smile on his face, knelt beside Contarini and carefully withdrew the iron gag from his mouth.

At the same instant Aristarchi's hatchet chopped through the hawser by which his vessel was riding, and he took the helm himself to steer her out through the narrow channel before the wind.

CHAPTER XXIII

When Pasquale had let Zorzi in, he crossed the canal again, moored the skiff with lock and chain, and came back by the wooden bridge. Zorzi went on through the corridor and came out into the moonlit garden. It was hard to believe that only forty-eight hours had passed since he had left it, but the freshly dug earth told him of Giovanni's search, about which Pasquale had told him, and there was the pleasant certainty that the master had come home and could probably protect him, even against the Ten. Besides this, he felt stronger and more able to move than since he had been injured, and he was sure that he could now walk with only a stick to help him, though he was always to be lame. He had looked up at Marietta's window before leaving the boat, but it was dark, for Pasquale had wished to be sure that no one should see Zorzi and it was long past the young girl's bedtime.

Pasquale came back, and produced some more bread and cheese from his lodge, for both men were hungry. They sat down on the bench under the plane-tree and ate their meagre supper together in silence, for they had talked much during the long day. Then Pasquale bade Zorzi good night and went away, and Zorzi went into the laboratory, where all was dark. But he knew every brick of the furnace and every stone of the pavement under his feet, and in a few minutes he was fast asleep in his own bed, feeling as safe as if the Ten had never existed and as though the Signors of the Night were not searching every purlieu of Venice to take him into custody. And early in the morning he got up, and Pasquale brought him water as of old, and as his hose and doublet had suffered considerably during his adventures, he put on the Sunday ones and came out into the garden to breathe the morning air. Pasquale had no intention of going over to the house to announce Zorzi's return, for he was firmly convinced that the most simple way of keeping a secret was not to tell it, and before long the master would probably come over himself to ask for news.

Beroviero brought Marietta with him, as he often did, and when they were within he naturally stopped to question Pasquale about his search, while Marietta went on to the garden. The porter took a long time to shut the door, and instead of answering Beroviero, shook his ugly head discontentedly, and muttered imprecations on all makers of locks, latches, bolts, bars and other fastenings, living, dead and yet unborn. So it came to pass that Marietta came upon Zorzi suddenly and alone, when she least expected to meet him.

He was standing by the well-remembered rosebush, leaning on his stick with one hand and lifting up a trailing branch with the other. But when he heard Marietta's step he let the branch drop again and stood waiting for her with happy eyes. She uttered a little cry, that was almost of fear, and stopped short in her walk, for in the first instant she could have believed that she saw a vision; then she ran forward with outstretched hands, and fell into his arms as he dropped his stick to catch her. As her head touched his shoulder, her heart stopped beating for a moment, she gasped a little, and seemed to choke, and then the tears of joy flowed from her eyes, her pulses stirred again, and all was well. He felt a tremor in his hands and could not speak aloud, but as he held her he bent down and whispered something in her ear; and she smiled through the shower of her happy tears, though he could not see it, for her face was hidden.

Just then Beroviero entered from the corridor, followed by Pasquale, and the two old men stood still together gazing at the young lovers. It was on that very spot that the master, when going upon his journey, had told Zorzi how he wished he were his son. But now he forgot that he had said it, and the angry blood rushed to his forehead.

"How dare you?" he cried, as he made a step to go on towards the pair.

They heard his voice and separated hastily. Marietta's fresh cheek blushed like red roses, and she looked down, as shamefacedly as any country maid, but Zorzi turned white as he stooped to pick up his stick, then stood quite upright and met her father's eyes.

"How dare you, I say?" repeated the old man fiercely.

"I love her, sir," Zorzi answered without fear for himself, but with much apprehension for Marietta.

"And have you forgotten that I love him, father?" asked Marietta, looking up but still blushing. "You know, I told you all the truth, and you were not angry then. At least, you were not so very angry," she added, shyly correcting herself.

"If she has told you, sir," Zorzi began, "let me—"

"You can tell me nothing I do not know," cried Beroviero, "and nothing I wish to hear! Be off! Go to the laboratory and begin work. I will speak with my daughter."

Then Pasquale's voice was heard.

"A furnace without a fire is like a ship without a wind," he said. "It might as well be anything else."

Beroviero looked towards the old porter indignantly, but Pasquale had already begun to move and was returning to his lodge, uttering strange and unearthly sounds as he went, for he was so happy that he was really trying to hum a tune. The master turned to the lovers again. Zorzi had withdrawn a step or two, but showed no signs of going further.

"If you are going to tell me that I must change my mind," said Marietta, "and that it is a shame to love a penniless glass-blower—"

"Silence!" cried the old man, stroking his beard fiercely. "How can you presume to guess what I may or may not say about your shameless conduct? Did I not see him kissing you?"

"I daresay, for he did," answered Marietta, raising her eyebrows and looking down in a resigned way. "And it is not the first time, either," she added, shaking her head and almost laughing.

"The insolence!" cried Beroviero. "The atrocious boldness!"

"Sir," said Zorzi, coming nearer, "there is only one remedy for it. Give me your daughter for my wife—"

"Upon my faith, this is too much! You know that Marietta is betrothed to Messer Jacopo Contarini—"

"I have told you that I will not marry him," said Marietta quietly, "so it is just as if I had never been betrothed to him."

"That is no reason for marrying Zorzi," retorted Beroviero. "A pretty match for you! Angelo Beroviero's daughter and a penniless foreigner who cannot even be allowed to work openly at his art!"

"If I go away," Zorzi answered quietly, "I may soon be as rich as you, sir."

At this unexpected statement Beroviero opened his eyes in real astonishment, while Zorzi continued.

"You have your secrets, sir, and I have kept them safe for you. But I have one of my own which is as valuable as any of yours. Did you find some pieces of my work in the annealing oven? I see that they are on the table now. Did you notice that the glass is like yours, but finer and lighter?"

"Well, if it is, what then?" asked Beroviero. "It was an accident. You mixed something with some of my glass—"

"No," answered Zorzi, "it is altogether a composition of my own. I do not know how you mix your materials. How should I?"

"I believe you do," said Beroviero. "I believe you have found it out in some way—"

Zorzi had produced a piece of folded paper from his doublet, and now held it up in his hand.

"I am not bargaining with you, sir, for you are a man of honour. Angelo Beroviero will not rob me, after having been kind to me for so many years. This is my secret, which I discovered alone, with no one's help. The quantities are written out very exactly, and. I am sure of them. Read what is written there. By an accident, I may have made something like your glass, but I do not believe it."

He held out the paper. Beroviero's manner changed.

"You were always an honourable fellow, Zorzi. I thank you."

He opened the paper and looked attentively at the contents. Marietta saw his surprise and interest and took the opportunity of smiling at Zorzi.

"It is altogether different from mine," said Beroviero, looking up and handing back the document.

"Is there fortune in that, sir, or not?" asked Zorzi, confident of the reply. "But you know that there is, and that whenever I go, if I can get a furnace, I shall soon be a rich man by the glass alone, without even counting on such skill as I have with my hands."

"It is true," answered the master, nodding his head thoughtfully. "There are many princes who would willingly give you the little you need in order to make your fortune."

"The little that Venice refuses me!" said Zorzi with some bitterness. "Am I presuming so much, then, when I ask you for your daughter's hand? Is it not in my power, or will it not be very soon, to go to some other city, to Milan, or Florence—"

"No, no!" cried Beroviero. "You shall not take her away—"

He stopped short, realising that he had betrayed what had been in his mind, since he had seen the two standing there, clasped in one another's arms, namely, that in spite of him, or with his blessing, his daughter would before long be married to the man she loved.

"Come, come!" he said testily. "This is sheer nonsense!"

He made a step forward as if to break off the situation by going away.

"If you would rather that I should not leave you, sir," said Zorzi, "I will stay here and make my glass in your furnace, and you shall sell it as if it were your own."

"Yes, father, say yes!" cried Marietta, clasping her hands upon the old man's shoulder. "You see how generous Zorzi is!"

"Generous!" Beroviero shook his head. "He is trying to bribe me, for there is a fortune in his glass, as he says. He is offering me a fortune, I tell you, to let him marry you!"

"The fortune which Messer Jacopo had made you promise to pay him for condescending to be my husband!" retorted Marietta triumphantly. "It seems to me that of the two, Zorzi is the better match!"

Beroviero stared at her a moment, bewildered. Then, in half comic despair he clapped both his hands upon his ears and shook himself gently free from her.

"Was there ever a woman yet who could not make black seem white?" he cried. "It is nonsense, I tell you! It is all arrant nonsense! You are driving me out of my senses!"

And thereupon he went off down the garden path to the laboratory, apparently forgetting that his presence alone could prevent a repetition of that very offence which had at first roused his anger. The door closed sharply after him, with energetic emphasis.

At the same moment Marietta, who had been gazing into Zorzi's eyes, felt that her own sparkled with amusement, and her father might almost have heard her sweet low laugh through the open window at the other end of the garden.

"That was well done," she said. "Between us we have almost persuaded him."

Zorzi took her willing hand and drew her to him, and she was almost as near to him as before, when she straightened herself with quick and elastic grace, and laughed again.

"No, no!" she said. "If he were to look out and see us again, it would be too ridiculous! Come and sit under the plane-tree in the old place. Do you remember how you stared at the trunk and would not answer me when I tried to make you speak, ever so long ago? Do you know, it was because you would not say—what I wanted you to say—that I let myself think that I could marry Messer Jacopo. If you had only known what you were doing!"

"If I had only known!" Zorzi echoed, as they reached the place and Marietta sat down.

They were within sight of the window, but Beroviero did not heed them. He was seated in his own chair, in deep thought, his elbows resting on the wooden arms, his fingers pressing his temples on each side, thinking of his daughter, and perhaps not quite unaware that she was talking to the only man he had ever really trusted.

"I must tell you something, Zorzi," she was saying, as she looked up into the face she loved. "My father told me last night what he had done yesterday. He saw Messer Zuan Venier—"

Zorzi showed his surprise.

"Pasquale told my father that he had been here to see you. Very well, this Messer Zuan advised that if you could be found, you should be persuaded to go before the tribunal of the Ten of your own free will, to tell your story. And he promised to use all his influence and that of all his friends in your favour."

"They will not change the law for me," Zorzi replied, in a hopeless way.

"If they could hear you, they would make a special decree," said Marietta. "You could tell them your story, you could even show them some of the beautiful things you have made. They would understand that you are a great artist. After all, my father says that one of their most especial duties is to deal with everything that concerns Murano and the glassworks. Do you think that they will banish you, now that you have a secret of your own, and can injure us all by setting up a furnace somewhere else? There is no sense in that! And if you go of your own free will, they will hear you kindly, I think. But if you stay here, they will find you in the end, and they will be very angry then, because you will have been hiding from them."

"You are wise," Zorzi answered. "You are very wise."

"No, I love you."

She spoke softly and glanced at the open window, and then at his face.

"Truly?"

He smiled happily as he whispered his question in one word, and he was resting a hand on the trunk of the tree, just as he had been standing on the day she remembered so well.

"Ah, you know it now!" she answered, with bright and trusting eyes.

"One may know a song well, and yet long to hear it again and again."

"But one cannot be always singing it oneself," she said.

"I could never make it ring as sweetly as you," Zorzi answered.

"Try it! I am tired of hearing my voice—"

"But I am not! There is no voice like it in the world. I shall never care to hear another, as long as I live, nor any other song, nor any other words. And when you are weary of saying them, I shall just say them over in my heart, 'She loves me, she loves me,'—all day long."

"Which is better," Marietta asked, "to love, or to know that you are loved?"

"The two thoughts are like soul and body," Zorzi answered. "You must not part them."

"I never have, since I have known the truth, and never shall again."

Then they were silent for a while, but they hardly knew it, for the world was full of the sweetest music they had ever heard, and they listened together.

"Zorzi!"

The master was at the window, calling him. He started a little as if awaking and obeyed the summons as quickly as his lameness would allow. Marietta looked after him, watching his halting gait, and the little effort he made with his stick at each step. For some secret reason the injury had made him more dear to her, and she liked to remember how brave he had been.

He found Beroviero busy with his papers, and the results of the year's experiments, and the old man at once spoke to him as if nothing unusual had happened, telling him what to do from time to time, so that all might be put in order against the time when the fires should be lighted again in September. By and by two men came carrying a new earthen jar for broken glass, and all fragments in which the box had lain were shovelled into it, and the pieces of the old one were taken away. The furnace was not quite cool even yet, and the crucibles might remain where they were for a few days; but there was much to be done, and Zorzi was kept at work all the morning, while Marietta sat in the shade with her work, often looking towards the window and sometimes catching sight of Zorzi as he moved about within.

Meanwhile the story of Contarini's mishap had spread in Venice like wildfire, and before noon there was hardly one of all his many relations and friends who had not heard it. The tale ran through the town, told by high and low, by Jacopo's own trusted servant, and the old woman who had waited on Arisa, and it had reached the marketplace at an early hour, so that the ballad-makers were busy with it. For many had known of the existence of the beautiful Georgian slave and the subject was a good one for a song—how she had caressed him to sleep and fostered his foolish security while he loved her blindly, and how she and her mysterious lover had bound him and shaved his head and face and made him a laughingstock, so that he must hide himself from the world for months, and moreover how they had carried away by night all the precious gifts he had heaped upon the woman since he had bought her in the slave-market.

Last of all, his father heard it when he came home about an

hour before noon from the sitting of the Council of Ten, of which he was a member for that year. He found Zuan Venier waiting in the hall of his house, and the two remained closeted together for some time. For the young man had promised Jacopo to tell old Contarini, though it was an ungrateful errand, and one which, the latter might remember against him. But it was a kind action, and Venier performed it as well as he could, telling the story truthfully, but leaving out all such useless details as might increase the father's anger.

At first indeed the old man brought his hand down heavily upon the table, and swore that he would never see his son again, that he would propose to the Ten to banish him from Venice, that he would disinherit him and let him starve as he deserved, and much more to the same effect. But Venier entreated him, for his own dignity's sake, to do none of these things, but to send Jacopo to his villa on the Brenta river, where he might devote himself in seclusion to growing his hair and beard again; and Zuan represented that if he reappeared in Venice after many months, not very greatly changed, the adventure would be so far forgotten that his life among his friends would be at least bearable, in spite of the ridicule to which he would now and then be exposed for the rest of his life, whenever any one chose out of spite to mention barbers, shears, razors, specifies for causing the hair to grow, or Georgians, in his presence. Further, Venier ventured to suggest to Contarini that he should at once break off the marriage arranged with Beroviero, rather than expose himself to the inevitable indignity of letting the step be taken by the glassmaker, who, said Venier, would as soon think of giving his daughter to a Turk as to Jacopo, since the latter's graceless doings had been suddenly held up to the light as the laughingstock of all Venice.

In making this suggestion Venier had followed the suggestion of his own good sense and good feeling, and Contarini not only accepted the proposal but was in the utmost haste to act upon it, fearing lest at any moment a messenger might come over from Murano with the news that Beroviero withdrew his consent to the marriage. Venier almost dictated the letter which Contarini wrote with a trembling hand, and he promised to deliver it himself, and if necessary to act as ambassador.

Beroviero had already called to Marietta that it was time to go home, though the midday bells had not yet rung out the hour, when Pasquale appeared in the garden and announced that Venier was waiting in his gondola and desired an immediate interview on a matter of importance.

He would have come on Contarini's behalf, if for no other reason, but he had spent much time that morning in laying Zorzi's case before his friends and all the members of the Grand Council who could have any special influence with the Ten, or with the aged Doge, who, although in his eightieth year, frequently assisted in person at their meetings, and whose Counsellors were always present. He was now almost sure of obtaining a favourable hearing for Zorzi, and wished to see Beroviero, for he was still in ignorance of Zorzi's return to the glass-house during the night.

Marietta was told to go into the deserted building, containing the main furnaces, now extinguished, for it was not fitting that she should be seen by a patrician whom she did not know, sitting in the garden as if she were a mere serving-woman whose face needed no veil. She ran away laughing and hid herself in the passage where she had spent moments of anguish on the night of Zorzi's arrest, and she waved a kiss to him, when her father was not watching.

Zorzi waited at the door of the laboratory, while Beroviero waited within, standing by the table to receive his honourable visitor. When Zorzi saw Venier's expression of astonishment on seeing him, he smiled quietly, but offered no audible greeting, for he did not know what was expected of him. But Venier took his hand frankly and held it a moment.

"I am glad to find you here," he said, less indolently than he usually spoke. "I have good news for you, if you will take my advice."

"The master has already told me what it is," Zorzi answered. "I am ready to give myself up whenever you think best. I have not words to thank you."

"I do not like many words," answered Venier. "But if there is anything I dislike more, it is thanks. I have some private business with Messer Angelo first. Afterwards we can all three talk together."

CHAPTER XXIV

Zorzi sat on a low bench, blackened with age, against the whitewashed wall of a small and dimly lighted room, which was little more than a cell, but was in reality the place where prisoners waited immediately before being taken into the presence of the Ten. It was not far from the dreaded chamber in which the three Chiefs sometimes heard evidence given under torture, the door was closed and two guards paced the narrow corridor outside with regular and heavy steps, to which Zorzi listened with a beating heart. He was not afraid, for he was not easily frightened, but he knew that his whole future life was in the balance, and he longed for the decisive moment to come. He had surrendered on the previous day, and Beroviero had given a large bond for his appearance.

There were witnesses of all that had happened. There was the lieutenant of the archers, with his six men, some of whom still showed traces of their misadventure. There was Giovanni, whom the Governor had forced to appear, much against his will, as the principal accuser by the letter which had led to Zorzi's arrest, and the letter itself was in the hands of the Council's secretary. But there was also Pasquale, who had seen Zorzi go away quietly with the soldiers, and who could speak for his character; and Angelo Beroviero was there to tell the truth as far as he knew it.

But Zorzi was not to be confronted with any of these witnesses: neither with the soldiers who would tell the Council strange stories of devils with blue noses and fiery tails, nor with Giovanni, whose letter called him a liar, a thief and an assassin, nor with Beroviero nor Pasquale. The Council never allowed the accused man and the witnesses for or against him to be before them at the same time, nor to hold any communication while the trial lasted. That was a rule of their procedure, but they were not by any means the mysterious body of malign monsters which they have too often been represented to be, in an age when no criminal trials could take place without torture.

Zorzi waited on his bench, listening to the tread of the guards. As many trials occupied more than one day, his case would come up last of all, and the witnesses would all be examined before he himself was called to make his defence. He was nervous and anxious. Even while he was sitting there, Giovanni might be finding out some new accusation against him or the officer of archers might be accusing him of witchcraft and of having a compact with the devil himself. He was innocent, but he had broken the law, and no doubt many an innocent man had sat on that same bench before him, who had never again returned to his home. It was not strange that his lips should be parched, and that his heart should be beating like a fuller's hammer.

At last the footsteps ceased, the key ground and creaked as it turned, and the door was opened. Two tall guards stood looking at him, and one of them motioned to him to come. He could never afterwards remember the place through which he was made to pass, for the blood was throbbing in his temples so that he could hardly see. A door was opened and closed after him, and he was suddenly standing alone in the presence of the Ten, feeling that he could not find a word to say if he were called upon to speak.

A kindly voice broke the silence that seemed to have lasted many minutes.

"Is this the person whom we are told is in league with Satan?"

It was the Doge himself who spoke, nodding his hoary head, as very old men do, and looking at Zorzi's face with gentle eyes, almost colourless from extreme age.

"This is the accused, your Highness," replied the secretary from his desk, already holding in his hand Giovanni's letter.

Zorzi saw that the Council of Ten was much more numerous than its name implied. The Councillors were between twenty and thirty, sitting in a semicircle, against a carved wooden wainscot, on each side of the aged Doge, Cristoforo Moro, who had yet one more year to live. There were other persons present also, of whom one was the secretary, the rest being apparently there to listen to the proceedings and to give advice when they were called upon to do so.

In spite of the time of year, the Councillors were all splendidly robed in the red velvet mantles, edged with ermine, and the velvet caps which made up the state dress of all patricians alike, and the Doge wore his peculiar cap and coronet of office. Zorzi had never seen such an assembly of imposing and venerable men, some with long grey beards, some close shaven, all grave, all thoughtful, all watching him with quietly scrutinising eyes. He stood leaning a little on his stick, and he breathed more freely since the dreaded moment was come at last.

Some one bade the secretary read the accusation, and Zorzi listened with wonder and disgust to Giovanni's long epistle, mentally noting the points which he might answer, and realising that if the law was to be interpreted literally, he had undoubtedly rendered himself liable to some penalty.

"What have you to say?" inquired the secretary, looking up from the paper with a pair of small and piercing grey eyes. "The Supreme Council will hear your defence."

"I can tell the truth," said Zorzi simply, and when he had spoken the words he was surprised that his voice had not trembled.

"That is all the Supreme Council wishes to hear," answered the secretary. "Speak on."

"It is true that I am a Dalmatian," Zorzi said, "and by the laws of Venice, I should not have learned the art of glassblowing. I came to Murano more than five years ago, being very poor, and Messer Angelo Beroviero took me in, and let me take care of his private furnace, at which he makes many experiments. In time, he trusted me, and when he wished something made, to try the nature of the glass, he let me make it, but not to sell such things. At first they were badly made, but I loved the art, and in short time I grew to be skilful at it. So I learnt. Sirs—I crave pardon, your Highness, and you lords of the Supreme Council, that is all I have to tell. I love the glass, and I can make light things of it in good design, because I love it, as the painter loves his colours and the sculptor his marble. Give me glass, and I will make coloured air of it, and gossamer and silk and lace. It is all I know, it is my art, I live in it, I feel in it, I dream in it. To my thoughts, and eyes and hands, it is what the love of a fair woman is to the heart. While I can work and shape the things I see when I close my eyes, the sun does, not move, the day has no time, winter no clouds, and summer no heat. When I am hindered I am in exile and in prison, and alone."

The Doge nodded his head in kindly approbation.

"The young man is a true artist," he said.

"All this," said one of the Chiefs of the Ten, "would be well if you were a Venetian. But you are not, and the accusation says that you have sold your works to the injury of born Venetians. What have you to say?"

"Sometimes my master has given me money for a beaker, or a plate, or a bottle," answered Zorzi, in some trepidation, for this was the main point. "But the things were then his own. How could that do harm to any one, since no one can make what I can make, for the master's own use? And once, the other day, as the Signor Giovanni's letter says there, he persuaded me to take his piece of gold for a beaker he saw in my hand, and I said that I would ask the master, when he came back, whether I might keep the money or not; and besides, I left the piece of money on the table in my master's laboratory, and the beaker in the annealing oven, when they came to arrest me. That is the only work for which I ever took money, except from the master himself."

"Why did the Greek captain Aristarchi beat the Governor's men, and carry you away?" asked another of the Chiefs.

Zorzi was not surprised that the name of his rescuer should be known, for the Ten were believed to possess universal intelligence.

"I do not know," he answered quite simply. "He did not tell me, while he kept me with him. I had only seen him once before that night, on a day when he came to treat with the master for a cargo of glass which he never bought. I gave myself up to the archers, as I gave myself up to your lordships, for I thought that I should have justice the sooner if I sought it instead of trying to escape from it."

"Your Highness," said one of the oldest Councillors, addressing the Doge, "is it not a pity that such a man as this, who is a good artist and who speaks the truth, should be driven out of Venice, by a law that was not meant to touch him? For indeed, the law exists and always will, but it is meant, to hinder strangers from coming to Murano and learning the art in order to take it away with them, and this we can prevent. But we surely desire to keep here all those who know how to practise it, for the greater advantage of our commerce with other nations."

"That is the intention of our laws," assented the Doge.

"Your Highness! My lords!" cried Zorzi, who had taken courage from what the Councillor had said, "if this law is not made for such as I am, I entreat you to grant me your forgiveness if I have broken it, and make it impossible for me to break it again. My lords, you have the power to do what I ask. I beseech you that I may be permitted to work at my art as if I were a Venetian, and even to keep fires in a small furnace of my own, as other workmen may when they have saved money, that I may labour to the honour of all glassmakers, and for the good reputation of Murano. This is what I most humbly ask, imploring that it may be granted to me, but always according to your good pleasure."

When he had spoken thus, asking all that was left for him to desire and amazed at his own boldness, he was silent, and the Councillors began to discuss the question among themselves. At a sign from the Chiefs the urn into which the votes were cast was brought and set before the Doge; for all was decided by ballot with coloured balls, and no man knew how his neighbour voted.

"Have you anything more to say?" asked the secretary, again speaking to Zorzi.

"I have said all, save to thank your Highness and your lordships with all my heart," answered the Dalmatian.

"Withdraw, and await the decision of the Supreme Council."

Zorzi cast one more glance at the great half circle of venerable men, at their velvet robes, at the carved wainscot, at the painted vault above, and after making a low obeisance he found his way to the door, outside which the guards were waiting. They took him back to a cell like the one where he had already sat so long, but which was reached by another passage, for everything in the palace was so disposed as to prevent the possibility of one prisoner meeting another on his way to the tribunal or coming from it; and for this reason the Bridge of Sighs, which was then not yet built, was afterwards made to contain two separate passages.

It seemed a long time before the tread of guards ceased again and the door was opened, and Zorzi rose as quickly as he could when he saw that it was the secretary of the Ten who entered, carrying in his hand a document which had a seal attached to it.

"Your prayer is granted," said the man with the sharp grey eyes. "By this patent the Supreme Council permits you to set up a glassmaker's furnace of your own in Murano, and confers upon you all the privileges of a born glassblower, and promises you especial protection if any one shall attempt to interfere with your rights."

Zorzi took the precious parchment eagerly, and he felt the hot blood rushing to his face as he tried to thank the secretary. But in a moment the busy personage was gone, after speaking a word to the guards, and Zorzi heard the rustling of his silk gown in the corridor.

"You are free, sir," said one of the guards very civilly, and holding the door open.

Zorzi went out in a dream, finding his way he knew not how, as he received a word of direction here and there from soldiers who guarded the staircases. When he was aware of outer things he was standing under the portico that surrounds the courtyard of the ducal palace. The broad parchment was unrolled in his hands and his eyes were puzzling over the Latin words and the unfamiliar abbreviations; on one side of him stood old Beroviero, reading over his shoulder with absorbed interest, and on the other was Zuan Venier, glancing at the document with the careless certainty of one who knows what to expect. Two steps away Pasquale stood, in his best clothes and his clean shirt, for he had been one of the witnesses, and he was firmly planted on his bowed legs, his long arms hanging down by his sides; his little red eyes were fixed on Zorzi's face, his ugly jaw was set like a mastiff's, and his extraordinary face seemed cut in two by a monstrous smile of delight.

"It seems to be in order," said Venier, politely smothering with his gloved hand the beginning of a yawn.

"I owe it to you, I am sure," answered Zorzi, turning grateful eyes to him.

"No, I assure you," said the patrician. "But I daresay it has made us all change our opinion of the Ten," he added with a smile. "Good-bye. Let me come and see you at work at your own furnace before long. I have always wished to see glass blown."

Without waiting for more, he walked quickly away, waving his hand after he had already turned.

It was noon when Zorzi had folded his patent carefully and hidden it in his bosom, and he and Beroviero and Pasquale went out of the busy gateway under the outer portico. Beroviero led the way to the right, and they passed Saint Mark's in the blazing sun, and the Patriarch's palace, and came to the shady landing, the very one at which the old man and his daughter had got out when they had come to the church to meet Contarini. The gondola was waiting there, and Beroviero pushed Zorzi gently before him.

"You are still lame," he said. "Get in first and sit down."

But Zorzi drew back, for a woman's hand was suddenly thrust out of the little window of the 'felse,' with a quick gesture.

"There is a lady inside," said Zorzi.

"Marietta is in the gondola," answered Beroviero with a smile. "She would not stay at home. But there is room for us all. Get in, my son."

NOTE

The story of Zorzi Ballarin and Marietta Beroviero is not mere fiction, and is told in several ways. The most common account of the circumstances assumes that Zorzi actually stole the secrets which Angelo Beroviero had received from Paolo Godi, and thereby forced Angelo to give him his daughter in marriage; but the learned Comm. C.A. Levi, director of the museum in Murano, where many works of Beroviero and Ballarin are preserved, has established the latter's reputation for honourable dealing with regard to the precious secrets, in a pamphlet entitled "L'Arte del Vetro in Murano," published in Venice, in 1895, to which I beg to refer the curious reader. I have used a novelist's privilege in writing a story which does not pretend to be historical. I have taken eleven years from the date on which Giovanni Beroviero wrote his letter to the Podestà of Murano, and the letter itself, though similar in spirit to the original, is differently worded and covers somewhat different ground; I have also represented Zorzi as standing alone in his attempt to become an independent glassblower, whereas Comm. Levi has discovered that he had two companions, who were Dalmatians, like himself. There is no foundation in tradition for the existence of Arisa the Georgian slave, but it is well known that beautiful Eastern slaves were bought and sold in Venice and in many other parts of Italy even at a much later date.